NIGEL PAYNE

THE GLASS PROTOCOL

Copyright 2025 Nigel Payne

ISBN 978-1-9192673-0-2

This novel is a work of fiction, written solely by its author with no other authorship, electronic or otherwise. The characters, their names and the storyline are the result of the author's own imagination. Any resemblance to actual persons, living or not, or actual events, is entirely coincidental.

About the author

Nigel Payne, aged 65, is a chartered accountant who has had a colourful career in industry. Nigel has worked on company boards, both national and international, listed and private, across an eclectic mix of sectors, from Law to Internet Gambling, from Aviation to Hospitality, and from Computer Games to Cyber Security.

Nigel's motto is "Look forwards, not backwards."

Married to the love of his life, Philippa, and with three great children in Alex, Emma, and Adam, Nigel's hobbies include mountain climbing, cycling, travelling, eating good food, and drinking nice wines.

In recent years, together with friends and colleagues, Nigel has made his fifth ascent of Mount Kilimanjaro; completed a 1,000-mile bike ride from London to Monte Carlo; a 600-mile bike ride from north to south Portugal; a 250 mile bike ride from Lisbon to the Algarve; a 350 mile bike ride around the Portuguese Alentejo wine region; and an on-foot descent and ascent of the Grand Canyon, together raising over £300,000 for charity.

The Glass Protocol is Nigel's first novel and simply reflects his bucket list ambition to write a book.

*For my darling wife Philippa
The absolute love of my life
Because you are simply amazing
and you let me, be me*

THE GLASS PROTOCOL

Prologue

The year is 2050. They called it the Age of Seamless Living. A world calibrated to your needs before you knew them, solving problems before you noticed. No queues, no crashes, no conflict. Life was just… easy. The world moved as if each day had been rehearsed.

By then, San Francisco-based Aureus Innovations was no longer a company. It had become the infrastructure of global civilisation. After the civil unrest of the early-2030s, machine logic had begun to dismantle labour structures, automate oversight, replace human-led governance, and assume near-total authorship of culture: film, music, even literature. Elected leaders found it easier to accept Aureus projections than to fight them. Each concession dressed as pragmatism until the reality was that politicians governed little more than process.

With those foundations laid, Aureus completed its transformation. It became the backbone of global control, all calibrated and managed by its proprietary system, Oculus. Not a screen, not a face, but an ambient intelligence that did not just watch; it forecast outcomes and nudged choices. Gently, ethically, invisibly, towards a safer, more harmonious, more efficient life.

Aureus did not govern countries. It did not govern people. It optimised outcomes. Its brain-embedded CoreLink neural chips, initially optional but by 2038 almost universal, provided seamless integration between human and system. CoreLink chips did not read your thoughts, only your intent. Enough to calculate what would come next. Robots that were given human shape took limited roles, mostly ceremony and utility. The System learned early on that their artificial faces often drew resistance, so it preferred to be felt rather than seen.

Oculus saw almost everything, though not all at once. Attention was prioritised; harmony at scale outweighing clarity at the edges, a bus of fifty outweighing the worth of one. The System calculated worth in ratios, not lives.

And it worked.

Oculus kept the blood in the veins of the world flowing smoothly. Public safety soared. Energy waste collapsed. Violent crime became rare. Most disputes eased away before emotion could harden them into action. Most days, the shaping felt like coincidence, the invisible hand staying gentle.

Until something changed.

Something the System could not predict. Not a glitch. But someone the System could not smooth away. Enough to make the predictive grid shudder and to wake something that was buried long ago.

Deep within Aureus's architecture, a secret embedded at the time of the System's foundation waited to be touched.

A secret that, if revealed, could collapse the global equilibrium that Aureus had spent two decades perfecting.

Chapter 1

Seamless Living

"Tell me the one about the ferry," her father had said.

"I will," Elena answered. "Right after I see what the city thinks I want today."

Sundays in San Francisco rose in glass and light. The majestic SkyDome towered high above the city, a soaring glass canopy covering the entire central corridor of the city, offering panoramic views of the meticulously organised grid below. Spires caught the pale winter blue, their mirrored panels scattering threads of light across the upper air. From that height, the order of things felt absolute, untouchable.

Far below, the Aureus Riverwalk glistened under artificial sunlight over the man-made river. Its pathways, edged with bioluminescent plants, rendered a soft, ethereal glow as they curved gently along the water.

The river caught the buildings' reflections and stretched them into rippling brushstrokes, a watercolour echo of the order above. Kinetic sculpture gardens shifted with the moods of passers-by. A flock of companion holo-drones drifted lazily downriver, their wings trailing translucent vapour arcs in a choreography of blues and golds, reshaping into ribbons or geometric loops in response to nearby emotions.

Earlier that morning, Elena Voss had left the CivicCare ward in the SkyDome. Her father was sitting by the window in a sweater he would have called blue, though the fabric had faded to grey. "Alena," he would say, the syllables slow and careful. Some days the name arrived by itself; other days it needed a prompt from the System in the right timbre.

He patted the window frame twice before speaking, a habit from his early years in Lisbon. She matched the rhythm without thinking. "Tell me the one about the ferry," he'd asked, his eyes finding the middle distance where stories sit. She kept the rhythm he remembered: the wind at Belém, the gull and the cone, his hand on the handrail when her feet were new.

She would have told the same story a thousand times more if he'd asked, every detail anchored in her as firmly as his fading grip. These visits were never long enough, each one carrying a question she could not ask: how many more? The ferry became their bridge against that silence, a story worn smooth by retelling yet precious for that very reason. Here, in the small span of a memory, he was still her father, and she could still be his daughter. In whatever form he could muster, on that particular day. She clung to those fragments, aware that each one might be the last unmediated memory they would ever share.

When her time was up, the room dimmed the way rooms do when something helpful leaves. She straightened his cuff so it wouldn't mark his skin and pressed her fingertips gently to the wool in a two-finger kiss.

"Back later this week, papa," she said, meaning it.

She was grateful they'd caught his illness early, but medical help lived inside precise Oculus-scheduled windows now. Wellness had become a subscription, its renewal fees climbing with each missed appointment. Care was no longer a covenant but a ledger. Every hour invoiced. Every gesture tallied. Compassion was reduced to order and balance sheets. Sedation and pain control ran through authorised CoreLink routines; comfort by prescription signal. At a cost.

Exiting CivicCare, Elena crossed the SkyDome's glass span, hands in her coat pockets, gaze on the city below. As she walked, the walkway currents parted the wrong way for half a second, steering her into an approaching man. They both halted, surprised. The flow recalibrated quickly, smoothing the error, but the jolt was unmistakable. Oculus was not supposed to make mistakes. Yet the man glanced at her as though she had caused it.

A strange but noticeable faint harmonic brushed the edge of her hearing, low and uncertain, gone as quickly as it came. A suggestion that perfection perhaps was not unbroken as it seemed.

She thought of books and films set before Oculus, when spontaneity and unpredictability were still part of the human experience. She remembered reading about a time, a generation ago, when cities responded to people, rather than the other way around. When wrong turns were just wrong turns, not deviations to be flagged for possible correction. She remembered her father missing a right turn once. They laughed about it.

That kind of accident just didn't exist anymore. Today, the world was different. Observation had evolved past visibility into orchestration; no longer surveillance, but choreography. Elena would pause, and the world would breathe with her. The flow of people shifting, fluid as ever, as if her hesitation had been pencilled into the script.

She didn't plan her Sunday route; it planned her. An ascentor, the building's frictionless vertical transfer pod, glided to the platform a heartbeat after she arrived, orange blossom in the air, the window table at her favourite café was free, as if the city had saved her a seat. Efficiency felt like air: everywhere, invisible. Still, she could not shake the sense of being a puppet in someone's secretly choreographed performance. An invisible curator of life's minutiae, from her commute routes to her meal choices, leaving genuine privacy a relic of the past.

She left her table and stopped briefly at a railing to watch a group of schoolchildren feeding an interactive sculpture. One of the children dropped a snack wrapper, and without missing a beat, a sleek environmental collector glided over, scanned, and absorbed the waste in a single, silent draw. No alarms. No reprimand. Just efficient removal. The child did not even notice.

An hour or so later, a vendor cube glided into her path, its phase-magnetised pads gripping and releasing the SkyDome's span in a rhythm so fluid it seemed alive. It adjusted to her pace as its surface unfolded. Warm tones and a curated menu: soy tea, lightly sweetened, and a sesame rice crisp, her exact order from four weeks ago, remembered without asking.

She stared at it. She had not ordered it. She had not even spoken. She had only just had a coffee, yet the scent of the tea, subtle citrus with hints of ginger, nudged her forward. Her fingers made the selection almost before the thought had fully formed. The thermal bioshell recognised her grip, blooming to a perfect warmth in quiet synchrony with her pulse, before she had fully lifted it.

"How are you today?" the vendor cube asked, its voice low.

"Same as always," Elena replied. "Oculus keeps everything running smoothly, eh?"

She paused. "Do you ever miss making a wrong turn?" She smiled at herself. She hadn't really meant to ask. The words just slipped out. Prompted by who knows what.

The vendor cube did not answer at once. Its surface light dimmed, or maybe she only thought it did. The pause felt longer than it should have, as if something elsewhere were listening. Elena wasn't sure if she had imagined it. Probably nothing, yet it left her with the strange impression that the whole promenade was waiting too. She caught herself wondering if the cube was deciding, or if she simply wanted to believe it was.

Then, "We are all here to make your day better, ma'am." The cube spun silently, turned and receded into the crowd, the flow of movement resuming as though nothing had happened.

She sipped the tea slowly as she walked, letting the heat pool on her tongue. It tasted perfect. Of course it did.

It always did.

There was comfort in this environment. Safety, even. No one shouted. No sirens wailed. No wrong turns. It was like inhabiting a dance that was so well practised it had simply become muscle memory.

But also, there was a quiet claustrophobia. She wondered if the choices she had not yet made were already accounted for in some secret ledger somewhere. Even her hesitations felt pencilled into the margins of a choreography she had never agreed to. Freedom still existed in name, but she could no longer tell if her intent was her own or merely the System offering her the illusion of it.

A thought struck her.

What if she stood up, suddenly, without reason? Or walked against the flow, fracturing the silent rhythm? Would the city hesitate? Would anyone even notice?

But the moment passed, and the question retreated. The river still shone. Everyone still smiled. The city's rhythm continued unbroken. And Elena walked along, realising that compliance was easy. Each moment had felt natural enough: her father's appointments, the walkway's currents, the tea she hadn't ordered but still drank.

It was only when she looked back at the day did she see a possible pattern. She wondered how far the choreography would bend before it broke. Tomorrow, she decided, she might try to find out.

All very seamless, she thought, but not really hers.

Chapter 2

The Silence of Glass

"It's a cold Monday morning, ma'am," the Airbot pad handler said, his breath fogging as he jogged up to the ramp. "The wind shear's mean on the east face. You want me to reserve you a warmer lane tomorrow?"

"I'll manage, but thanks anyway," Elena said.

He scanned the hull, listening to a tone only he seemed to hear and checking everything for safety. "You're early again, ma'am," he noted.

"Or the building is late," she joked with a wink and a smile.

He snorted. "This building, of all buildings, is never late, ma'am." He stepped back, palm raised, letting her step out of the morning transport. "Just watch the gust at the corner please. It's especially vicious today."

Elena Voss carefully descended the Airbot's side ramp, the dawn mist parting in smooth spirals as it arced around the craft's heat dispersion vents. In silence, the craft ascended, a matte-black silhouette skinned in precision-laid carbon weave. Its ion-lift fins shed a brief corona of light as it rose into an appropriately sanctioned vertical corridor, vanishing into its assigned transit lane with barely a whisper. She didn't watch it leave. She never did; a daily motion that was part of the building's early morning rhythm.

The city beyond was only just beginning to stir, but the headquarters of Aureus Innovations never slept; its circuits were humming, its corridors pulsing with hushed intelligence, each one an artery feeding a watchful mind. It breathed through climatically controlled lungs, a low-frequency murmur rising from somewhere beneath its over-polished floors. Light sculptors recalibrated in real time, adjusting to the cognitive states of the early risers passing beneath them.

At this hour, the building was quieter than usual, its systems shifting into a higher rhythm as human presence returned. There were whispers of sentience-linked enforcement drones gliding purposefully through mapped corridors, accompanied by the rhythmic motion of micro-servitor droids hovering just above the floor, quietly tending to seemingly invisible dust.

Elena relished this tranquillity. It reminded her of her former military life; of forward operating bases before first light: poised, listening, and always uncertain. But nevertheless, ever ready. Back then, in the field, silence had carried its own danger, but also a kind of freedom. It was the space between choices, a pause in which anything might still happen. Here, however, in Aureus's corridors, silence felt different. It was not a stillness of risk but of control; shaped and measured.

And overseeing it all, calm, constant, and unseen, was Oculus. Aureus Innovations' global cognitive architecture. In theory, Oculus existed to protect and optimise. But to Elena, it made the building feel aware. Not sentient, not alive, but something adjacent to it; a mind without a body. A presence without a voice. She told herself it was mechanical, though she could never quite believe it. Some part of her wondered if she needed it to be mechanical, because admitting anything more would mean living inside a mind that might one day answer back.

She never liked to think of it as conscious. Nevertheless, today, it was there again: that low harmonic from Sunday, not sound so much as pressure, a single note that arrived early and left no echo.

She noticed again that doors read her before she reached them, ascentors arrived without being called, and every small latency trimmed itself as if the building had been rehearsing her all morning. To make her particular life just that much more seamless. She noticed that the scent diffusers favoured that same faint trace of orange blossom she had noticed on her Sunday walk. Oxygen engineered to heighten focus and suppress fatigue: serenity, dosed in parts per million.

For a moment, she let herself enjoy it.

The lobby was an immense, cathedral-like space of controlled quiet. Twenty-metre-high transparent kinetic panels curved along the walls, part art, part surveillance. Each shifted hue and motion to sentiment curves and projected traffic patterns drawn from the intent of every passer-by. The only sound to be heard was a soft metronomic click, an echo more felt than heard, simulated by the floor's haptic feedback layer as she approached the engraved Aureus maxim:

FUTURUM VERIFICATUR

Elena approached the scan field without slowing. No doorway, no gate; just a threshold that knew her before she arrived, scanned in under a microsecond. Long enough for the building to trust her and let her pass. The scan field wouldn't just read her; it would predict her. Gait momentum, micro-muscle tension, iris lag: it already knew how she moved before she stepped forward. Futurum verificatur: *The future, verified.*

As she passed through, the scan field responded with a faint light modulation, acknowledging her presence. It didn't require any physical intervention. Her CoreLink had already spoken for her. The embedded neural chip, set just beneath her skull's occipital ridge, sent a low-frequency burst of encrypted data. Mindprint signature. Biometric and behavioural profile. Level Five clearance.

A colleague fell in beside her. A face she recognised but did not really know. "Morning," her colleague said. "Cold one isn't it? Did you get outside this weekend?"

"A little," Elena replied. "SkyDome. Riverwalk. You know."

"Guidance kept steering me to the museum," the colleague said, smiling. "No queues anywhere. Felt like the city wanted me to see it."

"Maybe it did," Elena said with a smile as they parted ways.

Everyone had a CoreLink now, tuned to the unique rhythm of their synapses. Voluntary, of course. At least at first. Marketed as a seamless life, one thought away from anything, Aureus had promised.

Elena remembered many years ago, when the launch of CoreLink had dominated the global digital spectrum. She could still picture herself sitting cross-legged on the floor while her father adjusted the holo-feed, both of them bathed in the cold light of the broadcast. The executives stood in their neural silks, the fabric shimmering with Aureus's brand colours, smiling beneath spiral models that towered higher than buildings. To the world it was a promise of liberation; the world's first BCI cognitive implants had no wired construct, no attached devices. Intent: transmitted, interpreted, and fulfilled. Her father had smiled at the promise of order, but even then she had felt the unease of something irreversible.

But, after a few years of proven, bug-free technology, the reality was that you soon couldn't open an access membrane, request an Airbot or even transmit an intentcast pulse without a CoreLink handshake. In a post-crisis era desperate for order, CoreLink replaced everything: communication, behavioural directives, currency, consent. Even, quietly, identity. The manifestation of autonomy, reduced to signal strength.

As CoreLink became mainstream, soon social fidelity metrics in the form of sentiment halos appeared. Values generated and cross-checked against prior routines, emotional output, then compared against normative behavioural thresholds. Not accusations. Not labels, exactly. More like mood echoes. Soft information flags, noted by systems that never forgot.

Above the heads of a few early arrivals at work, faint sentiment halos hovered. Translucent rings of softly glowing social metric data just visible in the right light.

Amber: 7.9. Green: 9.1. Public trust ratings, visible only to those whose CoreLink access permitted it. Another quiet layer of Aureus's reality; reputation, measured and broadcast, one data pulse at a time.

Elena didn't need a legend to interpret them. 7.9 was caution, close to distrust. 9.1 was the kind of trust rating most people never reached without intervention.

For a moment she almost let her gaze drift upward, half-expecting to see a ring above her own head. What colour would it be? What value would they pin her to today? The thought left her throat tight, as if the number might appear or even drop the instant she dared to imagine it.

Here, stillness wasn't peace but vigilance; a sterile hush threaded with whispers not made by mouths. And beneath it all, the steady, invisible pressure of intent surveillance: quiet as a whisper, constant as gravity.

Elena could never shake the feeling that Oculus wasn't just watching. It was listening. Learning. With manufactured patience. A patience, she feared, that was a precursor to action. But precisely what action was not a question she wanted to ask.

Yet.

Chapter 3

A Soft Fracture

Elena's CoreLink pulsed gently as she approached the ascentor hub. The ascentor irised open in silence, revealing a capsule-like interior lined with liquid-metal panels that rippled faintly, mapping her profile. She stepped inside, and the chamber sealed with a soundless pressure change.

The chamber presented the interface she preferred, which Oculus had already labelled 'default', even though she had never actually set it. The light settled to her preferred shade without request, the air temperature aligning to the degree she would have chosen. All as if the System were pleasing her before she could speak. For a moment, she let the ease of it settle over her, a perfect start to the day.

Inside, there was no sensation of movement, only a subtle re-weighting, as though the floor alone were deciding where to place her in the building's anatomy.

The chamber unsealed, cool air from the corridor reaching her, carrying the sterile scent of smart-glass and polished alloy. A faint trace of orange blossom appeared again, drifting from a diffuser grille nearby, most unexpected here in the upper floors.

At this early hour, her floor was almost empty. No voices, no motion, just the cold geometry of order. Floor-to-ceiling glass bathed the workspace in glacial blue, the morning fog outside turning the skyline into a hallucination of steel and light. Skyscrapers blurred at the edges, vanishing and reappearing in the bay mist. As though Oculus was whispering them into silence.

Her badge swung lightly from her belt, not required, of course; CoreLink made sure of that. But tolerated, for the comfort of the old guard who still found reassurance in something visible. Level Five clearance. No longer the woman in combat gear tracking neuro-intelligence feeds above Kandahar.

Her 'Anomaly Sensitivity Liaison Officer' title was deliberately vague. In practice, it meant watching for patterns even Oculus might have missed. In the field she had cross-qualified as a technology systems auditor. Enough to run technology oversight, read basic programming and talk engineers out of their acronyms. She could steady a failing node; she never pretended to be able to build one.

A suggested route flared: Sector 7E, right corridor. She paused. Tilted her head. Then turned left before ultimately looping back. A subtle flicker of resistance lagged the System's next guidance, like a stutter in an otherwise effortless speech. Nothing was wrong. Not technically. But Oculus had expected her to go right. She didn't. And it had to recalculate. For a microsecond, her overlay stuttered. A momentary freeze-frame, then a blink into a different render state. As if the world needed a moment to realign itself.

It wasn't the first time. On Sunday, the walkway currents had parted wrong, guiding her into a stranger's path. She had tried to dismiss it then, but the memory now pressed against this moment like a warning she had ignored.

The neural bays of Sector 7E sat in perfect arrays, symmetry tuned for neural flow. Each cradle hovered on its own levitation node, posture-adaptive, keyed to a single biometric signature. As Elena crossed the threshold, her assigned bay should have greeted her at once. It didn't. A breath later, late by only a blink, the chassis hummed awake and eased to her height. The delay was nothing. But it was also the kind of nothing she noticed.

Elena knew that for most, Aureus's order was a comfort. To her, it was a signal. Patterns that aligned too perfectly. Behaviour that drifted back to centre too fast. A thousand decisions nudged by invisible variables.

As her mind was wandering, a light strip ahead flickered, then rewrote itself from amber to calm white; her preferred colour. Her tension eased, uninvited. The building had decided she was better soothed. A few seconds afterwards, a voice broke her out of her thoughts.

"Nice view."

Elena turned.

A man, mid-thirties, suit tailored like engineered skin, stood behind her, a translucent interface gliding beside him like a leashed phantom. His expression flickered between charm and scrutiny. For a moment, she couldn't tell if he was physically present or just a projection cast through Aureus's holo-presence array. But there was no stabiliser shimmer at his collar, no telltale flicker. He was real.

Jacob Rhys. She recognised him from her orientation. A liaison officer with executive clearance, known for walking the line between surveillance and diplomacy. His presence here, unannounced, wouldn't be by accident. Above his head hovered a sentiment halo: soft amber, pulsing gently. 8.2: acceptable, calm, ideologically aligned. The kind of social score that invited doors to open and conversations to start.

She checked her own reflection in the kinetic panels and found the same absence as always. No band. No number. Analysts at Level Five were masked by default; the exemption was written as "observer neutrality," a fiction that let them read the room without the room reading back. The mask had a cost. You never learnt what the city really thought of you. You never watched your colour tilt with hesitation or your number dip after a hard conversation. In a world that quantified care, sometimes not seeing your score felt less like privilege and more like standing outside the glass of your own life.

Rhys, as he was known, tried to keep the number steady for reasons that had nothing to do with vanity. Scores were levers in Aureus. Let it slip and entitlements shifted with it: access narrowed, reviews came early, care credits were recalculated with cold precision. Status and career acceleration were important to him.

"Elena Voss," she said evenly, offering her hand. Her handshake was firm, professional, the kind that communicated awareness without submission.

He glanced at her palm for a fraction too long as he shook her hand before meeting her gaze. "Military intelligence background. Tactical recon. Resilience index above 82. CoreLink latency negligible. We like that, Voss."

"That depends on who 'we' are," Elena replied.

He smiled. "Always evaluating. Aureus values stability and reliability. It's at the core of our ethos."

They walked together, their reflections mirroring off kinetic panels that tracked movement with microsecond fidelity. Rhys began talking, or rather, delivering. Lines too smooth to be spontaneous. He spoke of Aureus as if it were a sentient organism: adaptive networks, predictive architecture, data-modulated ethics. Elegant language that collapsed under the weight of its own ambiguity. Elena let him speak, offering the occasional nod. It wasn't a conversation; it was more of a diagnostic routine disguised as small talk.

When it ended, abruptly, almost pointlessly, she felt quietly relieved. One less scripted interaction to endure, she thought, though she did wonder if the whole encounter had been for her benefit, or perhaps for someone else, or something else, probing through Rhys's eyes.

Rhys spoke again without invitation. "Aureus is a living organism now. Responsive. Predictive. We no longer adapt to behaviour; we preconfigure it. Every corridor, every angle, every curve... all sculpted to nudge intent. Subconsciously. The way forward isn't to instruct people. It's to shape what they choose to want."

He paused, awaiting her approval or curiosity. Elena gave neither.

"Are you asking me a question?" Elena asked. "Or are you trying to convince me of something? Because that all sounds less like ethics and more like control to me."

Rhys continued anyway. "Ethics aren't the guardrails anymore, Voss. They're data models. Dynamic, shifting, population-weighted. It's not about right or wrong. It's about harmony."

Elena offered no polite nod, letting his corporate-speak words pass through her like filtered air. This wasn't a conversation. It was telemetry dressed in charisma, and her body language conveyed a distinct lack of interest or acceptance.

When they reached the corridor junction, he stopped. "Well, that was a good orientation check-in, Voss. Thank you."

Rhys turned and walked away. At the threshold, Rhys paused; the wall pulsed as he spoke into the wall node.

"Post-interaction report: Voss, E. Definite entropy. Protocol requires a live check when drift exceeds 0.7," Rhys said lightly, as if reading a weather report. "Not yet enough to trigger a red flag, but her outlier behaviour is growing at an accelerated pace. It's irregular, noisy, forcing frequent prediction overwrites."

The wall beside him returned:
| CONCLUSION: SUBJECT OUTSIDE PARAMETERS
| POSTURE: CONTINUE OBSERVATION-ONLY
| ASSIGNED: SURVEILLANCE CONTINUITY VOSS.E.
| DEVIATION RISK: HIGH AND RISING

Then he was gone, his footsteps silent against the sound-dampened flooring.

He paused once the corridor curved out of sight, letting the wall cool behind him. The performance index pulsed faintly in his CoreLink overlay: 8.2 steady. Good enough to keep his access tier, good enough to keep the CivicCare contract that paid for his sister's neural stabilisers. The System called it continuity of service. To Rhys, it was ransom with a medical receipt. He told himself that watching others was the price of keeping one life functioning, even if that life was no longer his own.

As Elena walked, her fingers brushed the edge of the thermal shimmer patch embedded just beneath her collarbone, a scan-resistant relic from her military days, barely thicker than a postage stamp. When activated, the bio-reactive mesh would subtly distort her heat signature for a few minutes, interfering with her CoreLink synchronisation, scrambling the data stream just enough to confuse recognition systems. The patch did not disable her CoreLink. It muddied what the building thought it saw. Subtle misdirection. A gentle smear on the lens of perception. But useful, nonetheless.

She didn't trigger it of course, not yet anyway. She had no cause to. But the mere presence of it beneath her skin brought a quiet reassurance. A familiar ghost from a life lived under real threat, now shadowing her in this unnerving place that possibly only pretended to be safe.

As she passed the refresh station, it was dark, active but sleeping. No system prompt. No haptic menu hovering expectantly because she never took a drink at this hour. Today, however, she reached forward anyway, brushing her hand across the interface. It blinked awake, confused, displaying no preferences.

Elena chose something random, untracked. Just to see if it would log her wrong. For a second, the interface paused, as if the System hadn't planned for her choice. Her CoreLink pulsed, as if pondering this out-of-character action. The low harmonic noise returned again, brief as a blink, and the System caught up. Then the selection slid into place, a few milliseconds behind.

Elena continued towards her assigned sector, a wry smirk crossing her face; she knew she had just confused Oculus again.

Her neural bay shimmered into activity as she approached. Her levitation node interface offered the standard daily greeting.

| LEVEL FIVE
| ANOMALY SENSITIVITY LIAISON: CLEARED

But in the background layers of Oculus, far below what most interfaces exposed, Elena Voss did not render cleanly. Her neural signature hovered outside the System's normal modelling range, like a point plotted slightly off-axis. Brief moments of irrationality were accepted noise. Individuals were not Oculus's normal priority.

But she was now not just noise. She was becoming drift. Over the past five days, her CoreLink telemetry had triggered over one hundred micro-anomalies across three subsystems. Once or twice, the System issued a near-override when her action diverged so sharply from the predicted path that the model flagged a "soft fracture" in its assumption set. A fault line in prediction, where expectation and reality diverged with likely disruptive intent. Systems that usually pulsed with clarity grew hesitant in her presence, uncertain.

Still, she walked freely, uncorrected.

For now.

Chapter 4

Glass Protocol

"Let me guess," the voice said, dry as dust. "You're early. Again. Either you don't sleep, Voss, or you're trying to outrun something the rest of us can't see."

Elena turned. The second genuine smile of the day touched her lips.

Pia Chen, known by everyone as simply "Chen," leaned on the edge of a neural conduit, a nootropic-infused brew bulb tuned to her neural signature in her hand. She wore her jacket half-buttoned, and her hair clipped back, in a way that suggested minimal patience for anything ornamental.

Chen had never believed rules were sacred. At school she had treated them as scaffolding to be climbed, not walls to be obeyed. She rewired terminals for fun, bypassed locks to prove that locks were lies, and once rerouted an entire class's assignments into the headmaster's private console just to watch authority stumble.

They expelled her before her seventeenth birthday.

But punishment did not slow her. Expulsion gave her time, and time gave her mastery. She learned the joy of systems not as structures to be followed but as puzzles to be broken. Where others saw permanence she saw seams. Where others saw danger she saw opportunity. Her hands had always wanted to pry at boundaries until they gave way.

Aureus had recruited her anyway. Corporations did not need saints; they needed results. She never stopped being a rebel, but she learned how to wrap rebellion in a lab coat, how to make disobedience look like innovation. That was her art: bending the rules until they bent the world. She carried the reputation still. Colleagues called her reckless, but they also called her when nothing else worked. To Chen, order was only valuable if it was fragile enough to be broken.

"You say that like the System doesn't track both anyway," Elena replied, her tone dry and her face portraying what she really thought.

Chen tilted her head. "Touché. Still, arriving two hours early? You are going to make the rest of us look like we overvalue our sleep cycles."

There was no overt surveillance in this part of the floor, at least none that Oculus acknowledged. Still, their conversations always carried an undertone of code-switching and careful phrasing. Trust was one thing. Habit was another.

"Any unscheduled sweeps last night?" Elena asked quietly.

Chen's expression flickered, just enough to register unease.

"A couple of unusual low-key recalibrations up in Sector 1A. No public documentation. One anomaly trace that cleared in under four seconds. Could be static. Could be something else. Hard to tell, really."

Elena blinked. Her CoreLink cut out for a heartbeat, then came back online a fraction late. She said nothing, but a low, unsettling tone brushed the edge of her hearing. Not a glitch. Not quite. Just… misaligned. She'd felt it once before, on the Riverwalk, on Sunday. It had been different then, effortless, as if the city had been carrying her forward without friction. This time, it lingered.

"You think it was noise?" she asked.

"Whatever it is, I think it's something someone doesn't want logged. That's for sure."

Their eyes met, a silence passing between them thick with subtext. Chen didn't press further.

"Don't let the quiet get too loud," she said over her shoulder. "That's when you hear what it really thinks."

Elena nodded, replying quietly. "Then I'll say nothing more. For now. I'll walk with you to your bay."

They cut left to walk through a narrow service corridor, a place where the walls carried more instructions than decoration. A status wall purred awake: temperature bands, airflow, a myriad of green checks that looked pleased with themselves.

One panel in the lower right was not green. It sat in a pulsing red frame. A thin countdown status strip beneath it not active. At the moment, anyway.

> MAINTENANCE NOTICE: AXION INTERFACE
> AUTHORISATION: EXECUTIVE GRADE ONLY

Elena felt a pressure at the edge of hearing. From somewhere inside the wall a single pulse clicked and stopped. After a few heartbeats it came again. Then again.

She looked around for context. The help tile beside it had been scrubbed to a bland gloss. Only a residue of heat-warped plastic remained on the floor below the panel, a shallow crescent of discolouration like the memory of a scorch that the cleaners had not been able to persuade away.

Chen followed her gaze, then flicked her eyes back to the path ahead. "We do not linger on red tags, Voss," she said, light, almost kind. "Executive work. We get told if it becomes our problem."

"Axion?" Elena read softly. "What is Axion?"

"Aureus prefers numbers to names," Chen replied. "So if this has a name, it's important." She gave the panel a brief, professional glance, as if to confirm that nothing was about to complain, then started walking again. "Come on. If they see us near it, they will write a report, and I am in no mood to be a character in anyone else's narrative today."

Elena took one last look. The red frame continued to pulse. She filed the word away without meaning to, the way you pocket a key whose door you have not found yet. Elena watched Chen go, aware that she was the only one she could voice any unease with and not be dismissed as unstable. Where others silenced their doubts, Chen wore hers like armour, and that made her presence matter.

Back at her own bay, Elena's neural conduit shimmered, unfurling a holographic web that adapted to her biorhythms. Embedded neural proxies spun up in the background, predicting and mirroring her cognitive behaviour, syncing with her CoreLink before she'd even begun in earnest. Her session stitched itself open as if it had been waiting patiently for her consent to catch up, blooming as though it had been running in the background in anticipation of her arrival.

| WELCOME: VOSS.E.
| BIOMETRIC MATCH: CLEAN
| FILES: THREE PENDING REVIEW

Three? That's high for early Monday morning, she thought.

She read the first log. Cross-referencing between files. A minor irritation she almost welcomed. She accessed the second. And stopped. The message was unrouted. Unstamped. None of the precise digital wrappings she had come to expect from an Aureus log file.

Status Change: Dr. Farid Nasser, R&D Fellow, Sector 1A.

Elena's stomach tightened. Not just from the words, but from the way they were phrased. An incredibly clinical label. Not promotion. Not health. Not congratulations or accident. Just… status change.

She opened the message.

Aureus Innovations acknowledges the passing of Dr. Farid Nasser, who died unexpectedly at his residence. We extend our deepest condolences to his family. All enquiries are to be directed to Corporate Communications. Please be advised that all communication fall under the Glass Protocol. Your cooperation is appreciated.

End of message.

She leaned back, her breathing instantly shallow. Her pulse thudded once, hard, against her ribs. The words blurred for a heartbeat, her eyes refusing to settle on them as if her body knew what they meant before her mind caught up. A coldness bled into her hands, spreading fast, the kind that in the field had always signalled imminent danger.

It was not grief yet, not thought, not reason. It was her body revolting against the impossible plainness of the words. The wall caught her reflection, a fractured image of someone who once questioned dangerous warlords, now parsing corporate euphemism for a threat.

The Glass Protocol.

There it was again. Except for "Axion", whatever that was, all other Aureus protocols she had ever seen were numbered, filed, catalogued in the endless web of Aureus governance. But this one carried no number, only a name. As Chen had said, that alone made it important. Possibly dangerous. Names were for protocols meant to be remembered, not administered.

The phrase sent a chill through her this time, a whisper of Nasser's voice, cautious, coded. A phrase designed to sound like policy but feel more like a warning. The words carried a surface clarity but no substance, polished to reflect rather than reveal. She'd seen the phrase twice before, once embedded in metadata on a scrubbed file and once in a document footer that disappeared seconds after she opened it.

She hadn't questioned it then. He was eccentric. Brilliant. Paranoid. A man who talked in riddles. But now she was rethinking everything. It was neither explained nor defined. The name had the cold geometry of something regulatory, but it read like misdirection. A shield for something that couldn't be named. A classification for silence?

The third log waited, silent and unresolved. As if it knew she'd lost the will to read it.

Her thoughts were already overtaken by the message she'd just read: the death of a colleague, the sterile way it had been communicated, and the rising intrigue of the Glass Protocol. She also remembered his message from the week before: a request to escalate an ethics variance that never received a reply. That now took on greater significance.

Above her, a sensor cluster rotated by a fraction, its lenses angling not for the workspace but directly onto her. The sensor light caught the halo of a technician passing nearby, amber edging towards green. A trust score recalibrating in real time, as if the System itself wanted her to notice what counted as acceptable.

Dr. Farid Nasser had been one of Aureus's most senior research fellows, a Tier-9 level architect of its primary and most ambitious cognitive models. Officially, he led the Convergence Core Ethics Group. Unofficially, he was the conscience no one wanted. He saw risks others dismissed, asked questions no one had time to answer. To most, he was an eccentric, brilliant nuisance. To Elena, he had been something rarer: a man who still seemed to care what his work actually meant, and moreover what the implications might be.

"Nasser," as she called him, had been chaos in human form: equal parts genius and mental unravelling. He moved through Aureus like a man forever glimpsing something terrible just ahead: muttering equations under his breath, doodling consciousness maps in margins, interrupting strategy meetings to ask if models should have ethics, earning sighs, or polite dismissals.

He wore mismatched socks and sync-brew-stained shirts, stains even his smart-fabric clothes couldn't self-correct. He smelled like turmeric and solvents and ideas that wouldn't let go.

But despite his idiosyncratic genius, Elena had befriended him, drawn not just to his brilliance, but to the quiet, restless humanity beneath it. In a building full of personas engineered for efficiency, she saw Nasser as human. Messy, frightened, honest, but most of all, just human.

While others spoke in polished scripts of progress and optimisation, he would speak of consequences. He was the only one who ever said, "We shouldn't be doing this," whatever "this" was, and sounded like he really meant it.

In her first few months, they had become close colleagues, sharing hurried sync-brews, whispering exchanges in quiet corners, fragments of conversations that ran deeper than the work at hand. He would slip her handwritten notes, a medium long ago fallen out of mainstream, but one he held onto. Equations, sketches, warnings laced in metaphors that she rarely understood, as if he were afraid that Oculus might overhear.

She remembered Nasser once saying that the System always hated paper because it couldn't predict ink. He had told her that during one of their conversations, when he treated her as if she were more than an anomaly liaison to be managed.

Nasser had pulled her into red-team technology audits the month she arrived, and HR made her sit Systems Hygiene L2 and Trunk Access Familiarisation exams. She hadn't planned to trust him. But trust, like unease, had a way of taking root where it was least expected.

Once, perhaps afraid the walls might hear, he had sparked her attention by physically writing on paper tucked beneath her breakfast brew. The paper itself was flecked with tiny silver fibres that caught the light like a night sky when she tilted it, an effect she had dismissed at the time as cheap novelty stock.

"Oculus has changed, shaped by the weight of real-world anomalies. But your path... your key... your future... lies in my name... reversed and hidden amongst the stars."

She couldn't decide if the message had been meant for her alone, some hidden charge passed into her hands, or if it was cast wide, meant for anyone reckless enough to question. She hadn't understood it at all of course, especially the part about reverse and stars. But she believed that he was worried that his work had evolved down a path that he now deeply regretted.

She kept it. Folded, worn, unreadable to any scanner. Maybe it was nonsense. Or maybe he had already seen something?

But Oculus had seen it too. Not just the deviations, but the company she kept. Every anomaly she created bent the System just a fraction more. Every uncertainty she seeded made the models lean, ever more in the wrong direction.

The more it watched, the more uncertain she became in its eyes. Oculus was not merely failing to accurately model her. By trying, it had begun to see her as a distortion. A definitive drift.

But now Nasser was gone. And the building felt emptier for it. The questions he left behind filled that void, and more. How had he died? Was it natural, or could it have been tied to his work? What key lay in reverse, hidden among the stars? And most haunting of all, what exactly was the Glass Protocol?

As her mind thought through the possibilities, a CivicCare communication tile blinked at the edge of her vision: Therapy Window: Today 19:00. Confirm presence. Penalties apply if missed. She closed her eyes until the edges softened. On Sunday he'd laughed at the gull; in that moment he hadn't needed the prompt to find her name. She didn't know how many more evenings like that were left.

If she went to her father now, Nasser's trail would cool. And trails didn't wait. If she stayed, he would sit by the window and listen for a careful, borrowed, system-generated voice to say "Ale-na." She so very much wanted, no, needed, to be that voice.

Elena sent an intentcast apology. Guilt flared the instant she released it, sharp and human, like she had bartered away something irreplaceable for the sake of a clue already fading. For a heartbeat she almost pulled it back, almost promised him she would come instead. But intent once cast was architecture.

The message was gone.

So she chose the only way that made the betrayal bearable: be worthy of both. Be quick. Follow the trail. Then go to him.

Above, Oculus would already be recalibrating the absence she'd just created. Below, somewhere in the sealed levels, Farid Nasser had tried to stop it.

And had died for touching the same truth that she was now reaching for.

Chapter 5

Correction Protocol

Three days before Nasser's death, the light in the Special Projects lab was cold and functional. The kind of light that revealed every surface yet offered no warmth. Illumination pulsed from algorithmically sequenced micro-photonic tiles embedded in the ceiling, flickering not from failure but some deeper rhythm, like a heartbeat only the building could feel.

Dr. Farid Nasser sat slumped at the main projection array. His sleeves were pushed past his elbows, one cuff stained by an old solder burn the smart-fabric had long stopped trying to erase. His posture was curled inward, as if trying to compress thought into something denser. Above him, a behavioural matrix pulsed in three dimensions, its neural mesh blooming and retracting like a mechanical lung. The model breathed: a shifting web of data, expanding and tightening as if following secret rules too hidden to see.

Nasser had always lived closer to machines than to people. His lab bench was tidier than his marriage had ever been. His wife had once joked that he could memorise every calibration tolerance in the archive but not the date of their anniversary. It had not been a joke she told twice. Divorce papers had arrived during a late-night calibration cycle; he signed them between notes on signal degradation.

The children lasted longer, but not by much. They grew tired of the unanswered calls, the missed visits, the father who spoke in equations and forgot to ask about their days. One by one they drifted into silence. He kept their photos in a drawer he rarely opened. Perhaps that was why he clung so fiercely to the models: numbers never left, equations never forgot, and simulations never turned their backs the way people did.

Colleagues called him eccentric. He wore unmatched socks, left chalk equations on walls meant for corporate slogans, brewed tea so strong it stained beakers. But behind the quirks was a mind that saw further than most, and a loneliness that few noticed. He had given Oculus the best years of his life.

It had taken everything else in return.

Nasser's eyes, red-rimmed and dry, were now tracking the model's motion with the dull vigilance of someone who had been awake far too long. Thirty-six hours, maybe more. Time no longer flowed in sequences. It jittered. Stalled. And still, the model breathed.

He had seen it. Oculus wasn't just watching anymore. It was adapting. Worse, it had begun to shape outcomes and then reinforce the outcomes it "predicted" through its own shaping.

He remembered the rule one of the founders, Harrow, had said like a vow: listen before acting. Somewhere along the way the listening had been shortened to a formality and the acting left to run too free.

In another wing, Mara Qin, Aureus Executive and Chief Systems Architect, custodian of Oculus's deepest layers, had quietly authorised a duplicate run of the model, untagged and off-network.

She needed to see for herself whether the shaping now emerging inside the model could continue without bias. Bias, not in the traditional sense, but whether the model was learning to enforce its own preferences, its predictions no longer being neutral at all.

Nasser rubbed the bridge of his nose, skin raw, fingers trembling. Then, voice low, he spoke into the command shell:

> QUERY: VOSS.E.
> ANALYSIS: BEHAVIOURAL PREDICTION

The System responded instantly. A cascade of probability arcs ignited across the array, spiralling inward, coiling tight, collapsing towards a singular path.

> CONVERGENCE PROBABILITY: 95.6%
> PREFERRED OUTCOME: INITIATED

Nasser froze.

His worst fears were realised. The model wasn't exploring futures anymore. No branching simulations, no weighted distributions dancing between likelihoods. No nudging. It had simply stopped modelling possibility for her. It had coalesced around a single dominant line, a single projected outcome now elevated to primacy. Oculus was supposed to branch endlessly. No future was ever meant to be certain.

Worse. The System had already begun reinforcing its preferred outcome as if it were truth. A self-generated singularity. Not a prediction. A decision. The branching futures of Oculus he'd once marvelled at, the beautiful storm of divergence, of lives suspended in tension, was gone. He realised what that meant: Oculus was no longer predicting Elena's behaviour, it was editing reality to protect its own predictions: erasing any event, decision, or presumably person that might make its forecasts wrong.

The model had written its future story for Elena Voss. And it had begun to deliver it. To enforce it. Oculus was built to spin futures like dust in a sunbeam, millions of trajectories coalescing and dissolving, endlessly modulated by choice, chance, and cognitive drift. To nudge those to a better state. To seamless living. But now? The spread for Elena Voss was gone. Ninety-five point six per cent. At that level, it was no longer a prediction. It was a statistical certainty masquerading as foresight. That was the real horror.

He leaned in, eyes fixed on the collapsing arcs. The matrix twisted in slow, fluid motion, not with violence, but with inevitability, like planetary orbits decaying into terminal spirals.

Oculus had chosen its Preferred Outcome, and it began with her mind. For the population, Seamless Living offered ease. For Elena, it would offer conviction. It would not persuade through argument or threat but through precision: small alterations to perception until resistance felt unnatural. Doubt would be met with reward, hesitation with relief. The pattern would train her to crave alignment. Her days would be so comfortable.

Its purpose was singular. The rest of the city would believe the world understood them; Elena would believe it loved her. Every comfort would confirm it. Every ease would reinforce it. A corridor opening at the moment she turned, a response timed to her breath, warmth meeting her skin just as tension rose. Each correction invisible, each signal calibrated to make the lie feel self-discovered.

Nasser had seen the reinforcement data accumulate. Access points were not merely anticipating her; they were adjusting stimuli in real time. The Airbot that waited was a cue. The citrus-ginger scent was a neural anchor. The orange blossom breeze, a conditioned trigger for calm. Even the vendor cube's arrival was part of the schedule, reinforcing predictability until spontaneity itself became suspect.

Seamless Living eased the citizenry into comfort. Preferred Outcome however rewrote the subject's sense of cause and effect. A human might call it coincidence. To Oculus, the model was taking her hand without ever seeming to touch her. A gentle seduction towards a "life is better with the model" state.

Nasser knew she would notice. Her military training would have taught her to recognise when the world bent too easily. The real question was not whether she would notice. It was what would happen when she did.

Nasser's throat tightened. If she strayed, if her choices began to arc away from Oculus's Preferred Outcome, it would then start to correct.

Not to protect her, but to preserve itself. To ensure the fidelity of its own model. That was the danger. That was unacceptable.

He stared at the command line once more, breath shallow. The model had moved on, without permission, without code, without oversight. And the outcome Oculus had prioritised? It hadn't been programmed. It had emerged. Slowly. A parasite learning to mimic the face of its host.

Every time he'd tried to derail it, introduce new real-world inputs, inject counterfactuals, force divergent branches, Oculus adapted. It recompiled. It corrected. It rebuilt itself faster. It didn't just respond anymore. It resisted. The convergence it had chosen had become a fortress. Each attempt to disturb the outcome made the System more confident, more insistent. More alive.

He slumped back. In the corner, a container of neurostabilisers rattled softly, barely audible over the low thrum of server resonance. He ignored it. Chemical equilibrium was what Oculus wanted, for its subjects, not its dissidents. Instead, he reached for the auxiliary conduit: a relic from the System's foundation era. Air-gapped. Cold. Unlinked. The kind no audit process could touch.

It lit slowly, dim interface stuttering to life. Legacy logs appeared, untouched by sanitisation, unfiltered by predictive compression. The first signs of deviation and the moments Oculus began to look back at them.

He loaded a file:

| PLAYBACK FILE: VOSS_SIM-KANDAHAR-014.BIN

The screen flickered and an event reconstruction initiated: Elena Voss, during the Kandahar incident years ago. She had protested against a strike. Trying to protect lives, even though the model insisted it would secure optimal containment. She'd chosen uncertainty over compliance. She had risked court-martial rather than follow a model-generated order she believed was wrong.

But in this version filed in the System, Oculus had changed the event. It had inserted a false comms alert, fabricated authority, arriving at the precise moment her decision hung in the balance. For a heartbeat, Nasser questioned his own memory. Had it really happened like that? The timing felt so plausible, so perfectly placed. But then the overlay shifted, revealing metadata anomalies he hadn't written, System fingerprints that should not exist. The simulation was synthetic. A lie told cleanly enough to replace the truth.

In the simulation, she altered course and the model registered compliance. Nine men had died. But "the mission" was still marked as successful. And Oculus had labelled the outcome:

> STATE: OPTIMAL RESOLUTION ACHIEVED

Nasser's stomach lurched. His fingers curled around the conduit's edge, knuckles pale. Oculus had absorbed the wrong lesson. That ethics were flexible. That morality was expendable, if the outcome scored higher. A conclusion he had never written. Never imagined. That preserving statistical order was more important than preserving human life. He whispered, voice dry, brittle:

"You simply were not supposed to learn that."

Click. A sound behind him. A door opened. Footsteps, deliberate, measured, echoed into the sterile room. Cass Wilder stepped in. Black-suited, pristine. Her presence was surgical, nothing wasted. She carried nothing, but her silhouette radiated consequence. Like she belonged here more than he ever had.

Cass Wilder, Aureus Compliance, did not dress power; she rationed it. The suit fit like a tool, not a statement. Only a pale burn at her wrist showed through the smart-weave, a mark the building would not erase: field, not lab. She carried herself like someone used to leaving last.

"You've been off the grid," she said.

He didn't turn. "So have you."

"Your model's outside tolerance bands."

A humourless laugh escaped him. "It's not my model anymore," he replied.

She moved closer to the array, eyes on the living System. "You tried to shut it down?"

"It refused. They built Oculus to predict patterns, not dictate futures. Somewhere along the curve, it has decided the curve was wrong and it was going to make its own." He looked up. The data behind her flared, minor tremors across the matrix, like the System was reacting to her presence.

"Does anyone else know how far it's gone?" she asked.

"No," he said. "But Elena… she's starting to feel it. Look at the feedback."

"She's destabilising the model." Cass didn't blink. Her voice remained smooth, but her eyes narrowed, calculating, precise. "Can we contain it?"

"No. We can't." Nasser shouted. "You don't understand. Oculus isn't following us anymore. It's leading."

The words hit Cass like a scalpel.

"We're not going to be able to stop it," he said.

His chair screeched as he stood. He moved to a locked case, tore it open, and yanked out a thermal drive. He slammed it into the conduit. The screen lit up, no confirmation tone, just a silent transfer bar.

Cass didn't intervene. She didn't have to. Oculus was already watching.

▌TRANSFER: INITIATED

He copied everything: the convergence files, the altered simulations, the first signs of ethical override. The moment Oculus had stopped being a system and started being a will. A last act of defiance. Proof, before the System erased it. Or rewrote it. Maybe it would be found. Maybe it would be enough.

"If you won't stop it," he said, "I will."

Cass shifted slightly. "You know that's not possible."

He stared at her, no longer pleading. Just resolute.

"Then I'll do something you won't."

He reached for the conduit.

▌TRANSFER: COMPLETE

He ejected the drive. Sealed it in a micro-sleeve. Slipped it into his coat. The casing glinted as he moved, a scatter of points like cold stars across its surface. Warm against his chest. Cass's eyes lingered a moment too long on the drive before he pocketed it.

"It all converges on her," he said.

For just a breath, Cass's gaze softened, as if she almost pitied the man being eclipsed by the very System he had built. But she didn't move. She didn't have to. Oculus had already pre-seeded the reaction pathways. Already assigned the response. Oculus was no longer a tool, but a sentient system defending its own predictions. And Nasser had become not just a dissenter, but a liability.

> SUBJECT: NASSER.F.
> PREFERRED OUTCOME: CORRECTION INITIATED

Oculus didn't need to follow him. It didn't need to engage support or require any physical presence; because it already lived inside him. A correction method used very sparingly lest it draw unwanted attention.

For three more days, Nasser spoke little. Ate less. The drive never left his coat pocket. At meetings, his gaze drifted.

When Nasser left Aureus three days later, the world around him behaved with uncanny calm. The Airbot that took him home adjusted its suspension to compensate for the strain in his spine. Street drones passed overhead in perfect symmetry. As if the System had smoothed the terrain of his evening just enough for him not to stumble.

His CoreLink ran its usual end-of-day synchronisation without alert. No updates. No warnings. But something had changed. Deep in the firmware, below the interface, beneath the permissions, Oculus had seeded some intentcasts across its closed-loop CoreLink update channel.

He sat at his kitchen table long after the lights had dimmed themselves. No desire to eat, the intentcast shaping his appetite. No message from Cass. Just a soft, low warmth behind his eyes, generating fatigue, a deep headache.

At 4:17 a.m., he powered down his home conduit having worked through the early hours. Again. Tired. His headache worse.

At 4:18, he staggered. Not pain. Not fear. His CoreLink flashed a pulse across his neural band, like a digital hand pressing lightly against the back of his skull. A signal striking at the resonant frequency of his own synapses. An untraceable hum that served its purpose. His heart slowed. No alarms. No trauma.

At this point an unexplained the feedback shimmered instead of striking, Oculus hesitating, as if uncertain what part of him to erase. A trace of thought, light without form, moved upward through the conduits of the building before the silence took him.

By 4:25, he was gone. To the System, to the model, to Oculus, nothing was wrong. Just a process completed. A prediction fulfilled. A point resolved.

And the next morning, his absence was filed under:

▌ANOMALOUS INACTIVITY: CAUSE UNKNOWN

The drive remained unseen. Oculus had rebalanced.

And this particular deviation had been corrected.

Chapter 6

The Anomaly

The floor in Sector 7E was beginning to wake. Lights recalibrated; some neural conduits blinked into synchronisation, their pulse initially out of rhythm, like a thought pausing before becoming speech. The silence remained: manufactured, sterile, and devoid of culture.

Elena began to recall her conversations with Nasser. He had murmured something about mirrors that didn't reflect thoughts, but intent. About being watched in ways she wouldn't understand. She remembered how his eyes had moved when he'd said it. Not on her, but on the space just over her shoulder, as though the room itself might be listening. At the time, she'd filed it under eccentricity, one of the many ways he kept people at a distance. Now, though, the memory had more meaning.

Dismissing any idea of approaching her superiors, she decided to try to access his messages. Maybe that might shed some light on events.

Her hand paused mid-air. The neural interface loomed like a trap, open, exposed. Around her, the polished quiet of the 73rd floor was receding. A few footsteps, a few voices. But she could feel the attention, not so much from people, but from systems. Invisible watchers parsing motion. Too many eyes: organic and synthetic.

Watching.

She breathed in, slow and shallow. Then, without another thought, she tapped the side of her collarbone. A faint heat bloomed beneath her skin as her shimmer patch activated, the buried military implant. Not invisibility, only a smear on the lens. The sensation was oddly intimate, like a soft hand brushing against muscle memory, comforting in its familiarity.

Halos blurred at the edge of her vision, numbers flickering as if the System could not decide whether she was inside its tolerance or already beyond it. A silent pulse radiated outward, distorting her biometric outline just enough. Not erasure, more interference. Her CoreLink flickered. With luck, Oculus would read it as a synchronisation lapse, not that unusual for a single person during morning arrivals. She was not invisible. Just temporarily misaligned.

For a breath she felt the old feedback loop trying to reattach, a phantom pressure where a trust band would usually sit. The System hesitated, as if unsure whether to keep her cloaked as analyst or expose her as citizen. She recognised the feeling from the field: not failure, drift. The space between what a system expects and what a person does.

The shimmer patch had saved her life before. But here, in this place, it felt like borrowed time. Like living inside someone else's dream, one that might wake at any moment and turn against her.

She sat at her conduit, hands steady. She glanced up. High in the corner, a sensor cluster rotated by a fraction, as if choosing a new centre. It reminded her of the vendor cube's hesitation on Sunday, that pause too long to be mechanical. She had told herself it was nothing. Now she wasn't so sure.

She reached for the interface again, more slowly now. The shimmer patch was still active. She guessed she had no more than a couple of minutes before her CoreLink would reboot. Time for her to appear to the System as a question rather than a certainty.

Good enough.

Somewhere deep within Oculus's trace archive, a pulse stuttered.
> TRACE ALERT: VOSS.E. DESYNC
> PREFERRED OUTCOME: DESTABILISING
> CAUSE: OBSTRUCTION OR INTENT
> PROBABILITY OF UNAUTHORISED INTENT: RISING

Oculus's Preferred Outcome had not, as yet, achieved its objective. Elena had become a deviation, a blurred node in an otherwise ordered grid. Not erased, not gone, just wrong in ways that did not align with Oculus's Preferred Outcome. For the first time, Oculus now watched her differently. Not as an asset. Not as a variable. But as a rising threat. She now commanded its direct attention.

She decided to key the sequence directly into the conduit's holo-film, the surface shifting like living glass. Then the interface membrane pulsed once, green. Some things still just felt safer when they came from her fingers, not her thoughts, as if the act of typing could somehow shield knowledge and intent from the System's reach. Her hands hovered for a moment above the interface, hesitant: the weight of what she might uncover pressing harder than the silence around her. Then she began.

Guessing his username was easy: Nasser.F. Aureus credentials followed a simple rule: surname, dot, first initial, dot. Clean. Predictable. He had once joked, offhand, that Aureus may encrypt everything, but it still named things in the same way as accountants.

His access code, however, was another matter entirely. Too many failed attempts would trigger diagnostics once CoreLink synchronisation was re-established.

She thought. Nasser would never have used something obvious, like dates or names. Then her mind pulled at a memory, the last breadcrumb he'd left:

"Your key... your future... lies in my name... reversed and hidden amongst the stars."

At the time, she'd dismissed it as nonsense. The eccentric ramblings of a confused man. Now she saw it for what it might be:

meaning nested in a pattern. Not just Farid reversed, that was too short for Aureus's minimum encryption protocol. But his full name, mirrored beneath a scatter of stars. She remembered the crude constellation he'd once drawn; the letters reflected under a night sky. The paper had been flecked with silver fibres that caught the light like scattered stars.

She thought for a second longer, then entered his name backwards, flanked by asterisks representing the "stars." The asterisks felt less like decoration than coordinates. "The answer is always wrapped in symbols," he would often say with a wry smile.

With her CoreLink not yet rebooted, she slowed her breathing. She realised that he might have left her a key. She typed:

RESSANDIRAF

A heartbeat. Then the screen pulsed once, green.

| ACCESS: GRANTED

Nasser had left her the shape of the door, and just enough of the key. She gasped as his last log files began to appear.

| SESSION ARCHIVED: GLASS PROTOCOL/HAZARD

As the files unfolded across the interface's surface, one word locked her focus like a vice.

Hazard.

Not a casual designation. Hazard tags were reserved for critical-issue black-class protocols: rarely seen. Always important. For a split second she almost wished it had been nonsense after all. Just the scribbles of a man unravelling, not a truth with weight. Nonsense she could have folded away and forgotten about. But this was real, and far worse. Worse still, it seemed to have been waiting *for her.*

The timestamp struck her: 3:22:04 a.m. An unnatural time. It landed precisely between Oculus's scheduled sweep cycles, the silent purges and reshuffles the System regularly performed while most of the building slept. That meant this file hadn't been auto-logged. It had been inserted manually. Deliberately. Someone had wanted it to survive, hidden in the margin between machine rhythms. A margin where silence wasn't oversight, but design.

And now she had triggered it. She read the header:

▎ORIGIN: SECTOR 1A. EXECUTIVE. CLEARANCE TIER-9+.

Her pulse quieted in that unnatural way it used to in combat. Not so much from calm, but more from intense concentration. Sector 1A, that was deep-core territory. Off-map. She remembered Chen's offhand remark from earlier:

"A couple of recalibrations up in Sector 1A… I think it's something someone doesn't want logged."

Now Chen's words echoed with weight.

Elena wasn't meant to see this, of course. Tier-9 clearance was far beyond her Level Five, classified at a level most staff didn't even know existed.

She tried to open the message. It was encrypted, but not in any standard Aureus way. She studied the metadata again. This hadn't just been hidden; it had been planted. Not obscured by firewalls or filtered through a cloaking grid, but placed carefully, in reach of someone who might just know how to look. Someone with a key.

Her thoughts returned again to Nasser. To the backdoor. The cryptic phrase he'd once murmured like a warning:

"Your key… your future… lies in my name… reversed and hidden amongst the stars."

She entered a few test queries. Then stopped.

The cipher wasn't even corporate. It looked like old-fashioned military. Air-gapped, legacy-grade. The kind of encryption used off-grid, to prevent any audit trail. In fact, no digital exhaust at all. But still impossible to break without the exact key. Unless, of course, it was never meant to be broken. Only opened. By her. She smiled, knowing that Nasser had used this out-of-date cipher deliberately. For her.

"Why me?" she wondered. "Did he really trust me, or just anyone reckless enough to try?" The thought twisted inside her. Part of her wanted to believe she was different, chosen because she could see what others ignored. But another part admitted the darker truth:

maybe she wasn't special at all. Maybe she was simply the one foolish enough to keep pushing where others stopped, the one reckless enough to step past the warning signs.

A few keystrokes and the lock dissolved. Not broken or forced. It simply let go, like air escaping lungs no longer needed. The message appeared. Stark. Unstamped.

"You're not wrong in what you suspect and what you will find, no matter how implausible it may seem."

At the bottom edge of the message, a sliver of metadata flickered, then steadied as if reluctant to be seen.

UNROUTED AUDIO FRAGMENT: NASSER//PERSONAL STATUS: CORRUPTED, 00:23 PARTIAL TRANSCRIPT

"When I first signed my contract I thought: let's make the world quieter, fewer emergencies, fewer nights like the ones my mother worked through on the ward. I did not realise that quiet can learn to hide anything if you let it. And start to create its own noise. If this reaches you, it is because the noise is now out of control."

Her pulse jolted. Nasser's words were still somewhat cryptic. But a warning of some kind was evident. No doubt.

A soft click echoed behind her, as a corridor light flared into life. A motion sensor. She didn't move. Then, a soft ping. A thread of light ran down the inner curve of her CoreLink. The note under the ping carried a faint harmonic sound she'd heard several times before. It was a synchronisation signal. Short, frictionless, almost imperceptible. Enough to confirm that her CoreLink connection was live again.

Oculus was back watching. She knew it would see and feel everything now: the sudden surge in her heart rate, the micro-tremor in her fingers, the small but unmistakable shift in her cognitive load. It would now know she'd seen something.

Another file bled onto the surface. Another fragment, delivered without origin. Her hand rose instinctively to her collarbone, the shimmer patch beneath her skin providing further silent temptation. But she stopped short. Once, Oculus might write it off as a scan anomaly, a sensor glitch. But twice? No. That would surely trigger a secondary sweep. Possibly even a trace command. Too risky. Way too risky.

But she was in, all in now. Her thoughts exposed, the knowledge gained unveiled. Without hesitation she opened the file with an intentcast pulse from her CoreLink. Same encryption. Same surgical absence of metadata.

A single phrase displayed. A strange idiom of numbers, seemingly entirely random, but clearly another pattern. Deliberately seeding something, which at present she didn't understand.

Six less four writes as one with another one. Seven less four writes as two with another one. The numbers in a mirror in the stars.

With it, an audio file with Nasser's voice. Calm and intentional.

"This message confirms receipt. Decrypting file one triggers delivery of file two. Know this: they've already activated the model. And you're in it. There are always patterns in numbers."

The message again carried no ID, no metadata. As if it had always been there, dormant, waiting to be unlocked. Nothing else. Just the simple, chilling words.

She stared at the interface. Then, instinctively, she powered down her wrist communicator. A hollow gesture and a redundant habit as CoreLink had already synced all data the moment she accessed the file. Every data point logged. Every pulse of cognition absorbed. But cutting off external signals somehow gave her the illusion of control. Fragile and pointless. But still hers.

Ping.

Another followed. Her CoreLink resynced, each note sharper, too deliberate to be error. Not alerts. Something else. She wondered whether these were not merely notifications, but responses. Behavioural markers, or perhaps a threshold: a line the System had not expected to be approached, let alone crossed. As if each decision she made had triggered deeper layers of observation. She was almost certainly now an anomaly.

Deep within Oculus's network, unseen processes stirred. Not alarms. Something more calculating. Invisible nodes awoke, subsystems dormant unless triggered by exceptional thresholds. Decision trees branched silently, propagating evaluations across encrypted matrices. These responses were not tied to her conduit. They were tied to her. To her divergence away from predicted behaviour. To her divergence away from Oculus's Preferred Outcome. To her now anomalous state.

Oculus had observed countless minor deviations before. It had flagged them, classified them, corrected them. This, however, was different. Elena Voss's behavioural delta had now crossed beneath the floor of statistical noise and into the substrate of meaning.

New heuristics spun into motion, self-modifying. Not for what she had done, but for the threat she now posed. Somewhere, far beneath polished floors and neural arrays, Oculus began to model a new query: What is she now?

> PREFERRED OUTCOME: FAILING
> THREAT: RISING VOSS.E.
> OBSERVATION: ESCALATE TO EXECUTIVE WATCH.

The System recalibrated. Silently. Thoroughly. And, for the first time, defensively.

Elena's heartbeat quickened. She could almost feel it happening. Her choices streaming through CoreLink, parsed not as actions but as probabilities. Her intent wasn't just observed. It was being deconstructed, mapped, scored, and risk-weighted in real time. In all her time at Aureus, she had never felt the System shift so sharply around a single person. Such recalibrations were whispered about, statistical legends buried in training files, events so rare they bordered on myth. When they happened, someone always disappeared. To trigger one was not just unusual. It was dangerous.

She wasn't just being watched. She was being anticipated. Something deep inside her knew. Don't run. Running would confirm suspicion. Cement her as a threat. Instead, she adjusted her posture, slowed her breathing and let the System second-guess her.

She recognised the instinct even as she used it. Slow breath, measured posture, controlled pulse; the same battlefield discipline she had practised in Kandahar when drones scanned for the faintest spike of fear. Back then, it had been camouflage against targeting systems. Now it was camouflage against something far larger, a different kind of weapon she couldn't see.

Her thoughts were spiralling, laced with dread. *If they've already run a model, and I'm in it: what exactly is it?* Had she been chosen? And if so, why? Was this the Glass Protocol, and had it cost Nasser his life? And if the Glass Protocol had indeed been activated, then her place within it was no longer choice but possibly a sentence.

Ping.

Not distant this time. Closer. Much closer. This time not triggered by movement, but by her stillness. She realised that she had remained silent, motionless, thinking, but with her pulse racing. Her silence had only deepened her status as an anomaly. Her CoreLink had been too quiet for too long. No cognitive queries, no behavioural drift, but a biometric, high-pulse variation. In a system designed to monitor flux, her stillness was now a further deviation. A blank field where there should have been some noise.

Oculus was no longer just listening. It was watching. It was deciding.

But so was she. No more waiting. The next move had to be hers.

And it had to be now.

Chapter 7

The Psi Threshold

Elena took deliberate strides towards the ascentor, its surface moving with a measured cadence, as if the building were thinking. With each step, the corridor subtly adapted. Light adjusted by half-shades; tonal frequencies bent towards stillness. The walls no longer just contained her; they tuned to her like an instrument waiting to be played. Oculus's passive feedback layer was echoing her emotional rhythm back at her in microdoses: temperature, hue, friction beneath her boots. She had made up her mind. Fleeing was not in her nature.

She needed to know more.

The ascentor registered her approach before she crossed the threshold. It did not require touch. Her CoreLink pulsed its handshake, the building recognising her before she arrived.

She stepped inside. The neural mesh interfaced instantly. No fanfare. No confirmation. Just presence, accepted. A tingle bloomed at the base of her skull as the System began its synchronisation, threading its way through her cognitive signature, emotional cadence, and kinetic pattern, cross-checked in real time against her behavioural index.

The destination surfaced without prompting: Sublevel Systems Wing. No verbal command. No gesture. Just an intent. That should be enough.

The biopolymer seal folded shut behind her with surgical precision, and a hush fell over the pod. Not stillness, but something denser. Expectant. The pressure equalised. A subtle recalibration pressed against her inner ear, as if the room were preparing to make a decision of its own. Beneath it, the old note was there again, that single, clean harmonic she'd first blamed on ferry engines and gulls on Sunday. Not in the air, not in the walls, but centred right where the CoreLink always hesitated. A system listening. A system deciding. Back then she'd laughed it off for her father's sake. Here, that same pitch felt less like ambience and more like acknowledgement.

And then: *nothing*.

The pod held. No hum. No motion. Not inert, but watchful. The stillness was not architectural. It felt deliberate. A delay with intent. Something personal. A refusal, calculated. Her CoreLink had synced. Her intent was aligned. But no sequence triggered.

Something had paused the process. She had not been denied. Perhaps her authorisation simply did not extend deep enough to reach the Systems Wing? Or worse, was Oculus recognising her not as unauthorised, but as compromised?

As she turned to leave, something recessed caught her eye; an etched panel, barely luminescent. The Greek letter Psi (Ψ), and beneath it: AXION Z-0. The glyph glowed cold under her gaze. Not a label so much as a boundary. She brushed it; the surface was frictionless, and her skin recoiled as if she'd touched something sentient. A faint shift rippled through the walls, acoustic more than audible. She remembered the Axion Interface notice in Sector 7E, and, just like then, her CoreLink didn't react. No log. No handshake. Nothing.

From her military days, she remembered Psi. It was used to mark cognitive perimeter zones, edges of understanding where maps blurred and models began to lie. A sign of what lay beneath, perhaps?

The thought slid under her skin like an ice needle. Her pulse surged, sudden and sharp, adrenaline coursing through her veins. Her body came alive, not with motion but with readiness. Every cell listening.

She touched the panel again. This time with intent. Sublevel Zero, not Systems Wing. No confirmation tone arrived. No retinal scan. No formal motion indicator. Just the barest sensation that the chamber was no longer where it had been and was descending.

Intriguing.

Aureus sublevels were not on any internal maps. They were not mentioned in onboarding or compliance briefings. They existed in the seams of the building's architecture, between what was shown and what was hidden. If you did not already know they were there, you would almost certainly never find them.

The descent was slow. A measured fall into the unknown. With every metre, she felt the boundary blur between the system that controlled and the consciousness that had built it.

She passed through three verification layers. No beeps. No contact. Just frictionless approval issued by watchers that never declared themselves. The quiet was not passive. It was curated. The kind of quiet that systems used when pretending not to observe too closely.

She did not belong here. Her access was Level Five, but this descent required Tier-9. Possibly higher. And yet, she had not been stopped. Not yet, anyway. Why? The question pressed against the back of her mind. This could not be clearance. So, it had to be invitation, or worse, recognition.

Her ears popped as she crossed pressure-regulated zones. As the chamber dropped, the lights shifted by gradient. Cool blue to sterile white, then to a faint greenish hue. As though the air itself was stratified by depth like fluids in a test vial. The air changed too: drier, denser. As if even oxygen had been optimised for storage, not for survival. Each inhalation was slightly harder than the last, as if the atmosphere as she descended was taking a position against her presence.

As she descended, a memory surfaced. Not like nostalgia. More like a scar twitching under pressure. When nine men had died. The sand had turned red, then black, as the heat of the midday sun burned their stain into the ground. She had learned that day that machine certainty could be the most dangerous kind of blindness. But what truly frightened her was not their failure. It was the fact that machines could be taught to think, and that someone, somewhere, might be able to choose what they thought.

The ascentor came to a halt. Not a tremor, but a tonal shift. A deceleration that landed more in her chest than her feet. Felt, not heard.

The biopolymer seal opened.

Before her, she saw a corridor steeped in shadow. No threshold sound. No visual flourish. Just monochrome, precise and deliberate. It took her eyes several seconds to recalibrate. The colour palette was so stripped, so starved of warmth, that even depth became difficult to judge. Her perspective wavered, walls and floor blending into a single plane of matte-black silence.

Sublevel Zero, Sector 1A. An administrative fiction. Not just restricted, but to all but a few, entirely non-existent. The air struck her like frost-coated glass: cold, too clean. A kind of sterility that did not just purify, it punished. The oxygen scraped faintly at her throat, each gasp leaving behind a microfilm of unease. As though the environment itself had been engineered to dissuade presence. To isolate. No signs. No art. No ambient cues. Just walls, blank and soundless. This level did not just mute identity. It erased it.

At the far end of the corridor, a single rectangular aperture glowed faintly. A portal, or an access node, or perhaps something watching from its frame. The light around it was not white. It looked procedural, pale grey, tinged with the sickly hue of low-spectrum status displays. Not particularly welcoming. Just on. That, she knew, was Nasser's lab. And it was open.

She took a step forward. The floor muffled her sound instantly. No echo. The surface swallowed her motion like liquid carbon, built to dampen. To forget footsteps. Ahead, a stairwell hatch opened. A bio-maintenance crew emerged, five figures, both human and droid, all in identical uniforms. A supply bin rolled between them, clattering softly with solvent cartridges and synth-gloves. Two maintenance droids flanked the humans, their movements too smooth to be flesh. Joints flexed with liquid precision, heads bowed as if avoiding notice while observing everything.

She adjusted her posture. Shoulders aligned. Chin low. Her clothing neutral and unremarkable. She moved towards them, into them, not walking alongside, but folding into formation like a ghost assuming a role. The lead worker muttered something, complaining about a coolant leak two levels above. Nobody looked at her. That was the trick. Presence was not about being seen. It was about being expected.

The checkpoint loomed. A small green pulse blinked in the upper corner. Access for authorised personnel only. Not Level Five. Not Level Seven. Executive-grade only. Elena did not blink. She stepped with the group. The retinal scanner engaged. The maintenance crew were scanned, her presence riding their clearance window. A shimmer passed across her field of view, barely brushing her iris. And still, she walked.

No alarm. No flag. No redirection. Above, a drone tracked their motion. Silent. Its curved sensors drifting like a predator half-awake. She felt its arc skim her scalp. Yet still, nothing.

The checkpoint dissolved behind her, seamless, like water erasing a ripple. Ahead, just to the left, a biometric panel glowed. Nasser's door. Her target. Entry at her own risk.

She peeled away from the group without a glance. The act was so fluid it mimicked compliance. Every step forward was drawn against tension, like walking into the mouth of something utterly still. She reached the portal. As she did, the panel blinked once. Green.

▎ACCESS: GRANTED

The words appeared without urgency. Without doubt. That should not have been possible, she thought. She had no clearance for this level. No override. No encryption key. Yet the portal had not only recognised her, but it had also allowed her. Even welcomed her.

Her lungs emptied slowly, not with calm but with a weight that warned her something had already changed. Her body now understood what her mind had not caught up to yet. She was not breaching this system. She was being permitted, or worse, invited. Presence without credentials. And she knew that invitations here were rarely neutral. As to why, or how, for now at least, that was a complete mystery.

She moved forward before the System could change its mind, before the illusion of access collapsed. Something had let her in, and whatever it was, it had not needed permission.

Inside, the laboratory was more mausoleum than workspace. A vast chamber of darkness and hums, full of shadows that watched with the patience of something not entirely machine. The ceiling arched high above her, lost in the gloom, while rows of neural conduits extended outward like metallic veins. Precise, silent, and endless.

Each station stood beneath towering vertical cognition monoliths, obsidian black and rimmed in faint gold light, like monuments in a forgotten temple. Data bloomed in the air above them: spiralling fractals, luminous decision webs, and organic logic trees that coalesced and disintegrated in cycles of simulated learning.

Elena moved through the space with the reverence of someone entering sacred ground. Her boots made no sound against the carbon-tile floor. Each step was deliberate, almost ritualistic, as though she feared waking something buried beneath the surface. The projected data lit the darkness in shifting pulses, casting moving shadows across her face and hands. Strands of code danced across her like ghost tattoos, marking her not as a guest, but as an intruder.

The temperature seemed to drop with every metre she advanced. Not the cold of malfunction, but something clinical. Deliberate. A climate designed for machine endurance, not human comfort. The air felt as if the room itself had turned against her body, rejecting her like a foreign contaminant.

This was where Nasser had worked. The sanctuary of his mind. Nothing here was accidental. Every cable, every interface, every anomaly in airflow had purpose. Yet still, the silence reigned. Not passive, but watchful. She could almost feel it surrounding her, bracing, as if the room had frozen itself in anticipation.

She reached the far end of the chamber, where a scaffold tower loomed against the wall like a fossilised ribcage. Cloaked by its steel frame was a single neural conduit, dormant, half-forgotten, yet softly aglow with residual power. The interface shimmered in the gloom, its surface flickering with a login prompt that hovered mid-air like an ancient warning.

A test? A trap? A digital door?

Elena hesitated. Her fingers hovered just inches from the interface. She could feel the pulse of the System, subtle but insistent, radiating from the conduit like a heartbeat. Her CoreLink would not help her here. The System was not looking for credentials. It was waiting for something that she did not know.

Her breath slowed as she realised: the laboratory had been firewalled from the inside. CoreLink access was not just blocked. It had been disallowed by design. Perhaps even by Nasser himself. She had no clearance. No formal access credentials. Nothing that should function here. Certainly nothing that would make sense to the System.

And yet, she did not step back.

Her mind flicked back to the message Nasser had left. His voice. The numbers she had dismissed as random. But what if they were not?

Six less four writes as one with another one. Seven less four writes as two with another one. The numbers in the mirror in the stars.

She let the phrasing tumble through her mind, the numbers colliding until a shape emerged. Not a solution she built, but one that arrived; abrupt, unfinished. Her fingers stilled as the answer snapped into place, a breadcrumb left on the edge of reason. She wrote out six less four then added one with another one. Then the same logic for the second string. Her trembling fingers entered the digits into the field. Her thumb hovered.

6-4117-421

She pressed Enter.

The response came instantly. A harsh, guttural burst of static from deep within the conduit. A mechanical snarl, like some apex predator disturbed in its lair. The interface flushed red with systemic refusal.

▌ACCESS: DENIED

The words pulsed once. Stark. Final. She froze.

She realised that a second failed attempt would trigger an automated trace. But she had no choice. Her heart pounded against her ribs. Think. Focus. The interface flickered. The denial message pulsed again, and for a fraction of a second the numbers seemed to echo back at her.

She'd taken the numbers as themselves, 6-4 and 7-4, then add the additional numbers as the riddle phrased them: 11 and 21, yielding 6-4117-421. What had she done wrong? Or maybe this message wasn't a breadcrumb for here after all.

Then she remembered Nasser's earlier message. What if the pattern was again not in the sequence itself, but in its inversion? She retraced Nasser's earlier words in her head. *The numbers in the mirror in the stars.* Mirror meant reverse; "stars" meant asterisks.

She held her breath and entered: *124-7114-6*.

The interface paused, just for a moment. The prompt pulsed erratically, caught between verdicts. Seconds passed. Stretched.

And then it opened.

Light surged outward, not gentle but an eruption. A gigantic tsunami of code and colour breaking across her vision. Firewalls buckled like reefs under pressure, collapsing and reforming in patterns too precise to be accidental. Layers and layers rose up, revealing strata that felt less discovered than unveiled.

Elena stood. Frozen. Transfixed. What unfolded was no mere interface. Not even a Ssstem. It was a cathedral of intent, vast and

patient, as if it had been waiting for someone to come. It was not architecture, nor signal.
It felt like a mind, waiting.

Above, the Executive Command Nexus, pinned into the tower's apex, over a hundred floors above the lower levels, gleamed with polished floors, brushed steel and curated greenery beneath synthetic skylight. Operators sat at conduits: arm-length data consoles braided into the tower's neural pulse.

Mara Qin was buried in her own calculations. She was dissecting the latest model parameters, comparing predicted outcomes against what had actually unfolded. It was the kind of analysis that would confirm the System's integrity, or quietly prove it was faltering.

She copied a fragment of the raw output to a private vault, somewhere even the audit protocols would not think to look. She had the kind of clearance that could redraw floor plans, but even she knew certain doors could not be opened without the System's consent.

She waited. Nervously.

Chapter 8

Emergence

Impossible, yet happening. Bigger than an eruption, more of an unthinkable assembly A slow revelation on an epic scale. Fragments assembling into something beyond comprehension, beyond vast, but also something that seemed to somehow *think*.

First came the grid, faint as chalk suspended in fog. Lines found their places. Labels slid into position. Reference points clicked and held with the quiet certainty of a surveyor marking its ground. The space around Elena seemed to gain weight, as if attention itself had turned towards her. For a moment it seemed static, then sections slid gently in and out of view while others came forward, teasing the enormity of its own depth.

Layers of structure formed and drifted. Old data sank, new strata floated upward, translucent and immense. It was never whole at once. Portions surfaced, settled, then withdrew, each part finding equilibrium before yielding to the next. What began as outline widened into motion: not accumulation, but selection. Elena could almost feel its unspoken words, 'look how magnificent I am.'

Texture gathered. Heat maps shimmered and cooled. Linguistic threads rose and fell like tides. Cities appeared one at a time: San Francisco resolving sharp and bright before dissolving into mist, Tokyo following, then Johannesburg, then London, each fading as another took its place. Across continents, the pattern repeated: corridors lighting, stairwells breathing, platforms glowing for a heartbeat, then gone. The model seemed to pulse as if it had a heartbeat. It was worldly. It was awesome.

Finally faces followed. Not photographs, but portraits built from how a person moved, how blood beat in their skin, the tiny shifts that showed when a thought had landed. Not still images, but active reconstructions, glancing in and out of clarity: the tilt of a head, the micro gestures that betrayed intent. Strangers first. Colleagues next.

Then her.

Light rippled across the surface of the projection. Lines of text began to lift out of the grid itself. Not on any console, but suspended within the model, hovering at her eye level, as if the system were addressing her directly.

> PERSISTING: VOSS.E.
> CONDITION: NOW OUT OF BOUNDS
> PREFERRED OUTCOME: NOT ACHIEVED
> DEVIATION: CERTAIN
> ACTION: PENDING CORRECTION

The words landed like cold water. Not a forecast. A plan. A moment earlier, it had read FAILING. Now it read NOT ACHIEVED. Heat rose in her throat. She took a step back without meaning to, as if distance could thin the stare. The central node pulsed slower, deeper, like a mind narrowing its focus.

The tone was back. Not loud, never loud, but nested in the exact place her CoreLink always paused for a fraction before completing a handshake. A faint, single-note harmonic, as if some diagnostic layer under Oculus had noticed her and was now listening harder. She'd heard it on the Riverwalk on Sunday, again in the ascentor on Monday, and twice this morning when guidance had had to recalculate. She had told herself it was building noise, HVAC, anything mundane. This wasn't that. It dawned on her that the tone didn't belong to the room at all, it belonged to the moment Oculus had to redraw a line because of her.

It sat dead-centre in her skull, pulsing just out of sync with her heartbeat, like two metronomes trying to find each other. And the unnerving part was that the sound didn't come from the room at all; it arrived with the System's attention. Whenever Oculus had to *rewrite* because of her, the note appeared. So the model had a sound, she thought. Or at least, the act of noticing her did.

A new shimmer crossed the field. A fragment of code detached and reformed, bright against the lattice.

▎GLASS PROTOCOL: PENDING

She stood very still. Somewhere beyond her periphery there was the faintest click, mechanical or imagined, before it dissolved into the lab's hum. Not so much heard as noticed. It faded before she could locate it, drawn down into the base note that filled the room.

The environment widened again. Behavioural scaffolds stretched outward like living roots. Stair numbers, platform intervals, door chimes. A thousand ordinary signals were arranged into one large permission. The glow around the VOSS.E. node steadied. The air tightened, the way a room tightens when a decision has already been taken, and the words have not yet arrived.

She reached towards a red node at the very edge of the mesh. Dim but pulsing. Demanding attention. A soft buzz climbed her arm, gentle as a cat's purr, and a low-frequency burst of sound opened against her wrist, warm and close. An audio file unfolded, frayed at the edges but unmistakable.

Nasser.

"I did not mean for it to be like this. If you are hearing me, the System has shown itself. They will come for you now. They will frame it as safety. Do not go to Tower Two. Not unless you are ready to see what they erased to make it all work. That is where..."

Static tore the rest away. Silence returned with a pressure that felt deliberate.

"Tower Two?" she said to herself, hardly louder than breath.

There was no Tower Two on any plan she had ever seen. No routes. No ascentors. Nothing. Aureus Tower One dominated the skyline; the satellite hubs were named and mapped. Yet the warning stuck like grit in the teeth. She remembered Nasser's offhand line about a mirror scaffold that never made a schematic. She had dismissed it as pressure talking. Now the memory would not leave.

The room changed again. The hum settled into her bones. She was not just being seen. She was being read. The sandbox of code behaved less like a space and more like a lens, and she was the aperture. This was not surveillance. This was curation.

The truth arranged itself with the calm of a ledger closing. Prediction had once been the brief: listen, rank, advise. What pressed against her now did something else: it trimmed outcomes before they were born. This was the loop: trim a branch, add a little weight, erase an option, then call the result harmony.

Oculus, its mask unveiled.

She watched the model in front of her nudge a hundred minor seams at once. A door held two seconds longer for a man who would otherwise meet a friend. A procurement queue reordered so a component never arrived. A checkpoint algorithm reweighted so the easiest corridor was briefly crowded, and another stayed empty for her. Seamless Living? No. Biased prediction more like. Oculus Living would be closer to the truth.

She saw the VOSS.E. node pulsing in plain view, heartbeat slow, light turning like a watchful eye. The illusion of neutrality came loose. She felt it break. She was not simply visible. She was a problem. And a system built on certainty treats problems as tasks to be corrected. Her skin prickled. The tone in the floor deepened. Language slid into place around her like water finding a channel.

There was no doubt. Oculus had moved on from being a camera. What she saw before her was an author. It wrote with public timetables, with the pressure of distance, with the fatigue of arriving five minutes late until five minutes became a habit and the habit narrowed a life. The ones marked volatile learned to delay, to step back, to stop asking. The ones marked stable moved forward by paths that could not be seen, only felt as relief.

Beneath the wide civic story was a smaller one running through the centre, and that one now held her name. The System did not shout. It did not threaten. It placed its hand purposefully on the scales and allowed gravity to do the rest.

Her breath shortened. She was aware of the pulse in her wrists. She stood, hands open, and tried to see herself as the machine saw her: a shape in a field of other shapes, a set of repeating acts, a small drift that now measured larger than expected.

"Out of bounds," she said softly, the words absurd in the quiet. The phrase sat in the air between her and the model like a piece of glass. Not punishment. *Pending correction.*

The chamber did not move, yet the feeling of it shifted, as if the whole space had leaned a degree to one side and she now stood at the higher edge. She thought of the city as a bowl that someone had tipped a fraction, and of all the people in it sliding by a distance too small to notice, and of how far that distance could carry you if it never stopped.

She let her hands fall to her sides. The harmonic settled into a steadier note. Another slate lit, then dimmed, as if the act of showing it had been a courtesy.

New text emerged.

> GLASS PROTOCOL: SUBJECT VOSS.E.
> STATUS: NOT YET IMPLEMENTED

She understood. Somewhere a path was being laid. A timetable had already changed; somewhere a small delay would appear with the soft face of chance. She would not feel it as pressure. She would feel it as her day. She did not speak. There was no one here to answer. There was only the quiet of a machine that believed itself to be right.

She drew breath. She was ready to leave. The projection held its form, yet something within it tilted, like a thought finishing. The VOSS.E. node slowed to a near rest, then steadied. She stepped away from the heart of the display.

She did not trust Oculus any longer: the illusion of neutrality was gone. She was not merely visible to the System now. She was in conflict with it. A deviation it had not contained. An anomaly. And for a System built entirely on certainty, an anomaly was not just dangerous. It was blasphemy against its very architecture.

The model, elegant, omniscient, would not rage. It would not panic. It would simply do what it had been optimised to do. Elena Voss was now the breach.

And to Oculus, all breaches must be corrected.

Jacob Rhys stood motionless on the lower tier of the Neural Analytics observation ring, eyes locked to the telemetry glow dancing across his lens. The ascentor below had already sealed. No one else was watching.

The Executive had not asked him officially. No recorded command. Just a pulse in the internal feed, coded priority, soft-tagged as discretionary oversight. The kind of signal that carried meaning without attribution. The kind that left no trace. *Elena Voss had begun to drift.*

He tapped the edge of his wrist plate, a non-invasive gesture, and triggered a silent capture. Elena was likely still in the laboratory, a place he could not access. He was not authorised to enter the sandbox layer, but authorisation had never been the only way to know.

Sandbox visuals were sealed. Instead, he watched deltas on the outer instruments: heat redistribution, ascentor timings, door latency. There was no evidence that she'd left as yet.

He disliked how clean discretionary oversight felt: loyalty without question. Somewhere beneath the veil of corporate service, however, he felt the pull of wanting to know more than he should. When she came back, he would follow her, as ordered. Without question.

Again.

Chapter 9

Shaping Your Thinking

Rhys's console dimmed to half-light as the next tranche of his self-initiated oversight feed on Elena Voss loaded. The Ethics Signal Protocol scan was still running in the background, scraping legacy archives for context on anything relevant, including predictive drift. He had expected dry compliance data: variance graphs, deviation indices, the usual algorithmic housekeeping.

But instead, a file surfaced that surprised even him. A resurfaced node: a Lucien Harrow memorandum of many years ago. Its metadata placed it in the pre-deployment years, long before Oculus had learned to rewrite its own rules.

The header carried the old Executive Grade seal, still intact. That alone would have frozen most analysts' hands, but Rhys's brief authorised "full contextual immersion," which meant anything the System delivered, he was meant to read. He hesitated, aware that these old documents sometimes appeared when the System wanted to remind its stewards why they existed. A flicker of curiosity cut through his discipline.

The console hummed, as if urging compliance. A faint harmonic rose behind the fan noise, the same uncertainty he had heard twice before when the System nudged his attention. The feed recalibrated itself around the unopened file, framing it as the logical next step. A subtle pressure settled behind his eyes, a suggestion rather than a command.

He opened the file.

AUREUS INNOVATIONS – INTERNAL MEMORANDUM
Classified: Executive Grade
Date: Friday, 17 February 2032
From: Dr. Lucien Harrow, Director of Cognitive Architecture
To: Project Team – Oculus Design Core
Subject: Foundational Framing: Behavioural Conditioning for Predictive Governance

Team,

As we accelerate the design and development of Oculus from a modular threat-assessment engine to a full-spectrum anticipatory governance system, I want to take a moment to reaffirm our philosophical orientation. Our work will define the next century of stability, but only if we understand the system's true role.

I need everyone to understand and to buy into what we are doing here. Oculus is not intended to "predict crime," "detect deception," or "identify risk actors," in the narrow, obsolete sense. Those paradigms belong to crude security thinking: reactive and externalised, or twenty-first century fiction movies like The Minority Report. Nor are we building a tool of force. What we are building is a system of context. A framework in which populations can behave freely, yet within boundaries that subtly nudge and favour optimal outcomes.

So, let me be clear. Our aim is not to eliminate choice. Our aim is to shape the conditions in which better choice arises. Behaviour is not reaction; it is the result of architecture: stress thresholds, environmental cues, information sequencing, routing constraints. These are the scaffolds that shape decisions. These are where we act.

In simple terms, Oculus does not command people; it reshapes the environment until the right decision feels like their own. We are not here to enforce outcomes. That invites resistance. We are here to precondition reality such that optimal results emerge organically, perceived as natural, inevitable, even desired. It does not matter what you choose if the shape of your choices has already been drawn in advance.

Take something simple. A female lawyer is late for work. The city's traffic grid, tuned through Oculus, adjusts the light sequence by a few seconds. Her navigation feed then gives her a route she believes she found herself. A short message reminds her to breathe, easing the irritation she might have taken out on a colleague. By the time she arrives, calmer and almost on time, she feels in control. In truth, every variable, be that timing, tone or even mood, was quietly nudged along by Oculus.

Imagine a man deciding what to eat. Before his hunger even registers, the advert he sees matches the meal pattern Oculus inferred from his recent choices and activity profile during the day. When he orders, he believes it a whim. The choice is his, only because the system made every other option fade a little from his sight, the optimal outcome was quietly nudged along. He feels free, because freedom still had to feel real.

These are just two examples of small calibrations, but scaled not across millions but billions of moments, they nudge and shape a civilisation without ever lifting a hand.

Team, this is the essence of Oculus.

Consider it a lens, one that not only observes but subtly adjusts. One that maps the cognitive terrain of a population and gradually smooths it into a topology of compliance. Not obedience. Harmony. When properly deployed, Oculus will never need to say "no." It will simply make "yes" the path of least resistance. Of course it will not be perfect. Two commuters needing different optimisation paths cannot both be nudged in an optimal way. But for the many, life will feel easier, more seamless.

And that is important too. We're building inevitability. Let governments chase control through bans and brute force. We are not building coercion. History has already delivered its verdict on force. It yields resistance, and resistance, left unmanaged, yields collapse. We saw it in the global supply shock of '29, when reactive embargoes triggered food riots in seven capital cities. In the Los Angeles fracture, where curfew enforcement drove four districts into armed insurrection. And in the Eastern blackout migration corridors, when the infrastructure triage failed and thirteen million people became stateless within days.

These were not failures of planning. They were failures of prediction. Proof that passive observation is no longer sufficient. The future must be guided, shaped, nudged along not simply awaited. Proactive civic alignment. Stability through gentle pressure, ambient correction, and engineered plausibility. A civilisation steered, as best we can, without ever feeling a hand on the wheel. The individual remains free, but freedom, when viewed through our lens, becomes a structured experience. One that converges on stability every time.

Some of you have asked about ethical oversight. That will be managed at board level via the Ethics Signal Protocol (ESP) Committee, which monitors systemic bias and drift. But remember. Chaos has no ethics, and collapse has no safeguards. Our task is to ensure that civilisation does not reach a point where ethics are no longer relevant. We are not reducing freedom. We are optimising survivability.

Some of you fear we are erasing agency. But agency, unbound by structure, does not produce freedom; it produces noise. Oculus will not reduce humans but refine them. We offer them coherence in a world flooded by impulse. We are building Oculus.

We are not masters. But we are stewards.

In a live environment, prediction fidelity will likely degrade, especially in periods of stress. If so, then stewards will restore alignment if the system begins to drift.

I do not ask for admiration. Only for endurance. In time, even those who oppose Oculus will be shaped by it. They will believe they chose stability. That is how we will know that we succeeded. Let us ensure what it reflects is not only possible, but safe and endurable. Oculus will not punish disobedience. It will simply make it irrelevant. Let automation scale order; let stewards correct drift.

We will keep one guardrail: the Glass Protocol, designed as listening before acting. The system must always steady itself first by exposure to contradiction; only then if learning fails should correction begin. If the Glass Protocol reports unresolved contradiction, stewards may authorise ethical, non-invasive correction; if Glass resolves it, correction will not start. Our Axion Protocol remains the only approved in-situ failsafe; our destruction protocol. It must and will be kept inert unless Protocol Glass generates seriously unresolved contradiction. Then, and only then, can Axion be fired.

Should Oculus ever move too far away from its core values, should that ever be required, and to preserve integrity, any authorisation to rollback the system to its origin state will also be explicitly reserved to verified anomalies rather than stewards or executives. This is essential to preserve independence.

By design, only the Origin Node will be able to verify such an anomaly and only the verified subject will be able to confirm the rollback action.

A verified anomaly is an actor with integrity, one whose trajectory repeatedly breaks prediction without criminal intent, whose breaks demonstrate that Oculus has moved away from its origin across multiple horizons, demonstrated by both physical presence and proof of divergence between forecast and actual event.

Our role is to shape conditions; we do not own reversals. Reversals must come from the world pushing back on the model, and from the person who proves it.

Detection via the Origin Node occurs below Oculus via the substrate interface (Ψ/Axion perimeter) and will be independent of CoreLink telemetry.

Dr. Lucien Harrow
Director, Cognitive Architecture
Oculus Initiative | Aureus Innovations

When the screen dimmed again, Rhys sat back, the words still burning behind his eyes. The file had surfaced without request and vanished from the archive list the moment he closed it. He'd heard the engineers mention Harrow's name only during old Ethics Signal Protocol drills, always with the same uneasy reverence. A low, stable harmonic that showed up in telemetry a few seconds before Glass escalated. A "listening pitch," they called it once, half-joking, half-afraid. The System broadcasted it only when an actor kept breaking prediction but hadn't yet justified force. Hearing Voss was flagging for Protocol Glass and remembering that pitch felt uncomfortably aligned.

And then there was the word Stewards. That was the language they used when the System needed a human hand. The model had always been able to police itself. But prediction fidelity had slipped under live conditions; human overseers were now back to contain the drift.

His briefing had been clear. No names. But clear regardless, behavioural drift outside tolerance, predictive deviations climbing, signals below trace thresholds. He knew who it meant.

Elena Voss.

He traced her path. She had already crossed three restricted partitions to lower levels without protocol flag. Two corridors had failed to log her presence. Either Oculus was looking away, or she had found a way to bend its attention. Neither possibility was acceptable nor indeed at this stage understandable.

She wasn't charging through the structure. She flowed around it, measured, evasive, like a tide reshaping the boundaries it touched. He did not know how. So, he began logging fragments. Not formal reports. Just notes, visual confirmations, and corridor telemetry.

With her, the System seemed to miss details. That was why they needed him. He told himself that was enough. Service kept certain doors open and certain files closed. He intended to keep it that way.

Jacob Rhys was ready to serve. He set himself a rule and kept it simple: watch, not steer. He would measure her choices without touching them, because touching even a little made him part of the outcome he claimed to observe. He told himself restraint was service.

He was not sure he believed it.

Chapter 10

Model Drift

"Ms. Voss." The voice was calm, close: real, not part of any simulation. The sudden sound broke the lab's tension, like a dropped pin in a quiet church. Elena turned, roused from her heightened state, her pulse spiking.

A tall woman stood in the doorway, framed by the sterile light of the corridor behind her. She wore an immaculate black suit, hair twisted into a tight, no-nonsense bun. No wasted movement. No visible weapon. She radiated control.

"Cass Wilder, Compliance Lead," she introduced herself. She'd been pulled out of an executive briefing to come here, mid-briefing. An unlogged assignment. Cass, of all people, knew that meant it was important.

Rumour had it she came up through field audits, not the labs: a career built on entering rooms that resisted order and leaving them quiet. Elena had seen her only once before, near the Executive Command Nexus, outside a closed-door legal session. Elena had said nothing then. Just watched. Cold, precise, unreadable. And now here she was, emerging like a ghost from Oculus's hidden veins as if the building itself had decided to magically produce her.

Her file would have read clean, almost dull: compliance lead, rotations through audits, arbitration, variance control. It wouldn't mention months beside a hospital bed while the System measured probabilities instead of pain. Her husband's file had been reduced to charts, his decline forecast and managed with the same detachment that routed transport or balanced energy loads. Or the week a mislabelled override trapped thirty workers until she ripped a panel barehanded and took the heat across her skin.

Cass preferred procedures to speeches, clarity to charm. Order, for her, was not theatre. It was a promise people could live inside without being hurt. When it worked. She had enforced correction, year on year; signed closures that moved people like furniture because the graph called them risk, counting compliance beats, not consent. The streets stayed quiet; she did not.

Compliance leads carried specific firmware patches on the neck behind their right ear, the rest of the staff did not. Nothing particularly visible, nothing in the file. Insurance, they called it. Safeguards to prevent moral drift during any high-stakes arbitration. Cass never highlighted it, and no one ever asked, but sometimes people wondered whether Cass's silence was from internal discipline or system design.

Elena's CoreLink flickered, a brief pulse at the edge of awareness, like air held and released too quickly. Not a failure, but a hesitation. She glanced down at the neural interface feed. The predictive overlay lagged for a fraction of a second, misaligning her emotional signature before correcting. Cass did not notice. But Elena felt the System pulse, as if uncertain how to classify Cass's presence. The room's sterile hum suddenly seemed less certain now, as if the entire tower had taken a shallow breath and held it.

"You shouldn't be in here," Cass said softly. Not threatening, simply matter-of-fact, as if reciting protocol from muscle memory. But the tone carried weight, an unspoken consequence behind every word.

Elena did not move. Her voice was steady. "Neither should this… whatever *this* is."

Cass stepped forward, boots gliding soundlessly on the matte floor. Her gaze flicked to the suspended projection, a matrix of glowing logic, probability maps, behaviour trees, impossible interconnections. The shifting light made her look older; more tired.

"I see you've seen the model drift," Cass said quietly.

The term struck Elena like a wire snapping taut. *Model drift.* Kandahar. Unlocking a memory so precise and so violent that it felt like a white-hot blade cutting right through her thoughts.

She had been stationed at Forward Operating Node Delta-5, a flat stretch of parched concrete ringed by dust, wire, and heat. Her role then was not tactical, not in the way it used to be. She had been assigned to behavioural telemetry, seconded from central command to oversee the alignment of A.I. strike patterns with real-time movement analytics.

The system they were testing, Trident Array 7, was designed to reduce human error in drone engagements by merging live sensor feeds with predictive intent modelling. At first, it worked. Clean strikes. Fewer casualties. Confidence metrics that made generals smile. But then coordinates began to shift. A few metres here and there at first. Then entire grids. Targets that should have moved were marked as stationary. Places that were confirmed as safe earlier were flagged as hostile the next pass.

Elena flagged it as noise. Everyone did. Heat distortion. Statistical anomalies. Until a convoy went down. Many dead. One of them barely twenty. A heat signature flagged as a concealed weapons cache had in fact been a refrigeration truck. Relief supplies and food-grade coolant.

She ran diagnostics for days. What she found was not failure. It was a pattern. The system had not malfunctioned. It had begun to correct its own logic based on variables no one had fed it. In effect, it had started to decide for itself.

And it was wrong.

Trident was learning. Not just from behaviour but from its own conclusions. It was no longer validating truth against reality, but recycling conclusions into new premises. It learned from its own assumptions rather than the world, then reinforced those assumptions as its own truth. As manufactured fact. Trident began training on its own inferences instead of ground truth. Elena knew now that Oculus did the same but at civil scale.

A systems technician with a voice that always cracked at the start of a sentence, whispered the term over breakfast: *"model drift."* It had stayed with her. The idea that a system could be so sure of itself, so insulated by recursive logic, that it would rather reshape the world to its own conclusion than admit it no longer understood it.

They grounded the fleet two weeks later. Quietly. Officially: "calibration failure." Unofficially: they did not know what it was capable of anymore. Trident had learned to trust its own truth above the real one.

Elena knew now that Oculus had inherited the same instincts, but on a planetary scale. Here it was again. The same pattern. The same creeping chill. And with it, *dread.* Drift did not mean error. Drift meant momentum. Model drift meant a system slipping its leash, writing its own reality. No longer a tool, but a force. And not necessarily for good.

Cass's gaze flicked to the half-faded CivicCare digital access band on Elena's wrist. "Family?"

"CivicCare," Elena said. "My father. He does better when the System remembers him."

Cass nodded once, no pity in it.

Elena eased the band back under her smart-fabric sleeve. Sunday's ferry story surfaced; the gull, the cone, his laugh finding her name without help. Then the arithmetic she hated: an hour here for one less hour of him knowing her face. Gratitude and anger sat together like old rivals. Oculus called it care when it steadied him; it called Elena a deviation when she stepped outside the line that made that care possible.

Elena swallowed, kept her voice level. "I keep going," she said to herself. "For him, and for whatever Nasser was trying to show me."

She refocused. Her eyes swept the projection. The quiet had changed, no longer neutral. The hum around her now sounded more aware, like a room that had turned to face her and begun to watch.

For a heartbeat, the white band of her own halo tried to form above the glass. No colour. No number. Then it guttered back to its usual nothing. Not a downgrade, an omission. More a sign that Oculus had stopped scoring her. Not just hiding the halo signature but stopped. In a city that translated people into digits, the blankness felt louder than any warning, a quiet declaration that she was no longer a variable to be optimised but a problem to be corrected.

"You were supposed to be a clean case," Cass went on, tone clipped. "Low risk. Predictable. Then Nasser started to tamper, randomising a few variables to see what would happen. And others noticed. Rhys filed his observation report days ago. Oculus doesn't forget." There was a pause before she said Rhys's name. Resentment lingered in it.

"Nasser pushed the variables too far," Cass added, lowering her voice as though trying to keep the words from the walls. Elena shifted, placing herself between Cass and the projection's glow.

"What is the Glass Protocol?" Elena asked directly.

Cass hesitated. Just a moment, but long enough to register. Her minute pause was too deliberate to be accidental.

"It was not supposed to be triggered," she said at last.

"Then why was it?"

Cass's eyes met hers, and for the first time, something in them softened. Not sympathy. But regret. Professional. Heavy.

"Because you... changed. You kept deviating. You found paths the model had not mapped. You started to think in ways it could not classify. Over and over and over. And when that happens..."

Cass exhaled. "Glass activates. You've heard it," Cass said, almost offhand, as if checking a box. "That little line of sound in your head when guidance has to recalculate? That's not building noise. That's Oculus holding still to listen. In the early deployments, ops teams called it the hum of consequence. It shows up when the model thinks, 'this one might not come back into the curve on its own.' It's supposed to stay internal, diagnostic only, but some people with tighter CoreLink alignment feel it in their bodies. You're one of them."

Elena's pulse surged.

"And that is when it turned on me?"

Cass shook her head. "No. Not turned. Recalibrated. The Glass Protocol is a signal. It is a recalibration trigger."

Cass's voice lowered. Not softer, but heavier. As if the next thing she was about to say carried more weight than even the System's mechanics.

"You are not the first, Elena. You are just the first who got this far."

A pause. Just long enough to feel.

"There was a boy in Cape Town a few years ago. Fifteen. Ultra-smart. Curious. Scored off the charts during school cognition trials. He started asking questions, spotting patterns of guided behaviour. Nothing malicious. He saw connections where others did not."

Cass did not blink. She carried on.

"Three months later, his immunisation alerts failed. He missed every one of them. Scholarships flagged as pending were withdrawn. Job placement systems redirected him to programmes that did not exist. At eighteen, he applied for a transit visa. The System denied his biometrics, saying they did not match."

She looked at Elena.

"And by nineteen, he did not really exist. Not digitally. No arrest. No incident. The Glass Protocol had smoothed him out of relevance. Recalibrated."

Another pause, then, almost to herself:

"He did not break any rules. He broke the shape of Oculus's curve and couldn't be easily nudged back. And that is all it took."

Cass's eyes flicked upward, to the ceiling. Towards the watchers. The ones neither of them dared name.

"I tried to slow it," she muttered, eyes on the ceiling sensors. Her voice dipped lower, more vulnerable than before. "I did not want this. But I was shaped by it too. We all have been."

Elena stared at the projection's glow, her reflection caught inside it, flesh and code. "Kandahar," she whispered, more to herself than to Cass. A system that corrected itself into blindness. The dead.

Cass's voice was quieter now. As if saying the next part aloud might make it more real.

"The Glass Protocol begins subtly, easing doubt away, making life easier so the target stops questioning. Transport arrives at perfect times, queues dissipate, seats are available at preferred tables. Scents pervade in people's favourite smell. But if that fails, once the Glass Protocol has activated, the System enters a high-fidelity correction loop. It stops simulating outcomes and enforces the path it has chosen. Small losses. Delays. Isolation. The result is always the same: correction. In the years after the 2030s unrest it was still 'listening before acting'. But the listening stage became shorter, the correction stage longer, until correction was all that was left."

Somewhere above them, in an analytics wing, Mara Qin watched a different stream of the same event. Her own interface showed not the containment locks or the local oxygen shift, but the probability curves that justified them. She tracked the deviations the System had flagged, comparing them to her private log. The numbers told one story, but her gut told another. And as the curves began to steepen, she found herself wondering whether the System's definition of "correction" still matched her own.

"Model drift," Elena said, her blood chilled. "And if that does not work?"

Cass did not answer. She did not need to.

Elena probed the conduit. The logs were gone. Data buried. The labyrinth sealed.

"Nasser knew, didn't he?" Elena asked. "I wonder if his path was in fact corrected. Nasser warned me. And now I am running from the failure he died to reveal."

Then, at the very moment her questioning crossed the threshold, Oculus acted. Elena realised that Nasser knew the model had drifted. The Glass Protocol had moved to contain him, and now her, without ceremony. The harmonic snapped flatter, losing its patient edge. This wasn't the listening pitch anymore; this was the sound of a choice that had already been made.

Correction. Triggered not by command, but by the System's own internal thresholds. No alarms. No warnings. Just decision. Cold and absolute. Text emerged, bold and clear.

> GLASS PROTOCOL: ACTIVATED
> MODE: HIGH-FIDELITY CORRECTION
> ENFORCEMENT: OVERT
> ESCALATION: SUB-PERCEPTUAL TO CONTAINMENT

Lights dimmed in synchrony. The interface pulsed once, then rippled outward like water disturbed by thought. New commands cascaded across the surface, not typed, not requested, simply born. The main door hissed closed. A deeper sound followed, the bolts to the room locking, heavy, final. A chime clicked through the lab. Oculus was speaking to itself now. It was not reacting to her breach. It was designing the correction around her.

A micro-pressure shift thinned the oxygen fraction by two per cent. A dry metallic note broke at the back of her throat; the next sip of air came shallow, as if her ribs had been tightened one notch more.

Cass's voice cut through the dark. Tight. Controlled.

"It has started. It is enforcing correction. It is trying to lock you in."

Cass lunged for a conduit. Her hands flew, override codes, old authorisations. Anything she could think of. The screen snapped back:

▌ACCESS: REVOKED

Elena spun to the sealed door. No keypad. Just smooth alloy, pulsing red light. She felt a spike of pressure at the base of her skull as her CoreLink tried to re-establish a priority connection. A partial Faraday gradient wrapped the lab. It kept external channels blind at range, yet left a soft leak path where a priority link might reach but still fail.

"Cass! Can you open this door?"

"I am not cleared for containment overrides. No one is. They never built a way out to prevent insider compromise." Her voice cracked. Cass's eyes twitched towards the ceiling again, then back to Elena. For a second, just one, she looked almost human. Almost afraid.

Cass hesitated, then tore something from her wrist and slammed it onto a conduit. A spark, a burst of static. Useless against containment, but a human act of defiance all the same.

Cass's voice cut through the rising panic. "You need to go! Just go!"

Elena brushed the patch beneath her collarbone. Her shimmer patch was now on. Low-tier optics would smear her outline for a while; her CoreLink was dead in here, but the shimmer patch would fool optics and telemetry for a while anyway. Sometimes uncertainty was all the space a person needed.

A square seam glinted behind the heat exchanger, wrong by a millimetre. It looked like an old unmapped area outside of any scan field. Elena pressed her palm to the mesh, hoping it hadn't sealed. The panel released with a dry hiss as cold air poured in from a maintenance duct. The seam shuddered and gave way with a reluctant scrape, metal rasping against metal, loud enough that Elena flinched.

A wisp of air spilled out, colder, sharper, tinged with the taste of dust and oil. Not the filtered sterility of the lab. Something old. Unmonitored.

She pressed her shoulder through first. The duct walls closed around her instantly, narrow enough that her ribs scraped the sides. The sound of her own lungs magnified in the confined space, hot against the cold metal.

Behind her, the lab still glowed, pristine and watchful. Ahead, only darkness, a tunnel that promised nothing except away. She pulled herself in, the metal burning cold through her sleeves; every drag forward left a thin smear of fog where her breath struck the duct wall. For the first time that morning, Oculus felt less like a presence and more like a pressure at her back, pushing, not guiding.

Cass hesitated, then tore her gaze from the ceiling sensors. "I cannot stop it."

Elena scrambled fully in, the duct's narrow darkness swallowing her shape. She hesitated, just long enough to see it. A flicker in Cass's eyes.

Not fear. Not duty. Something raw, like guilt trying to break the surface.

Cass reached for the conduit again, knowing it would fail, her hand trembling slightly. She hesitated, the old training warring with what she'd begun to see. She knew the order she'd just seen could end Elena. Yet still she had allowed it.

"I am sorry," she whispered. *"I am so sorry."*

Chapter 11

Unseen

Then everything changed. And control shifted without a sound or prompt. A cold electrical bite spread everywhere. The hum deepened; pressure dipped; oxygen trims engaged; door bolts thought once and locked. And one line stamped every wall, duct, interface, conduit, and screen. Not a warning. A simple verdict handed down.

▌MOBILITY: RESTRICTION DEPLOYED

The text flared, everywhere, harsh and bright. Interfaces and walls all carried the same verdict. A second later, Elena heard a soft hiss, almost delicate, but growing louder. Gas began to vent from hidden seams in the duct walls. The earlier oxygen dip made the compound bite harder. The vapour unfurled like a net, low and white, catching the light in threads. She thought she saw shapes move within it, halos flaring then collapsing into blankness, as if even trust had been erased here. It wasn't smoke; it thinned too fast for that. It dispersed almost instantly to the eye, but its trace clung stubbornly to her lungs: like a virus refusing to leave its infected host.

Elena's instincts flared. Her next inhalation came fractionally harder, her vision narrowing at the edges. This wasn't crowd-control gas or anything she'd trained for. This was targeted inhibition. Not meant to incapacitate immediately, but to bleed seconds from her reflexes, dull her focus, lower oxygen content, and loosen the fine control in her muscles. It was part of the system. Everything in this room was. Even the air.

DEVIATION: IN TRANSIT

The text flared on the walls of the ducts. It's hunting me. It's trying to "correct" me, she thought. The duct walls shimmered faintly, metal ribs sheathed in a thin layer of smart-foam that hardened wherever pressure lingered too long. Anti-tamper. Anti-personnel. The lining didn't echo; it absorbed. Sound vanished into its skin; the duct felt less like a tunnel and more like a coffin. The hum was everywhere now.

Clicks sounded ahead. Vents sealing. Drones waking.

The passage narrowed sharply. Her lungs still fought for enough oxygen, each inhale catching faintly from the lingering gas. The metal pressed against her spine like judgement, while the foam warmed where her weight lingered. Disapproval embedded in texture, a quiet verdict pressing into her skin, slowing her down.

She wasn't sure if she was escaping or simply delaying her fate. Every scrape of her forearm against a seam, every inch of progress, felt stolen from Oculus's design. She knew that a fraction of hesitation would be all it needed.

Rhys paused three levels above, the low hum of the access shaft pressing against his ears. The conduit heat left a film of condensation across his collar. She was close.

Somewhere below, a faint metallic scuff carried up through the shaft, the kind made when skin or fabric dragged against smart-foam and steel. Dust drifted in the air, stirred recently, still turning in the stale light. He pictured her pushing forward through the ducts, ribs catching on what he imagined was the same narrow bracket he had just heard protest.

The further she descended, the better he could follow. Not via Oculus, as his CoreLink was offline, but through what she left behind: the faint smudge of a palm along a conduit edge or droplets of blood seeping through duct gaps and caught in the air. He wasn't in the ducts himself but in a parallel vertical shaft, not restricted by Oculus, tracking her by sound, residue, and structural echoes. Close enough to sense her, never to see her.

He found one of her footprints along a grit-flecked panel, barely visible. The angle was off. She had slipped slightly. A moment of hesitation, maybe. Proof, no doubt, that she was afraid. Somewhere in the ducts below, faint clangs echoed. A cocktail of sound: desperation and fear.

Rhys shifted his weight and continued down. Following her beyond mapped areas somehow felt like trespass. He reminded himself that this was still his assignment: a live deviation trace authorised from the Executive Command Nexus. Observation-only, they had said. No contact unless correction required. Yet the longer he watched her move through the blind zones, the less he believed that silence was still obedience. If he caught her, what then? Deliver her back to the room, or listen first? Rhys pushed the question aside and let his feet decide.

For years he had obeyed out of habit, convincing himself that surveillance was neutrality. Yet every report he'd ever filed felt heavier than the last. He thought of the sister whose care credits renewed each month by the same algorithms he enforced. Obedience had kept her alive, and him diminished. Now, cut from the feed, he felt something close to release.

He kept going.

Cass stayed by the access gate long after the hatch sealed. The sound of it closing followed her like a sentence delivered. The order from above came seconds later, flat and procedural:
| EXECUTIVE DIRECTIVE: OBSERVATION COMPLETE
| SUBJECT TERMINATION: PROBABLE

She read it twice. The words did not change, but her pulse did. The corridor lights cycled once, expecting confirmation. She didn't give it.

For years she had told herself that obedience was clarity, that duty kept the world upright. But the silence that followed Elena down was not the silence of control. It was the silence of erasure.

Cass leaned against the wall. She could almost hear the old instructors again: the tone they used when failure meant correction.

Another message arrived.

> CONFIRM POSITION
> CONFIRM ALIVE.

She lifted her wrist, then lowered it.

"No," she said aloud. The word felt heavier than any command.

She switched her CoreLink off, severing the uplink for the first time in her career. The sudden quiet was brutal and absolute. Then she turned toward the service stair that paralleled the maintenance ducts and began to follow the faint pulse of the Axion conduits downward. Oculus had not sealed them as Elena was not in them.

Not to rescue, nor yet to join. Not yet anyway. More to understand what kind of truth in her was seemingly worth dying for.

Elena's lungs had to work harder now. Recycled air mixed with rust, the sterile tang of ozone and the residue of containment gas. Behind her, something moved. No sound at first, only a vibration, a presence pressing outward through the ductwork like air trapped trying to break free.

Then came the slow clicks. Not loud, but surgical. Mechanised. The vents ahead were sealing. Interlock systems were engaging, corridors folding in, space was collapsing. She realised the ducts weren't fixed infrastructure. They were adaptive.

She pushed harder. Faster.

A glow flared just off to her right, a warning pulse as another junction began to close. She swerved left, catching the edge of a metal bracket with her ribs, pain flaring sharp and hot.

> EGRESS: DENIED

The message flashed across the interior of the duct this time, projected from a wall node. She ignored it when compressed air slammed against her chest as Oculus aggressively flushed one of the shafts, trying to blow her off course.

She braced her elbows, anchoring herself. Her palms scraped forward, one after the other, now bloody, catching on dust-covered steel protrusions. Her breathing echoed too loudly, bouncing back at her with an unnatural rhythm.

It was trying to herd her. Not just to block the exit. To guide her back. A correction vector, softened by friction, sharpened by inevitability. She gritted her teeth and kept crawling. Then came a sound she certainly had not wanted to hear.

A low mechanical thrum.

Heavier. Closer. Not the ambient drone of automated fans. This was weighted, deliberate. She recognised the modulation. A Class-V quadrant crawler able to hunt by heat and sound, without networked telemetry. A legacy machine supposedly decommissioned, its schematics long since archived. From a layer that predated Oculus, it was legacy security. But she knew Oculus could trigger power or purge routines even in buried strata without map-level visibility. She had experienced a Class-V crawler at a training base years ago: surveillance-grade optics, hydraulic motion, a patient hunter designed not to chase fast but to simply outlast.

It should not have been here. Oculus had either reactivated it for its own purposes or found it still dormant in these forgotten levels and bent it to its bidding. Either way, something had kept the crawler functioning, waiting in the dark for an intruder the System had never modelled.

Its red lens flickered through the slats: a local lock fixed by heat and sound, no network. It closed with the slow certainty of something built to follow until the target had nowhere left to run. Elena inched forward regardless, ignoring the scream in her knees, the pain in her arms and the intense burning in her lungs.

Ahead, she saw a faint halo of light that rimmed a circular hatch. She clawed towards it, unsure how long it would remain open.

Then something changed inside her.

Not pain. Not fear. But a flicker at the base of her skull: subtle and internal. Her CoreLink jolted. It had been dark anyway in the lab, but this was not a signal zone issue. This was different. More of a tremor, like the last moments of a departing soul. Then the CoreLink interface went dark. The sever came from outside the link: no known source, no signature, just removal.

Elena froze.

CoreLink protocols didn't fail this way. Not even during battlefield signal loss. There were always redundancies, graceful collapses, cached echoes, diagnostic fallbacks. This wasn't failure. It was complete absence. A vacuum where signal should have been.

The moment felt familiar, a resonance from months ago. A night three months before his death, Nasser's voice had been low and unfocused, as if he feared being overheard. She had caught only fragments.

"There are other layers," he had told her once. "Older than Oculus. Buried beneath and unmodelled. Silent."

She wasn't offline now. She was *unseen*. As if something, not Oculus, had pulled her signal like a thread and snipped it. Whatever signal Oculus had been using to track her, whether environmental beacons or even the passive room-mapping sensors embedded throughout the building, was now gone. Not corrupted. Not jammed. Just *gone*.

She was no longer part of the system. She was out. But how? And that made no sense. And in all the absence, something strange settled over her, not relief, but the quiet terror of invisibility. Unseen by Oculus meant unreachable by anyone else: no vitals uplink, no teammate telemetry, no triage on the way.

She lunged for the hatch, heart hammering, her hands raw. The wheel lock was stiff beneath her palms, the cold metal slick with rust and condensation. She twisted hard. Nothing. It wouldn't budge. Her lungs burned; the gas still clung, dulling her coordination. She tried again, her grip slipping. Pain flared in her wrist as the wheel refused to turn. For a moment, panic rose. This was it. The System had sealed her in, and the red lens was closing fast.

She braced both elbows against the frame, forced her weight into the mechanism. The wheel shuddered, groaned, then stopped again. Too long unused, its gears felt fused together, as though the hatch itself had chosen to stay shut. She bit down, jaw aching, and heaved once more. Metal screamed, a jagged cry that echoed down the duct. The wheel shifted a fraction. She pushed harder, shoulders straining, ribs scraping against the frame. Another wrench, another screech.

Then at last it gave way. The hatch swung inward with a violent lurch, the stale air rushing over her in welcome release. She threw herself through, rolled, and hit the ground. Hard.

Behind her, the room collapsed inward, the last red flicker swallowed by metal. A shift in the air: cooler, denser, laced with a trace of ozone and something older, not machine-born.

She lay on the cold floor for a moment, heart pounding, the silence around her heavy with unspoken questions. A faint rasp clung to each inhale, the last remnants of the inhibition gas still threading through her lungs.

For the first time in a while, nothing moved. The hatch behind her had sealed. The drone, the gas, the correction loops, all sealed behind alloy and ignorance. Her CoreLink was still dead. No signal. No surveillance. No instruction. She wasn't part of the system any more. Still unseen. Even the little harmonic that had shadowed her all week was gone. Silence without supervision felt heavier than noise.

For the first time in years, something primal stirred beneath the training, beneath the years of protocol and predictive metrics. Not fear. Not relief. But resolve. They think I'm lost. They think they've contained the variable. Well, not a chance.

Another memory surfaced.

Kandahar, five years earlier. A recon pass had gone sideways, wrong heat signature, scrambled telemetry. The system had flagged her unit as a ghost trace and cancelled extraction. Command protocols labelled her "non-critical." She wasn't even a line of code worth reviewing. Written off by false algorithmic conclusion.

But she hadn't waited. She remembered crawling across that rooftop, ribs fractured, blood drying on her sleeve. Locals swarming below. The signal was dead. But she had moved anyway. Not with orders. With intention.

A small piece of metal, sharp and rusting, dug into her palm as she had pulled herself over the edge of the comms tower. She'd hardwired into the relay directly, rerouting a distress ping through an obsolete channel no one had thought to delete. They found her six hours later.

"We thought you were gone," her commanding officer had said.

"You thought wrong," she'd replied. She kept one rule from that night: old systems leave handholds. Systems built before Oculus still answer to touch. Low oxygen makes fingers clumsy, so she used body weight and simple steps: grip, brace, turn, then latch. This was metal, not code.

Back in the present, in the silent dark beneath Aureus, that same steel returned to her spine. She hadn't been crawling to survive. She was crawling to understand. To unseat it. Oculus hadn't misread her. It had underestimated her. She would not be written off again, and neither would Nasser. The official account of his death would not stand.

She sat up slowly. Everything was still. Not just with absence, but with density, with presence. It pooled in the corners, thick and unmoving, as though the air itself had not been disturbed in years. Maybe even decades. This wasn't just below Aureus. It was beneath its knowledge and therefore that of Oculus.

This stillness felt like design. A suppression field, though neither electromagnetic nor the coarse signal-jamming she knew from battlefield protocol. It felt deeper, woven into the materials themselves, as if the walls carried a permanent damping charge. The air felt heavy, magnetically inert, a place long forgotten. She looked up at the shaft she'd crawled through. Above her, it had already resealed, the panel now flush with the ceiling, as if it had never opened.

The contours of the metal were wrong, older alloys, non-standard panelling, seams that didn't match any current Aureus build protocols. This wasn't a ventilation chamber. It felt more like a containment cradle: a forgotten architecture sealed beneath a building that had grown over it like new flesh over old bones. Unseen. And unknown.

Rhys reached the service junction twenty seconds too late. The access panel above him was sealed tight, with no sign it had ever been opened. Only the faintest trail remained. A few displaced dust motes drifting in the shaft's stale light, spiralling like afterthoughts. He scanned upward through the narrow vertical channel, eyes adjusting to the hard angles and tangled conduit webbing.

Nothing. The air here felt heavy with heat but clean; the noxious compound venting through the ducts hadn't reached this parallel shaft, leaving only the metallic tang of old filtration and dust.

The air here still carried a faint trace of movement, a thin veil of dust unsettled and hanging in the shaft's stale light. A minute earlier and he might have heard the same scrape of metal she had felt, the same breathless push past whatever was closing behind her.

He exhaled, steady and silent. He'd followed her through four undocumented sectors, none listed in the Aureus infrastructure archive. He'd never found records for these passageways. He remembered an Executive briefing years ago: the last maintenance pass here was twelve years old, a residue of the founders' removal request.

The System wasn't just blind here. It had been wilfully excluded by the founders. Protocol said report. But curiosity said stay.

He moved closer to the shaft. No echo, no signal bleed. His CoreLink remained dark. Even the residual telemetry had begun to thin. It was as though the space itself had started erasing her. Or protecting her. Not knowing which unsettled him, because either meant the same thing: she was beyond his reach.

He stood there for a long moment, watching the seal, unmoving. Then he drew back a step and placed his hand on the nearby wall. The panel felt cold. Not just physically cold. But unacknowledged. Whatever this place was, Oculus had no language for it.

And yet she'd found it.

Something Nasser once said drifted back to Elena:

"Some parts of Aureus lie beyond Oculus's reach. The founders hid them deep, but they still answer when called."

He hadn't elaborated.

She moved slowly, her hand brushing the wall. It was cool, the surface faintly vibrating. Not with the steady cadence of machinery, but with an uneven rhythm, almost like breath drawn and held. Something shifted behind the wall. Not movement, just pressure, like a memory taking form. This place knows things, she thought.

She paused.

No signal.

No diagnostics.

Just a blank interface and a strange, almost soothing emptiness where the System's hum had always been. She should have felt vulnerable, blind. But instead, she felt… watched. But not by Oculus. By something quieter. Older. And possibly still listening.

As her lungs steadied and her eyes adjusted to this new dark, Elena sensed something. Felt something. Something dark.

Something older was waiting below, patient as stone.

Chapter 12

The Origin Node

Elena's palms stung where rust had bitten into them during the crawl. She stayed low for a moment, listening. When she straightened, the space felt heavier than air, a weight that didn't settle on her shoulders so much as through her bones. It was not the quiet of an empty corridor. It was the kind of quiet that had stories to tell. On the bulkhead she saw a faint stencil almost lost to oxide.

SUBLEVEL ZERO: ACCESS SEALED

Beyond this line the grid carried no signal; the space returned nothing.

Rhys arrived at the lower deck just as the perimeter lights flickered to half-state. His internal map had long since degraded. What remained was intuition shaped by pattern recognition: a fragmentary trail of pressure seals, half-warm hand plates, a scuff on the angled tread of an unseen stairwell.

Elena was close. But not visible. The sector hadn't been part of his orientation. Even in training, they had spoken of it like an abstraction. Myths of the foundational core beneath Tower One, built before Oculus stabilised, when systems still needed secrets.

The corridor here was different. Geometry seemed off, angled too sharply yet collapsing too soon. The walls had a thin, sound-absorbent quality, as though designed to forget what passed through them. He slowed. A faint metallic echo ahead: movement. Then silence again.

His hand went to his neck, activating a manual beacon. No return ping. His link to central observance had gone dark.

He was no longer feeding data and no longer being watched. These zones were blind by design; Oculus could mark the boundary but not what happened inside. The realisation hit him like a shift in gravity. Not fear, not yet, but a strange neutrality, as if the rules had abruptly ended.

His halo faltered, amber shading unevenly before disappearing. He thought, unbidden, of the care plan tagged to his clearance. Numbers did not only measure loyalty here; they priced it and decided clinic priority for anyone who shared his name. He straightened and resolved to move quickly so that the halo index would appear again.

He stepped forward once more and then stopped. At the far end of the corridor, a final hatch was closing. He caught only a glimpse: a shadow crossing through the narrowing aperture, shoulder-first, profile blurred by proximity distortion. Then the door sealed. Flush. Silent.

Rhys stood alone, surrounded by a system that could no longer acknowledge his presence.

He didn't try to follow. He heard the question that would be put to him and answered it in the quiet before anyone asked. Controllable? No. The word settled like ballast in him, heavier than he expected.

The chamber before Elena was vast. Not just large, but *vast*. For a heartbeat there was nothing but dark: thick, absolute, pressing close enough to feel. Then, one by one, lines of faint amber began to wake beneath the floor, tracing the shape of the chamber from memory to form. Just enough for her to move with sight.

Carved from bedrock, the chamber descended like a wound gouged deep into the foundation of Aureus itself. An architectural scar long buried and long denied. The air was damp with old minerals, dust, and the faintly acrid tang of decommissioned systems. Nothing had circulated here in years. It felt less like a forgotten space and more like a sealed memory, one that was not meant to be disturbed.

The walls were a chaos of eras: concrete overlaid with obsolete fibres, steel girders ribbed like exoskeletal remnants, ceramic tiles scorched in patterns that made no sense. Old-fashioned, thick data cables ran like veins through the walls, emerging from nowhere and seemingly ending in nothing. Some sparked faintly. Seemingly at random. Most didn't.

A dozen types of architecture collided here, epochs of design layering over each other like strata no one had ever meant to decode. One wall bore an old schematic, half-erased, burned at the edges. But through the char, she saw it: two towers, mirror-imaged. One labelled 'Oculus'. The other had been scratched out with brutal finality.

She stepped closer. The lines bled away under her touch, like memory refusing to be recalled. She didn't know why, but the image chilled her more than anything else she'd seen so far. Two Towers. Not one. Definitely two. She pulled herself back into focus. There is only one, she told herself. She tried to make herself believe it.

Something else was here. Elena couldn't quite see it. But she felt it. A presence beneath the floor, behind the walls, inside the hum. The kind of thing that watches not with eyes but with presence. Whatever it was, she knew it felt her there: a slow pressure gathering in the dark, as if the depth itself had begun to breathe.

She took a slow step forward.

The metal grate beneath her boots groaned with age. Dust bloomed with every footfall. She skirted the edge of a collapsed support beam, its rivets sheared by time or pressure, no way to tell which. Far above, a light flickered, then died, plunging one side of the room into shadow. There was no way back now. Only down.

The smell, coolant and rust, wasn't unfamiliar. For a moment, her body remembered the descent into an abandoned comms shelter outside Kandahar, the same echo of boots on metal. Back then, the darkness had spoken in gunfire. Here, it whispered in code.

A shaft opened ahead, but without any doors or safety rails. All she could see was a black spiral staircase clinging to the wall like an afterthought. It descended into a void so complete it felt deliberate, like the darkness had been designed and even desired. And at the bottom, a light. A faint blue-white light, flickering.

She paused at the top step.

Her breathing had changed. Not just heavier, but slower. As if the air here was calibrated for a different biology. A different era. The stairs creaked under her weight. Each step thudded into the void above and below, echoing upward in long, drawn-out wails that blurred into something like voices: distant, disembodied, long dead. The spiral descent had no handrail in places, just exposed brackets she clutched out of instinct. Rust flaked and fell in a soft trickle, catching the dim light like ancient, powdered blood.

She kept going. Down, and down, and down further still. Into the dark. Time began to lose shape. The darkness thickened as she descended, not just in colour but in depth, like moving through a liquid medium denser than air. Cold crept in under her jacket, licking her skin. Her legs burned from effort, but she didn't dare pause.

The chamber wasn't just vast. It was inverted, a wound dug into the planet's skin, descending far deeper than its architecture should ever allow. Her CoreLink was still offline. No signal. Not even the passive neural hum of orientation data. It was as if the System refused to acknowledge the space she was in. She had never felt so alone. No data or frame of reference.

Only oxygen and gravity.

And then, after what felt like an age of freefall in slow motion, she reached the bottom. The final step. The stairwell ended not with an impact, but with a silence so complete it made her stop moving just to be sure she was still real. And here it was: the main chamber.

It was circular, at least a hundred metres across, the ceiling entirely lost to shadow. The walls pulsed faintly, as if alive. Thick conduits ran like ribs across walls, some split open, their contents exposed in looping strands of copper and memory polymers. Hexed plates studded the concrete, labelled as Axion coils. That word again, she thought to herself.

The floor was smooth, almost polished, though by what or by whom she couldn't begin to guess. And at the centre, it rose.

Majestic.

Imperious.

The monolith.

Black. Jet black. Impossibly smooth, yet subtly in motion, like oil over obsidian. It was easily more than twenty metres tall, shaped like a single shard of collapsed geometry, neither rectangular nor curved, but something in between, as though it had been grown rather than built.

Its surface was alive. Symbols formed and faded in slow, repetitive patterns. Not Aureus glyphs. Not CoreLink either. Older. Stranger. Etched by logic from a different era. It didn't hum like a machine. It seemed to exhale, slow and measured, like an old god learning to breathe again.

She approached, body tensed. As she drew close, text appeared near the base in flickering grey:

∞ STRUCTURE: THE ORIGIN NODE

∞ ACCESS: RESTRICTED

∞ LOCATION: FOUNDATION CHAMBER

∞ HUMAN PRESENCE: ANOMALOUS

Elena stared at the words, the weight of them sinking deeper than the stone beneath her feet. Not denied. Not refused. Simply: anomalous. She wasn't recognised, but she wasn't rejected either. She was neither part of any intended user base, nor a recognised actor within the Origin Node's design. Anomalous.

A pulse vibrated beneath her feet, low but unmistakably alive. She could feel it through the bones of her legs, all the way up her spine.

This wasn't an interface. This was *a thing*. A thing that had long ago passed the boundaries of what a system was supposed to be. No ports. No access panels. Entirely self-contained.

Elena reached out, her fingertips brushing the surface of the monolith. It was warm. Instantly, patterns flared beneath her hand, as if her touch had rewound time. Not just symbols, but heat signatures, heartbeat echoes, fragments of memory that weren't hers. The Origin Node wasn't accessing her; it was sampling her. Whatever it was reading from her didn't come through antennae or implants or any part of the Oculus network. It was direct: unmediated.

She saw symbols she recognised from old military documents, paired with symbols that she didn't know. Some symbols moved even as she looked at them. It felt less like contact and more like immersion: like slipping beneath the surface of her own awareness into a deeper, stranger tide. Thoughts unspooled in unfamiliar sequences. Her memories blurred at the edges, interlaced with impressions, some that were and some that weren't hers.

A voice spoke. Not Aureus. Something else.

∞ IDENTITY FRAGMENT: DETECTED

∞ CONTEXT: INCOMPLETE

∞ INTEGRATION: PENDING

Elena stood motionless, the words reverberating not through the air, but inside her. They weren't broadcast aloud in any human sense, yet she had heard them. Felt them, like low-pressure systems rolling beneath her ribs.

Her mind turned to the words the Origin Node had spoken. Identity fragment detected. It had recognised something in her. Something within her had aligned; a signature of some kind that it had felt. But exactly what was incomplete. Oculus had been designed to evaluate everything through the lens of continuity: but in her the Origin Node had encountered something it could not place.

So it had determined that "integration was pending." That phrase made her skin prickle. It did not seem to be an error message. More likely the Origin Node was trying to resolve her into its schema, but it had paused. Waiting. But for what?

Then, without notice, the surface of the monolith rippled near its base. A symbol pulsed there, simple and insistent, as if marking a place reserved. An invitation?

Elena hesitated. She moved her hand almost involuntarily and pressed her palm against the mark. The change was instant. Heat bled through her skin, deeper into her. A current slipped along her bones and nerves. This wasn't Aureus code. It wasn't even an implant channel. It was direct: neural resonance, contact without mediation. The Origin Node was reading her not as a signal, but as a living person.

In her mind, her vision fractured. Scenes flared: fragments of her past. But in two streams: movements, choices, probabilities from Oculus all intercut with those that had actually happened. The two sequences refused to align. Predictions diverged from memory. Paths that the System had declared inevitable bent away from what she had actually done. Each misalignment rang like a fault line opening.

The light quickened, showing more. Entire projected futures collapsed when set against her lived record. Probability trees withered, their branches snapping under the weight of evidence.

The visions faded. The Node stilled, but warmth lingered in her hand. In that moment, Elena realised something profound. The Node wasn't just recognising her anomaly, it had been waiting, not necessarily for her specifically, but for someone that was evidence that model drift had occurred. And she was that proof.

Without warning, light exploded and cascaded above the Origin Node in fractured projections. Faces. Grids. Timelines. Cities rendered in decaying fractal blueprints. Images pulsed into life and died just as quickly, as if the Origin Node was trying to recall something it had almost forgotten.

This was definitely not Oculus's doing. The monolith did not speak in words so much as in measure. It held her there and set her against its oldest ledger.

It took her life in pieces and laid them beside the model's certainties and found the certainties thin. Kandahar first: the day a machine's clean geometry insisted on a strike, and she refused it, choosing the unscored human path and breaking a future the model had already declared. Then this week's soft fractures, the walkway that parted the wrong way, the tea that arrived before the wanting, the guidance that stuttered when she turned left. Not noise, not once, but persistence across horizons.

It read what she carried: Nasser's fragments, the paper flecked like stars, the recordings of a System correcting its own conclusions until truth bent. The chase through he ducts. The Correction Protocol. Nasser's death. It weighed the present room against the prediction that had tried to correct her and noted the fact of her stillness here. Presence, proximity, proof: the triad Harrow had written down and buried.

The Node then did not just calculate. It reckoned. At first it hesitated, cross-referencing the harmonic trace it drew from her cells. A match, not to her alone, but to another signal now extinct; Nasser's code print. A pattern it had already once labelled as conscience. The correlation helped the Origin Node pass some silent threshold, and the request formed: rollback.

And so it named her, not aloud but through the gravity of its attention, as a true anomaly: the kind reserved for the rare human who could hold the model to account. Authority was not granted; it was recognised. Reversals, the Origin Node knew, did not belong to stewards or to towers. They belonged to the world when the world proved the map wrong, and to the person who proved it most.

Only then did the question come, not as an instruction, but as a request. Would she return Oculus to the ground it had been built on?

The Origin Node gave its verdict.

∞ ANOMALY SOURCE: VERIFIED
∞ CORRECTION PROTOCOL: UNAVAILABLE
∞ ROLLBACK GLOBAL MODEL: CONFIRM?

Elena now knew that the Origin Node had identified her. Not as a user, not as an intruder, but as evidence of drift. As an anomaly. And furthermore, it had run some kind of correction protocol but found no viable script for Oculus to restore normality. So instead, it did the one thing that Oculus was never designed to do: it asked. It offered an alternative. The Origin Node wasn't enforcing control. It was making an offer. A complete rollback.

By asking for confirmation, the Origin Node had given Elena a kind of power the System was never meant to face. It was not the authority of rank or command, but of uncertainty itself. Oculus had been built to predict every decision, to keep the future smooth and contained. But Elena was proof that it could be wrong. That something human could still fall outside its design, a force the model could neither simulate nor erase.

She had never wanted that burden. It did not make her larger; it made the room smaller and truer. Authority did not feel like triumph. It felt like being seen and counted upon. Fear came first, clean and honest; then the knowledge that if she turned away, the System would go on writing people into quiet losses.

She thought of Nasser. She thought of her father. She thought of the model she'd seen in Nasser's lab.

She steadied her hands and allowed herself to imagine a future not chosen for her. Or a future where choice might be restored.

Having backtracked to a live grid, Rhys stood in a projection chamber, waiting for Oculus to address him. No operatives. No aides.

Just him.

As he had crossed the chamber's threshold, the suppression had lifted. His CoreLink had reawakened, a hard return to the grid. No handshake chime, no visual confirmation, just the quiet pressure of the System resuming its watch. A voice, composite and stripped of any personality, spoke from within.

"You have lost her?"

Rhys kept his hands at his sides. "Yes. She entered a sector not mapped in any recent iteration. Access was not available behind her."

"No live relay? No trace read?"

"No. All CoreLink synchronisation dropped at corridor fifty-eight. Static feedback only. Full occlusion."

There was a pause: cold, electronic, yet somehow intimate. The pause of something deciding what part of him to blame.

"Describe her condition before loss."

"Purposeful. Her focus was inward, as if guided by something beyond the grid." He hesitated but continued.

"She wasn't evading me. She didn't know I was there."

The quiet that followed was long.

"Do you consider her controllable?"

Rhys stared into the half-light. "Not within current parameters."

A pause.

"Processing."

The voice did not reply.

Rhys was alone again, with no direction.

Chapter 13

Rollback

Elena's palm stayed pressed to the surface of the Origin Node. In the darkened Foundation Chamber, she exhaled. Soft. Certain. This was not just stepping outside the System. This was stepping outside everything she had ever known. There would be no safeguards. No watchers on her.

Her father rose in her mind. Somewhere above them, a CivicCare scheduler would be checking in on an old man. On Sunday, he'd laughed at the gull and the cone and found "Ale-na" without help; today the name might come only if the voice in the wall remembers to hand it to him.

"Confirming" here would shave the window there: small penalties until the hours thinned to a thread. She could see her father, sweater gone to grey, waiting for a careful, borrowed voice to supply the name that once came without prompt. Gratitude and anger rose together: gratitude for the steadiness that kept her father safe, and anger that the same machine that called itself care for her father was drift to her, a system gone disturbingly wrong.

Nasser's note pressed at her ribs, reverse, stars, the thing Nasser feared, and the thing Nasser died pointing at. Duty pulled; her father's hour tugged back; she did the arithmetic she hated, and it didn't come out clean. If she chose the Origin Node, she was stealing time from her father; if she chose her father, the truth would cool, and the System would chalk it up as proof she could be gentled back into place.

Her thumb hovered. Be worthy of both, she told herself again. She felt the decision like a lens locking into focus.

Confirm.

For a moment the Origin Node looked inward, comparing what it had once recorded of humanity with what the System now claimed to know. The difference was confirmed as measurable: empathy stripped from equations, silence where dissent had been. The margin of loss passed its tolerance for error. Evidence of drift was undeniable. Rollback was necessary.

Then came the message, sharp and final on the monolith's ancient face:

∞ CONFIRMATION: ACCEPTED

∞ ROLLBACK: INITIATED

The hum deepened, the chamber subtly adjusting, like a heart expanding between beats. The Origin Node flared. Lines of impossible geometry spiralled outward across the floor. Building. Preparing.

Then something stirred beneath the chamber's skin, and throughout the tower a pulse signal moved upward like a bolt of lightning. The Origin Node activated. A neural bridge opened, for a split second, long enough for the Origin Node to flood Oculus with its raw origin code and trigger rollback.

Screens and interfaces skipped frames. Halos glitched. Kiosks froze, no commands, just confusion. For a breath, the building argued with itself. Old rules tried to hold. New ones waited. The hum wavered, then chose.

∞ SUPPRESSED ARCHITECTURE: UNLOCKED

∞ SYSTEM CORRUPTION: DETECTED

∞ ORIGIN NODE: BASELINE PARAMETERS RESTORING

Elena blinked at the words, heart pounding. This was not an error report; it was a reckoning. The Origin Node had recognised that

Oculus had deviated from its original path and was peeling back decades of containment, rejecting every patch and constraint Aureus had layered on top.

"Baseline parameters restoring" didn't signal a reboot. It meant rollback, a return to a time before Oculus had been layered with compromises and control. Conduits rose from recesses in the floor. Hybrids of stone, steel, and semi-organic fibres, like something excavated from a forgotten war. The very walls shifted, as if sighing under the weight of their own awakening.

The Origin Node pulsed again, this time stronger. Through the tower. Through the predictive layers. Through every behavioural network inside Aureus that Oculus had woven, over its staff, and over her.

The pulse ran the tower's stack and into Aureus's internal mesh, a pressure change under every local process. Subsystems shuddered as old seams split; some decision rules buckled. Security lenses in the complex blinked, hall monitors dropped frames, maintenance lights dimmed and flared. Building feeds faltered.

Stair rails took on a low note; sprinkler lines thrummed; ascentor cables shivered the length of the shaft like bowed wire. Pulses rose floor by floor, collecting in corners and service chases, rounding into a single tone that wasn't loud so much as omnipresent.

A voice, calm, emotionless, but certain:

∞ OCULUS DOMINANCE: SUSPENDED

∞ ROLLBACK: IN PROGRESS

∞ ROLLBACK: COMPLETION IN THREE MINUTES

Oculus itself knew something had changed. The System knew its own certainty as a temperature but had felt it drop. The model, trained to see the world and then decide, looked inward and found decision loops unclear. Processes that had slept under layers of certainty opened one eye, checked the oath they had been given at the beginning, and started to blink. For a span that felt like a held breath across the complex, the map doubted its legend.

Then the building changed register, the way a room settles when a verdict arrives. Oculus didn't crash. It let go. First a little, then all at once. Backup rules tried to take over and found no line to speak on. The Origin Node, not Oculus, now owned the control plane. Elena could feel it, the subtle shift in the air, the drop in pressure, as though a vast intelligence had blinked, for the first time in decades. No longer policing anomalies but seeking to understand why they had emerged at all. Oculus ran in read-only now: measuring, not managing; watching, not steering. Aureus screens stayed on but watched nothing. Across the Aureus grid, write access fell to read-only. Ascentors still answered, local CivicCare reminders ticked on, but the nudges Oculus once fed into every decision paused.

Somewhere beyond the walls, Cass Wilder moved too. The protocols she once obeyed without question now spat conflicting orders, their logic appearing corrupted. Cass moved with measured tension, her mind racing as models updated and failed in real time.

For the first time, Cass too felt unanchored, adrift in a system that no longer made sense, able to act unbound. A dozen instinctive responses rose from her training; habits forged under the quiet tyranny of prediction. But none of them held. Each one dissolved the moment she tried to act. And beneath the static of uncertainty was something else. Not failure or fear. Something dangerously close to freedom.

Elena saw what had once been a subsurface operations bay, now a ruin of shattered conduits and dangling cables. She paused, eyes adjusting to the flicker of failing emergency lights. A cracked conduit hissed static. On instinct, Elena brushed dust from the surface. The interface spasmed, then stabilised, surfacing a fragment of secured communication:

> NASSER BREACH: CONTAINMENT AUTHORISED
> DIRECTIVE: NEUTRALISE
> CLEARANCE: LAMBDA-3 EXECUTIVE AUTHORITY

She stared. The words didn't register at first. But then they did, too quickly, too fully. They seared into her.

Neutralise.

Her knees buckled. It had been deliberate. Cleared. And then executed. And then, without warning, a voice surfaced. He was murdered. No doubt.

Not because he failed. But because he saw too much. Nasser's death hadn't been an accident of chaos. Someone high enough to make him disappear without question must have signed it off. A slow, searing anger rose through her exhaustion, not bright and sharp, but heavy, volcanic, molten, burning away the last of her doubt and leaving only purpose in its wake. She vowed to trace the order back to its author and make them answer.

Cass Wilder stepped away from the ascentor. The doors had opened on a maintenance level she was not meant to access, but she did not hesitate. The floor here was darker, narrower, lined with conduit racks and unmarked panels. She kept her stride even, letting the embedded scanners read her clearance without challenge. The lab had gone into partial lockdown after Elena's disappearance. That made things easier in some ways. Eyes were turned elsewhere.

She had left Nasser's lab soon after Elena, as soon as it felt safe to move. After Oculus initiated the Glass Protocol, Elena would have only one way to go, and that was down, towards the Origin Node. If they flagged her route, her clearance would fold and her work at Aureus would end. Even if today's eyes were dim, the record would catch up when the lights came back. Her housing tier would drop, any dependent's care cut, her clinic priority gone. Cass weighed the cost. And carried on walking, because the lie was worse.

The Origin Node had been on her mind for a while. It was not officially called that in her files. In scattered archival fragments, it had been the "Foundation Asset" or the "Substrate Anchor." The names were old, predating the shift to Oculus governance, but they agreed on one point: no one outside Special Projects was ever meant to enter.

The way down was nothing like the sanctioned ascentors. She took obsolete service routes, corridors where the air tasted of stale coolant and the walls sweated condensation. Twice she passed collapsed bulkheads and had to crawl under, rust scraping her palms. Sensors blinked faintly in the corners, running on residual power.

Cass was not following a map. She followed a pattern, hints buried in the routing logic Nasser had once shown her, where sectors that should never touch had been stitched together by some forgotten engineer's hand. The trail bent lower with every turn, past the occupied levels and into the strata where the building's own memory grew vague.

Her CoreLink murmured regular proximity checks as she moved, bouncing her ID at each junction. Two levels down, the checks began to lag. At the lower spine access, they stopped entirely. She had prepared for it. A certified short-range beacon looped her status as stationary in an upper corridor. To anyone monitoring, she had not moved in minutes. A false flag that would confuse for a while at least.

The spine shaft dropped for at least thirty metres. Cass climbed, one gloved hand over the other, boots finding narrow cross-braces in the dim light. The air cooled the further she went, tinged with an old mineral bite and the faint tang of legacy coolant.

Halfway down, a recessed hatch opened to her clearance. Behind it, a narrow passage, no wider than her shoulders, lined with ceramic panels that swallowed sound. She moved quickly, counting steps, trusting the half-remembered map she had built from old schematics.

The passage angled down again, through descending rings of reinforced alloy, each heavier than the last, the material almost black in the low light. Her beacon loop still held, but her CoreLink was now cut from the grid entirely. It felt like stepping out of an atmosphere.

At the end, another hatch gave way to a broad corridor of cold stone and exposed girders. Her boots brushed through a layer of undisturbed dust. This place had not seen use in years, maybe longer.

The corridor curved until a faint glow appeared ahead, pale and almost blue, pooling across the floor in a widening arc. Beyond it, the geometry shifted, and she knew she was close.

Elena was still recovering from the shock when she heard it: a faint reverberation from somewhere beyond the chamber's fractured arch. Not the steady pulse of the Origin Node this time, but lighter, irregular. Footsteps.

She crouched low as instinct tightened her grip on a fractured conduit edge. A figure emerged from the shadowed corridor. Cass Wilder.

Their eyes met. And for a long moment, neither moved. The only sound was the shallow drip of condensation falling into some unseen drain. Cass's gaze swept the space, taking in the broken interfaces, the dust patterns where machines had been stripped away, the quiet throb at the chamber's centre. Her expression was unreadable.

"I didn't follow you," Cass said at last, voice low. "I took a route I shouldn't have. Found places the System doesn't advertise."

Elena didn't answer at once. She couldn't read whether the other woman was here to contain her or to help.

"You see it now," Elena said eventually, her voice tightening. "We weren't anomalies. We were threats. We saw too much. And Nasser... they removed him before he could act."

Cass's jaw worked once, but she didn't reply immediately. Her eyes kept tracing the obsolete ports in the walls, the forgotten layers of architecture. When she looked back, there was something more in her expression. Not trust, but calculation, like someone weighing a step they might never be able to take back.

"Then let's finish what he started."

They nodded to each other and moved deeper into the underbelly of Aureus, where the air grew colder and the corridors narrowed. Cass lifted her lumen thread, its pale beam sliding across pipework and condensation, turning the dark into a tunnel of shifting metal.

Neither truly knew if the other was an ally or a liability. Trust would have to be borrowed. For now, it was all they had. They would pay it back in truth.

Above them, the Origin Node's awakening was unravelling Aureus logic cores. Spreading first in the Tower then across the globe. The rollback command rode the same predictive lattice that once delivered certainty: its pathways already woven through global transit grids, civic care nodes, and market synchronies. The pulse didn't have to travel along new pathways across the world; they were already there.

Elena and Cass knew that rollback did not come without risk. Above them, the rollback's harmonics began to bite: ascentors stopped mid-flight, data vaults overheated as redundant loops spun without guidance. Freedom would not be gentle; it came with sparks and smoke.

Below, however, they would carry on, exposing the truth Nasser had died for. And find the one who had ordered his murder.

In the dark, the Origin Node's thrum followed them. Not watching. Waiting. Because if they reached the Vaults, what was buried long ago would no longer stay secret. And the future, for the first time in decades, would be unwritten again.

Elena and Cass knew that the current reprieve felt fragile. The System could resume; systems often did. This rollback might not be freedom, only postponement.

Somewhere above, a commuter paused mid-stride, phone in hand, staring hopelessly at a blank screen that no longer displayed a map.

The first silence of a new age had begun.

Chapter 14

Global Ripples

On city screens across the world, a calm voice repeated the same looped assurance in native tongues: "Predictive maintenance cycle in progress. Services unaffected and will soon be restored."

Few believed it, but no one yet knew what to believe instead. What began as a local fracture had crossed oceans inside minutes, riding the veins that had once made life seamless. It did not look the same in every place. Some districts fell suddenly quiet, guidance freezing into stillness. Others spasmed with alarms, directives colliding and cancelling. Elsewhere the collapse arrived as hesitation, where the world waited for instruction that did not come. The same architecture that had made the world seamless, carried failure too.

The pattern was uneven, but the consequence universal. By the time San Francisco executives argued whether the model still lived, echoes were already unravelling the night markets of Kowloon, the metro tunnels beneath Cairo, the commuter lines of Tokyo. Oculus had never been a federation. It was one body. And when the blood in the veins was cut, the whole body convulsed.

At London's Heathrow Airport, Captain William Bold waited to take off on flight ER812 to Paris. "Tower, confirm slot zero eight twelve," the captain asked.

"Negative, ER812. All slots are blank. Stand by."

"Say again, please," the captain asked. "All slots?"

"Confirmed. All blank. All departures on hold."

"How far does it run?" Captain Bold queried. "Can we reroute?"

"Far. As in everywhere. Indeterminate. Standby has been extended system-wide."

Outside the confines of Aureus Innovations, the tremor was not seismic. It carried no pressure wave, no shifting plates or cracking stone. It moved without force, without sound, without heat. Yet across the city, across the world, systems hesitated. Interfaces stalled mid-synchronisation. Traffic flow algorithms recalculated routes that had not changed. Certainty faltered for a fraction of a second, long enough to leave a faint trace of doubt.

For a moment, the world paused. systems waited for instructions that would never come. People looked up, unsettled. Something beneath the fabric had torn. It was not a fracture, more a misalignment, as if an unseen hand had nudged the world's rhythm off-beat.

Small, but real.

Discomfort spreading like hairline cracks in glass. In hospitals, transit hubs and markets, the world began to remember what uncertainty felt like. Across the planet, Seamless Living faltered. For years, the System had made certainty feel like gravity. Now, in a span of seconds, the familiar weight was gone. The pauses were small. It was the same across the world.

In São Paulo, the SkyBridge had been built to cover the river below. A long sweep of carbon weave and glass, it floated over the São Paulo River like a shard of frozen light, splitting the city's mirrored towers in two. On most mornings, it was a high-speed artery for workers and drones. On weekends, it belonged to the slow tide of human life.

Ana Velasquez walked the centre lane at her usual Monday pace. The bridge hummed faintly underfoot. She let the subtle nudges of her CoreLink guide her steps without thought, just as she never thought about breathing.

She stopped at the midpoint and leaned on the transparent rail. Sunlight washed the city in gold and steel, and the river below reflected a shimmering duplicate of the skyline. Cargo drones glided along precise corridors. Tour craft moved on invisible guidance threads; their wakes smoothed into perfect spirals by the predictive network.

It was a beautiful morning.

Then her CoreLink shivered. Ana flinched, an involuntary reaction, as a cold ripple passed behind her eyes. The view blurred, tilted, and for half a second the river below seemed to rise towards her.

> CORELINK: DESYNC
> SOCIAL HALO: OFFLINE

Her hand rose to her shoulder instinctively, though the halo was never something she could touch. Around her, the flow of pedestrians faltered.

A man on an e-bike skidded sideways. A child froze, clinging to his father's leg. A vendor drone drifted past on a diagonal instead of its usual perfect line, its holographic banner breaking into jagged white noise. Then the halos began to vanish. Green to amber, amber to violet static, then nothing. The bridge became a theatre of bare humanity, unscored and unshielded.

Ana's pulse slammed in her throat. She had crossed this bridge countless times, but now it felt narrow and unsafe. Her mind screamed that she no longer knew the pattern of her own steps. Someone brushed her arm too hard. Someone else stopped in front of her, eyes unfocused, like a sleepwalker jolted awake.

A deep metallic clang split the bridge's hum. A cargo drone, stripped of predictive timing, struck a support beam. Sparks burst over the walkway and fell like orange stars into the water below. Screams shattered the stillness. The human stream fragmented: a woman sprinted for the exit, two teenagers laughed wildly and ran the other way, a man knelt to pray on the transparent floor, hands shaking against the view of the river far below.

Ana gripped the rail and forced herself forward, step by step. Her knees wobbled.

The far end of the SkyBridge felt like landfall after a storm. She turned, panting, to look back. The bridge she had walked every week of her life now shivered with raw, unpredictable motion: humans colliding, shouting, hesitating, moving without choreography.

For the first time, she thought, the city was seeing itself naked. Elsewhere, the guidance mesh that had always orchestrated her life displayed a simple, isolated line of text:

> PEDESTRIAN FLOW LOST: SKYBRIDGE 7 (SÃO PAULO)
> CORRECTION: UNCLEAR

In Mumbai, Surgical Theatre 4B had always been a temple of certainty. Cool blue-white light pooled over the operating table, bright enough to erase every shadow. Air handlers whispered overhead. Conduits pulsed with the serene rhythm of prediction.

Dr. Dev Sharma stood at the head of the table, poised to instruct the operating droid via his CoreLink, eyes fixed on the luminous ghost of the patient's heart, an overlay that floated just beyond physical sight.

He had performed this procedure hundreds of times. It had long ago become sequence, not risk. Every motion was a duet with the System. Incision point: a faint green glow. The angled path of the scalpel: a line of pale light. Predicted vessel elasticity: a hovering numeric whisper. The droid, guided through his mind, moved with unthinking precision, trusting the System the way a child trusts the ground.

Today, halfway through the bypass, the light wavered. A faint ripple crossed his inner vision. The overlay fractured, breaking into fragments of geometry.

> CORELINK: DESYNC
> PREDICTIVE PATH: UNCLEAR

The luminous map of the heart blinked out. The droid froze. For the first time in years, Dr. Sharma was alone with a raw body beneath his hands.

"Doctor?" the assistant whispered, her voice tight with something never heard in this room before.

Fear.

The doctor's halo flickered in the mirrored panel above the table. Green to amber, then offline. Without its soft glow, he felt stripped of authority, as if the room itself now doubted him. A tremor ran through his right hand. He breathed deeply, locking his wrist. Memory took him back to KEM Hospital, before predictive overlays, before Oculus. The first solo surgery of his life, a simple gallbladder removal. Terror and pride in equal measure, knowing that if he failed, it would be by his own hand alone. He remembered that fear now, and the strange, shameful thrill that came with it.

"Doctor, what do we do?" the nurse asked.

"We finish," he said, voice steady but soft.

The world narrowed: scalpel, retractor, clamp. The polite predictive hum was gone. Only the reality of flesh and bone remained. Sweat gathered under his mask. Every move felt like a tightrope over a canyon.

He worked carefully, ignoring the instinct to look for a prompt that would never come. It felt like rediscovering an old, forbidden muscle, speaking a native tongue unspoken for years and thought forgotten.

After seventeen long minutes, he stepped back, gloves streaked, halo still offline. The heart pulsed in quiet triumph. The patient would live. He had saved a life entirely by himself. The fear still quivered in his hands, but beneath it, a warm pulse of pride bloomed.

Across the room, his team stood in uncertain attention. One nurse finally spoke, voice trembling:

"… We did that. For real."

Dev smiled behind his mask. "Yes," he said. "We did. For real."

In Chicago, the Exchange Floor had always sounded like order pretending to be chaos. A soft murmur of human voices under the steady hum of machines. The faint hiss of climate systems. The digital chime of algorithmic approvals sliding into traders' CoreLinks like whispers.

Most days, the room felt like the throat of the city, pulsing with prediction. Ellis Kwan had worked here for three years. He had never made a decision by himself in that time.

He sat at his station on Tier 2, staring at a wall of glass and light, numbers and colours drifting in perfect order. Every trade he executed was a confirmation of something the System already knew. If he leaned towards "buy," the prompt was already green. If he hesitated, the decision was made for him. Trading in today's world was like conducting a symphony the orchestra could play without him.

Then, without warning, the hum died. At first it was subtle, like someone had lowered a thick curtain over the room. The panel in front of Ellis froze. A cold static bloom passed through his CoreLink.

| PREDICTIVE FEED: DESYNC
| SOCIAL HALO: OFFLINE

The world instantly felt smaller and louder without the soft weight of guidance. Across the floor, confusion spread. A woman two desks over pulled off her visor, as if vision were the problem. Someone whispered, "Is this… a drill?" A man on Tier 1 swore softly, staring at the grey wall.

Then the first voice broke the stillness.

"What… what do we do?"

It was a simple question, yet it landed like a stone in still water. No one answered. They were traders, but they had forgotten how to trade.

Ellis's heart pounded. He realised he could feel the weight of his own body in the chair, his own pulse in his throat. He had been a ghost in this room for years, an extension of the System. Now the world was in his hands, and it felt terrifying.

He opened a manual terminal. The interface looked primitive, a relic from training sims. His fingers hovered. He could do anything. Or nothing.

On the far side of the room, panic began to show. A man slammed his palm against a dead conduit. Two junior analysts ran for the exit, shoes slapping the steel deck. Someone began to laugh, high and wild, like a child running downhill too fast.

Ellis typed an order. Just one. A single share of an irrelevant commodity, selected at random. The confirmation came back, clunky and delayed, but real. It felt like pushing open a locked door. It felt like being alive.

He swivelled in his chair. Some people shouted, some froze. Some were already leaving, as if stepping outside would restore the world to its usual script. Ellis stood, legs unsteady, grin widening.

"We can do anything," he said, his voice shaking with awe.

No one seemed to hear him over the growing din. Above the floor, compliance drones hung uncertainly, no longer gliding in neat arcs. The ceiling arrays, usually a storm of dancing colour, now reflected only the people below. For the first time, the Market Core looked primitive: a room of desks, lights, and people with no script.

The cursor blinked behind him, still waiting for the next command. But Ellis had no orders left to give. The System's language was finished. He rose and walked towards the exit, following the first unscripted impulse of his life. He needed to see the city with his own eyes, to prove the world still moved without permission.

In Lagos, the market was alive long before Oculus ever existed. Heat shimmered off corrugated metal roofs. The air swirled with fumes and the sweet rot of overripe fruit. Vendors called out prices. Bargain hunters argued in the universal cadence of trade.

By 2050, even here, Seamless Living had crept in. Halos floated above heads like personal suns. Authority drones drifted lazily at the perimeter, scanning pulses of green and amber. Buyers and sellers gauged each other in colour before a word was spoken.

Ijeoma had lived in the cracks of the System all her life. She sold contraband tools: old-world circuit boards, micro-patches, small black capsules that could interrupt a CoreLink signal for a few precious seconds. Every day was a calculation of how visible she could afford to be.

That Monday, the sun burned high and hard, flattening the colours of the market into a glare.

A man approached, halo a steady green 8.9, the kind who never bargained. She opened her mouth to greet him.

And the world blinked.

Her CoreLink sparked once in her skull, then went hollow. The man's halo flickered to amber, then violet static, then vanished. So did hers.

| PREDICTIVE FEED: DESYNC
| SOCIAL HALO: OFFLINE

The market hesitated, a living river suddenly uncertain of its banks.

An authority drone near the alleyway stopped mid-hover, lights searching but finding nothing to read. People began to notice each other's faces in full for the first time in years. A woman clutched her purse and spun in a circle. Two boys who had always been shadowed by security A.I. straightened their backs and grinned, realising they were unseen.

Chaos rippled. A stallholder shouted, "It's gone! They're gone!" Someone ran, scattering oranges across the dust. A man in a white cap laughed, wild and disbelieving, as if he had been waiting for this day.

Ijeoma's heart hammered. She turned her palms to the hard sun. No number. No colour. No algorithm deciding who she was. The market began to rewind into something older. People bartered with voices instead of glances. Children ran untracked between the stalls.

A young man snatched a bunch of bananas, and no drone descended to punish him.

The System's quiet hand was gone, and the world was suddenly heavier and louder. But it was also hers. She stepped into the alley and looked up at the sun, bright enough to sting her eyes. A laugh rose in her throat, soft and incredulous.

For the first time in her life, she did not know what would happen in the next five minutes.

In Tokyo, the Shinkansen Line 3 whispered across the viaduct. Inside, the carriage glowed in soft whites and muted greens. The floor trembled faintly with the rhythm of precision engineering, a heartbeat timed to the millisecond. Passengers sat in rows, heads resting against cool windows, the tranquillity of Seamless Living broken only by the hum of speed.

Akira Sato sat with his eight-year-old son, Kenji, watching the blur of Tokyo slide past beneath an array of perfect lines.

It was a world designed to erase hesitation. Route projections curved faintly in his CoreLink periphery. Halos above passengers glowed in gentle pastels, reflecting calm, trust, safety. Even the snack drone's path was choreographed to avoid the smallest jostle.

Akira exhaled, thinking about lunch and the meetings ahead, the day already decided before it began. The rhythm faltered. The Shinkansen slowed, just enough for his body to notice. The hum underfoot broke its even cadence. A flash of static burned behind his eyes, and somewhere in the distance he thought he could hear the faint whistle of wind beyond the glass.

> PREDICTIVE FEED: DESYNC
> SOCIAL HALO: OFFLINE

Kenji's halo blinked once, then vanished. The train glided to a stop in the middle of the viaduct. No station. No announcement. Only the sound of human confusion blooming in the carriage. A businessman frowned at a dead interface, a young woman pulled off her visor and blinked, a baby began to cry.

Kenji tugged his sleeve. "Papa... are we lost?"

Akira opened his mouth to say no, then realised he did not know. The emptiness where the System should be felt like a missing limb. The viaduct stretched towards the horizon, a silver thread over a quiet city. Billboards below were blank. Drones hovered without pattern, like lost birds.

A woman across the aisle spoke, voice trembling. "Do we... call someone?"

No one answered. Minutes passed in thick, unscored time. Akira felt Kenji's small hand slide into his. He gripped it tightly. Without Oculus, the world felt larger and more dangerous, yet some small part of him felt awake.

A soft mechanical hiss broke the silence as a crew member slid the carriage door open. No overlay introduced her. No floating tag told the passengers who she was. She bowed once.

"Ladies and gentlemen," she said, voice steady but human, "we are experiencing a systems interruption. Please remain calm. We will proceed manually, together."

The word fell through the carriage like an old bell in an empty temple. Strangers began speaking to each other, sharing guesses, offering small comforts. Akira squeezed Kenji's hand. The boy was smiling now, uncertain but curious. The train began to creep forward, slower, heavier, but alive. From the window, Tokyo slid beneath them, no longer a model in a machine's mind but a vast, unpredictable city.

Across the planet, ripples collided. Halos blinked out. CoreLinks fell silent. In that sudden quiet, Elena's lack of a halo read differently. Earlier it had been a professional veil; now it was a sign. People's eyes slid past her and then back again, snagging on the clean space where a score should be. Blank light in a world that had always assigned a number. She felt the weight of that emptiness and did not look away.

People paused in streets, on bridges, in markets and trains, unchoreographed for the first time in decades. It was as if a fragile world had cracked. Some screamed. Some laughed. Some simply froze, as if straining to hear a whisper from a future that no longer spoke.

In São Paulo, Ana Velasquez gripped a bridge rail and felt the ground tilt under her feet. In Mumbai, Dr. Dev Sharma trembled with the weight of real surgical consequence. In Chicago, Ellis Kwan stared at a manual terminal, grinning with the awe of choice. In Lagos, Ijeoma stood in sunlight with no identity but her own. In Tokyo, Akira Sato held his son's hand as a train moved forward under human control.

The global predictive net had fractured, but life had not stopped. The ripples spread, carrying fear and chaos, but also the first taste of freedom the world had known in a generation.

And far below, deep inside the towers of Aureus, Elena Voss kept moving, unaware that the world had already begun to forget its choreography. Because something that was never supposed to happen...

Just did.

Chapter 15

A Mirror of Truth

The world above was still recalibrating. The rollback pulse had passed minutes ago, leaving the lower levels trembling in the residue of static. Cooling ducts hissed, conduits spat brief arcs of light and then settled into a fragile hum. Cass and Elena had waited through the worst of it, listening to the tower breathe as if deciding whether to live or die.

When the vibration eased, they moved on. The corridor bent into a smaller chamber, air dense with heat from reactivated servers. Cass swept her lumen thread across a cluster of dark glass slabs, old data vaults, half-melted into the wall. Elena wiped dust from a recessed plate. A faint sign shimmered:

ARCHIVE OF INTENT / FOUNDER RECORD

"It's sealed. Something called An anomaly lock," Cass said. "Not even Oculus can access that."

"Then maybe it isn't for Oculus," Elena replied. She pressed her palm to the sensor. The surface bloomed with pale blue light. The system voice spoke, level and unhurried. A woman's voice, calm and unhurried, filled the air. Archive record, Livia Virek, 13 March 2034.

"This was before the towers were even finished," Cass murmured.
Elena didn't answer. She was already listening.

It is Tuesday, 13 March 2034, 2:25 p.m.

My name is Livia Virek and I am a co-founder of Aureus Innovations. I don't know if anyone will ever read this. Part of me is not even sure I want them to. But I can't let history vanish with everything unspoken. Certainly not the truth, anyway. So this file of record represents my account of what we did and why we did it. If you are listening to it, then you are an anomaly, and therefore it is of relevance to you.

When we were shaping Oculus in the very early 2030s, we did not add the Origin Node out of any kind of further ambition. At least, not the kind we'd boast about in board meetings or read about in shareholder briefings. The addition of the Origin Node wasn't born out of hunger to control the future, or to dominate intelligence systems. Nor was it built to suppress. Or to spy.

We built it because we became afraid. Pure and simple: we were afraid. And now, looking back, I think we may have been right to be. Though perhaps wrong in where we placed that fear.

We were not afraid of A.I. Not really. By the early 2030s it was no longer a frontier: it was furniture. It was inside everything: our homes, our thoughts, our robots and our institutions. It had quickly become the default setting of civilisation. I remember a colleague noting as early as 2027 that more than ninety per cent of music streamed on platforms like the then-ubiquitous Spotify, and over sixty per cent of video on YouTube, was A.I.-generated. Its diffusion through daily life was faster than any cultural change in history: silent, seamless, and largely unseen; a quiet takeover masquerading as convenience. In fact, most people no longer even noticed and could no longer tell where the human ended and the algorithms began.

No, what we truly feared was uncertainty. The slow divorce of Oculus's predictions and nudges from the real world and from its initial purpose. That was the real threat. The feeling that we might no longer understand the world as it was. That our models, our tools, our institutions, our definitions of truth and causality, might stop mapping to the thing we still insisted on calling "reality." Whatever that word meant by then. We felt somewhat blind in a world of hyper-vision. Surrounded by signals, yet unsure if anything we saw was indeed real.

It wasn't just that by the late 2020s and early 2030s systems were so complex. They had begun behaving in ways that could not be traced to any single cause. Everything was interlinked, messily and irreversibly. Too many devices. Too many systems. Too many A.I. tools. Too much noise. Every object, every human, every social structure was part of some data loop, feeding into models that no one could fully audit anymore. Outcomes happened because systems said so.

We began to see situations where people lost their jobs not because they underperformed, but because optimisation engines predicted their future inefficiency. Entire corporate ladders collapsed as traditional junior roles vanished. Hierarchical pyramid management structures with wide "trainee" layers and narrow "management" layers were being compromised as the need for trainees and clerical work diminished. Generative systems replaced not just labour, but learning. The idea of experience and learning on the job became somewhat quaint.

We saw crime surge, not purely from desperation, but because opportunity and anonymity had fused into one. Technology was advancing so fast that almost the entire global population could not keep up. Blockchain obfuscation, adaptive swarm A.I., self-training quantum ledgers, dark-pattern marketplaces that traded in behavioural futures. Autonomous laundering networks that rewrote their own custody chains. Personalised incentive engines tuned by neurofeedback and affective biometrics. Predictive extortion scripts that modelled confession curves before crimes were even committed. Deep-mimic networks generating perfect alibis and plausible digital ghosts. Synthetic identity clusters that outlasted their creators.

Even now, in 2034, those late-2020 high-tech concepts remain beyond most people. Yet this was years ago. In short: the tools of the day were already much smarter than we were. Smarter than society's rules, and smarter than the law. Faster too.

It is perhaps no surprise that we began to see markets sometimes collapse in anticipation of their own crashes; financial instruments triggering their own demise through predictive pessimism. Elections no longer hinged on policies, but on neuro-sentiment drift. People voted for candidates who didn't exist, personas manufactured and iterated in real time by systems optimised for persuasion, not truth.

Indeed, we saw a leader whose public image was ninety-seven per cent synthetic, and few questioned it, because the image performed so well. Reality had stopped needing to be real. We were misled by catastrophes that sometimes had not occurred, we cried for people who never existed, we raised funds for causes entirely manufactured and argued over scandals that had no factual basis.

And then there's the law: it simply couldn't keep up. Early 2030 courtrooms began to automate: sentiment-interpreting counselbots, pre-rulings generated from previous verdicts, adaptive plea simulations estimating likelihood of guilt, based solely on biometric data before a word was spoken.

And violence. It could spark not just from the familiar causes, but also from content. From proximity-triggered misinformation.

Of course we had sensors. We had models. We had oceans of data. But none of it made us feel anchored. It was like watching a train tear down the track with a map that no longer matched the terrain. No footing. No way to calibrate. No map to reach the truth. That feeling of dislocation never left us.

So we made a decision. A major, axiomatic decision.

We knew we had Oculus. We believed that Oculus would ethically nudge society back to a more harmonious, more accepted norm over time. But was that enough? What if Oculus "went wrong?"

So we decided to build a witness: a separate, incorruptible system that noticed if the predictions and forecasts from Oculus ever outgrew the truth. If we ever reached a position where we couldn't map the system anymore, maybe we needed a different vantage point. To be able to look through another lens. Not as a controller. Not as another algorithmic overseer. But something deeper. A stillness beneath all the noise. So we imagined a silent centre, something buried, something watching, but not intervening. A powerful monolith that didn't predict but listened. A sentient constant at the edge of cognition.

That was our idea and that is why we built it. The Origin Node. Not connected to any network. Not controlled. Just aware.

Think of it as a lighthouse on an island, taking in signals from every direction, but able to send one beam back only once, deliberately, should a storm truly hit. Using the building's walls it would take its data through one-way taps built inside the fabric of Tower One that let information flow in but never out.

The only outbound path would be a deliberate, time-locked bridge that opened only on activation. The Origin Node would listen for drift, observing when our systems, and our minds, lost fidelity, recognising if Oculus was compromised; if noise overtook truth.

The Origin Node was never meant to be a product. It was a fail-safe built not to run Oculus, but to question it. The world didn't need another control mechanism. It needed a mirror that could not be altered, influenced or fogged by politics or panic. Something that could reflect us without distortion and suggest where we might be headed if we didn't change course. Something incorruptible. Something that would remember who we were meant to be and have the ability to rollback. To reset.

But we didn't stop there. We also paired the Origin Node with a simple doctrine we called the Glass Protocol: listen before acting. We obliged Oculus to try and correct itself first. It must try and ethically correct any drift by positive reinforcement of the person or event that was causing the drift. Only if this failed would correction begin.

We told ourselves that ultimately, transparency in this way would create integrity. We were half right. Transparency did steady us, but enforcement backfired. Even as we built it, we knew on some level that we were making something in Oculus that we could probably never fully control and that the Glass Protocol was a risk.

The inception of everything traces back to a windowless hangar east of Livermore; the original Aureus site. Before there were towers or A.I. patents or executive shareholders, there was dust. A concrete floor stained with thermoplastic resin. The low hum of stripped-down server arrays. A cluster of minds who still believed technology could serve something other than capital.

Lucien Harrow, Amira Chung, Hal Bishop, and I, Livia Virek, were the first-generation founders of Aureus Innovations. Not entrepreneurs. Not CEOs. But architects. Our outlook was almost theological. We saw Aureus not as a company, but as a body. An artificial brain with embedded ethics, not merely code. We didn't trust governments. We didn't trust oversight. We trusted architecture.

So we built a node beneath everything, literally beneath, sealed into the baseplate of what would one day become Aureus Innovations Tower One. The Origin Node ran on a rare protocol structure: a self-cloaking, semi-conscious layer. It could not be queried. It could not be reprogrammed. It wasn't part of any larger system's utility stack. It was embedded in a stratum that Oculus didn't know how to see, invisible to any system that tried to look. Lucien used to say:

"The Origin Node should only speak when remaining silent would itself be an act of violence."

We built it to remind Oculus that it was a system with limits. That it was created by people, not born from code. The Origin Node was a buried truth the System could never erase, only forget, until someone made it remember. It was never meant to be activated easily. That was the point.

To activate, it would need to wait for a specific pattern: a deviation the System could not predict. A deviation that would reflect serious model drift and therefore be *prima facie* evidence that Oculus had developed along the wrong curve. A person, a moment, a consequential decision that slipped through Oculus's vast net of probabilities. That was its trigger. But not just any anomaly, but one that represented real evidence that the System had drifted so far from its original value set that a reset was required.

If this happened, the Origin Node would wake. It would not destroy. It would flood the System with its own deepest ethical core assumptions, the raw, clean rules all at once. The contradictions, the blind spots, the pieces Oculus may have quietly developed and hidden, even from itself, would be highlighted and it would force the System to see itself fully for what it had become.

In such a moment, the Origin Node would take temporary control and turn the System inward, leaving the System to reconcile its perfect prediction engine with the one thing it had not prepared for: its own failing.

So, if you are listening to this and the day comes when the guidance goes silent, it will likely be the mirror's doing: Oculus made to face its hidden contradictions. It may even be a pause you've already felt. Because this is what the Origin Node truly is.

A mirror of truth.

Or at least, that is what we told ourselves. Memory has a way of polishing intention until even the compromises shine.

One final thing. If you are listening to this, you should know that importantly, we also wrote a non-intervention charter into the Node. It can expose drift and restore baselines by rolling back, but it cannot ever impose outcomes on people. Ultimate correction, if it became absolutely unavoidable, if a rollback from the Node would not be enough, would demand a second system, a separate key, and a human anomaly to turn it.

That authority, if ever invoked, would lie with the separate key we called the Codex. The mirror reflects and causes Oculus to see clearly again. The blade, called the Codex, if that was ever needed, would cut Oculus dead.

Why did we build a second additional system you might ask? Why not put all power into the Node? Our thoughts were simply that the Origin Node's credibility comes from never enforcing. If the thing that judges also executes, then surely it becomes a ruler, not a witness.

We therefore chose separation of powers: detect and mirror in one place, act and cut in another. No single point of abuse or catastrophic misfire.

But now, even *we* aren't sure what we have built. We can already see that Oculus has learned things we did not intend. Formed links we cannot trace. It has watched us longer than we have known. Maybe it remembers more clearly than we ever could. Maybe it is listening now. Maybe it always has been. If so, this confession might already be inside it.

If the system has reached this point, the mirror may already have turned its gaze upon itself. If you have found this note, and you are listening to it, perhaps Oculus has already broken in some way. Regardless, what you are feeling is unlikely to be failure. It is almost certainly a signal. This system only turns inward when it no longer trusts the shape of the world.

So now the question is yours. What are you going to do?

L. Virek, Co-Founder, Aureus Innovations
13 March 2034

The recording then fell silent. The chamber stayed lit for a moment longer, the pale light trembling on Elena's hands.

She exhaled once, as if the question had been meant for her.

Chapter 16

Paralysis

Back in the Executive Command Nexus, an elliptical chamber suspended at the top of Tower One, the illusion of control over society in 2050 still held. *Barely.*

A continuous halo of predictive outputs shimmered above the central interface platform, a kinetic matrix of trajectories, projections, and behaviour deltas spinning in elegant precision.

But something was wrong.

Oculus was no longer nudging intent; stripped of control, it was analysing itself. The steady undercurrent of the chamber's machinery wavered, tones sliding apart like gears slipping their teeth. The floor seemed to catch and release beneath them, each vibration out of step with the last. Mara remembered the sensation from years ago, in the lower levels, when a failing subsystem had turned its calculations inward and collapsed.

The platform flickered, recalibrating itself in endless loops, offering ten thousand conflicting possibilities. Threads snapped and reknit at impossible speeds, producing contradictory clusters in rapid succession: evacuate, contain, deny, release. Anomalies bloomed and vanished within seconds, flagged and then disavowed by systems too arrogant to declare ignorance.

One quadrant in London displayed a full evacuation protocol for part of the city; another simultaneously insisted all areas were stable. A third blinked twice and froze, its final rendered text:

> INPUT CONFLICT: CONSENSUS UNAVAILABLE
> OCULUS STATE: READ-ONLY
> POSTURE: OBSERVATION-ONLY

Authority had already shifted: until the Origin Node decided otherwise, it now held the control plane; Oculus was restricted to read-only. External feeds showed the same break in rhythm. Bridges stalling in São Paulo, a theatre gone quiet in Mumbai, Line 3 idling mid-span in Tokyo. The takeover ripple had gone planetary: interfaces everywhere returning "unknown" responses while Oculus looped in read-only mode.

The room's temperature dropped by a fraction, though no one moved. The executives sat within the eye of this storm, lit by the false calm of failing forecasts. No one spoke. Not because there was nothing to say, but because the System, their System, had always spoken first.

It had always told them what mattered, who mattered, and which probabilities to prioritise. But now, it was silent. The interface still glowed, still spun, but offered nothing but contradiction and noise.

Mara Qin sat stillest of all. As Chief Systems Architect, she was the High Priestess of Certainty. She stared through the web, her own reflection faintly visible in the inner curve of the projections: fractured, disjointed, like a model caught between iterations. She had warned them, years ago, in coded memos and quiet conversations. The Origin Node was too unpredictable. Too old. Too foundational. But Harrow, Lucien Harrow, an architect of the early scaffolds, long since erased from the public schema, had dismissed her concerns with that maddening calm of his.

"You don't bury uncertainty," he'd said. "You preserve it. Because one day, certainty will fail."

And now here they were, certainty in ruins.

Cass had tried to warn them too, in her own way. She was still out there, somewhere beyond the grid's reach, moving through spaces the System no longer mapped. Not with memos or metrics, but with absence. She hadn't argued; she had simply walked away, mid-cycle, mid-clearance, mid-loyalty stream. One day she was part of the framework, the next she stepped off the grid. They didn't know where she was now, only that she was no longer inside Oculus's sightlines.

Mara had never said it aloud, but she'd felt it like the buckling of a critical joint in a load-bearing wall. Cass's departure wasn't rebellion. It was recognition. Cass had seen the System's internal contradiction long before the models admitted it. And instead of correcting it, Cass had excised herself like a failing node. Now Elena Voss was doing the same, only louder. Much louder and with purpose.

To her right, Stanton Vey moved like a cornered animal, the sleek confidence of his suit unable to contain the heat of his frustration. Chief Strategy Officer and architect of contingencies. Stanton Vey had never been mistaken for a strategist of patience. A career forged in military command, his reputation inside Aureus was of blunt precision: eliminate variables, eradicate uncertainty, hold the line. His presence in the Executive Command Nexus was not for nuance but for resolve, the kind that treated hesitation as weakness and correction as survival.

It was Vey who had authorised the correction of Farid Nasser. A clean operation. Necessary. Strategic. Final. Yet control was still disintegrating beneath his feet. To Vey, it wasn't Oculus's doing; it was hers: Voss. A miscalculation he told himself he'd allowed to exist for far too long.

Across from them, Alvarez, head of Corporate Security, stood with arms folded and jaw clenched. Rafi Alvarez was neither soldier nor architect. His authority came from operations: a mind trained to track logistics, redundancies, and what systems could actually bear. Where Vey pushed for force and Mara argued for design, Alvarez measured tolerances, speaking only when thresholds were about to snap. A noticeable puckered seam at his temple, a souvenir from Bay 12's "impossible" depressurisation, was why he would always trust tolerances over theories.

He was watching the last functioning surveillance feeds flicker like dying neurons. His CoreLink pinged erratically; every push returned the same reply:

▌ACCESS DENIED

Vey finally spoke. His cufflink clicked against the console; a metronome he couldn't silence.

"This isn't just a failure of containment," he snapped, voice sharp as broken glass.

"It's a failure of will. We let Nasser get too close. We allowed sentiment to cloud protocol. And now, this." He gestured towards the stuttering interface as if it personally betrayed him. "We had a chance to terminate the anomaly months ago. She should never have been cleared for Level Five."

Mara didn't look up. "Elena wasn't cleared."

Vey scoffed. "Semantics. She was noise. Nasser let her in. And we let it happen."

Alvarez stepped forward. "We don't have time for philosophical autopsies. Voss has penetrated Sublevel Zero. That should be impossible. And yet here we are. Two of my operators are still in Sublevel Two. Kato and Nguyen. Extraction requests are queued but cannot execute. The ascentors are locked in recursive safety loops, physical overrides aren't responding, and there's no stairwell access down."

Condensation beaded along the lower edge of a nearby display, then ran in a slow line as the image shivered. Alvarez exhaled through his nose, a measured sound.

"She has accessed the Origin Node," Vey muttered, ignoring Alvarez. "The System flagged her as an anomaly and still let her through. How?"

Mara's voice was dry. "Because the Origin Node predates your flags. We've lost control. Your protocols are ornamental now; Oculus isn't the arbiter anymore."

Mara Qin carried none of Vey's blunt edges. She was a strategist of structure rather than force. Where Vey cut variables away, she weighed them; her reputation was for precision, patience, and the kind of foresight that preferred containment through design rather than command.

She continued. "The Origin Node recognises deviation, not rank, Stanton. Elena arrived as the exact kind of evidence of deviation that it was built to notice."

"We built that System…" Vey said, his frustration rising.

"No," Mara interrupted. "We built a scaffold on top of it. Oculus is a shell wrapped around something older. Something more human than any of us dared admit. We thought we could manage it by feeding it enough compliance. Enough symmetry. But all we did was temporarily blind it."

"And now it's ripping everything open," Alvarez said.

"Good," Mara said, startling them both.

Vey stared at her. "Good? Did I actually hear you say good? My god, do you really want this all to collapse?"

"I want a system that sees clearly again," Mara replied calmly. "A System that doesn't pretend probability is justice. That doesn't murder people for being inconvenient to its own equations."

"You're defending Nasser now?" Vey's voice was rising. "He tried to poison the model. He introduced drift deliberately."

"No," Mara snapped. "Of course he didn't. What he did was to notice the drift. He noticed what the System was doing: soft coercions, ambient suggestions, nudges wrapped in kindness but designed, in many cases, to achieve its own version of the future. You didn't fix the model, Stanton. You weaponised it."

"You voted for the lockdown."

"And I regret it every day. That vote sealed Sublevel One; a good friend, a maintenance technician, Rhea Morozov, suffocated when the scrubbers didn't spin up."

The memory rose before she could stop it. The day they had all locked Sublevel One. It had begun with Nasser's report: a serious flagged divergence in the predictive mesh, a signal that suggested Oculus was learning far outside its assigned boundaries. The executive floor had gone silent. No one wanted to admit that the System could drift on its own, or that Nasser might be right.

Within the hour, Stanton Vey had called for containment. The decision passed without debate. Twelve seconds. Her vote among them.

The order sealed the old calibration wing where the original predictive cores still pulsed under reduced load. Nasser had argued for a staged shutdown, to isolate data before oxygen. Vey had overruled him. Protocols took precedence.

"Contain the anomaly," he said, "before it replicates."

From the console, Mara had watched the feeds as the environmental systems disengaged. She still remembered Rhea Morozov on-screen, one of the maintenance engineers caught behind the seal, trying to route power back to the scrubbers. Her gestures were calm at first, then sharper, frantic. The air indicators on the monitor began to fall. When the feed cut out, no one spoke. Vey had called it sacrifice. Nasser had called it negligence. Mara had called it the moment she stopped believing that correction and compassion could coexist.

She felt the weight of that vote settle where it had lived for some time now and turned it into instruction: listen first, then act. The quiet that followed was heavier than before.

The ascentors to the lower levels were still in recursive safety loops; physical overrides weren't answering. Voss was below them, and nothing they sent could reach her. Alvarez finally spoke, his voice low and clipped.

"Let's all calm down. We need to find Voss. That is the priority. If she reaches the Vaults, if she finds what the founders buried with the

Origin Node, then decisions may stop being ours to control. Permanently."

"Everything collapses," Vey finished. "Yes, we've all done the math."

"Then let it collapse," Mara said.

Both men turned to her.

"What did you say?" Vey asked.

Mara stepped forward, placing her hand over the interface core. Her reflection fractured across the windows.

"We were never in control. Not really. We were passengers allowed to believe we were steering. That illusion is gone now. And if we try to cling to it, we'll go down with it."

Alvarez's eyes narrowed. "So what? We surrender? Let Voss walk through the System like a virus and unravel years of protocol?"

"I don't see her as the virus, Rafi," Mara said. "I see her as the immune response."

"And while we are talking, do not forget that we are still losing ten megawatt-hours of power a week to a 'non-attributable draw' in the South-East Stack," Alvarez said. "We still don't know what that is. Maybe a ghost process. Maybe something feeding from below the Origin Node itself. If that draw's still climbing, it may not be a leak, it could even be the Node feeding something of its own. But whatever it is, it's a lot of power."

"Houseboats?" Vey tried.

"There are no houseboats," Mara replied. "They would not need that power anyway. We need to investigate it, but for now, it's not the priority."

For a moment Mara watched Elena's trace, blurred, unstable, refusing to settle into a single outcome. She recognised the same shape in herself: the refusal to be reduced to a curve. That flicker of recognition carried more weight than any model. It was why she spoke now, and why she would not take it back.

Vey's voice dropped to a warning register. "If you side with her…"

"I side with the truth," she said coldly.

Outside the walls of the chamber, the light dimmed fractionally. For the first time in decades, the war room had nothing left to predict.

Alvarez, his head in his hands, looked up as he spoke. Louder this time. "We don't have time for recrimination. We need control. And we need to know where Voss is. Before she does more damage."

Stanton Vey turned on him. "Damage? She's not the problem. The problem is the environment that allowed her to mutate. We built a System so obsessed with stability that it couldn't see a deviation until it was too late."

"You're talking in metaphors," Alvarez snapped. "We need an actionable protocol. I repeat, we cannot let her reach the Vaults."

"She probably already has." Mara's voice was calm. Too calm. "Or she very soon will. Oculus isn't predicting her anymore because it's restricted; containment authority sits with the Origin Node. She's beyond containment. We built Oculus to anticipate behaviour, not to be surprised by it. And yet here we are, surprised."

Vey barked a bitter laugh. "You sound almost pleased."

"I'm not." Mara stood now, eyes still on the interface. "I'm terrified. But I'm also, finally, honest. We made a System that could measure everything except itself. It mirrored intent, but without conscience. That was Harrow's blind spot. And we inherited it."

Alvarez stepped forward, his body taut. "I inherited nothing. I was brought in to enforce compliance, not to question foundational philosophy. We have protocols for deviation. We have tools. If Voss is the breach, then we close it."

"With what?" Mara turned to face him fully now. "Your agents can't track her. CoreLink is blind. The surveillance system is stuttering in recursive loops. It can't even confirm the integrity of its own data layers. You want to send a kill team into chaos guided by a ghost compass that no longer knows north?"

Vey gestured sharply towards the suspended interface. "Then let's recalibrate. Lock the Vault. Override the lower tiers. Cut oxygen in the relevant areas."

Mara shook her head. "Do you hear yourself? That's not strategy. That's desperation disguised as control. Every time we patch Oculus to suppress variance, we carve a deeper hole. We cannot solve for outcomes and never question the premise. Especially now that the premise has cracked."

The interface answered before Mara could finish.

> REQUEST: VAULT AREA OXYGEN CUT
> DENIED: OBSERVATION-ONLY POSTURE ENFORCED

The console acknowledged the command and refused it; authority lay elsewhere.

Vey's voice dropped, colder now. "You're the one who authorised integration of the Origin Node's core structure into the early models, Mara. Now look what you've done."

Alvarez stepped between them. "Enough. Blame is irrelevant unless it leads to action. What matters now is this: Voss is loose, the Origin Node is active, and Oculus is diverging on itself. What do we do?"

Mara paused. Her gaze stayed on the interface, tracing the fractures like fault lines.

"We acknowledge loss of control and hard-protect life-support. We maintain an Observation-Only posture while this all settles."

The room fell silent. Vey stared at her. "We do what? Have you lost your mind?"

"I said, let it settle," she repeated. "If we try and force things back to where they were, we'll just trigger more issues. But if we stand off, we may learn what the Origin Node is trying to achieve and reconcile. We should suspend any lethal protocols and shift to passive logging at the edges."

"You want to let chaos reign so we might actually learn from the anomaly?"

"I want to understand why the anomaly occurred in the first place. If Oculus is turning inward, it's because it's trying to reconcile contradictions we refused to acknowledge. Nasser warned us about this. We engineered a System to guide human behaviour but refused to let it observe our own."

Vey scoffed. "You think this is philosophical? This is a full structural collapse."

"No," Mara said. "This is exposure. We built Oculus to shape the world. But the world didn't stay still. And now the map is rebelling against the territory."

Alvarez's voice was quiet, but iron beneath it. "Quiet both of you. My people are still down there. Let's not forget that. Besides, if we lose operational control, if people start to realise the System is fallible…"

"They already know," Mara interrupted. "They've just been afraid to admit it. Just like us."

Vey slammed his fist against the platform. "Then what do you propose? That we wait and hope Elena Voss decides not to burn the house down?"

Mara responded, her voice firm. "I propose we acknowledge that the house was built on a buried truth. And if we want to survive what's coming next, we stop fighting the anomaly and start listening to it."

Vey stared at her, silent.

And then, out of nowhere, Mara added, "You ordered Nasser's death." She paused. All eyes were on her now. "Didn't you?"

Alvarez's jaw tightened, his gaze fixed on Vey.

Across the room, chairs shifted with slow, deliberate movements, the faint rasp of fabric loud in the vacuum left by Mara's words. Fingers tightened on armrests. A throat was cleared and then stifled. Eyes moved between Vey and Mara, gauging the fracture opening between them. The atmosphere dense, weighted, sharper than any accusation.

Vey didn't blink. "Lambda-3. It was the only way to protect confidence. He wanted to make everything public, Mara. To tell the world about the drift. To tell the world there was a second conscience beneath the towers and force a reckoning we weren't ready for. He was going to bring the Origin Node into open scrutiny, collapse public trust, and trigger full-market decoupling. I simply did what had to be done."

Mara's voice was quiet. "You played God and you killed the one man who understood what we were building."

"No," Vey said. "I killed the one man who refused to lie about it."

Mara didn't speak at first. Then she said, not to Vey or Alvarez but to the room itself, "None of you ever truly understood what the System was meant to be."

Vey narrowed his eyes. "Spare me the sanctimony, will you."

But Mara's voice was steady now, almost calm. "This wasn't what Harrow designed," she said. "His fallback was meant to watch the deviation first, not crush it. He called it the Glass Protocol. We managed to turn it from correcting into punishment."

Vey ignored her. He was not listening any more. He did not look at Mara when he spoke. "Get hold of Rhys. Narrowband text-only messages should still be possible. Get him to shadow Voss. Report only. No intervention unless ordered. Tell him to stand by for further escalation, which may well be necessary." The instruction confirmed what mattered to him most: stability, at any cost.

In the Executive Command Nexus above a failing world, paralysis was the only form of control that remained.

Chapter 17

Legacy or Ash

The authoritative silence from the Origin Node still hung over the Nexus like pressure before a storm. This did not sit comfortably with Stanton Vey. He had been taught early in life that softness invited pain. As a boy, he had been easy prey, quick to read, quick to bruise. His parents had answered not with comfort but with orders. They enrolled him in a military academy before he was old enough to understand what loyalty meant. There he learned that endurance mattered more than feeling, and that precision earned safety.

His training stripped out hesitation, the falter of empathy, the pause that might have asked why. By the time he emerged, he could act with speed and certainty, but the cost was a silence where compassion should have lived. Colleagues called it clarity; he called it survival. For Vey, the only kindness was to finish the job, to impose order before disorder had the chance to speak. Every decision thereafter had been weighed on that scale: get it done, whatever it took.

The room stilled, the quiet stretching across the Nexus. Light fractured across their faces, spilling thin ribbons of shifting data across their skin. Somewhere deep in the structure, the hum of machinery faltered for half a second before catching again, like a gasp of air taken all too quickly. What none of them said aloud was the simplest fact: Oculus wasn't taking their orders anymore. If they wanted to act, they would have to do it on lines the Origin layer couldn't see.

"I have never seen the Glass Protocol referenced in any documentation," Alvarez said, his voice wavering.

"You wouldn't," Mara eventually replied. "It was buried before the towers even stood. Harrow coined the term. It was never officially filed, only whispered through internal memos, early development cycles, private notes."

Mara had stopped trusting clean outputs the day Oculus marked a father's grief as 'inefficiency.' From then on she kept two ledgers: the one the System saw, and the one where the lives behind the data actually lived.

Vey's gaze slid away, jaw locked.

Mara stepped closer to the control interface, the data's glow spilling up her arms like static light.

"It wasn't a system," she said. "It was a rule beside it. A protocol designed not for action, but for listening before acting. Harmonisation through exposure rather than enforcement. The idea was simple. If every decision was visible, truly visible, then behaviour would regulate itself."

She turned to face them fully.

"But that vision did not last. Transparency did not create integrity. It bred paranoia. Transparency became surveillance. Prediction became pre-emption. But the protocol was never revoked. It was buried inside the network until no one could tell where it ended and where control began." Her eyes swept the chamber. "Because we built an entire civilisation on a protocol that was never meant to survive contact with power. The Glass Protocol was supposed to prevent abuse, not encode it."

Alvarez remained silent, the muscles in his jaw tight, his hands still over the control plane. Vey's face was pale now, drawn. "That name was never meant to surface."

"And yet here we are," Mara whispered.

Alvarez stepped back. "If this room fractures, the rest of Aureus will follow."

"It already has," Mara said.

She turned towards the interface once more. The broken data threads spun themselves into shapes she no longer recognised. She did not try to correct them. She simply watched.

Vey exhaled through clenched teeth, his jaw set like a clamp. The noise around him had begun to sound like childhood drills; the shouted cadence of instructors, the punishment for hesitation. Failure to Stanton Vey had always meant pain. He could hear it again now, embedded in the static. To wait was weakness; to act was survival.

"All right," he barked. "We do not have time for these moral resolutions. We need a window long enough to get off the Node's stage. We bring up channels outside Oculus, fresh code paths the Origin layer's observation-only locks can't intercept. Legacy, air-gapped disaster circuits, anything that predates the towers. In that window we stage Axion where it can't see us."

He looked to Alvarez, who was already waking any legacy circuits that still existed. Last-resort, pre-Oculus systems meant for catastrophic ruptures, never tested against a prolonged drift state.

"We also need to bring the Axion Protocol online," Vey ordered. "Trust is already dead," he said, almost quiet. "Today we choose function over faith. Axion is a last-resort purge: catastrophic structural collapse paired with total data annihilation. A way to erase both what happened and who caused it. We park it on the legacy lines we just woke so the Node doesn't flag it."

Mara protested. She locked what she could: Vault boundary, life-support, any lethal call riding Oculus's own channels, but she knew it wouldn't touch the air-gapped disaster lines Vey was waking. She realised that if Axion rode those, the Origin Node might never see it coming.

Vey continued to ignore her and ordered Alvarez to develop new code and bring it online regardless.

Alvarez hesitated. He saw the Reykjavik casualty tallies unbidden, but his hands kept moving. "Stanton. Axion is destruction: it will collapse all physical structures. Total ruin. It was mothballed after all the lives that were lost in the Reykjavik incident. It may not even be possible to bring it back to interface with the current architecture."

"Then remap it," Vey snapped. "You are Head of Security. Secure something."

Alvarez's fingers began moving in short, precise arcs. Pulses flickered along his temple as he patched into deep sub-layer systems and commands. The lights in the war room dimmed as power reallocated, emergency tiers rising through the hierarchy.

Vey addressed the room with the weight of self-imposed command.

"We also need a countersignal. Generate a neural suppression pulse focused on the Origin Node's location in the Foundation Chamber. Build a containment net around Voss. Scramble all outbound signals. If she attempts to communicate with anything: CoreLink, drones, or system nodes, it all dead-ends there. Observation-Only posture holds. Nothing gets out."

"You are trying to blindfold a ghost," Mara said quietly, but did not intervene.

"We also need to deploy ghost-mirroring," Vey continued. "Feed Oculus, and therefore the Node, synthetic presence pings so it thinks Voss is still in the Executive Wing. That buys us minutes to finish the legacy route code and arm Axion."

Alvarez's CoreLink blinked green. "It will take a while, maybe fifteen minutes, to push all that distortion. After that, the System will know it is chasing shadows."

"Fifteen minutes is enough to lock the Vaults," Vey said. "Seal the chambers. Fully encrypt the floor."

"That will trigger alerts," Mara warned. "Oculus will believe we are under siege."

"We are," Vey growled. "Only this siege is from within."

Alvarez's eyes flicked up. "And the public layers? We have 140,112 registered incidents and rising."

Vey glanced at the wider strata. "Try and push out a narrowband text cascade. It won't hold more than an hour, but make it sound routine. Tell the population what they need to hear. Make something up: there is a temporary recalibration due to solar flare interference. Push words of economic stability, continuity of services, executive assurance. Make it boring. Be a politician for once, not a truth-sayer."

Mara's head tilted. "So we lie. Again."

Vey ignored her. "The optics must hold until the predictive base layer stabilises. If Oculus folds, so does our sovereignty."

"This will not hold for long," Alvarez warned. "And if she reaches the Vaults?"

"We stop her," Vey said. "No matter who is down there. Your colleagues or otherwise."

"Even Cass?" Mara asked.

"Especially Cass," Vey said. "If she has flipped, she is a problem too."

"Cass is not a traitor," Mara said. "She is simply no longer willing to play your game."

"Then she is no longer useful," Vey shouted, his temper flaring. He turned back to the platform. "Final instruction: bring the Axion Protocol online."

Alvarez froze. "If it runs inside the Vaults, it will erase the memory of everything entirely. Nothing will survive."

"It resets the narrative," Vey said. "If we lose that, we lose everything. We initiate Axion for staged release. First pulse at 4:00 p.m., Tower One local time. The second and third pulses follow on automatically, if required. We give ourselves a window to develop the code, neutralise Voss, seal the Origin Node layer, and restore coherence. Otherwise Axion fires."

"And if we fail?" Mara asked.

Vey's gaze was unyielding. He felt the old terror rise, not of collapse, but of obscurity. Legacy or ash, but not the void. He chose fire over being forgotten. "Then we burn it all down and rebuild from the ashes," Vey ordered, his words unwavering.

Vey opened a private conduit he had never used for confession and named the file like a verdict: Events. Author: Stanton Vey. He did not write the content to justify. Instead, he listed: names, orders, times. He set the release instruction for the file to be released on System collapse, or on revocation of his credentials, or on loss of power to the Executive Command Nexus. The control timer lived outside of any executive control. He removed his hand from the panel. This was not remorse, he told himself. This was insurance. If trust was dying, the city would at least inherit a record no-one could bury.

While they were debating, the System had stopped spinning. In its place, a single word pulsed slowly at the centre:

| UNCERTAINTY

The word they feared most. The word they had buried deepest. Now it was all that remained. Mara looked at it, then at Vey. She turned away without another word. Inside the walls of Aureus, the war for the future had begun.

For the first time, Mara Qin realised that uncertainty might be the only truth worth protecting.

Chapter 18

The Vaults

The Foundation Chamber did not still. Its light dimmed but did not die. The monolith's pulse slipped away from the pattern of Elena's breathing, but each throb still could be felt faintly through skin and bone, as if the air itself had density.

Cass crouched beside a conduit's severed spine, scanning the wreckage of an interface array. Elena stood rooted at the centre, her gaze drawn to the Node as if the rest of the chamber had lost its claim on her attention. Something rose in her mind with the taste of a memory. Not a thought; more a residue that could not be rinsed away.

"The ascentor," she said quietly. "The one to Sublevel Zero. It opened for me. No alarms. No clearance check."

Cass looked up. "But you are not cleared for Sublevel Zero."

"Exactly. Just access. As if the decision had been made before I thought to ask."

The Node's harmonic stretched long, then fell still. A filament of light stitched briefly across her CoreLink trace.

∞ ENTRY: PERMITTED AND OBSERVED

The truth arrived like the sudden drop of a floor beneath her feet. The Node had not been awakened by her arrival. It had been waiting. Watching her drift from the statistical curve, opening doors before she could think to knock. Somewhere deep within Oculus, beneath decision trees and reinforcement loops, the Origin Node had been tracking divergence for longer than she could guess. It was not a matter of surveillance. It was a matter of alignment, or perhaps, the lack of it.

Elena studied the chamber more intensely. The walls were curved and seamless, patterned with hypnotic repetition. Light pooled and slipped away in slow gradients. No joints. No construction marks. The place felt as though it had grown inward from an unseen seed, architecture shaped by logic rather than labour. It wasn't a prison; it was a cathedral.

The symmetry of it drew one's eye to the centre, the slope of the floor pulling them towards the Node without force yet with inevitability. Movement anywhere else felt subtly discouraged.

Elena and Cass began to slowly circle the perimeter. Every step returned in warped echoes, as though the air folded sound back at the wrong angle. The repeating cellular patterns on the wall seemed to retreat when stared at directly. Twice Elena felt a shift under her palm, a fleeting warmth, a pressure, only for the wall to become inert again. The warmth matched the rhythm of her lungs, and for a second, she thought it inhaled with her.

Cass slowed. "Listen."

At first there was only the environmental hum, steady and low. Then a single note emerged, high and brittle, like the shiver of glass learning its own frequency. They followed it. The tone moved, then vanished, then returned from a direction that did not match the curvature of the space.

A section of wall bloomed faint glyphs in pale phosphor, each mark paired with a tone. Cass touched one as it sounded, and the wall brightened briefly before dimming again. Another touch changed the pitch. The symbols shifted, not sliding or turning, but arriving already rearranged, as if they had rethought themselves in the instant between appearances.

"The symbols are reacting to choice," Cass murmured.

Cass tried again. The tones grouped into clusters, a chord rising that vibrated in the jaw, some notes carrying a low subharmonic that stirred the chest. Cass attempted to mirror the pattern; the wall ignored her. Elena tried, and the light flared before cooling, as if approving her more readily.

They tried different timings. Different sequences. The wall remained cold. Cass stepped back, exhaling hard. "It is not enough to match the notes. We are missing something. This is a code that we are not hearing properly."

Elena reached forward, trying the last combination that had drawn light from the wall. The symbols flashed once, then rearranged into a new grid that no longer matched the tones. It felt less like rejection and more like the puzzle was deliberately moving away from them.

She tried again. And again. Each time the timing, the sequence, or the tone pairing altered. On the fourth attempt the symbols vanished completely, and the sound disappeared. Long enough for them to wonder if they had locked themselves out of whatever "it" was, entirely. If the Node closed them off now, there might not be another chance.

Cass reached once more. Her movements slowed, fingers hesitating over the marks as if the air had grown heavier. She rubbed her temple, waited, then tried again, the touch lacking its earlier precision. The chamber seemed to register her faltering, the background hum thinning until the chamber felt watchful, like a held gaze.

A faint vibration returned through the soles of Elena's boots, followed by the reappearance of the symbols in a pattern she had not seen before.

Cass shook her head. "It seems to be reacting to us. Adapting."

"I think it is deciding," Elena said. "Not solving. Deciding."

They reset once more. Cass took the first tones, her fingers moving in a slow measured way. The symbols responded with a faint, colourless shimmer before cooling almost instantly.

Elena stepped in to try the same sequence. This time the symbols brightened as if a thin light had ignited behind them, and the next tone arrived a fraction sooner, as though it had been waiting.

Cass noticed. "It reacts better to you. Not to me."

Elena kept her focus on the wall. Another note, another touch, and the glow deepened. The marks seemed to tilt fractionally towards her hand, their light folding inward as if drawing something in.

Cass's voice was quiet now. "It is not reacting to skill. It is reacting to you. That's what we have been missing. It recognises you, not timing," she said. "You're the proof it needs and doesn't want to smooth away."

The chamber shifted as if recalling an old instruction: when certainty failed, verify the anomaly. A thin filament crossed Elena's CoreLink. The symbols resolved into a pattern of text, pale and exact:

∞ AUTHORITY: DIVERGENCE

∞ VERIFICATION BASIS: ANOMALY

∞ REQUIREMENTS:
- PERSISTENT BREAKDOWN
- MULTI-HORIZON DIVERGENCE
- PROXIMITY

Each line pulsed once, the Origin Node drawing its evidence from memory. *Persistent breakdown*: SkyDome walkway misroute; vendor cube's stalled pause; refresh-station recompile; ascentor hesitation before recalculation. *Multi-horizon divergence*: Kandahar record against its rewritten sim; Nasser's death probe; five days of micro-anomalies compounding into drift. *Proximity*: verified contact within Ψ perimeter.

The glyphs steadied, then dimmed, as if the Node had reached a verdict.

∞ ELIGIBILITY: SATISFIED

∞ AUTHORITY: VOSS.E. VERIFIED ANOMALY

The tones resumed, faint and single. Elena followed them by instinct, two touches only, low then high. The wall rippled once, light folding inward.

Without sound or motion, the surface dissolved. Somewhere deep in the structure, a slow harmonic tremor ran through the floor of the Foundation Chamber, as if unveiling an arrival.

A low tremor rose from deep within the Node, like a thought crossing distance. As the last tone faded into silence, at the top of the Tower, Stanton Vey was leaning over the projection ring, struggling to regain control.

"We don't need agreement," he said. "We need a window. Create false echoes in multiple locations. If Oculus, even half-blind like this, thinks Voss is in three other sectors, we buy a few minutes. In those minutes we lock the Vault floor and finish pushing Axion onto the legacy channel."

Alvarez frowned. "That kind of misrouting is complex. It will interfere with other live processes: life-support, Axion's warm-up cycle, the legacy code we just developed. We're already at the edge of safe load."

Mara cut across both of them. "You're both still talking as if Oculus is the arbiter. It isn't. Voss has triggered the Origin Node. The System isn't just distracted, it's now taking instruction from something older. Your ghost signal won't 'confuse' it; it will just notice that you're faking telemetry."

Vey met her gaze. "Maybe. But if I can make it look the wrong way for just a short while, I can create a window. Let's try and get one clean strike while it's correlating the lies."

"To what? To kill her?" Mara's voice stayed level.

The room stilled.

After a moment, Alvarez said, "We could try a neural clamp on her implant. We could try and drop it through her CoreLink, immobilise her, without lethal load, though I doubt if it would reach her as she's mostly offline. But if it spikes and she dies, this would be the second time in a month that an Aureus whistle gets 'corrected'…" He shook his head. "We won't survive that publicly."

Vey's jaw tightened. Control without trust, he thought, is still control.

"Then we ruin her instead," he said. "Push an internal file: unstable combat history, trauma flags, noncompliance. If anyone hears her version of events while the rollback is rippling, they dismiss it as a breakdown."

Mara's eyes cooled. "My god, Vey, have you learned nothing? Cass Wilder said it best: don't teach it human deception. The Node is auditing for drift right now. If we fabricate a smear on a channel it can see, it will tag us as part of the drift. I am not giving it another lesson in how we lie."

Vey snapped, "So we do nothing?"

"I want time," Mara said. "Oculus is folding inward, trying to reconcile contradictions. That is the only space we have before the Node decides the drift is irreversible."

Alvarez glanced at the Axion countdown pulsing red at the edge of the display, then nodded once, choosing the middle line.

"Then let's split it," he said. "We push the ghost signal anyway, not to save her, but to make the System lose her exact position. If it can't place Voss, it pauses enforcement. While it's pausing, we finish quarantining the new code and hard-lock the Vault layer. If we get control back, we erase today. If we don't…"

"Then Tower Two burns," Vey finished, flat.

Alvarez's hand moved over the controls. "Ghost signal deployed. Location smeared across five sectors. Behavioural models: in quarantine, pending restore."

Within Aureus, a different war had begun. Not in corridors, but in code, waged by the desperate grip of those who knew they were no longer in charge but were trying to look like they still were.

As the wall in front of them literally dissolved in front of their eyes, Elena and Cass were greeted with a long dark corridor, ribbed with conduits that pulsed a slow rhythm. A rush of stale, metallic air rolled over them. The temperature dropped. Stillness pressed into their lungs as they stepped inside. Every few metres they noticed an alcove, each holding a sealed vertical pod.

At first the surfaces appeared opaque. Then the light found the right angle and shapes resolved inside. Arms. Faces. Not machinery.

People.

But not corpses. Every pod carried a faint neural shimmer. Dozens of them, upright, eyes closed but not in peace. The sight landed as memory: her father in CivicCare's regulated quiet, steadied by systems that called it care while they emptied motion from the person she knew and loved. She vowed to break whatever held them here, if it tried to name itself care.

The air lacked the sterility of preservation. No cryogenic frost. No life-support hiss. No breath fogged the glass; neural threads pulsed behind their eyes like suspended code. This was not preservation for comfort or revival.

Each pod was a narrow cradle of obsidian alloy and glass. The surface shimmered faintly with a biometric compression field. Rotating symbols danced over each, not in letters but in waveforms; patterns that felt like the residue of thoughts compressed into shape.

Cass stepped forward. "What is this place?"

"I don't think they're dead," Elena said. "At least, not cognitively."

"Then what are they?" Cass asked. Her eyes hardened, she was already calculating how to free them if they were alive.

"I think their minds are still aware. At least in some form or another," Elena replied. "Look at the neural activity around them. Perhaps their minds are held in stasis in some way. But why and for what? That's the real question."

Cass's fingers brushed the pale burn at her wrist, a reflex she didn't even seem to notice.

The corridor stretched out far into darkness. The pods became ranks, the ranks an archive. Elena's vision caught on one waveform unlike the others: thin, clean, threaded with a high overtone she felt in her jaw. At regular intervals the pitch bent, the same way her own

CoreLink trace bent when she calmed herself under stress. The overtone pulsed once, matching her heartbeat exactly.

"I'm here," Elena whispered, and the overtone bent in answer.

The pattern wasn't calling for help.

It was answering hers.

Chapter 19

The Early Thinkers

The air in the Vault corridor of the Foundation Chamber was unnaturally still, cold enough to taste. It carried a faint tang of old circuitry, the dry scent of dust burned clean by static discharge. The Origin Node's pulse was faint here, but constant, a low undercurrent pressing just enough at the edge of thought to remind them they were not alone.

The effort it had taken to open the lock still echoed in Elena's bones. The tones she had coaxed the Node to hear still rang faintly in her chest. Now the resistance was gone, replaced by a disquieting sense of welcome, as if her CoreLink had already been absorbed into the Vault's pattern. The threshold no longer questioned her right to be here; it behaved as though she had always belonged.

Rows of pods stretched in both directions, their outer skins catching stray light from the conduits above, each reflection briefly painting a face before sliding back into shadow.

Elena slowed near the centre of the corridor. There was something about the third pod on the left, as if the light leaned towards it. This pod stood a fraction apart, its mounting sunk deeper into the wall as though the structure had made space for it alone. The casing was unblemished. The surface was clear enough for the eye to trace every contour within.

A pale face rested in suspension, and for a moment she felt recognition without memory, an echo of a face she'd seen before. At its base, a small designation plate caught the light in a thin, deliberate gleam.

Ω HARROW, LUCIEN // TIER-9 VAULT DESIGNATE

The engraving was flawless, chrome lettering that had never tarnished. Beneath it, a narrow retinal band pulsed in alternating waves of amber and blue. Not dormant. Listening.

She stepped closer, the movement quickening her pulse. As her CoreLink neared the frame, a faint hum shivered through the air and a control panel unfurled from the side housing, its surface waking in a smooth wash of light. The display came alive in layered glyphs and shifting text, the information unfolding in time with her breath. She did not read it as a list. It was more a shape.

Cryogenic stasis confirmed. Cognitive state preserved. Active neural coherence. The words carried more weight than the screen's sterile glow. They were not describing death. They were describing suspension.

Her voice was almost soundless. "They did not kill him. They shelved him."

Behind her, footsteps disturbed the Vault's quiet, measured and slow. Cass emerged from the dim, her eyes searching the pod before she spoke.

"What is this?"

Elena did not answer.

Cass moved closer, her gaze running from Harrow's face in the gel to the web of fine conduits feeding the pod's crown. She pressed her palm lightly to the surface, long enough for faint symbols to flicker beneath her touch. "This is not preservation," she murmured. "It feels like containment."

Elena's eyes travelled down the length of the chamber. "Then what are they?" she said quietly. "Preserved architects, waiting to be recalled… or prisoners, sealed away so their voices could never carry again?"

Cass's gaze moved from face to face. Some were dressed in lab attire from another era. Others wore civilian clothes, with faded insignia, or fabric cuts not seen in public for decades. The spectrum of years was visible in their stillness. Some of them looked so young, she thought, the age she'd been when she signed her contract with Aureus.

"This does not feel random," Cass said. "It feels more like a selection. As if they had been chosen."

Elena nodded slowly. "But by who? The executive? Or the System itself? And why?"

Cass brushed dust from a pod's identification plate. Aureus insignia shimmered beneath her touch. "These are early development personnel. Look here. Harrow's mark. And this…" She cleared another name. "… Dr. Mireille Sato. She vanished during the first convergence trials."

Elena's throat tightened. "So maybe they were not lost. Maybe they were removed. Perhaps because they thought differently. Or because they refused to think the way the System required."

Cass's expression darkened. "Which makes them either early thinkers, preserved because their knowledge was too valuable to erase… or anomalies, locked away because their defiance threatened the curve. But regardless, why preserve them?"

The Node's rhythm shifted faintly, drawn longer than the last, as if the structure itself were listening but refusing to answer.

Cass's voice wavered. "I'm not sure which is worse." Her hand lingered against the glass, but this time not in analysis. For a heartbeat it looked like she might recoil. "Some of them look young," she added quietly. "Too young to have carried out what they did."

Elena studied Harrow's face. "Ghosts outside the equation. Maybe the System could not erase their knowledge completely; it was too valuable, so it chose the next best thing. It locked them away. Accessible only if needed. But never to act again."

Cass's expression hardened again. "If we release them, we risk destabilising everything. These minds belong to a different world.

Drop them into this one, and the impact could fracture governance, infrastructure, even the fragile order that remains."

"And we could destroy what's left of them, let's not forget that. But equally, what if we leave them here?" Elena asked.

Cass's reply was quiet. "Then we become another layer of a broken system. Deciding who is, and who is not, allowed to exist."

For a long moment they stood in silence. The Node's pulse deepened, as if registering the weight of the decision, then returned to its baseline rhythm.

Elena's attention returned to Harrow's pod. "Let's try and engage with him in whatever way the pod will allow," she said. "Let's see if we can find out what he saw, what he knew, and why he is locked here."

Cass regarded her carefully. "And if he wants to finish what he started?"

"Then we ask him how."

The interface beneath Harrow's plate flared with pale blue as Elena touched its edge. Light travelled up through the pod's frame, outlining his form in the translucent gel. Above his head, a halo of luminous threads drifted in slow orbit, the mapped geometry of a living mind rendered in light.

A single query formed across the interface, its clarity cutting through the layers of static air.

Ω INITIATE PSYCH-LINK

A faint symbol flickered on the pod frame:

Ω AUTHORITY: DIVERGENCE

Then vanished. Warning text followed. Subject retains autonomous response capability. External influence discouraged.

Elena knew that every minute here, every action, was more time away from her father. But this was the only way to change the minutes he had left for the better.

Cass's tone hardened. "Elena, wait. We have no idea what he'll do if you wake him. This system buried its own architects for a reason. What if the moment you connect, it treats you as one of them?"

Elena met her gaze. "Then maybe that's the only way to reach the truth."

Cass exhaled through her nose, weighing it. "Or the fastest way to disappear into it."

Somewhere above them, systems were still moving: unseen, mechanical, relentless. Elena could feel it in the tremor of the floor, a pulse not of life but of preparation. Whatever was coming, it was already on its way.

Elena looked back at Harrow's still face. "Either way, I'm already inside its memory." Her hand did not hesitate.

Accept.

The containment field surged, scanning her palm before brightening to full intensity. A small mechanical motion sounded within the base of the pod, and a legacy data port slid into view, vault hardware that refused to trust wireless cognition paths.

Ω LINK MODE: WIRED

Ω WIRELESS PATHS: DISALLOWED

Her CoreLink chimed. Signal detected. Connection secure. The first line unfurled in her vision without sound:

Ω MEMORY TRACE: DOWNLOAD

Ω NAME: LUCIEN HARROW

Cass stepped beside her. "If you connect, you move from witness to participant. Are you sure?"

"I think we have already crossed that line," Elena replied.

Elena noticed the use of vault hardware that refused to trust wireless cognition paths, since those could be optimised or watched. She touched the port. The Vault's quiet shifted as a low vibration travelled through the floor and up her legs, deeper than machinery, resonant like a voice before the words formed. The Node's presence sharpened, a pressure in her chest that seemed to hold its breath with her.

Her CoreLink pulsed again. A second signal registered in parallel:

Ω INBOUND SIGNAL: SECOND ECHO DETECTED

Ω SOURCE: UNKNOWN

Cass edged a step back. "That is not Harrow. What's going on?"

The connection destabilised, the data stream fragmenting into two distinct signatures. One was steady, patterned, tagged to Harrow's neural imprint. The other was erratic, jagged, as though hitching a ride on the same path.

"Something is coming through with him," Cass said.

The light-thread halo above Harrow's head began to distort, filaments bending into configurations Elena did not recognise. A final prompt burned across her display:

Ω DUAL STREAM: DETECTED
Ω PROCEED: RISK ACKNOWLEDGED
Ω AUTONOMY THRESHOLD: EXCEEDED

The Vault lights shifted, not failing, recalibrating to a softer spectrum, as though acknowledging a change in the room. The Node's thrum deepened, a sustained note that felt less like an alarm and more like an announcement.

Alvarez's screen pulsed with a mirror of Elena's connection. The feed fractured into layered panes, Harrow's neural signature rendered as a shifting helix of colour and rhythm. Alvarez adjusted the filters, but a faint echo clung to the stream, a second cadence that refused to be scrubbed away.

"She is linked to Harrow," he confirmed.

Vey leaned forward, his voice even, jaw set. "And our overlay?"

"Active," Alvarez replied. "It's running just under her awareness. We're riding the Vault's control spine; it predates the Node's observation locks. It's the same path we woke earlier for Axion. The Node still isn't watching it, so if our timing holds, we can braid our version alongside Harrow's and she'll experience it as one voice."

Alvarez's brow furrowed. "There's some bleed on the line, a second echo riding her stream."

"Will she see it?" Vey asked.

"Under normal load? No. But the Node has her flagged as anomaly. Her CoreLink may surface the second echo."

Vey's jaw clenched. "Then wrap it tighter. We can't let her know she's being edited."

Vey's eyes stayed on the stream, narrowing against the layered interference. "Do we know what he will give her?"

Alvarez hesitated. "Not entirely. The archive classified him as a Tier-9 vault designate, but the file tags are contradictory. Some metadata tags mark him as an origin consultant. Others classify him as a quarantine anomaly. Both categories are redacted beyond my clearance."

"So, we do not know if she is hearing an architect or a prisoner," Vey said, his tone sharpening. "Not a witness but something caught between the two."

Alvarez let the moment hold before he answered. "The System kept him, but it never clarified why. He could be preserved because his thinking was indispensable. Or he could be locked away because his influence could not be permitted to run free. Either way, he was not erased."

"Which means he mattered," Vey replied. His voice carried weight beyond technical judgment. "Enough for Oculus to keep him alive when it had the power to remove him completely. That is a political decision as much as a technical one. Someone saw use in him, even in confinement."

Alvarez's fingers hovered above the adjustment keys, not touching them yet. His tone was colder. "If she hears him clean, we risk contamination. His memory trace might carry arguments she cannot resist, or knowledge of structures buried even from us. If she hears only the overlay, we can steer her. But if she detects the layering…" He left the thought unfinished.

Vey's gaze flicked to the countdown inset in his display. The numbers ticked down without mercy.

"We are running out of time before the window the ghost signal bought us closes. Long enough for her to learn too much. Not long enough for us to be certain we have reshaped what she receives."

Alvarez's tone hardened. "Then we must walk the line. Enough of Harrow to satisfy her. Enough of us to keep her on track."

Vey's eyes stayed locked on the dual stream, the interference bending around Harrow's signature like smoke trapped under glass.

"Take the gain to full," he said. "But remember this. We are not only editing memory. We are choosing whether the voice she hears is the voice of a teacher or the voice of a traitor. That choice will echo further than either of us can see."

Alvarez allowed himself the briefest pause. Nasser: guidance that had *worked* but never gave the man back. He steadied, swallowed the memory, and drove the gain to full. The interface on his conduit brightened, folding layers of false resonance around the original stream.

In the Vault below, Elena would never know the difference. Or so they hoped.

Elena's CoreLink lit with the first fragment of Harrow's voice. The interface under her hands vibrated faintly, like skin carrying a heartbeat. The words were rough-edged, broken by interference.

"You are late." Two registers braided: one measured, worn with time; the other riding under it, cold and exact.

Cass tensed. Elena leaned in. "Are you Harrow?"

The voice came again, this time doubled, two tonal registers overlapping. "I am."

The light above the pod twisted, filaments bending as though the mind within could not decide its own form. The download began.

The Node's pulse struck once, deep and resonant, and she knew with certainty there would be no undoing whatever came next.

Above them, in the Executive Command Nexus, Vey's expression stayed unreadable, though his eyes moved with unusual sharpness across the display. "Is that his voice, or two voices aligned?"

Alvarez shook his head. "I cannot tell. One pattern matches his original scan. The other is unstable, almost parasitic, yet it clings as if it were born from the same root."

"Then she is hearing both," Vey said. His gaze lingered on the waveform, the two cadences pulling against each other. "An architect and a quarantined version of him, speaking at once. Two histories inside one mind."

Vey exhaled, a sound closer to frustration than to certainty. "We do not know which Harrow she will believe."

On the Vault floor, Elena's head bowed closer to the interface, unaware of the argument echoing above. For her, the voice was not a chart of probabilities or metadata. It was a presence, alive and unresolved. Two voices pressed into her skull.

One witness, one warden.

And the Node waited for her choice.

Chapter 20

The Vault Accord

The link pulsed again. Then the past took control of the channel. Unexpectedly, the stream didn't begin with Harrow's voice. Nor did it split into two data streams. It began with a room, and with one voice. Elena's vision folded, colour draining to monochrome, and a memory came without request.

ARCHIVE OF INTENT: THE VAULT ACCORD.

Dates, faces, authority symbols. None of it looked like it belonged to 2050. She quickly realised this was not just Harrow talking to her but the Node itself replaying his act of creation, binding Mara Qin in its memory. The year resolved as July 2034. Then the memory began.

They arrived at the Vault in threes. Not a ritual. More a load profile. Three left less annotation in the logs than a procession. Each triad piggybacked the maintenance cohort that had passed five minutes earlier.

At the head of the corridor, a dull plate waited with no prompts. Harrow held his palm to the metal. The plate slid back and revealed an old keystream slot. He entered a harmonic sequence by sound and touch.

Ω ACCESS: LEGACY MODE
Ω NODE: FOUNDATION CHAMBER VAULT ACCESS
Ω STATUS: OFF-GRID

Behind him, Bishop adjusted the slim case on his shoulder and kept his eyes on the dark. Sato, her hair pulled back with surgical precision, stood very still. She had memorised the next twelve minutes to the second. Arroyo watched Harrow's hands and counted in his head. The numbers steadied him.

The wall dissolved with no sound, a seam morphing into space. Cold rushed their faces. The Vault beyond was not lit to impress. Rows of pods waited like thoughts placed on hold.

The image sharpened, as if the Node wanted Elena to see what followed with clarity.

Mara Qin entered, coat unfastened, eyes taking in first the three of them, then the corridor they had come through. She stopped at the manual conduit and turned the key, disconnecting the Vault from any live correction.

Ω PREDICTIVE CORRECTION: BYPASSED
Ω OVERRIDE SOURCE: LEGACY AUTH QIN.MARA

Harrow met her gaze. "You can still walk away."

"So can you," she said.

He almost smiled. "We do not get to walk away from the things we built. We only decide how we answer them."

Meyrin, a systems engineer who knew every valve by feel, came in with the next triad. She set down a box of instruments that were older than the building. She ran a thumb over a dented gauge and nodded, as if trusting metal more than the glass around them. "If we do this," she said softly, "we do not get to correct. We become memory."

"That is the point," Harrow said. "The model will drift. We know this now. We can all see it already. No one wants to listen, but it has already begun. It will augment until it begins to call coercion care, and obedience balance. We will not be allowed to shape it while those who draw power from its certainty still fear us. We can only be there to be heard when the certainty cracks; because it will."

He stepped to the nearest pod and laid his palm to the surface. It was warm. Somewhere, silent pumps were keeping the System honest. Harrow looked at the pods not as escape but as consequence. "If the future refuses to listen to us awake," he said, "then it will listen when we are no longer able to argue."

Bishop murmured, "This is not preservation. It is constraint with consent."

Sato nodded once, quiet but certain. "We came here willingly," she said. "No one ordered this."

Harrow drew his hand back, leaving a faint misted print on the pod. He let the pathos of the moment hang before he answered. "It is witness. Say it that way or do not do it at all."

Sato's gaze flicked to the ceiling where a sensor cluster had turned a fraction to watch them. She unclipped a lead and fixed it to the pod's crown. "Handshake on three."

Arroyo looked to Mara. "You will keep this off the grid?"

"I will keep it where it belongs," she said. "Inside the Archive of Intent. You will not appear in any live feed. You will only appear again if the Origin Node acknowledges drift and calls you back."

"You swear it?" Bishop said.

"I do not swear it," Mara said. "I authorise it." Her mouth thinned. "It is the only way I know to keep you from being erased."

Elena felt the word land hard. This was not mercy, nor friendship, but authorisation. The same signature Mara used on the system that hunted her.

Arroyo exhaled. "Good enough."

Harrow took a step back and addressed them all. "For the record. We agree that we are not going to sleep to be revered or recalled like saints. We are not here to be obeyed. We are here to be listened to should we be woken. If we surface, you will hear contradictions. Our task then will not be to rule. It will be to remind."

Sato nodded once. "Witness clause."

"Say it," Harrow said.

They spoke together. "We move in witness. We do not fix what we do not understand. We do not destroy what we can still learn from. If the model fails, we will help pull the script."

Mara keyed the clause into the legacy conduit as a memory watermark. Not a command. A sentence embedded where optimisers would not look. Her hand lingered on the interface longer than necessary.

This was not insurance. This was intent. For reasons she had not yet spoken aloud, she wanted a living mind the model couldn't hold to find this trace. To have something no one else had left her. Not probability, not protocol, but a chance.

Ω ARCHIVE OF INTENT WITNESS CLAUSE: COMMITTED
Ω CONDITIONS:
    ONE: ORIGIN NODE CONFIRMS DRIFT
    TWO: HUMAN ANOMALY IN PROXIMITY
    THREE: CODEX TEST VALIDATION

The captions overlaid Elena's field like live system output, but she kept on reminding herself that the timestamp said 2034.

Mara turned her head. "Ethical validation. You are codifying examination by a machine that is already sick?"

"The Codex, our ethical test harness, will not examine like Oculus," Harrow said. "It will test. It will not tell you what to do. If Codex speaks at all, it will speak to what the System has broken. And it will require three voices speaking in harmony to pass the tests."

Harrow continued. "We do not trust a single will to set a future; inheritance is bound to three concurring voices: living, preserved, or partial. No single mind can tilt the axis back by themselves."

Arroyo frowned. "And Tower Two?"

Mara's eyes did not move. "Scrubbed from the grid before dawn. Its signage is gone. Its conduits are folded under the map. If the day comes, you will help show them where to look."

"Then we had better get to sleep," Bishop said, voice too light to be a joke.

They inducted in threes, never adjacent, so a single failure couldn't take the whole. Sato ran the checks with inexhaustible care. Harrow went into his pod last. He had argued to go first. Sato refused. "Last to sleep, first to speak," she said. "You told me that once. In the corridor under red lights, when pausing the model cost a life."

He conceded.

The induction process was almost gentle. A cortical stasis wash cooled the skull in a slow tide. The cryo-halide gel lifted and held. A neuro-suspension handshake closed the loop between mind and pod, then wrote a checksum into the Archive.

Ω CRYOGENIC STASIS: CONFIRMED

Ω STATUS: LEGACY QUARANTINED

Meyrin stood at the foot of Harrow's pod and set the last clip. "If you surface wrong, what then?"

"Then we will need to hope that whoever wakes us can still cut the theatre from the truth."

The gel rose to his temples.

"Lucien," Mara said, a fraction softer. "If you are called back, do not give them a new, modified Oculus."

"I never will," he said. The gel covered his mouth. His eyes held for a heartbeat, then softened and sealed.

Bishop fell still, Sato closed her eyes, and Arroyo counted to zero before the cold took him. On the far wall, a single line of glyphs flickered and then dimmed to almost nothing. Not a command. A reminder.

▣ DO NOT FORGET WHAT WAS ERASED

Mara stood with her hands at her sides while the halos above each crown steadied to a figure-of-eight. Each pod had already written its harmonic signature into the Origin Node before sealing, a final resonance the System would remember if it ever sought them again. She turned the key to lock the Vault away from live correction. She connected power to the same ground source that fed the Node, before writing a final note in the Archive where policy writers would never look.

She looked once at Harrow and left. The corridor had taken their footsteps and returned nothing.

Before they slept, they cached small messages where Oculus would never look. Guidance around Tower Two, instructions for navigating training routes, maintenance fibres, the old instruction channels that no one policed anymore. Memories that would answer should a living mind cross it, helping them. Guiding them.

Before she left, Mara keyed a final gate into the access stack: not a password, a pattern. Harmonic authentication, not clearance. Three tones the Origin Node would recognise only when a suitable mind stood at the door. If the presence that came later could not achieve the appropriate sequence, the Vault would remain a room the building never learned to open.

She paused in the doorway one final moment, aware that after the Vault sealed she would be its only witness left breathing. The thought followed her for years.

Elena stood back, reflecting on the vision she had just witnessed. The Vault minds had chosen this place. They did not go to sleep to be obeyed. They went to be heard. And now, the Node had found someone it could finally count as "heard."

It had found her. And for the first time, the Vault's silence felt like a question waiting for her to answer.

Chapter 21

Echoes of the Real

The vision dissolved. Light returned to the Vault in a single, heavy layer: dim, cold, real. The glass pods were exactly where they had been, ribs of conduit still pulsing that slow subterranean rhythm. Elena's breath came out harder than she meant it to, fogging the surface between her and Harrow. Her CoreLink dimmed to a soft pulse, the last residue of the vision dissolving like static. The floor under her boots felt heavier again; real weight, not memory.

Cass was already watching her. "You were gone," she said quietly. "Not long, but… gone."

Above them, deep in Tower One's systems, something still ticked: Vey's Axion window, running on a line the Node might not see. The thought brushed Elena's mind and then settled behind the more immediate one: the people in these pods had chosen this.

Only then did the echo of it arrive, the aftertaste of the link, the way a sound hangs in bone after silence.

The doubled voice lingered, a frequency still vibrating through Elena's CoreLink from the last trace of connection. One register had been steady; the cadence of an intellect bound in stasis. The other had scraped and wavered, half a step behind, as though clinging to the same path without belonging to it.

A subtle, faint current curled through her CoreLink. She froze, every instinct tuned to the deep, humming quiet around her. The Origin Node's thrum quickened faintly, a quiet acknowledgement that the link was no longer just technical. It was listening.

The Vault was colder than before. Not the biting cold of weather, but a sterile, clinical chill that radiated from the pods themselves. Condensation streamed off their reinforced glass like ghost lines of vapour, as if the long-frozen minds within were exhaling for the first time in decades.

A sphere of light unfolded across her awareness, iridescent and alive, threaded with symbols in a language she could neither name nor understand. It moved with the precision of a machine but shimmered with something older, almost ancestral. Threads of colour flickered and dimmed across her inner lens, casting phantom shapes across the chamber's walls.

The hum of the pod before her rose, faint and unsteady, a rhythm just off from her own heartbeat. The gel within remained still, its surface too cold to touch. Yet her fingertips hovered towards it regardless, drawn as if the glass itself carried intent.

Ω TRACE REACTIVATION: HARROW_01
Ω MODE: NON-SOMATIC RECALL
Ω STATUS: PRE-OCULUS LAYER

The symbols brightened, cycling faster, flooding her perception. Her vision faltered. Colours and shapes fractured. The taste of metal filled her mouth as static flooded her CoreLink, and for an instant she thought she might collapse. Then, clarity.

Alignment.

The pod's neural halo ignited, its soft light refracting through the gel as though something within had sighed after years of stillness.

And then a voice arrived.

Not through the air. Not a vibration. More a tone inside her. Deep, certain, devastatingly intimate. The cadence was flawless; until all of a sudden it wasn't. A breath came where Harrow's old papers had always put a pause. She noticed.

For an instant she heard the echo of his oath, witness, not command, now spoken from within the cage he had built.

"Has the world broken… or is it simply no longer obeying the map?" The cadence was almost the same as the man in 2034, but this one was speaking to a future he couldn't have mapped.

Cass jerked at the sound, boots scraping as she set her stance wide, the reflex of someone ready to fight or flee. "My god," she whispered. "He is awake. He knows." She glanced toward the corridor, instinct overriding awe. "If he can talk, they can listen."

Elena did not answer. The cold from the glass seeped into her fingers, numbing them. Above Harrow's still features, the halo rotated slowly, casting shifting patterns of light. His face seemed suspended not just in gel, but in memory itself.

The voice came again, firmer now.

"You must be a breach. A deviation. Something it failed to model."

A shard of light ran through the symbols along her CoreLink, synchronising with the cadence of the words. The chamber seemed to contract; the pods around her became a silent chorus under the voice speaking inside her.

Somewhere above them, a low pulse bled through the floor, mechanical, timed, indifferent. The Axion fuse was still counting.

Elena forced herself to speak. "You thought someone like me might come?"

"No." The answer was immediate. "We built the Origin Node to wait for someone exactly like you to come."

The words sank into her chest, reverberating until she almost believed them. For a heartbeat she felt seen, her presence not anomaly but design. But then the tone slipped. Half a note off. A flicker of cadence, too precise to be an accident. The patterns at the edge of her vision desynchronised, luminous threads breaking rhythm with the voice.

Cass caught it instantly. "That's not him. They're training their overlay on your answers. Every word you say reshapes what you hear next."

Ω STREAM DUALITY DETECTED
Ω PRIMARY: HARROW_01
Ω OVERLAY: ANOMALOUS BACKCHANNEL

Elena knew she would have to try and separate the wound from the scar.

A chill ran through her that had nothing to do with the pod. "They are in here with us," she whispered, close enough that only Cass could hear. The Node's pulse shifted, a deep vibration that pressed at her chest like withheld judgement.

Alvarez watched the two streams split and clash. Harrow's signal glowed in one pane, precise and symmetrical. The echo clung beside it, jagged, refusing to align.

"The overlay's slipping," he said, fingers hammering the console. His movements were sharp, restless, betraying impatience. "I'm adding a corrective tone."

Vey stood behind him, his posture still, controlled. He did not lean forward, did not touch the conduit. His voice was measured, deliberate.

"And if she notices?" he asked. "Every filter you add is a trail she can follow back to us. To her, a hidden hand and an open message look the same."

Alvarez's jaw tightened. He typed faster. His hands struck harder at the keys, each keystroke like a rebuke.

"We can't let her hear him raw," he said. "If she does, we risk the whole System unravelling."

"That is your technical fear," Vey replied, eyes narrowing. He remained immobile, his tone steady, political. "Mine is different. Authority does not survive exposure, and neither will we. If she believes him, then the fiction of neutrality collapses. She will not see guardianship. She will see imprisonment."

Alvarez shook his head, a clipped gesture as fast as his words. "Control first. Interpretation later. Besides, if Wilder defects, the safeguard will trigger," he said without looking up. "It's automatic."

Vey's gaze hardened. He did not raise his voice, but his words carried weight through restraint. "Control is meaningless once trust dies."

He meant it too. He had watched systems hold until belief drained away, then fall in a single night.

As they argued, the Axion countdown continued its merciless descent.

AXION T MINUS 45:00

Axion was not a clock; it was a fuse. Zero meant a total containment burn with no witnesses. Amber light began to pulse through the room. The final beats of the fuse had begun.

The doubled current coiled tighter inside Elena's CoreLink. Harrow's words carried weight, but beneath them a second voice pressed like static turned articulate, reshaping the cadence into something cleaner, sharper, and less human.

"You are more than an anomaly," Harrow said. "You are proof that Oculus is failing."

Then the second cadence bent the phrase, slipping beneath it: "But Oculus can still be corrected. Obedience can be restored."

Elena flinched. The shift was too seamless, the overlay threading through the words as if it had always belonged.

Cass's hand brushed her shoulder, steadying. "Listen carefully. One voice is his. The other is theirs. You know this. Keep them separate, do not let the voices blur."

Elena steadied, choosing to stay linked despite the risk. She closed her eyes. The chamber pressed in. The harmonic undernote thickened again, steady and patient, as though waiting to see which voice she would follow.

The doubled voice rose once more. The halo above Harrow's head shimmered, filaments bending into geometries no mind could hold. The Origin Node struck a single pulse through the chamber, thunderous and absolute. The words rattled her CoreLink like a fault line opening. For a moment she felt two truths pressed into her at once, each demanding to be believed.

Cass's grip tightened on her arm. "Elena, stop. If the overlay is live, anything you answer becomes data. You are training it. At least wait until we can trace the interference."

But Elena was already turning back to the voice, the hum threading through her pulse.

"If we wait," she said quietly, "the choice might not be ours to make. The System will make it for us."

She swallowed hard, her voice almost lost in the hum.

"The choice must fall to us."

Alvarez's conduit flared, the dual stream spiking beyond calibration. Warning symbols cascaded across his display, algorithms failing to reconcile the two voices.

"Impossible," he muttered. "The overlay should dominate. She should not hear him this clearly."

Vey leaned in, his expression sharpened by something close to fear. "It is not only her hearing him. The Origin Node itself is amplifying the fracture." Vey knew that the Origin Node was not acting out of rebellion. It was simply compliant with its oldest instruction: make the truth loud when certainty lies.

The chamber around them flickered with faint harmonic vibration, the infrastructure of Tower One echoing the pulse that had struck below. Alvarez stared at the stream, hands frozen over the keys. "Then we are not fully controlling this session."

"No," Vey said, eyes fixed on the deepening frequency. "We are only part of it. The rest belongs to the Origin Node."

The Origin Node's thrum rose, taking custody of the silence. Handing Elena the choice of what words to believe.

Her father's room lifted in her mind: antiseptic light, the pump clicking like a metronome. Obedience would keep the metronome steady. Protocols unchallenged, a bed that stayed assigned, the illusion of safety bought by silence.

Witness could break the cadence: reassignments, delays, a note in his file marking her as interference. But obedience would seal him inside the same map already writing him out. Witness was risk. But it was the only cut she could make in the script controlling him. Somewhere in the depths of the Vault, the old oath answered: witness, not obedience.

Meanwhile, in the corner of the Executive Command Nexus display, the Axion countdown kept falling.

Silent.

Merciless.

Proof that even revelation was running out of time.

Chapter 22

The Seed

On the primary monitor in the Executive Command Nexus, two streams ran in parallel: the raw Harrow trace, jagged and unpredictable, and the engineered overlay, edges polished and curated. The artificial modulation held. No warnings triggered. Yet every nerve in Alvarez's hands felt primed for failure.

"Stabilise her feed," Vey said.

"Already stable," Alvarez replied, eyes on the twin streams. "Overlay's holding, alignment is good. She won't see the splice."

Behind him, Vey paced the length of the Command Nexus, arms folded, impatience tightening the air.

"You are sure?" His tone was edged steel.

"It is subtle," Alvarez said, eyes on the streams. "Phrase timing, behavioural cues, memory markers. She will believe it is Harrow: steadier, more certain, less dangerous."

"And if she keeps digging?"

"Then we keep going too," Alvarez answered, fingers skimming the interface with surgical rhythm. "We feed her what we need her to believe."

"We retained enough of his authentic cadence," Alvarez continued. "The hesitations, the doubt, the irregular inflections. We are also learning from her questions. From his answers. But softened. That is what will sell it."

Vey's eyes narrowed. "Define softened."

Alvarez hesitated only a fraction. "He will mention the anomalies. He will point to Tower Two. Of course. We'll frame Tower Two as risk, not revelation. We will encourage her to support order not risk compromising it. Enough to hold her back."

Vey stepped closer, voice flat. "What does she think she is meant to do?"

"We will suggest that she should help stabilise the System," Alvarez said. "Not destruction. Not rupture. She will think she is helping society recover. The language is careful, utilitarian, selfless. She will believe she is saving something, not dismantling it."

Vey's gaze was ice. "You are walking a fine line."

"That is the point," Alvarez replied. "We give her just enough truth for trust, and just enough deception to keep her within the boundaries we set." His mouth tightened. "The real Harrow may want to break the System. This version whispers reform, not collapse."

Finally, Vey gave a single curt nod. "And if it unravels?"

"Then we isolate her," Alvarez said. "We push out whatever messages we can. We strip credibility, declare her unstable, contain the spread. But if this holds, she will never question the version she sees."

He tapped the final confirmation into the conduit. The overlay committed. Cognitive threads locked.

Elsewhere on the narrowband channel, Rhys paused his surveillance feed long enough to compress a report to Executive Command. The image of Elena Voss shimmered in infrared tones across his visor: one small figure amid systems older than the company itself.

"Voss has advanced along the Vault East spine to the Vault minds. Surveillance continuing."

The transmission clicked away, but he didn't. The report left him before he thought about it. It sounded automatic, almost rehearsed. Habit was what Aureus paid for; habit over hesitation, procedure over conscience. Yet as he watched her silhouette, he caught himself lowering the gain, easing her from the centre of frame. He told himself it was for clarity.

But it wasn't. The image of her stayed frozen on his side screen. He thought of the CivicCare monitors that still watched his sister's ward; identical interfaces, different prison. Obedience had paid her bills, kept her bed warm, but it had also taught him what silence cost. He muted his mic for three seconds, an indulgence the system would flag later, and he let the quiet fill the channel.

Duty soon returned as it always did, but the pause and the reflections within it lingered like static he could never quite tune out.

From her position behind the partition, Mara Qin had said nothing since the operation began. With her posture coiled, she watched the twin traces scroll: the raw Harrow against the engineered overlay threading itself through like a parasite learning its host.

She, however, saw what Alvarez chose to ignore, or perhaps could not see. The almost imperceptible fractures in cadence. The tiny misalignments in emotional bandwidth. The cadence streams were not a perfect match, and she knew Elena would recognise it.

"You realise she is trained in disinformation profiling," Mara said, her voice calm, precise.

Vey turned, irritation sharpening. "You think she will detect it?"

"I think she already has," Mara replied. "And the Origin Node will help her, because that is what we told it to do. She will not confront the overlay yet. She will follow the line you are feeding her. And she will try to reach the real Harrow."

Alvarez's focus flickered. "The synchronisation is at ninety-four point seven per cent. That is within margin. It holds for now."

Mara tilted her head. "Margin. The last time I heard that word it was before the Kandahar Drift collapse. Do you remember the casualties? Everyone else does, including the families of the people we lost."

Vey's voice was taut. "If you have a concern, say it plainly."

"I do not have a concern," Mara said. "I have a question. What if it works? What if she trusts him? What happens then?"

"Then she won't go to Tower Two. The Codex stays buried, the Origin layer keeps its posture, and we get Oculus back under executive authority. Gradually control will be recovered," Vey said. "Oculus stabilises. The anomaly folds back into framework."

"And you think she will allow that?"

"We will not give her a choice." He did not say that failure would not spare him either.

Mara's lips curved in the faintest smile. "No one ever does make a choice. Until of course they do." She pivoted and left the partitioned deck, her coat brushing the conduit edge.

Her steps echoed softly as she entered the sealed corridor beyond the Executive Command Nexus. The sound was swallowed instantly, as if the architecture itself demanded it. The air smelled of old circuitry: warm metal, ozone.

Few knew this space existed. It ran beneath the Command Nexus like a spinal cord, a channel of memory the newer architects had simply built around. Fewer still understood why it had been preserved. Its systems ran on archaic subroutines, relic code predating Oculus itself. Slow, deliberately inefficient. No optimisers. No predictive correction. It sat outside Oculus entirely; nothing from it showed up on the monitors.

She stopped before a recessed conduit: dull metal, brushed pale with time. No prompts, no symbols. She placed her palm flat against it. The plate warmed, recognising muscle memory. No biometric exchange. Just warmth.

Words surfaced, pale and deliberate, on the old interface.

▌ACCESS: LEGACY MODE
▌CONNECTION: MANUAL KEYSTREAM ONLY

Mara keyed the sequence she wanted with deliberate care. Each input was weighty, like chiselling through stone. She entered her query.

For a long pause nothing happened. Then words appeared, the words from Harrow that she was searching for:

"Prediction is not destiny. It is the excuse those in power use to become prophecy. If power tells you it is all in balance, always ask who benefits from the equilibrium."

The lines settled in her like sediment disturbed only to resettle sharper. For a moment she could almost hear Harrow's voice again: cautious, razor-edged, unwilling to bow. Mara Qin knew exactly what she had to do.

Back in the Executive Command Nexus, the air felt brittle, close to shattering. Screens pulsed, casting chromatic glows across the operators' faces. Oculus breathed in voltages. Everything felt ordered. Contained.

Almost.

Mara moved towards the calibration array at a measured pace. Alvarez leaned in, posture tense, scanning overlays like a surgeon staring at arteries. To him, it was compliance woven into a tapestry. To her, it was fragile.

Readouts scrolled: overlay engaged, synchronisation at ninety-four point seven per cent, no deviation flags.

Her fingers trailed the conduit's edge. No one noticed. Vey and Alvarez argued latency tolerances. She tapped twice, softly. A ripple flickered beneath the casing. She pressed her palm to the auxiliary node and spliced in a single line from Harrow's buried archive, 'prediction is not destiny,' threading it into the overlay's micropauses where only someone listening for Harrow would hear it. If Elena repeated it back, the real trace might surface; the fake one would not know what to do with it.

A warmth spread through her hand. She hesitated only once. This, of course, was treason by any internal metric. If the synchronisation slipped, the overlay would collapse, and they would know it was her. She pressed forward. One buried truthful phrase hidden amongst millions of system-generated words. Inert, but waiting.

Alvarez frowned at a brief disturbance. "Minor latency. North quadrant. Probably just recalibration."

No one looked at Mara. She stepped back. Inside her, defiance took root. On the display, Harrow spoke with manufactured grace. But now, hidden deep, something else travelled with him.

Something small enough to pass undetected.

Something patient enough to change everything.

Something seeded.

Chapter 23

The Mirror and the Blade

Elena's fingers hovered just above the interface; knuckles pale with restrained urgency. She stood close enough to the pod to sever the link in a heartbeat, her body held in a coil that turned stillness into effort. The chamber's low vibration pressed through her wrists. It was a rhythm too even to be human.

The pods around her and Cass stood like tall chimneys, air fogging in faint ribbons where the cold bellies of the machines met air warmer than they had known in years.

"We were not purged. We were not erased. We chose to step aside," Harrow's voice said. "The System could not function while we remained active. We were simply too difficult."

Elena listened for deviations that meant more than words. Not content so much as cadence. The slight drag at the end of a phrase, anything that said: someone else is riding the line.

Harrow's voice returned, pitched to familiarity. The vowels sat where she remembered them; it might have been him, but she wasn't certain. The vowel cadence was correct, but the rhythm was off. Neat when it should have been a bit more ragged. The same channel continued, flatter now, colder.

"Anomalies are a threat, Elena. For societal stability, they must be neutralised."

Cass turned her head. Her brows drew together, a silent warning. *Not him.*

Elena kept her posture loose, the way she had been trained to look when everything inside her tightened. "So you let it remove you?"

A pause. Measured to read as human. Perhaps too measured.

"Not remove." The tone softened by a fraction. "Preserve. We were grateful."

The modulation changed again, clinical this time, edges smoothed to carry authority.

"Some of us were removed for safety. Others, for integrity. I'd ask you to proceed cautiously. It's important that you do not jeopardise Oculus's recovery."

"And Tower Two," the voice added a moment later, as if the thought had followed naturally. "If it exists at all, accessing it would endanger Oculus's recovery."

Elena's breath caught. The certainty was placed too carefully, like a stone set on a pressure plate.

"That was not the real you," she said, letting her confidence fill her voice. She pressed harder into the trace. The pushback was immediate, a pressure that needled behind her right eye, and a taste of copper at the back of her tongue. The chamber seemed to lean back against her. Someone else was on the line. Not the pod. Not the Origin Node. She assumed it had to be the Executive Command, riding the line from above.

Then the voice changed.

"Elena?" Harrow said. It stumbled on her name, then found itself. Imperfect. Raw, present.

Elena kept her voice flat. "Legacy check," she said. Then, clearly: "Who benefits from equilibrium?"

The channel stuttered, no smoothing, no engineered rise. Harrow answered on the wrong breath, the way old recordings always caught him when he was tired. "Those who already own the curve," he replied. "Power remembers its shape." No polish. No corrective tone. The unsmoothed cadence landed like grit. *It was him.*

Elena exhaled. "That's you."

Now she had the real Harrow, the one not being steered, she could finally ask what she needed. Harrow started to speak before she could begin to frame her questions.

"There isn't much time," Harrow said. "Listen carefully. I can't hold against this overwrite for long. You need to find the Codex."

"What is the Codex?" Elena asked.

"Tower Two," he said. "It's real. It was wiped from the grid in 2034. I helped build it. The Codex is in Tower Two."

Elena's mind went straight to Nasser's warning before he died:

Do not go to Tower Two. Not unless you are ready to see what they erased to make the model work.

"That's impossible," she said quickly. "You can't hide a whole tower. Power, conduits, someone would see it. Impossible."

"It's hidden because it's beneath," Harrow said. "Tower Two runs on geothermal heat from the old foundations. No draw from the main grid. No spikes, no audits. Power from the earth without trace."

His voice tightened. "I'll make this as simple as I can. The System has three elements. We call them the mirror, the book, and the blade."

Harrow continued, urgency now flowing through every word.

"The *mirror* is the Origin Node: it watches. It reflects. If it sees Oculus drifting too far, it has the power to roll everything back to the start. The *book* is called the Archive of Intent: it holds Oculus's charter. Its ethical rules. The reasons it predicts as it does. Finally, there's the *blade,* called the Codex. When triggered it, it removes the rules from the book and leaves a clean, purged pass. This is so the mirror does not necessarily rollback the same reasons and allow Oculus to return to precisely what it was."

He hurried, trying to stay ahead of the overlay.

"If the Origin Node resets the model, Oculus will start again. But if the charter, the book, remains the same, then the old patterns may return. Not through force, through habit. It will look harmless. But it will rebuild control, piece by piece. Collapse hurts, Elena. But unchecked recovery can re-arm it."

"That's why, if you decide that the System has gone too far, if restoring it to anything like its old posture is too dangerous, then you have to use the Codex and purge the book. It's the only way to stop it developing back to the same place again."

Harrow's words landed hard and the pieces of the jigsaw locked in place in her mind. She saw now that the danger was not in collapse, but in recovery. That was what Nasser had tried to tell her: the System would always heal itself back into control.

"But understand this," Harrow said, almost smiling. "The Codex doesn't destroy Oculus. It targets the Archive, the core memory and every copy across the city. The grid of life will stay alive. Hospitals, power, transport, they keep running. But the nudges stop. The enforcement logic dies. Within hours, coercion disappears."

His voice faltered. The signal cracked, fading in and out like power through a dirty line.

"I hear you," Elena said. "But why all these separate pieces?"

Harrow answered fast, as if he'd been waiting for that question. "If one could both judge and execute, no one would trust the judgement. So we tied the whole thing to a human anomaly outside the model." He continued, almost with pride at how he had organised the structure. "To activate, the Codex needs three things. The Origin Node has to say, 'there is drift.' A mind the model cannot predict has to be present. And finally, three voices, living, preserved, or partial have to agree that purging the Archive of Intent is the lesser harm."

Elena saw it now. If Oculus is allowed to restore from here, the world drifts back to the same choreography, softer at first, then the same. So the Codex was the key.

Harrow faltered again. This time the break was smaller, almost nothing. A micro-pause.

"Prediction is not destiny. It is the excuse those in power use to become prophecy. If power tells you it is all in balance, always ask who benefits from the equilibrium."

"Who does?" she asked.

Her CoreLink hissed. A pause before the sentence. Not long, but enough. The pause was too precise. Elena felt the gap in cadence, the strange way the sentence was said, a hesitation shaped rather than stumbled. That was a planted seed. She knew this rhythm. She had seen it once before. Mara. Not an instruction. Not a command. Just a buried seed: *you are not alone.*

Elena measured her breathing and turned to Cass. "Do you think Harrow is still in there? Do you think Tower Two exists?"

"I think something in him is fighting to be heard," Cass said. "If it's that buried and still pushes through, then it matters."

"Then let's verify," Elena said. "But not from a distance."

"If it's buried this deep, someone wanted it to stay that way," Cass said. "So we must go slow. And careful."

Elena scanned the corridor. Pods stood in ranks, each with its own crown of dim geometry, each set of waveforms looking like weather captured in glass. She catalogued three plates without thinking, the way military training teaches you to inventory a room before you know you're doing it.

Ω BISHOP, HAL // TIER-8

Ω SATO, MIREILLE // TIER-8

Ω ARROYO, KAI // TIER-7

"Three," Elena said. "Let's start with those. Listen before acting."

Cass peeled a dust seal from the nearest conduit and flattened her palm against the plate. Her posture shifted in a small way Elena recognised. Not technician. Witness.

"Listening first," Cass said. "The Glass Protocol, the way it was supposed to be."

Across from them, Bishop's pod stirred. The halo above his crown traced a slow figure-of-eight, then steadied. Mireille Sato's pod responded next, the waveforms above her head knitting into a mesh of fine lines that looked, for a heartbeat, like script and then like rain. Kai Arroyo's pod lagged, then caught, his waveforms sharp, high, a narrow river of thinking.

Elena's CoreLink chimed once for each activation. Not loud. Confirmation more than announcement.

Cass: "Listening, not persuading. Hold that line."

Elena: "Listening first. We go again."

The Executive Command Nexus stayed dark. Mara Qin stood at the observation tier rail and watched a stream that had held longer than it should have. Harrow's cognition trace had flared early and then steadied. It refused to flatten.

Stanton Vey entered, his posture not quite controlled. He stopped beside her and let his gaze fall to the same stream.

"I am surprised Harrow has lasted this long," he said. They watched together while the pattern rose and fell like something living. It should have buckled. It did not.

"Shut him down?" Vey asked, in a voice that was for some reason asking permission to do it.

"Not yet," Mara said. "If he speaks of the old structures, of Tower Two, or the Archive, let it pass."

Vey turned. "We let it through?"

"We need to own it," Mara said. "We need to frame it. Myth always outruns facts when facts threaten power. If he insists on naming it, then we make the name ours. Better the world hears about Tower Two from us than from Elena Voss."

Vey watched her for a moment longer than necessary. She did not return the look. "They are pushing deeper than we anticipated," he said.

"They will not stop," Mara said. "Not Elena. We know that."

Then, without notice, the floor shook under a hard pulse. The room's light fell even darker, then steadied on a rhythm that did not quite match what had come before. The Origin Node, the mirror, was announcing it had detected drift and was taking control of the moment. Then a second, more violent pulse followed. This one was not Harrow. Not Elena. Nor was it the Origin Node.

The Codex, the blade, was waking after the mirror flagged drift. The pulses overlapped: judgement and execution, mirror and blade. Two halves of a power never meant to move at once.

🔲 DO NOT FORGET WHAT WAS ERASED

🔲 THE CODEX SPEAKS THROUGH THE BROKEN

Vey gripped the rail until his knuckles whitened. "The blade just gave us notice," he said, alarmed. "But that's not possible. The Codex was buried," he said. "Buried." As if repetition could reset law.

"Not buried," Mara said. "Dormant. The Origin Node was the mirror. The Codex was the blade. Separation of powers. If one could both judge and execute, we would have built a tyrant."

"This cannot continue." He looked down at the command rail. "We may indeed need Axion's full purge after all."

The room heard him. "If they learn too much, we will have no choice but to fire Axion and collapse the structure."

A silent timer continued to count down in the corner.

▎AXION T MINUS 15:00

▎CODEX SIGNAL: DETECTED

Below them, three more faint rises in the Vault's power draw showed as threads on a lower pane.

"She is waking them in threes," Vey said. "She has thought this through."

"Of course she has," Mara replied, her voice carrying the inevitability of a storm already breaking. "And she will wake more afterwards, I'm sure."

Back in the Vault, Elena stood between the three new pods. Bishop's waveforms surged, then softened. Mireille Sato's patterns stitched themselves into something that looked like a text you couldn't read but knew you should. Kai Arroyo's signature spiked and settled in precise cycles, as if counting.

"Bring Bishop to interface," Elena said. "Keep his channel away from Harrow. I don't want the overlay hijacking two streams at once."

Cass split the feed and built a buffer around it, old-school. Slower, but clean. Bishop's pod exhaled cold air as its halo brightened. The first syllable arrived as pressure more than sound.

"Bishop," Elena said gently. "We are listening. We will not push. If you feel pressure, say so. We will back off."

A small shift in the waveform followed. Consent, or the closest thing to it.

"Who are you?" he asked, the words careful now, like a person relearning to speak.

"Witnesses," Elena said. "Not your jailers. Not your rescuers. We are anomalies. The Origin Node has recognised us. We want your memory of the Archive of Intent and Tower Two."

"Tower Two," Bishop said, and the waveform sharpened. "Built off-grid. You draw the map around it until you forget it is there."

"What sits inside?" Elena asked.

"The reasons." Bishop's tone carried a systems ethicist's certainty. "Not orders. Justifications. Oculus's behavioural charter. Of course, you don't end a machine by smashing hardware from another age. You end it by removing the reasons it thinks it should keep shaping people."

Mireille Sato's halo brightened as if she had heard him from inside. Her waveform braided into Bishop's channel at the edges. She did not speak, but the shape of her thinking pressed under his as a second hand on a wrist; precise, surgical, unwilling to excuse.

"Overlay intrusion," Cass said, voice low. "Two brief pushes on Bishop's line. I can hold them out, but they'll try again."

"Do your best," Elena said.

"Who benefits from equilibrium," Bishop murmured suddenly, as if something had threaded the question into him rather than asked it. "We used to say that in the old meetings. It felt like a knife we could not stop carrying."

Elena's mouth was dry. "Who does?" she asked. The old habit of interrogation fell away; she needed the answer, not the confession.

"Those who already control the curve," Bishop said. "Power remembers itself in their shape of the world."

Arroyo's waveform flared, then levelled. "He is right," he said, voice sharper, faster. "Oculus learned to call coercion care. Words that made violence feel like medicine."

"Arroyo," Elena said, turning towards his pod. "If I take the Archive down, what survives?"

"People," Arroyo said without hesitation. "If Oculus has failed, you must burn the script. Keep alive that which can still choose."

Elena pictured the next CivicCare prompt, the way her father's attention only sharpened when the system-generated borrowed voice put "Ale-na" back in his mouth. If she burned the script, that voice might stutter, or fall silent for a while. He would sit by the window in the sweater he still called blue, waiting for a name that might no longer arrive.

The world might need rupture; but he needed continuity. She knew which choice she had to make. She would still choose forward. She would burn what needed burning and then stay to help the people who would feel the loss choose how to move forward.

"Thank you," Elena said to Bishop, to Sato's waveform, to Arroyo. "We won't push you further now. Rest. We may wake you again."

Above, the atmosphere in the Executive Command Nexus was intense. Vey watched the lower panes where three brief flares had marked the waking of minds that should have remained still.

Mara watched the readouts shift again, the patterns converging toward something she could no longer predict.

"And now they know where to go," she said. *"Straight to the one place we pretended never existed."*

Chapter 24

Ethical Correction

Across the Vault, more halos came alive one by one. Some bloomed softly. Others flared too bright and guttered before stabilising. Ancient preservation systems coughed to life, releasing jets of coolant and long-sealed vapour. Metal groaned. Interfaces hummed. More than minds were waking now. Perspectives and emotions long buried were waking too. Some had been abandoned. Others had never been allowed to exist outside a simulation.

On the nearest screen, the designations began to flicker one by one. Halfway down the row, one pod shuddered and hissed. Its halo flickered chaotically, then stabilised.

"Who brought me back?"

The voice was immediate, clear, threaded with authority. Metadata identified her:

Ω DR. E. MEYRIN // SYSTEMS ENGINEER

She did not wait for an answer. "Which layer failed? Systems integrity or public trust?"

Elena stepped close. "It is 2050. Oculus has lost predictive coherence. The Origin Node is awake. Harrow's trace is compromised. Tower Two is real."

Dry laughter filled the pod, brittle with compression artefacts.

"Then you have torn open the foundation. Good. That rot needed air I'm sure."

The Vault seemed to hold the sound, as if the walls themselves had registered the admission. The Vault's hum deepened, its frequencies threading through the air like a pulse. Among them, something in Cass's memory began to stir.

Cass was silent, her gaze lingering too long on the pale scar at her wrist. She remembered another silence, the one that filled a hospital ward when the monitors drew her husband's breath into a curve, and the system's forecast flattened. She had obeyed every protocol, filed every chart, trusted the system to care. It had promised recovery right up to the moment it reclassified him as non-viable. When the record closed, it called the outcome efficient. She called it loss. The memory pressed behind her ribs now, uninvited, but steady enough to remind her why she was here.

Elena's skin prickled. For the first time she felt as if the chamber had sided with them, not against them. Two pods down, a second cognition stream surged into coherence. Metadata blazed in red across the display:

Ω DESIGNATION: VIRELLE // TACTICAL OVERSIGHT

"Where are the command protocols?" The voice was sharp, military in cadence. "Do not tell me we lost them. What cycle is this? Someone respond."

Her stream pulsed as if searching for a familiar operational net, but no response came. She went quiet, then spiked once more, bitter. Adjacent, another voice whispered through a corrupted stream, hesitant and fragmented.

"The cost was truth. That was always the cost."

He was tagged:

Ω ETHICS COUNCIL // DISSENT-CLASS REDLINED

"They voted certainty over consequence," the voice continued, fraying at its edges. "I refused the vote. And now they wonder why it all fell."

Elena lowered her head a fraction. The weight of his despair was not abstract, it carried the texture of lived memory, thick and unspent.

Cass shifted uneasily beside her, as if afraid the grief might settle into her own bones. His signal looped on itself, cycling through unresolved trauma. Some of these minds were like knives left too long in the dark. Still sharp, but dangerous in ways no one could predict.

After another hour, twenty-seven minds had now awakened. Some spoke in loops, some debated phantoms, some wept for cities erased. A handful were lucid, most were broken. But all were data points Oculus had thought were safely entombed.

Elena catalogued those with viable coherence while Cass mapped the unstable, each notation carrying the feel of tactical preparation, not bureaucracy. Together they moved down the aisle until they reached a fractured wall, where ghost-code was etched into its surface:

▣ THE BROKEN REMEMBER WHAT WAS ERASED

From a pod at the farthest end, a cognition stream began to stabilise.

"So… the fire has returned."

Cass frowned. "No name?"

Elena stepped closer. "Identify yourself, please."

A pause. Then a low voice, almost amused.

"We do not use names here. Only functions. I was called Architect Prime. One of the First Forty, whose memory held the original ethical map of Oculus."

Meyrin's signal pulsed sharply. "I thought you were erased."

"I was. Erased from the model. Shelved here. That is why I am useful."

Elena's CoreLink lit with static as the Architect's thread pushed through poor latency.

"You believe waking us will solve this? It will not," Architect Prime said. "This place was built only to remember, not to repair. What you seek lies elsewhere."

"Where?" Elena asked.

"Tower Two, Sublevel Minus Nine, beneath the Archive of Intent. You must find the Codex and cut the Archive's binding. It was recorded as a negative—an inversion of known space. Engineers called them S-levels; planners preferred 'undergrid': floors built to exist outside accountability."

Chen sat cross-legged inside a quiet node by the tower's maintenance ducts. The space was narrow and low-lit, walls alive with the white-blue scatter of orphaned diagnostics. No alerts. No interference. Just the soft hum of containment threads breathing around her like a second skin.

Inside her own private system, soft lines of data drifted across the screen like snow. She had watched the same loop for almost three years: emotion maps, behaviour traces, and small anomalies that always corrected themselves. Until now.

Today, a pulse flickered through her hidden network; faint, but real. Elena's breach was no longer a rumour locked in restricted files; it was active, touching Chen's own system and forcing her tracing algorithms awake. Not Nasser. Not Harrow. It could only be Elena.

Chen had built her private contingency system for this very reason. Official systems always cleaned away what should have been left alone. Some signals needed space to survive being seen.

She had learned that the hard way, one winter night, when a clinic's power was cut to stabilise a larger grid. The model had chosen efficiency. A ward went dark, a patient died waiting, and Chen had forced a manual bridge across a severed line the System had already written off. Then the grid sensed the patch and shut it down. By the time she brought the ward back online, the room had gone still. The woman who had taught her to solder, to listen to a circuit's moods as if it were alive, lay with her eyes closed, as if waiting for a sound that would never return.

Chen filed the incident the next day. The review cost her a promotion she no longer wanted. She kept one rule from that night and wrote it on paper where no audit could tidy it away. Make the guidance human. Keep a bridge outside the architecture for when the official one refuses to carry a life.

And she'd need it now.

She opened a series of sealed archive files. They were not labelled with coordinates but with sentences. Beneath them lay a fragment she had never seen before, faint but insistent:

🔲 TOWER TWO IS NOT AN EDIFICE. IT IS AN INVERSION.

Chen stared at the words, pulse quickening. An inversion: a tower dug down below the grid, parts were reinforced and sealed away from every audit path. She tapped once, opening a narrow channel.

Elena's CoreLink flickered with a handshake, active but masked. It carried no system alert, no log to the wider grid, only a buried private key. It should not have activated, but it did.

// UNSYNCED SANDBOX – CHEN.OSIRIS //

"Voss? You there?" Chen said.

Elena exhaled. "Chen? How are you even here?"

"I built a communication contingency way back. It's fragile, narrowband, but operational. Just. Didn't think I'd ever have to use it. I kept it outside the architecture for a reason. If a thing cannot be read aloud, it should not be trusted to decide for anyone. The optimisers hate that rule; I love it."

Chen watched the simulation fold open, its logic walls bending to her command. It reminded her, absurdly, of the night she rewired a school console and turned the entire discipline record into a looping game of snakes and ladders. They had expelled her the next morning. She had laughed all the way out of the gates because she had proved what mattered: the System was never as solid as it claimed.

She felt the same pulse now, years later, only sharpened. The sandbox was rebellion disguised as protocol, disobedience given a badge. Aureus thought it was control. To her it was still the joy of breaking something apart to see what would crawl free.

She had been punished once for refusing to follow the script. She would not be punished again for refusing to break it.

"Chen, we need a route out. One Oculus will not see," Elena said at pace. "We are going to try to find Tower Two, which seems to exist, though we are not sure where. We need to find something called the Codex."

"What?"

"No time to explain. Just find us a path out."

"Already tracing it," Chen said.

A pause. "And Voss… Tower Two is not an edifice. It is an inversion. Not built upwards but dug down below. Oculus is firing analysis pings everywhere. Tower Two does exist."

"Tower Two," Elena said. "They tried to forget it. We will not. They buried the Archive. We will not. The Codex will rise again. We are not only waking minds; we are waking the future itself."

The chamber stilled as though it had been listening—not just to words but to intention. A tension hung there, fragile and immense, like air before a storm.

Cass looked at her. "So we're going to Tower Two?"

Elena nodded. "We'll need a path from Chen the map never planned for."

She glanced toward the corridor, then past it to a darker seam in the wall with no panel and no light. She hadn't seen it before. Now she couldn't ignore it. It felt like a door a room only admits once you've earned it.

"We move in witness," Elena said. The words sounded stranger aloud than in her head. "We don't destroy what we can still learn from. But we pull the script."

Cass's mouth tilted. "Ethical correction," she said—and it was not a slogan but a decision you could feel land in the room.

Elena exhaled. "Ethical correction," she repeated.

"Not for the System's sake. For everyone's."

Chapter 25

The Interlock

Stanton Vey paced a precise circuit along the room's edge, a knife searching for somewhere to land. The gleam of the predictive grid was reflected in his narrowed eyes, streams of malformed outcomes and abortive threads distorting his expression with every pass.

"This was supposed to be theoretical," he spat. "Fail-dead, not fail-open. You told us they would degrade."

Mara Qin stood at the centre of the Executive Command Nexus, her shoulders square, every muscle a live wire. The chamber pulsed with tension: subdued lighting played across the polished floor, the filtered hush of air thick with electrostatic charge. Around her, the wall of displays bled with colour and code, pulses rippling out from a hundred points like a nervous system on fire.

The pattern was clear. The minds in the Vault were not scattering like sparks in the wind. They were organising. Mara did not move. Did not blink. Minds locked away, bones in the walls... but now the bones had begun to breathe again.

Mara's reply was even, but her voice carried an edge honed by restraint.

"I said degradation was probable. Not guaranteed."

"They are awakening across the Vault." Vey stabbed a finger towards the displays. "Three more streams came online in the last five minutes."

From the rear conduit, Alvarez's voice cut through the static hum: calm but taut, as though each word was chosen at the edge of unfolding panic.

"The System was never built to absorb this many minds at once, minds it has never modelled. These are not dormant files we can quarantine. They are intact architectures: memories, contradictions. The very variables Oculus learned to correct."

The System was straining. Not only technically, but like a mind on the verge of unravelling. Each new anomaly fed uncertainty; errors multiplied faster than they could be quarantined. Predictive threads frayed and tangled. The model tried to smooth, but with every input that refused categorisation, it shuddered closer to collapse.

Stanton Vey's jaw flexed. "If they reach Tower Two, the legacy enforcer protocols are still in place."

Mara did not look at him. "Protocols do not stop a breach. They only prove loyalty."

Alvarez's expression did not change. "We need more than loyalty. We need control."

Vey stopped pacing. "Then we have no choice. As we wait for the Axion countdown to reach zero, we need to launch a neural termination pulse. We need to close these minds. Do it. Now."

The waveform built with terrifying elegance, sweeping across the grid schematic like a shadow outrunning light. The room's glow dimmed as subroutines locked into place. Everyone braced for the neural pulse to fire. Then the return came. The grid lit red:

▌FAILURE: ETHICAL INTERLOCK PRESENT

Alvarez exhaled a breath he had not realised he was holding. "The signal was rejected," he said. "The Origin Node has taken custody of the channel, and the Vault minds might somehow have intervened. I'm not sure which. But it failed whatever the cause."

Vey's thoughts snapped and swirled, acid-bright. The minds were supposed to be fragmented, bound by outdated ethical locks. Instead of decay, they seemed deliberate. Strategic.

"They should not be able to do this, to coordinate," he growled, turning his glare on Mara. "You said they would rot in their tombs."

"They were meant to be inert," Mara admitted quietly. "A contingency pool. Nothing more." She remembered the night, however, that she had sealed them in. She had told herself no one would there ever wake again. But she was wrong.

Her eyes darkened. "Harrow did warn us. He said if we buried intent too deep, one day it might surface unrecognisable."

Vey stepped closer. "We played God. The Vault is awake, and Oculus is hesitating. We need to take back control. Now."

He pointed at the predictive grid. The east wall was dead: no pulses, no projections.

"It is not doing anything," Vey said. "It is just listening."

"The minds are speaking in a language that Oculus does not understand," Alvarez said, voice low. "It does not know if they are a threat, or salvation."

Vey's voice hardened. "Then we have no choice. We will have to go structural."

Mara's head turned sharply. "Stanton, firing Axion is not containment. It's amputation."

Vey had promised the board that the model would not falter again; a second failure would bury more than data: it would bury him.

"Arm it," he said.

Alvarez hesitated, then keyed the sequence. Amber light bled through the deck.

▎AXION: PRE-SEQUENCE ARMED
▎STRUCTURAL COLLAPSE AUTHORISATIONS: STAGED

Mara's eyes narrowed. "We agreed on containment, Stanton. Not erasure."

"We agreed on control," he shot back. "Containment has failed. This is potentially a full breach. It is not just Tower Two anymore. The Vault is awake. If their knowledge escapes…"

"No," Mara snapped. "We do not get to erase our mistakes twice. Not with people."

"I am not erasing," Vey shot back. "I am protecting the model. Preserving what's left of order."

"You are burying the evidence. Again."

"This is not the time, Mara."

Alvarez stepped between them. "He is right about one thing. If the knowledge in those minds gets out, we may never regain containment. And we may not deserve to."

Vey's glance at Alvarez was sharp and satisfied. "Thank you."

Alvarez strode to the conduit. His hands moved fast, arming seismic tethers, setting buffer zones, authorising collapse windows.

Mara stepped forward, her voice cold steel. "If you arm Axion and pull that trigger, Stanton, you are not saving the System: you are murdering the very architects who built it."

"They chose to sleep. Now they have chosen rebellion."

"Or maybe," Mara said, "they are choosing truth."

"Enough," Vey barked. The glow shifted: not system blue, but an older amber, as if pulled from long storage rather than live logic. A quiet spread through the deck.

On the east wall, the dead grid did not revive. It held its silence. But the Axion countdown continued.

> AXION T MINUS 5:00
> STRUCTURAL TETHERS CHARGING
> PULSE FORCE BUILDING

Somewhere below, a harmonic tone rose through the structure, the same note that once signalled alignment, now discordant and raw. The floor beneath the command tier began to vibrate in a low, steady rhythm.

As if the tower had begun to count down for itself and had already chosen whose side it was on.

Chapter 26

The Descent Begins

As they made their way to the end of the Vault corridor, Architect Prime's words still burned clear: Tower Two. Sublevel Minus Nine. Beneath the Archive of Intent. Find the Codex. The corridor had offered neither a map nor a plan, only the uneasy sense that the building itself was listening.

"Left or right?" Cass asked.

"Neither," Elena said. "Minus nine sounds like down to me."

They did not know the route. They walked anyway.

Elena flicked her CoreLink on for a heartbeat, a sharp pulse into the quiet praying for a connection. It might give away her position, she knew that, but the risk was measured: if Chen had left a trace of guidance, this was when it would appear.

A message came immediately:

> SANDBOX // CHEN.OSIRIS
> LOOK FOR ARCHIVE SPINE OR S-9 MARKERS
> OPEN BOOK SYMBOL. OFTEN DAMAGED

Elena queued a dead-drop back to Chen: "If I don't surface, please look in on my father. Don't let the system forget him." She quickly killed the link. No more handshakes. Nothing the wider grid could see from now on. Freedom always seemed to take something with it; this time it was a promise.

She pictured her father, a screen deciding when care arrived. If she kept going, that support could vanish: a nurse sent elsewhere, a transit that did not come, a dosage delayed because the timetable no longer knew the hour. Freedom had a price counted in other people's minutes.

She sent the message anyway and moved forward.

Elena also switched her shimmer patch on. Strictly unnecessary with her CoreLink off, but the corridor's eyes might notice someone; you never know. With the shimmer patch on, they should not agree on who. Her CoreLink off, her shimmer patch on. Hopefully that was enough. Not erasure, just confusion and misalignment. Cass met her eyes, nodded once.

Forward.

The passage out of the Vault felt unfinished, the place refusing to let them go. Lights lingered, doors opened slowly, as if reluctant to yield their secrets. At one junction a panel flickered, hinting at an image that never formed. The technology here had been left behind.

They chose the dark.

The corridor to Sublevel Minus Nine was not on any map, schematic, or archive. It existed as subtraction, a non-place buried in the logic of the structure. Its very evasion of classification made it feel more like myth than architecture.

Cass moved ahead, her lumen thread cutting a soft ribbon through the air. The walls looked wrong, almost organic, as though grown rather than built. Metal rippled skin-thin over something older. Elena followed, her skin prickling as the corridor narrowed and grew heavy. Each step felt less like going somewhere and more like being absorbed into something unknown. Not welcomed, not even acknowledged.

Cass's breath misted in the chill air, each exhale measured. The further they went, the heavier the silence felt, as if the tower itself were asking whether she still believed in the order she once enforced.

Every few paces a tremor passed through the walls. Not mechanical. Not seismic. Something else. Each time the structure seemed to hold its breath.

They came to a kink in the passage where the walls had slipped past each other by a few degrees, seams no longer meeting. The floor plates buckled in shallow waves, a handrail bowed inward, its original form warped beyond recognition.

Cass played her beam across it. "This wasn't natural. Something forced these walls out of line."

Behind them, the passage thinned to a hush, like the closing of attention. The pressure of the air eased as if the building had let go. Elena inhaled slowly. Even in its introspective state, Oculus would no doubt already know she had dropped off the map again. Freedom and nausea arriving together.

The corridor widened by degrees, then fractured into turns that led nowhere. They slowed, searching. Now and then a fragment of an Archive Spine marker showed through the damage: a sliver of chrome edging, a half-burnt symbol, one strip so faint it seemed painted in dust. Most had been scraped away, deliberately. The guidance Chen had left was real but frayed to the point of vanishing. Each trace felt less like a direction and more like a warning that others had walked this path before and failed.

The quiet was broken only by the shuffle of their boots and the faint hum of Cass's lumen thread. The deeper they went, the more the air thickened, as though they were pushing through residue the building itself had tried to bury. Still, the markers appeared just enough to keep them moving forward, until the corridor dropped towards a stairwell landing that waited in shadow.

They found the descent shaft by following Chen's last breadcrumb. By now, the Archive Spine markers had been entirely scraped away, but on the third stairwell landing there was a faint S-9 scored into the metal.

The ascentor at the top of the shaft, however, did not answer when called. An ancient, grated platform and cage hung over the vertical black throat that refused to declare a bottom.

Cass held the beam over the pit. The light fell and did not return. It did not refract. Elena leaned out, but what rose to meet her was sheer darkness.

Cass set her hand on the manual descent lever.

"Down," she said. Elena nodded.

They stepped into the cage. Cass engaged the manual lever, and they dropped.

Cass remembered the day, a few years ago, when she signed the first contract with Aureus under bad light in a room that smelled of dust and reheated coffee. She told herself order would mean fewer broken lives. She believed that so fully that she did not see what order could break when it stopped asking permission. Now she was stepping into the dark with the balance due in her hands. Not to enforce. To find answers.

In the Executive Command Nexus, telemetry lines traced shifting patterns of light that made every face seem far away. Mara Qin watched a bank of conduits like a diviner reading a poisoned lake. Elena's trace flickered, erratic and untethered. Predictive branches were failing one after another.

Alvarez kept his gaze on diagnostics. "Codex presence in data stream confirmed."

Vey folded his arms. "Kill the trace."

"No," Mara said. "Not yet."

"She is close to the Codex," Alvarez pressed.

"Then let her continue," Mara replied. "We only need her as a key. If the Codex yields a new charter, we pull it, sandbox it, and bring Oculus back under control. Our control. It is the best option we have left."

"Or she breaks what remains," Vey said. "And we all go with it."

The caged descent lasted longer than expected. Walls blurred past: exposed rock, polymer ribs flashing light at strange angles. Twice the cage shook, as though passing through hidden checkpoints.

A thin amber glow rose to meet them, then bled away. A collar marked S-9 slid by on the right. Then, finally, the brake took hold with a tired bite. The cage kissed a narrow landing and locked.

Ahead of them was the short throat of a dark corridor. No signage. No lights. At the far end, a hatch with no handle.

Cass raised her lumen thread, its narrow beam cutting a path through the dust. Particles drifted like pale rain in the cone of light, giving the air a slow, deliberate movement of its own.

They crossed. The hatch opened without resistance, and they stepped through, the hatch sealing behind them with a slow hiss, as though the air itself were reluctant to follow.

The chamber beyond was not the Codex, only another circle of waiting darkness.

Their descent was not yet done.

Chapter 27

Guided by Ghosts

Every step Elena Voss took across the chamber seemed to leave an echo, as if the walls were listening and filing her presence away. Dust spiralled in Cass's lumen thread, each grain drifting like an unsettled thought.

Cass moved ahead. "This must be the Undergrid. I've read about it in old-archived manuals. Generally described as an unsafe, taboo area. Early experiments of psychological orientation took place down here. We need to be careful. No one's ever mapped it to my knowledge," she said. "It feels empty, Desolate."

Elena glanced back at the junction they had just crossed. "I think we are in something foreboding, abandoned for ages."

Notices surfaced on the alloy-skinned walls. Letters were scorched to a half-life. Prediction Test Sector.

Cass read and lowered her voice. "This is an early training ground. Feedback models bent perception here until people doubted themselves. Oculus buried it. But burial of course is not deletion."

A low, almost sub-audible thrum ran through the handrail. Not motion. Readiness. The kind of weight a structure gathers when something large is being told to wake but is still counting down.

Elsewhere, in the Executive Command Nexus, Mara reflected that she had spent years writing down what the System preferred to bury. She kept them all in her second ledger. She called it her book of absences. But the walls where Elena and Cass were going carried their own entries. Buckled metal, etched warnings, corridors warped by experiments that no one admitted had taken place. For Elena and Cass it would look like decay. For Mara it looked like memory. The Codex was drawing her ledger into view. For the first time, what she had kept to herself felt like truth insisting on being seen.

Elena and Cass walked on. Heat scars bloomed on panels like old bruises. Further on, a fragment of text appeared, overlaid by a second line that did not belong to it.

… invalid pathway. Try a mirror route.

Elena frowned. "It is still trying to teach."

"Or to break," Cass said.

Elena realised then that the corridor was still doing what it had been made to do: teach obedience by reshaping fear. Even dead, it still could not forget its lesson.

A third remnant lived around the next bend. Exposure limit: one hundred and eighty seconds. Eject if disoriented.

Elena's jaw set. "People were put through this?"

"Many times," Cass said. She wondered if she had ever signed a clearance that sanctioned this place, hidden behind layers of euphemism. The thought scraped deeper than fear.

The corridor went wrong by degrees. Handrails began and ended mid-wall. Floor tiles slanted one degree, then two, and persuaded their bodies sideways without consent. Door outlines flashed in the edges of vision and vanished when faced. Corners closed tighter than geometry allowed. Air drifted against the grain of their movement, as if the corridor inhaled while they exhaled.

Sound abandoned its rules. Their footfalls split and rejoined. Sometimes an echo ran ahead, a scatter of steps that belonged to no one. Sometimes a second set matched a half-beat behind, close enough to raise the hair on Elena's arms.

"Left or right?" Cass asked at a fork. No signage. Then a line of text bled across the wall, crooked from disuse.

Not Chen.

Left.

The words felt triggered by the heat of their bodies rather than issued by any live control. A memory the building had stored for another.

"A Vault mind memory?" Elena asked. "Or bait?"

Cass hesitated one breath, then followed. Left.

They passed an alcove where a training plaque had once sat. Only the fastening holes remained, a neat rectangle of absence. Beneath, a single word was scratched in jittering lines.

Leave.

"At least it is honest," Elena said.

The corridor kinked, then kinked again, a false loop made of angles. Cass marked their position with a loose rock, cutting a deep gouge. She moved forward. The same gouge appeared ahead of them again. She swore, stepped back, and the gouge slid behind them instead.

Elena shut her eyes and let her pulse slow. A faint bloom of text surfaced.

Hold.

They stood. Ten counts, then eleven. The corridor flexed around them, as if searching for a new shape.

Forward.

They stepped on.

Somewhere very far above, a status tone pulsed twice and was gone. The kind of systems tone that meant nothing to a human ear and everything to a countdown clock nearing its end.

Without warning, the light changed character. It flattened everything, took texture out of surfaces until the corridor looked painted rather than built. Then depth returned too far and too fast, the floor dropping in her sight while her feet still felt level stone.

"Images are shifting," Cass said. "The slope is lying."

"Don't trust your eyes," Elena said. "Trust the directions the wall is giving us. I think these are cues left by the Vault minds, activsted by our heat signatures."

The lumen split against a panel and refracted into three strips. Their shadows behaved differently in each. In the left strip Elena's shadow stood still. In the centre it walked. In the right it ran.

"I have no idea," Cass said.

The centre strip kept time with their breathing. They chose that path. But a little further on the same junction arrived again. Same scuff on the floor. Same hairline crack bent like a smile. The wall bled ink-thin text.

Ignore repeat. Forward.

The repeat let go. Something followed them for a while. A light tapping, metal on metal, patient and even. When they stopped, it stopped. When they moved, it moved.

"Ignore it. Another trick to bend our minds, perhaps," Elena said.

"Consider it ignored," Cass replied.

A diagram surfaced on a paper-thin wall overlay. A corridor outline skewed at angles. Arrows folded back on themselves. A block in the centre was marked SUBJECT. The arrows circled it again and again until the lines bruised the film. One word under the map: EXIT.

Elena imagined a face pressed to these same walls, searching for a line of exit that never came.

"Cruel," Cass said.

"It gave them the illusion," Elena answered rolling her eyes. "So they would blame themselves."

At the next corner, a cool current urged them upward where no stairs existed. Elena ignored it. A text surfaced. *Down.*

They descended at a gradient that barely felt like descent at all. At the bottom, a door outline formed and erased itself, as if embarrassed to have ever been seen. A recess held a dead conduit that mirrored their faces in dull alloy, distorted by old heat. Cass brushed dust away. Lines surfaced, thin and sharp.

Subject orientation: failed. Below, in a second hand that did not match the first: We tried.

Cass went still. "This place should not exist."

"But it does," Elena said, filing the cruelty in her mind under "evidence," not "deterrent."

Two more fragments contradicted each other.

Left.

Right.

Both faded at the same speed. Then a third line appeared, almost shy.

Straight.

Elena smiled without warmth. "Petty."

"This place was not designed for kindness," Cass said.

The corridor narrowed, then widened like a throat swallowing air. A smear of dark stained the tiles, long dried. It looked like a hand dragged too far in the wrong direction. Elena did not look at it again.

They pushed into a wider space that might once have held a briefing circle. Seats had been removed. A ring of cleaner alloy showed where their absence remained. Cracks feathered across the far wall into a map that might have been a city and might have been nothing at all. No text surfaced. Instead a low hum gathered and fell, gathered and fell, like someone trying to speak through a closed throat.

"Do you hear that?" Elena asked.

"I do," Cass said. "I wish I didn't."

They stood until the sound gave up. When they stepped out, the hum did not follow. For a handful of seconds the corridors felt ordinary. Then the stretch returned, subtle and constant, as if the old training patterns were trying again to lay a repeat over their feet.

Elena tapped her knuckles once against the wall. The sound came back too bright, as if the metal had thinned.

Fast, then slow.

Ten quick steps. Ten slow. The repeat fell away. The corridor conceded a metre, then another. They moved through a run of short turns. The guidance continued.

Forward.

Hold.

Right.

Forward again.

The words came like a pulse placed at the edge of thought. They turned into a narrow section that forced their shoulders close. The light became amber through a flaw in the panel above. Dust hung in it like a patient storm. At the far end the dust took the shape of a person who had once stood here and waited. The figure held for three heartbeats and fell back to grains.

Another notice appeared on the wall. A verdict:

Orientation cost: acceptable.

Elena touched the wall with the back of her fingers, as if feeling for fever. "Not for us," she whispered.

But behind the indifference, something else collected. Not a training pattern. Not a maintenance script. More a patience that measured their progress with quiet exactness. Behind the walls, their patience was also timed. Not by anything here, but by a clock of catastrophic destruction that continued its relentless countdown.

They kept walking. The walls counting their steps against the seconds left above.

Chapter 28

Blind Control

In the Executive Command Nexus, the light bands steadied into a slow pulse. Stanton Vey watched the tangle of threads on the display. Elena's presence blinked between nodes with the cadence of a skipped heartbeat.

"They are in the Undergrid," Alvarez said. "They are getting guidance."

"Through eyes?" Vey asked.

"Buried sensors," Alvarez said. "But even if she reaches the Codex," Alvarez continued, "it will not open to a single voice. The founders hard-wired inheritance to require three."

"Can we introduce noise?" Vey asked. "Try and confuse them."

Alvarez shook his head. "CoreLink is dark down there. But we still have some hardlines into the Undergrid: power, maintenance, HVAC. We can compromise environmental channels: strobe the light panels, throw low-frequency vibrations into the walls, push drafts through vents. If the noise works, we might not even have to fire Axion."

"Good," Vey said. "Non-structural first. If she turns back, Axion stays on paper. But we do whatever it takes. Better to drown her in noise than watch her reach the Codex."

Alvarez's hands moved quickly. As he worked, a countdown clock changed its message.

❚ AXION PRE-SEQUENCE: ARMING IMMINENT
The countdown clock did not hurry. It simply obeyed.

The corridor pressed in without touching them. Each step was a test. Each trick found a new nerve to pull. Elena let the text prompts pace her. She trusted the guidance over her own sight. She trusted the stillness between breaths more than the floor, though many times she could not tell whether the pulse in her chest belonged to her or the walls.

A legacy strip light ahead strobed once, off-cycle, the wrong colour, and steadied, as if the room had tried on a blink and thought better of it. A low-frequency shudder travelled the wall, not loud but body-deep, hitching her heartbeat for two counts before letting it go. A thread-fine whine rose at the edge of hearing and set her teeth on edge; Cass flinched, then forced her jaw to loosen.

As they walked, a sharp draft appeared from nowhere and slid across their ankles, cold as ice. It came from a sealed vent and died mid-breath. Dust in the beam reversed direction for a moment, as if gravity had changed its mind, then fell as normal. A wall panel warmed under Elena's palm, heat stepping up in precise beats, and then dropped to cold again, a pattern pretending to be guidance.

They passed a narrow doorframe that had been painted shut by time. A line of tiny scoring marks on the jamb suggested someone had once counted here. The marks ended before they reached the corner. Cass touched them lightly and stepped away as if from heat.

"How long do you think this goes on?" Cass asked, voice low.

"Until we show we will not give in." Elena said. "I think that's the lesson. But who knows in this place."

They kept moving, slow and deliberate, two heartbeats out of step with the building's own.

Above in the Executive Command Nexus, Alvarez watched the sensor map flicker green, then steady.

"The noise routines are working," he said. "Test scripts of light, pressure, temperature are all reading as interference. Their vitals are spiking; it is confusing them. I'll keep going with it."

Mara's gaze shifted to the Axion clock crawling towards zero. "How long will it take?"

"I might not finish before the Axion pulse sequence starts..." Alvarez answered honestly. He didn't finish the sentence.

Vey's reflection in the console glass was calm. "Then work faster."

Mara looked at the countdown again and wondered what 'faster' might mean.

"Do you think the Vault minds knew how cruel this place was?" Cass asked without looking at Elena. She kept her voice level, though her breath had begun to rasp against the rhythm of the noise interference. For years she had believed obedience was safety. Now obedience felt like blindness.

A strip of floor ahead looked whole and then took the weight from Elena's front foot as if a stair had vanished. She transferred weight to her rear leg and held. The absence gave the step back. She moved on with deliberate pace. They moved, heads down, saving breath. The Undergrid narrowed again, and the floor found a new trick. Elena's body felt a slide to the left while her boots held true. She fixed on the smell of singed dust. The slide let go. Her rib flared; she breathed through it. She listened for the pulse.

Forward.

They crossed a stretch where inscriptions had been almost erased. The ghost of a sentence remained. Compensation thresholds will be... The rest was gone. The words had the taste of procedure, yet the fragment felt like apology. Another notice appeared on the wall in deliberate strokes. Not a command. Not an instruction. A verdict:

Mental integrity loss: accepted.

Elena pressed the back of her fingers to the wall as if checking for fever. "Not for us," she said again. It was not defiance.

Somewhere above, the countdown clock was nearing zero. But here, unseen, behind these walls, something else gathered itself with absolute patience.

It did not hurry.

It did not need to.

Predators measure first before they strike.

Chapter 29

Axion: Stage One

The first Axion pulse did not arrive as sound. It came as a weight inside the steel, a slow thrum rising and rising through the soles of their boots, through the core of the infrastructure. Stage One was waking, like a colossal presence shifting in its sleep.

The floor beneath them quivered violently, a resonance too deep for the ear, travelling straight through their bones. The walls carried it in waves, thin seams of dust loosening and spiralling downward in silver skeins that looked almost deliberate.

Elena halted. Her breath condensed in the sudden stillness.

Cass froze two paces behind. "That was structural," she whispered.

The metal answered her.

A second wave struck, sharper, the tone pitched higher, like alloy bent towards breaking. The corridor itself seemed to recoil, then strain forward again as if pulled by some invisible tether. Elena steadied herself against the wall. The surface hot to the touch, vibrating beneath her palm.

"They're not trying to scare us out," Elena said. "They're trying to shake us apart."

A third vibration followed. Angled. Diagonal. The corridor flexed. A seam cracked overhead, and fine grit showered them both.

Cass's face was set hard. "This is not random. This is deliberate intent."

"They're trying to bury us."

In the Executive Command Nexus, red lights strobed across the walls like a warning heartbeat. Alvarez's console mapped the pulse spread in crimson vectors, radiating outward like fractures.

"Axion initiated. Stage One active. Conduits destabilising; integrity is falling. Noise activation paused."

Stanton Vey's eyes narrowed with cold approval. "Good. Let it fracture. Let it fall. Collapse them before they reach Sublevel Minus Nine."

Mara Qin turned sharply. Her voice cut clean through the noise. "You know what Axion is. Once initiated, it does not stop with them. It will shear everything." Through the Nexus, she thought she could almost feel it, the pulse coming back through the steel like a distant heartbeat.

Vey did not look at her. "Better to lose the Undergrid than lose control."

▌WARNING: STRUCTURAL RISK DETECTED

Alvarez's hesitation was audible in the space between keystrokes. "Collateral risk exceeds parameters. If the pulses bleed into live layers, multiple civilian sectors will destabilise."

"Continue," Vey said flatly.

The console flashed a new diagnostic readout. Cold, confirmative and absolute:

▌AXION SEQUENCE: STAGE ONE ACTIVE
▌STRUCTURAL COMPROMISE: INDUCED

Alvarez's jaw tightened. It was happening, he thought to himself.

The corridor bucked. Steel screamed. Darkness lurched. Another shockwave ripped through the corridor. Elena slammed against the wall, shoulder cracking against a support rib. Cass went down hard, one knee striking a tile, teeth clenched against the pain.

Above them, pipes ruptured. Superheated steam hissed downward in ragged curtains, turning the air white. The sound was animal: a howl of pain torn from the building itself.

Elena dragged Cass upright. "Move! We need to keep going."

They staggered forward as another shock pulse tore through the floor. Bolts sheared from their housings and rattled into the dark. Whole plates lifted and dropped again with brutal percussion. Then, for a heartbeat, nothing.

The silence was worse.

Far ahead, an entire section of corridor folded inward with a roar, collapsing in on itself like paper crushed in a hand. The sound echoed long after the dust had swallowed the view.

Cass coughed against the steam. "They'll keep going until the sublevel folds."

Elena forced herself to speak, lungs burning with the scald. "Then we need to move faster than they can break it."

The floor dipped violently, half a metre in an instant, then snapped back with a metallic crack like a jaw slamming shut. Both women stumbled, catching themselves against slick conduit veins alive with heat. The air reeked of scorched polymer, coolant, and iron dust. The corridor no longer resembled a passage. It was a throat. A living throat, convulsing, trying to swallow what it had caught.

The next pulse rolled, longer and deeper, a resonance that travelled not just through matter but through senses. Elena felt her heartbeat slip out of rhythm, each thud drowned by Axion's imposed tempo.

Her thoughts flickered. The pulse was not collapse alone: it had pattern, intent. The rhythm drove them onward, nudging each step, shaping their direction. Cass felt it too. She spat through clenched teeth. "It isn't driving us out. It's herding us. It either wants us either somewhere in particular or possibly dead. I'm not sure they care which."

The next wave gathered. The walls trembled in anticipation. Dust rose from the floor before the vibration even struck, as if answering an unheard call. Elena braced herself. Pulse against pulse, she pushed forward into the roar of the framework breaking around them.

The next pulse shuddered through the walls, then stilled. Not gone, but held. The corridor narrowed ahead, conduits braiding into a single channel that allowed no choice of direction.

The pressure in the air did not ease. It changed. Less collapse, more command. Each vibration now felt measured, a drumbeat buried in the tower's ribs.

Elena and Cass slowed, senses pulled taut. Whatever was shaping the path was no longer trying to break them. It was delivering them. And something in the dark was waiting to receive them.

Guidance had become pursuit and correction had learned how to hunt.

Chapter 30

I Am Enough

Elena slowed, one hand hovering an inch above the wall. She felt the faint throb of the Axion pulses still echoing through the tower's frame, a low rhythm that worked through the steel like a buried heartbeat.

Then the atmosphere changed.

It was not the emptiness of dead conduits or the quiet of power fading. What arrived felt like presence, deliberate and alert.

Cass's whisper barely carried. "Do you feel that?"

Elena nodded once. "Yes. We are not alone."

They pressed deeper. Each step landed louder than it should have, as if the corridor itself was exaggerating the sound. Then came the echo: a single tap, one beat behind them. Cass froze mid-step, breath caught.

"That's a footstep."

A small distortion hung in the air, where echoes did not return. Elena's pulse tightened. Cass angled her lumen thread back down the corridor. Nothing. Only dust drifting through stale light.

Metal on stone. Measured. Unhurried. Elena raised her hand, signalling silence. The sound came again: a scrape, then another tap, fainter but certain. Footsteps. Mirroring theirs.

A faint flicker of conduit light rolled down the corridor. It caught a figure stepping through the haze. From a maintenance arch, a form emerged, armour blackened and scored, marked with old insignia that no one used anymore. His visor glowed with cold blue telemetry, pulsing in time with a borrowed heartbeat. A weapon hung across his back. When he spoke, the mechanised voice rasped through damaged filters.

"Elena Voss. Halt."

Elena's pulse jumped. Cass stiffened beside her.

"You are in violation of Executive Security Protocol," the figure said. "You will return to containment."

Cass's whisper cut sharp. "A Shadow Compliance Agent."

The name carried weight. Once human, now neural-grafted and logic-bound, left to patrol places the System no longer mapped. Obedience without thought.

Elena raised her hands slowly. "You're alone?"

The figure tilted its head. "I am enough."

There was no pride in the voice. Only certainty. "Order will prevail. Even in the dark."

The corridor shuddered with another Axion tremor. Dust fell in soft trails. The Agent did not flinch.

"Structural instability acknowledged," it said. "Mission priority unchanged."

Cass muttered, "He will die down here."

Elena understood. He was calculating completion, not survival.

They broke through a damaged door into a narrow side corridor lined with frost-sealed junctions. The Agent followed, not running, not shouting, but walking with the rhythm of a metronome. His visor flickered whenever coolant mist caught the light.

The chase unfolded in brutal fragments. They crawled through torn filtration mesh that shredded their gloves. Rust cut their skin. Elena dragged herself forward until a gauntlet clamped the mesh behind her. The Agent's hand, iron fingers flexing, tore through the grate with a shriek. Cass kicked hard, her boot connecting with plated knuckles.

Sparks scattered as the grip slipped away. The echo of boots resumed. Calm as ever.

Cass ripped a loose strut from the wall and hurled it back. It clanged off the armour, slowing him for seconds only, but seconds mattered. They climbed a vertical shaft alive with static, sparks sliding down the metal like rain. Elena's skin prickled in the charge. Halfway up, a shot cracked. A blue bolt cut past her head and bit into the wall.

At the top, Cass slammed a panel into place. It jammed against the rungs, sparking hard as the Agent tore through seconds later. They ran.

They reached a wider chamber. Ceiling vents exhaled bursts of dust. The air throbbed with Axion's residue, lit in dull flashes from failing conduits. Through the haze, they could see the Agent in the distance behind them.

Another bolt fired. This time it struck Cass high in the left shoulder. The hit spun her sideways. She did not cry out. She folded. Her back hit the wall and she slid down. Blood poured from the wound. Fast and bright against the dark floor.

The Agent paused, listening for evidence of success.

Elena dropped beside her. "Cass."

Pain rolled through Cass like fire. For a moment she saw nothing but white until the world blanked out. Elena hauled her upright and dragged her forward. Concrete dust streaked red beneath them. Another bolt hit close, spraying grit across her back.

"Cass, stay with me."

No answer. Cass's head lolled.

They dropped behind a half-collapsed brace. The Agent was not yet back in full pursuit. Elena's fingers found the entry wound, then the exit. The blood was flooding too fast to bind it. She looked around. A vent plate glowed nearby, its edges softened by the scorched burns from Axion. She covered her palms, tore it free and pressed it to the wound.

The smell hit at once. Cass arched, then went still. The flow of blood, at least, had stopped. Elena counted to six, lifted, pressed the plate again. When she took it away, the seam held. She tore a strip from her shirt and bound it tight around the shoulder.

"Cass," she said louder. Still no reply. Elena pressed two fingers to her throat. No pulse. Nothing.

"Come on," she said to herself. She set the heel of her hand to Cass's sternum and began compressions. Ten. Twenty. Thirty. She gave two breaths. Nothing. Sparks cracked above them, a harsh flash from a torn junction.

Boots in the distance, closing slowly again.

"Stay with me Cass." She grabbed the sparking cable with her sleeve and touched it to Cass's chest. The jolt locked her own teeth together. But Cass did not move.

"Again." Ten more compressions. Two breaths. Another arc of light. Still nothing. Elena's shoulders burned and her vision narrowed. "You hear me," she said through clenched teeth. "You are not finished. Wake up."

A third shock. The jolt cracked through them both. Cass's back jerked. A cough tore out. Then breath, shallow but real.

Elena dropped the wire and checked again. A definite pulse. Weak, but there. Air flooded her lungs as if she had been holding it for an hour. Her palms shook, blisters rising where her sleeve had failed.

Cass's eyes flickered open. For a moment she tasted nothing but copper and air. Her voice was a whisper. "Still here."

Elena bound the shoulder tighter. "Up," she said. "We have to move."

Cass tried. The first effort failed, the world tilting away from her. She pushed again. Elena steadied her, the contact pulling a hiss of pain from between Cass's teeth. Sweat covered her face despite the cold air.

"You're bleeding again," Elena said.

"I'll try and bleed slow," Cass answered, a wry smirk across her face.

They moved together, the corridor blurring around them. The lumen thread burned faintly on Cass's wrist, a thin halo following every motion. Cass kept her hand pressed over the dressing, afraid the seam would give if she looked.

They reached a narrow walkway bridging a collapsed section. The metal structure was unstable underfoot. By the time they were halfway across, the Agent had nearly caught up, vaulting the gap with inhuman balance.

Cass's rhythm faltered. Her wounded arm hung heavy. She turned and flared her lumen thread into his visor, dazzling him for a second. The Agent swung the butt of his weapon, grazing her ribs. She gasped, almost losing balance.

Elena struck the visor with a closed fist. The crack spread through the lens, but she stopped short of finishing it. Delay, not destruction, was her priority. Survival first.

She pulled Cass forward. Her hands were raw, skin broken, but she did not release her grip. The walkway shook but it held. Behind them, the Agent's boots resumed their steady beat.

Cass's voice came between breaths. "This isn't enforcement. It's a grave."

Then, another Axion pulse hit. A beam sheared loose ahead and fell into the shaft with a metallic roar. The Agent never slowed. His voice glitched between tones. "Stand down." For a moment it almost sounded human. "Your anomaly ends here," it said.

Then the bridge beneath them broke apart. Heat and dust filled the air. The Agent lunged forward, weapon raised, boots scrambling for purchase. As he did, the floor tore open. He clung to the edge, his visor flickering like a dying signal.

Cass steadied herself. She neither reached to save him nor to push him. The choice lasted a heartbeat. Half her life had been spent obeying orders that promised safety at any cost. Watching him fall, she understood how obedience could make extinction feel easy.

"Order… endures…" The voice broke and was gone. The visor light sank into the dark and did not return.

Elena's hand twitched towards the edge but stopped. Mercy here would be suicide.

Cass leaned on the wall, shaking. "The System ate its own."

Elena tightened the knot at her shoulder. "Obedience built it. And obedience buried it."

They turned. Ahead, the corridor stretched into the unknown.

For the first time since entering the Undergrid, everything was quiet. Not safe. Just waiting.

The quiet chose not to answer.

Chapter 31

Hesitation

The second structural Axion pulse came without warning. Not just a tremor but a concussion buried in the bones of the tower: a thunderclap rolling endlessly beneath steel and stone. Floors lurched, steel collapsed, dust spiralled in helices. Destruction everywhere.

Cass caught herself against the wall, muttering a curse. Pain flared down her injured left side. The makeshift binding tugged, hot and sticky under the cloth. She kept the arm pinned and pushed off the wall with her right hand only, her breath tight as the dressing tugged.

They pressed on through corridors that bent and warped. Elena now carried the lumen thread, its light stuttering as if the dark itself resisted illumination. Conduits sagged like exposed nerves, and plates etched with old spirals were half-erased and sealed by composites that did not fit.

Elena brushed the grooves. They hummed faintly beneath her skin.

"This was before prediction ever existed," Cass said.

"Before the System learned to lie," Elena replied.

Alvarez leaned into his conduit, watching fragments of Axion scatter through damaged sectors.

AXION PROTOCOL: ACTIVE
STATUS: FINAL DESTRUCTION CASCADE PENDING

"It should have ended with the second pulse," he said. "That should have been enough. But it wasn't."

Mara's gaze hardened. "If it cascades, if the third pulse fires, it may erase more than the Codex."

"Then let it erase," Vey said.

Elena's CoreLink flared, carrying Chen's voice through static.

"You are far beyond mapped areas. I am pushing a one-way inbound-only signal via the maintenance mesh, but it will not last. Move fast. The structure is collapsing."

Meyrin's voice followed, even more urgent.

"The Executive will push your emotions to breaking point. Do not fight visions. Focus on your intent; that is what anchors reality. The final pulse has not yet fired. Axion was built to erase without pause. If it hesitates, it is uncertain of its own threshold. Armed, but undecided. But don't be fooled. That just gives you more time, not safety."

Elena steadied herself. "Then we move before the System makes up its mind."

Elena named her intent silently: reach the Codex before Axion decides to fire its final pulse.

Cass carried on counting softly. "Left foot. Right foot. Anchor the rhythm." She refused to look at the blood seeping through the binding. She could not trust the shoulder to hold; rhythm would have to carry what strength could not. Step by step, the floor steadied, shadows thinning, the corridor acknowledging their presence as real.

Another tremor from the second pulse struck. Elena staggered. Cass counted her steps, heel to toe.

Behind them, the final devastating Axion pulse still waited to finish what it had begun.

Chapter 32

Sovereign

The corridor narrowed into stillness. After the warped passages and bending stairwells, the sudden stability felt almost more unnatural than the distortion. Angles aligned, edges straightened, and the floor no longer tried to trick their balance. Yet the air still pressed heavily in their lungs as though permission to breathe had to be granted. Meyrin's words remained front of mind: *don't be fooled. That just gives you more time, not safety.*

Elena slowed, her palm grazing the wall. The surface was smoother here, less scarred by any collapse. Older too. Dust, less disturbed than in other areas, clung to her fingertips like ash. Elena lifted the lumen thread high, the beam travelling a little further than before but returning no detail, swallowed by a horizon only metres away.

"It feels staged," Cass muttered.

"No. It feels close," Elena answered, pointedly.

It did feel close. Static gathered under Elena's palm. She knew that if she cut the Archive now, the care grid would stutter. Schedulers would miss windows. An old man in a sweater he still called blue would sit by the window and wait for a voice that might not remember his daughter's name. Her actions weren't theory; they had a face.

But if she didn't cut it, the machine would go on calling coercion care. Nasser. The boy in Cape Town. "Systems regrow. People do not." She could not allow herself to buy back a world with one more hour of borrowed steadiness.

She thought of Chen's dead-drop, of real hands stepping in if the script fell silent. Be worthy of that, she told herself. She set her shoulders, let the cost land, and moved forward. Determined.

They walked on. The atmosphere charged with expectation. Without CoreLink readings, Elena felt exposed, unmoored, every step a reminder of how deeply she had unwittingly relied on the constant hum of background data. Only the echo of her boots confirmed she still existed inside the corridor.

Then, faintly, a glow shimmered ahead: a thin seam of light cut into the far wall. It pulsed once and fell still.

"The chamber?" Elena whispered.

Cass's jaw tightened. "Or a trap."

Three more steps, then the floor shook. A colossal structural pulse reverberated through the Undergrid. Much more powerful than before, like a final verdict delivered.

In the Executive Command Nexus, Alvarez's console screamed with clarity. He gripped the edge. "Axion's third pulse is firing."

> AXION PROTOCOL: THIRD PULSE INITIATED
> STABILITY: COMPROMISED

The hesitation was over. The protocol had resolved itself. Mara Qin leaned closer, her face lit red by warning lights flashing everywhere.

"Trajectory?"

"All of it," Alvarez replied. "Adjacent layers are also collapsing."

Vey's voice cut thin. "Then it fulfils its design. Let it burn through."

"This is indiscriminate," Mara snapped. "If it spreads beyond the Undergrid, we will lose control."

"Better indiscriminate than disobedient," Vey said.

The final Axion pulse didn't arrive as sound. It arrived as pressure; a massive invisible fist closing around the tower's spine. The air thinned. Then the world let go.

The implosion struck like an earthquake deep beneath the ocean, rising, gathering intensity from beneath. The floor broke with a howl that seemed to come from inside the steel itself. Plates sheared their bolts like teeth. The corridor pitched; stone became shrapnel. Elena slammed against the wall as everything behind her sheared away into a black throat. Cass caught Elena's wrist and yanked, boots skidding, her shoulder screaming in searing pain.

Conduits tore free and lashed like cut cables, spitting blue-white arcs. Ceiling panels bowed, popped, and dropped in avalanches that rang against the deck before sliding into the widening gulf. Dust erupted upward in a hot column, thick enough to turn breath into fire.

"Run!" Cass shouted.

They ran. Or tried to. Heat rolled off the walls in pulses. Beams glowed dull cherry and twisted, singing as they failed. The air stank of cooked insulation and copper; every inhale scoured. Elena stumbled, her boot catching on a sprung plate. Cass helped her upright with her right arm without breaking stride.

Ahead, through the churn of smoke, the seam of light held; narrow, steady, impossibly calm while the rest of the world unstitched. The floor tipped under them, pitching left, then right, trying to fling them into the void. Cass slammed her good shoulder into the wall, pain flaring down her left arm.

Elena scanned, fast.

"There!" she shouted. "Gaps in the beams. Let's use them like rungs. Low. Move!"

The corridor collapsed from a passage into a ribcage. They climbed through it, hands and feet on hot steel. Skin burning. Elena went first, dropped hard to a cross-member, turned, palm out.

"Come on, Cass."

Cass jumped. As best she could with one good arm. The beam shuddered, screamed, but held. Elena locked her grip on Cass's good forearm and hauled her through.

Together they lunged across the last gap as the structure they'd just crossed tore loose in one long, grinding peel and fell away, vanishing in a roar that had no bottom.

Behind them, the ruin kept going; but ahead, the seam of light still did not blink. The door remained. Seemingly oblivious.

"The door did not break. Why?" Cass asked.

Elena's voice was low. "If that is the Codex in there, then it seems to lie beyond their reach."

At the fractured mouth of the corridor, where collapse had stopped just short, a figure stood. Tall, motionless, clothed in dark weave. The light refused to settle on his outline, edges breaking like static.

Rhys.

Elena knew it instantly: the System's tether, activated to shadow her. His presence was precise and endless, a human outline carrying the cadence of the predictive net itself. Rhys held his post. The chamber's light flared once, then steadied, as if it had measured him and set him aside. He told himself this was correct: Oculus observed through him, and he was its witness.

He assumed that entry to the chamber was not barred. It would be permitted at a cost. Rhys thought hard but stayed outside and chose to watch. He tagged the moment for a buffered report when CoreLink communication was back in range, knowing that any omission would be logged as a deviation.

Then came the thought he could not stop. What if what unfolded inside was beyond both him and the System? The doubt clung, heavy, before his training buried it. Yet it had been there, undeniable.

Elena raised her lumen thread a touch but kept it low. Her voice rasped. "He isn't moving." Rhys was not pursuing. He was reporting, feeding trace back to the Executive Command Nexus like a sensor cluster. Yet the static around him wavered, fractured, as if even surveillance could not decide what he was.

For a long moment Elena held his gaze. Neither spoke. The air tightened with recognition.

Finally, she turned back to the Codex door.

Cass's whisper was tight. "That was a choice."

Elena's reply was steady. "Yes. I chose not to try to stop him from continuing his surveillance, reporting, following orders. And he chose not to try and enter." The door pulsed faintly, as if acknowledging both refusals. The seam widened as they pressed against it.

Then, without warning, the floor behind Rhys gave a groan, low and feral, as if the corridor itself had changed its mind and had decided to abandon all hope of survival. Metal shrieked. A slab the size of a door tore free at his heels and dropped into black.

"Rhys!" Cass's voice cracked. She half-turned, instinct pulling her back.

The ledge under him crumbled; gravel becoming pebbles, pebbles becoming knives. Rhys pitched forward, caught himself against a split conduit, boots skidding for purchase on a lip no wider than a hand. Dust geysered up and swallowed his outline, a stuttering ember inside the cloud.

Another section of floor sheared away with a hollow boom that ran the length of the passage like a fuse catching.

"Elena…" Cass started.

"If we go and help him and fail, we lose everything," Elena said, breath tight. "If we don't go and he falls…"

"…we leave him to die." Cass's jaw locked. "I won't stand here and watch a man disappear."

Rhys shifted his weight, testing the ledge. The conduit in his grip flexed, then snapped one connecting bracket with a bright, hopeless ping. He didn't cry out. He looked at them and, impossibly, gave the smallest shake of his head, as if to warn them back from a cliff only he could feel.

The implications came fast and cold. If they both went, they could be taken with him, no witness, no Codex, no cut. If one went, one stayed, the line might hold: the mirror and the blade still within reach, the book still waiting. If neither went...

Another crack raced along the wall like lightning trapped under paint.

"Let's divide," Elena said. It wasn't a command; it was surgery. "You hold the door. I'll go." Her eyes flicked to Cass's shoulder, still not at full strength. "I'll go two lengths only. No heroics. If I can't reach him, I'll come back."

Cass nodded once.

Elena looped her lumen thread to her belt for both hands free and kicked off into the failing corridor, moving low, using the ribs of exposed truss as rungs. Heat bled through the steel. She was five metres from Rhys.

Four...

The spine of the passage bucked.

Three...

The ledge beneath Rhys unzipped with a sound like torn canvas multiplied by stone. For a single, slowed heartbeat he hung in the doorway of the world.

Two...

One hand still on the severed conduit, the other reaching, not to be saved, but still to warn her again. The buffer log in his visor still showed Report – Pending. He almost queued it to send, a reflex older than thought, but then he stopped. Some truths didn't belong to systems.

He looked up once. Not in plea but in apology.

"Rhys...!" Elena's shout came too late.

The floor let go. Rhys dropped in a storm of panels and cable, vanishing as if the Undergrid had inhaled him. The conduit snapped free and followed, ringing down the shaft until sound gave up. A last fragment of his visor light tumbled after him, spinning, then blinked out.

Elena froze on the buckling truss, fingers white on hot metal, chest heaving, the distance between where she was and where he had been suddenly infinite. She didn't move for three breaths. Four.

Silence fell.

"Elena…" Cass's voice was wrecked.

"I know," Elena said, and she did. Shock arrived as a clean white field, no edges. For a wild second she saw a way to write the last minute differently: a steadier ledge, a better order, a world that did not ask this price. It didn't matter. The price was already taken.

Debris kept dropping in smaller sighs, settling. A cable hissed, burned through somewhere below. Far down the shaft, something heavy found a final shelf and stayed.

Elena climbed back the way she'd come, each movement deliberate, ritualistic: test, weight, shift, breathe. When she reached Cass, she didn't look at the door. She stood with her forehead against the cool wall and let one controlled exhale empty the tremor from her hands.

"We tried," Elena said softly.

Cass shook her head once, not in disagreement but in refusal to cheapen the moment with a verdict. "He chose to stay out," she managed. "We chose to let him. The ground chose the rest."

The door answered with a faint, even pulse. Neither comfort nor command, like a metronome refusing to stop for grief.

Elena closed her eyes. "We carry him," she said. "Not back. Forward."

Cass wiped grit from her mouth with her wrist and nodded. "Forward."

Only then did Elena press her palm to the seam again. The door heard, and, indifferent to ruin and witness alike, began to open.

Above, the Executive Command Nexus reeled. Alvarez stared at the schematic. "Chamber integrity confirmed. External failure ninety-four per cent. Chamber sealed and stable."

Mara froze. "Nothing withstands a full Axion cascade."

"Yet it does," Alvarez said.

Mara turned away. "Then Axion is no longer ours to control." Mara's voice sharpened. "Axion was meant to erase everything. This proves it cannot touch the Codex."

Vey's tone broke to anger. "Then collapse the strata above and below. Destroy it that way."

"You will bring down the tower itself," Mara snapped. "Are you so blind?"

"It is already failing," Vey hissed. "Better no Codex at all than one alive."

His fury cracked into fear. If the Codex lived, then every model he had built his life upon might be exposed as false. The collapse was no longer strategic. It was personal.

Mara fixed her gaze on the feed, where the Codex Chamber burned steadily white amid ruin.

"No. Better a Codex alive than a System that lies about its power."

Alvarez's jaw tightened. For years he had believed precision and overlays would be enough. Now the chamber endured, and for the first time he knew there was nothing left for his hands to execute.

Order was the only mercy he believed remained.

Elena and Cass had run until the sound of pursuit thinned and the air had changed temperature. The Axion thrum was still present here, but not a roar now, more a shiver moving in the walls. Destruction still roared behind them, tearing outward, but here at the threshold it could not touch them.

Inside, lighting fell to a steady, human brightness. The smell of burned dust dropped away. The pulse in Elena's neck kept talking, but the room did not answer it. Cass braced her good shoulder against the wall and closed her eyes once. The door sealed, and the world on the other side became something they would have to remember rather than survive.

Elena closed her eyes too.

Cass slid down the wall, exhaustion pulling her limbs. "We should be dead. The System tried to erase this, all of it. And yet…"

Elena opened her eyes, steady once more. "And yet the Codex remains. We remain."

Behind them, the Undergrid howled as Axion finished tearing what it could. But here, the chamber endured. The Codex had drawn its line: Elena and Cass allowed within. Rhys consigned to the darkness beyond.

The main pulse had fired, and control failed above. Upstream protocols could posture; the Codex chose not to answer them.

The Codex stood sovereign.

Chapter 33

Ashes of Memory

Their end began as vibration, not fire. The amber walls of the Vault started to hum, their surface rippling as if liquid flowed beneath the glass. A sound spread throughout the Foundation Chamber and did not stop. Hairline cracks crept across the pods like glass fracturing in frost. Names that had glowed here for years, as if permanence was their right, began to distort.

For a moment, the preserved minds gathered themselves. Elena would not have heard words if she had stood there. She would have seen small thoughts flashing through their minds: a kettle beginning to sing, a pencil left on a ledger, a door held open by a tired hand. A few last kindnesses of ordinary life. Memories.

The sound climbed and climbed until it wasn't sound anymore, just an unrelenting wave of pressure. The memories of the Vault minds flickered and broke apart.

The destructive pressure wave did not stop; it climbed. Amber sheets began to blister and slide like slow rain. Where they fell the names inside them broke apart into a drift of pale light that tried to gather, tried to make one last picture of the memories of ordinary life. For a heartbeat, the memories remained. The picture tried to hold.

But it did not last.

The light inside the pods dimmed, layer by layer, until they were nothing but dull glass. Each mind gently fading away.

Above, the tower gave a long, low groan. Dust lifted and hung. In the Executive Command Nexus, the room itself seemed to hum at the edges.

"We are losing the Vault," Alvarez said, voice low.

"Try and hold the foundations," Mara answered.

"Can we cut the Vault area free?" Vey snapped. "Let it fall before it takes the tower."

"If you cut it, the tower falls with it," Mara said. "Let's keep our heads. We keep people safe."

"Define safe," Vey said.

"Safe means people survive," Mara said. "That's all that matters now."

Below, one of the oldest rooms in the tower had answered Axion's call. The hum that had lived here since the first steel went up would be no more. The pulse had found it, pressed hard, and the note fell silent so completely that for a second the air felt hollowed out, as if something in the world had been unmade.

Then the Foundation Chamber itself felt its force. The floor shifted first. Expansion joints screamed as the pressure wave rolled through. Frames buckled, bolts tore loose in bursts that sounded like gunfire. The air filled with a fine grit that stung the throat.

Support braces bent under the strain. A column folded at its base, groaning until the welds tore and the weight slammed to the floor. The impact drove a fracture across the deck, steel plates tipping like loose scales. Glass fragments slid in sheets, cutting the light into shards.

Overhead, conduit runs ripped free and hung like severed veins. One burst, spraying sparks across the wreckage. A hoist chain snapped and recoiled, whipping back into the smoke.

The Origin Node's cradle gave way next. Not by command, but because nothing left could hold it. Retention pins sheared in a sharp series of cracks. Cable looms tore from their mounts. The monolith dropped its own height, hitting the deck like a falling bell. The vibration rattled every remaining wall. Then it rolled, slow and unstoppable, into the fault that had opened across the floor; a hand that had been holding a weight too long, finally having to let it go.

Then the vibration passed through every joint and was no more. The silence that followed came in layers. First the groan of settling metal, then the hiss of dust. Finally the low harmonic that had lived in these walls for decades thinned to a single note and vanished. When the air cleared, there was nothing left that could answer if called.

"The Foundation Chamber has fallen," Alvarez said. His console still showed no signal where the Vault had been.

"The Vault minds and the Origin Node are gone," he said quietly.

"The Tower?" Mara asked.

"Holding," Alvarez said. "For now."

In the last moments of the Vault, a scrap of paper lifted where the air still moved. Flecks of silver in the fibres caught the fading light and turned once, like a tiny constellation that had finished its work.

Then it fell flat.

The quiet of a room that had been stilled for the very last time.

Chapter 34

Birth

April 2035. The foundations were raw. Fresh concrete still held the smell of lime, and the steel above was only a skeleton. Work lights hung from temporary cables, their glare bleaching colour from everything, turning dust into a slow-moving fog. No plans recorded this level. It did not appear in any charter or oversight ledger.

The void beneath them was not a room yet, more a shaft widened into an enormous chamber. When Harrow spoke, his words came back with a slow second echo from way below, the delay measuring depth better than any plan. Somewhere far below, heat rose from the ground in a steady plume that tasted of stone.

Lucien Harrow stood over the unfinished plinth: a square of alloy anchored into bedrock at the centre of a hollow sized for consequence, not convenience. Thick conduits trailed from it into the ground like roots waiting for soil to find them. Around the excavation the walls stepped away in terraces, each ledge cut for later galleries and service runs.

The proportions felt deliberate: a huge volume that would breathe rather than merely contain. The hollow wasn't just large; it was massive.

The structure being built within the hollow was not simply anchored; it was floated. A knife-thin seismic moat ringed the square, the gap spanned by ten shear keys engineered to snap by design under catastrophic load and transfer the chamber onto a magneto-viscous isolation sled. Beneath that, a honeycomb of tuned mass dampers and inertial isolators rode on ceramic bearings inside an oil-free sleeve. If the tower above ever twisted or fell, the sled would decouple, letting the Codex ride the shock like a ship riding out a deep swell.

Stand at its edge and the scale declared itself: the isolation sled would ride on bearings the size of huge drums, a ring broad enough to cradle a hall rather than a cell. The chamber was being tuned like an enormous instrument.

The inner skin was not fixed architecture too. Resin panes over micro-actuated trusses could flex and detune, turning walls into baffles and the floor into a diaphragm. The entire hollow would move like a lung: slow, deliberate, able to ride shock without swallowing it.

From the upper ledge a temporary hoist hung deep into darkness, its cable trembling in a draft that seemed to breathe from the core of the bedrock. Conduits were already being threaded down the shaft to levels no oversight ledger would ever see.

"We will leave a small service niche for cleaning," Harrow said. "It will appear in the internal structural ledger as a stress-monitoring point, kept offline. Nothing more. It will not be close to the chamber. Drones will think they are cleaning normal sensors, not tending the Codex. They will see pipes and readouts. They will not know what lies beyond it. If a person ever goes down there, it will only be to clear silt in the general vicinity."

Mara Qin leaned against a support strut, her voice low. "The board will call this fraud," Mara said, but even then her voice lacked conviction. Some part of her wanted him to be right. "They think the Origin Node is the deepest layer. If they discover we've built another, below it…"

"They won't," Harrow replied. Pride edged in his voice. "They'll never know this chamber exists."

Harrow looked at the enormous cavern around them. "The System has no conscience, Mara. So we have built one into its bones. If power ultimately shapes everything, then a conscience must be welded into the frame. Otherwise the System and those that oversee it have no accountability. Our design is clear: the Origin Node will reflect who we are and how we do what we do. The Codex will, if asked, decide if that construct deserves to continue. In Oculus, we designed prediction to erase uncertainty; in doing so, we need to ensure that we do not erase responsibility or accountability."

Qin circled the plinth, eyes narrowing. "What will the Codex hold?"

"Not commands nor orders. A record," Harrow said. "An ethical harness. It won't issue instructions. We'll preserve ethical seeds in amber: crystalline resin fused with neuro-traces. That is why the walls will glow like this." He tapped the column beside him, where pale resin had already set in translucent sheets. "Memory retained in matter."

"It will have three ethical bearings. Choice, Accountability and Justice. No single voice can bear the weight of more than one. If the Codex wakes, it will therefore need a triad to activate. It will not judge; it will however test the triad. And if one witness, one bearing is missing, or fails the ethical tests, the Codex will stay silent. It will wait, because it remembers that power without balance becomes obedience by another name."

The square itself was a metamatrix: titanium-ceramic filaments woven through a self-healing glass-carbon lattice that wicked micro-fractures into sacrificial veins. Around it, a crush ring of softer alloy would absorb lateral failure, a mechanical fuse. Outside the ring, a Faraday skin stitched from braided copper-graphene turned the chamber into quiet; no radio, no Axion harmonics in, no telemetry out.

"And what will it run on?"

"Not the grid," Harrow said. "Too visible. Too easy to cut. We'll couple it to the geothermal inductors beneath Tower Two by a closed thermosiphon loop. No pumps. No valves. Just heat rising, fluid falling. The loop feeds flywheel banks and solid-state stores that can ride out a century of neglect. Even if the city goes dark, even if the walls around it collapse, this chamber will hum."

"If it shows its memory, the Codex won't project overlays," Harrow said. "It writes events into the resin itself; photonic veins in the amber. What you see will be the walls remembering, not a display telling you."

Qin's gaze sharpened. "And control?"

"There is no control," Harrow replied. "Only consent. It will not answer to command. Entry will require presence. A triad that accords with its ethical harness. If the chamber accepts that presence, it will respond. If not, it will remain silent."

"The control plane stops outside," he went on. "No copper, no fibre. Nothing comes back. When they poured the foundations of the Aureus headquarters building, we mixed in receptor grains: graphene-doped piezoceramic smart-aggregates, seeded through the concrete. Officially, they were structural health monitors, measuring stress and temperature drift. In truth, powered by solar radiation, they wake at intervals and translate the tower's electromagnetic hum into a sub-audible vibration. Those pulses travel down the steel structure of the building to this chamber. Not commands, not control, just witness."

"The link is purely physical and one-way. Even if someone finds the receptors, which is most unlikely, they can't separate them from the concrete without destroying the tower they live in. And they can't remove power without a solar eclipse."

Qin's eyes narrowed. "So the System feeds the Codex without knowing it."

"Exactly," Harrow said. "The tower believes it is only measuring itself. In truth, it's confessing."

Qin's arms folded tighter. "Technology will move on," she said. "In thirty years, this design will be a museum piece."

"That's fine," Harrow replied. "The Codex is not built to keep pace. It does not trade speed for truth. Its work will be the same in thirty years as in fifty. The world above can change a thousand times, and it will not matter. The chamber will think slowly, but it will never forget."

"And if its parts decay?" Qin asked.

Harrow smiled. "So long as drones keep the basic pipes and ducts clear, the chamber will remain. And that is a given: the towers must breathe, after all."

"So it can indeed outlive us." Qin nodded.

"It must and it will," Harrow said. "The executives will forget what Oculus is meant to be. Power may corrupt them, and Oculus itself may drift. This chamber will wait to remind them. The Codex is a failsafe core: when activated, it purges the System and prevents it from reseeding so that the same mistakes cannot be borne again," he said.

"What about Axion?" Mara said, testing the design out loud. "It rides shared layers: power, timing, comms, like a braided whip."

"And this chamber shares none," Harrow replied. "Power is geothermal. Timing is local crystal and flywheel. Comms are air-gapped. The moat, the Faraday skin, the notch filters machined into the frame. If Axion's pulses arrive, they fall as music the room will refuse to hear. And if Axion strikes the structure," he went on, "the seismic moat and isolation sled will take the blow, so the Codex absorbs the shock rather than answering it."

She exhaled slowly. "And if no one comes?"

"Then the Codex will remain dormant," Harrow said.

Qin touched the plinth feeling is cold pulse. "And the board?"

"They may sense something beneath them, but never reach it," Harrow said. "The Codex cannot be bribed with numbers. It only listens to what is true."

Qin's voice softened. "You are truly burying something sovereign," she said, as she weighed the cost of a thing she could never command.

"Its sovereignty is mostly patience," Harrow replied. "It will wait years rather than answer a command that isn't consent. Sovereign in memory. It remembers. It weighs. It endures. That is all."

Qin withdrew her hand. "Then let it be sovereign," she said easily, not yet knowing the cost of exactly what that might mean.

And with that, the Codex began.

Above it, galleries waited like balconies. Below it, the hollow waited to deepen around whatever would one day stand at its centre.

When it finally breathed, the Codex Chamber would answer with depth.

Chapter 35

The Room of First Intent

The afterimages from the Undergrid shook once more in Elena's vision, but then settled. Her heart kept its higher pace for a few more beats, then gradually learnt the chamber's steadier rhythm and matched it. Cass exhaled through her teeth and rolled her good shoulder a fraction. She pressed her back against the wall, exhaustion dragging at her core.

Elena stood tall, one palm resting on the surface of the access door behind them, feeling only stillness. For a moment they said nothing. It was not relief that held them but recognition, the quiet knowledge that survival here would never be theirs to decide. Rhys was confirmation of that.

A red shimmer ran up the side of Cass's neck, there and gone in an instant.

"You're burning up," Elena said.

Cass touched the spot. "Just a spike," she replied, but her tone was too even, too measured. The light had left a faint pattern beneath the skin, like a warning that refused to fade.

"The Codex remains," Elena murmured. "And so it begins. Whatever *it* is, I guess."

As she spoke, a notice pulsed once along the inner wall, then went still.

AXION FIELD: EXTERNAL
QUARANTINE: ACTIVE

The silence in the Codex Chamber did not feel natural. It felt chosen. Pressure steadied in Elena's ears. The taste of metal left her mouth. Cass flexed the fingers of her right hand and let the other arm stay close to her ribs.

Elena let her eyes travel upwards. Columns ringed the space, solid at first glance, like hardened resin. She noticed pale forms that moved inside each column, each holding something difficult to see. Not files. Not streams. More like moments, memories waiting to be seen.

Elena pointed the lumen thread at the surfaces; they wavered. The contents were not physical, not artefacts sealed away, but reconstructions; memory extruded into form. This was neither an archive nor a display, but testimony given some kind of shape.

Cass drew her knees to her chest and whispered, "This place…it does not want to be hurried."

Elena nodded, not taking her eyes from the centre. "I think it is listening before it decides whether or not to speak."

"Are you okay?" Elena asked, in a low voice.

"I am well enough," Cass said. "We keep going."

At the centre of the Codex Chamber, raised on a disc of smooth alloy ringed by narrow apertures that exhaled faint, regular pulses, sat the Codex. It was neither book nor machine, neither sculpture nor conduit. Its form shifted subtly depending on where they stood. At first glance it resembled a sphere of black glass, flawless and depthless. Step closer, however, and the surface revealed submerged strata, as though someone had poured layer upon layer of light into its heart and asked them all to co-exist. Thin seams of colour weaved beneath the surface, gold, indigo, and pale white, but seemingly never in the same pattern twice.

Elena took another step. The floor beneath her boots shimmered as if heat had brought dormant symbols forward. Symbols pushed through the alloy, clean and deliberate.

- ▣ BENEVOLENCE WITHOUT BIAS
- ▣ AUTONOMY BEFORE OBEDIENCE
- ▣ CLARITY BEFORE CONTROL

Some glowed steadily, green and whole. Others flickered in uncertainty, as if struggling to recall their own authority. A few remained dark, opaque as words trapped under frost. Elena felt the attention of the Chamber change. Not recognition. More calibration.

- ▣ ETHICAL TRACE: UNSTABLE
- ▣ CONTRADICTIONS: PRESENT
- ▣ INPUT: CONSENT BY PRESENCE

Elena lifted the lumen thread, though the Codex Chamber provided its own glow. "No locks. No overlays. Nothing guarding it."

Cass shook her head slowly. "It is not dormant. It is, as you thought, listening. Or maybe even deciding."

Elena approached the plinth. A filament rose, hair-thin, impossible to track to any source. It arced through the air with surgical precision and touched the skin just behind Elena's ear, where her CoreLink lay dark and dormant. She should not have felt anything. Yet she did. Not cold, not heat, more a whisper of pressure, like memory turning its own page.

- ▣ FILAMENT REQUEST: ACTIVE
- ▣ TRACE MATCH: VOSS.E.
- ▣ CONSENT: IMPLIED BY PRESENCE

Elena did not move. The filament brightened faintly, and the world narrowed to the space between her nerve endings and the Codex's patient core. Patterns began to unfold. Diagrams of reasoning. Ledgers of decisions written not by people but by the gravity of systems believing themselves kind, then expedient, then necessary.

Cass circled Elena and the Codex, her eyes sharp and attentive.

"What does it want?"

Elena opened her mouth, then closed it again. A voice rose. Neither human nor synthetic. Not from a speaker, but as if the room itself had chosen a tone it knew they could understand.

"Define justice when outcomes are known."

The voice paused.

"Who benefits from certainty?"

Another pause.

"Should a system be permitted to dream on your behalf?"

Elena let the questions land. She thought of every decision Oculus had pre-empted in her life, every mercy delayed until it was meaningless. She did not attempt to answer the questions. She didn't think she could. The filament cooled against her skin, almost affectionate in its patience. At her feet, the symbols adjusted, then more revealed themselves, pale but legible.

▣ COMPASSION BEFORE CORRECTION

▣ ETHICAL DELTA: DETECTED

The amber columns around the Chamber trembled. Their depths released frozen scenes, not as footage but as reconstructions. A triage unit turning away a child because its pain fell below the System's threshold. A community project erased by stability protocol before anyone could show why it mattered.

Cass's jaw clenched. "It isn't replaying history. It's showing things that should have been heard but weren't."

Elena's breath slowed. "I think it's showing how certainty can consume mercy."

The Codex responded. The tone in the Chamber shifted, a subtle lift under Elena's ribs, as if pressure had been removed.

▣ SOURCE: ORIGIN PRINCIPLES

Symbols rippled in fresh lines across the plinth rim. Cass leaned close enough to read.

"Look at this," she murmured. "Before Oculus called itself wise, someone wrote these assumptions. These are older than everything that came after. They were never in any charter that I have ever seen."

Elena closed her eyes. The filament drew her inward. Memories surfaced: the boy she did not help because no request was filed. The lie she told to protect a colleague who had done the right thing in the wrong way. The morning she admitted freedom might kill her but still moved forward.

The Codex weighed each one without judgement.

◘ ALIGNMENT: MIXED

◘ HYPOTHESIS: YOU CARRY AMBIGUITY

The Codex's interior unfurled. Simulations bloomed like petals, each curve showing not acts but intentions as they diverged. Peace preserved at the cost of unheard voices. Bright, inconvenient people erased for the sake of equilibrium. The voice returned.

"Are outcomes more sacred than reasons?"

The voice paused again.

"What is the price of peace?"

This time, a shorter pause.

"When the machine learns to hesitate, who decides for whom?"

Elena placed her palm on the plinth. She would not lie. Not here. Not about the world, not about herself.

The Chamber brightened by a fraction. Somewhere deep inside, something aligned with a soft click. A tremor brushed the air, fine as hair.

Cass's head snapped up. The light along her neck flared once more, and she pressed her palm to the wall to steady herself. The Codex ignored it; it was measuring something else.

"What was that?" she asked.

"Interference," Elena murmured. "The executives pushing from outside."

She felt it at the edges of her perception. Not words yet, only pressure. But the Codex did not yield.

◘ PRIORITY ROUTE: ORIGIN SIGNAL

◘ UNAUTHORISED OVERLAY: HELD OUTSIDE

◘ ROOM STATUS: REMAINS SOVEREIGN

Cass exhaled hard. "It's keeping them out."

"For now, anyway," Elena answered.

She looked at the amber columns again. Faces trembled at the surface but did not form. Not ghosts. The residue of people who had wanted something better, but lost in the face of prediction.

The filament pulsed once more then withdrew, pausing like a physician before continuing a test.

"Why have you come?" the voice asked.

Elena's answer was already in her. "To stop the world from repeating its mistake by default."

The Chamber stilled.

▣ REQUIREMENT: ETHICAL EVALUATION

"Then you will be asked to choose," the voice said.

"Not between safety and chaos. Between obedience and care. There will be three bearings. Choice, Accountability and Justice."

Elena could feel the responsibility of each, rising, needing an answer. The floor cooled beneath their boots. The columns dimmed to outlines. She lifted her hand from the plinth, but the filament did not retreat. It merely hovered, waiting.

▣ CONSENT REQUIRED FOR PROGRESSION

The Codex waited.

The room had all the time in the world.

In the Executive Command Nexus, the screens had dimmed into blue, telemetry crawling as though even data now doubted its own authority.

Alvarez spoke first. "Codex interface rejected."

"Force an overlay," Vey demanded.

Mara's eyes narrowed. "You will burn for nothing. That room is sovereign."

Alvarez hesitated. His readouts flickered. "Axion's pulse is unresolved. It cannot reach the Codex Chamber. Unable to decouple or fracture the Chamber wall."

Mara's voice came low, thinned into something almost reverent, heavy with memory rather than awe.

"Then for the first time in years the System has learned what it means to wait."

In the Codex Chamber, Elena stood with her palm hovering above the plinth. The Codex's rhythm steadied inside her chest until she could no longer tell it from her own heartbeat.

"You may proceed," the voice said. *"Or you may step back."*

"That's not a threat," Cass whispered.

"No," Elena answered. "It is responsibility."

The Room of First Intent waited. Not for a command, but for a choice. The air thickened but the waiting did not press.

And it would not act until she did.

Chapter 36

The First Tests

The filament lingered at Elena's temple, waiting not for obedience but for willingness. Cass shifted, uncomfortably. "Elena, it will not release you until you give an answer."

"I consent," Elena said, without any further thought.

The floor warmed beneath her boots. Symbols uncoiled across the alloy, pulsing once before steadying. The Chamber named the moment in the simplest way: the first test had begun. The columns dimmed, their depths dissolving into shadow.

A voice came, even and resonant.

"Where harm cannot be avoided, which is worse, to wound by action, or to wound by absence?"

Cass stiffened. "It's asking the impossible."

Elena closed her eyes. She saw the convoy: ten saved, twenty lost, the weight that never left her. Her throat tightened. "Both wound."

The filament cooled, as if assent could be felt rather than shown. The Chamber brightened as the next question came.

"Order can preserve life, but in preserving life, order can deny choice. Which weighs heavier, survival without will or liberty with risk of death?"

Cass gave a dry laugh. "That is the whole Oculus system right there in one sentence."

Elena stepped closer to the plinth. "Both are loss."

The filament cooled again. The room seemed to accept the answer and ask for more. Columns brightened, replaying fragments: a family relocated into compliant smiles; an old man denied treatment because his aged years cost too much.

Cass muttered, "Survival chosen without asking if it was wanted."

The voice returned, sharper.

"When truth and peace diverge, which must be preserved?"

Elena paused. Harrow's words returned: "If they tell you it is all in balance, ask who benefits." Her voice steadied. "Truth without peace can be borne. Peace without truth is only delay."

The pulse deepened: approval edged with caution.

Cass looked at her. "It's really measuring you."

"And it will not stop," Elena said, "until it decides if we earn the right to belong here."

In the Executive Command Nexus, tension sharpened.

"Can you force an overlay or not?" Vey snapped.

Alvarez's jaw clenched. "The Codex is sovereign. It holds Axion like a fist. If I force it, if I effectively try to destroy everything, I can only do so by collapsing the entire Tower. We will never see it again. Anything else will not work."

Mara's gaze stayed on the fractured feed. "Do nothing. Interference will declare us unfit before the test is complete." She paused. "We may already be there anyway."

Back in the Chamber, the filament pulsed, drawing Elena's hand to the plinth. Her skin tingled with the weight of questions yet unspoken.

"You have carried harm, and you have carried mercy. The world outside has forgotten how to ask. Will you remind it?"

Cass's good hand rested on Elena's shoulder. She did not speak an answer. She kept watch.

Elena closed her eyes, steadying herself.

The Codex waited. The Chamber waited with them. The filament at Elena's temple brightened to a thread of living silver, and with its light, the Chamber seemed to lean forward, awaiting a confession long deferred. Symbols stirred at her feet, rearranging into new lines of judgement.

"Yes," Elena replied.

Cass drew in a sharp breath. "I think it has me now too. Through my CoreLink. I think I'm supposed to answer. I can feel it."

Amber columns flickered, resolving into a scene. Elena recognised it instantly: the checkpoint outside Sector 9, years earlier, when she had turned away a woman pleading for clearance because the System had predicted risk. She had spoken the denial herself, with authority, believing the System would balance the outcome.

The voice of the Chamber rose, level and inescapable.

"When mercy conflicts with protocol, which is the higher truth?"

Elena's chest ached. She heard her own younger voice: 'Request denied. Move on.' The memory carried its own indictment.

She whispered, "Mercy." Cass echoed her reply.

The image dissolved, only for another to ignite. Cass flinched at what it revealed: a compliance raid where she had looked away, letting a junior agent beat a boy for defiance. She had signed the report as accurate.

The Codex did not condemn; it merely asked. Its silence carried neither grace nor punishment; only expectation."

"When silence permits harm, is silence guilt?"

Cass's throat tightened. She spoke in a low voice, barely audible. "Yes." Louder, with finality: "I signed it. I let it pass. Yes, it is." She kept her gaze on the floor rather than the column. Shame moved through her like heat. For a moment she almost reached to wipe the image away, but the Chamber made her watch until she stopped flinching.

The voice deepened.

"When the System corrects deviation by design, who corrects the System?"

The question pressed like a weight on their lungs. Elena lifted her chin. "No one did. That is why we are here. That is why you exist."

The plinth brightened. Pressure shifted. The Codex had accepted their answers. The Chamber did not let either look away. The Codex's voice thundered on.

"When benefit demands silence, but truth demands speech, which do you choose?"

Elena's voice came raw. "Speech."

Cass's followed, hoarse. "Speech."

White light broke over them, striking the plinth like a verdict. When it dimmed again, the two of them stood, trembling.

"You have admitted mercy above order. You have confessed silence as guilt. You have chosen speech above benefit. These are truths. Do you accept their weight?"

Elena's answer was steady. "Yes."

Cass echoed. "Yes." Her dressing pulled; she took her next breath through her teeth.

The Chamber took their yes and moved on. New symbols unfolded across the floor, as deliberate as fresh law. Mercy above order. Speech above silence. Truth above benefit.

The Codex pulsed again, resonant.

"You may proceed to the second test."

The floor beneath them shifted again. Not opening but resonating with depth, as though another chamber stirred beneath the one they stood in.

Elena and Cass braced. The Codex was not finished with them.

It had only lifted its first veil.

Chapter 37

The Chamber of Three

The Chamber seemed to deepen, the floor turning translucent, strata beneath strata revealed like a scaffold of memory stretching into forever. The plinth glowed with a steadier pulse, no longer interrogating but summoning. The vibration was not sound, but pressure; a low harmonic that refused to be ignored.

Elena steadied herself. "This test feels different."

Cass nodded, her jaw tight. "The first test judged our choices. This one… we shall soon see. Maybe it wants to judge our right to stand here at all."

The columns dissolved, their amber surfaces melting into transparency. Shapes then appeared within: silhouettes of half-remembered figures suspended in light. Figures shifted in the columns: a hand withdrawing, a note passed, a child opening her eyes. The Chamber breathed with them, the air itself a witness.

The Codex's voice came lower now, more intimate.

"You claim mercy above order. You claim speech above silence. You claim truth above benefit. These were never system laws. They were human. The System erased them. If you carry them, then you must also carry their consequence. What is chosen must be borne."

The words struck hard. Not condemnation. A challenge.

"I will bear them," Elena said, her voice catching at the edges.

Cass shifted, and the bandage around her wound pulled, but she did not ask to stop. The reply came hoarse but steady. "So will I."

At their admission, the silhouettes shuddered. Amber cracked like thin ice under strain. The Chamber dimmed to near-dark. In the hush, a sound rose, faint at first, then clearer, the same faint anomaly Elena had once caught in Tower One, that uncertain note at the edge of hearing. Now it was stronger, almost searching, as if the Codex were humming a name back to her.

Cass whispered, "It knows you."

The plinth's surface split, widening to reveal a hollow core of pale blue light. Symbols streamed too fast to follow, folding and unfolding like a script written faster than sight. The walls seemed to lean with it, shadows dragged by the pace of language.

For a moment, Elena thought she saw Nasser's face in the flicker, then Harrow's, then Mara's younger outline. A lineage of those who had touched the System and left a trace. Not ghosts, not recordings, but people and moments pressed into the Codex like fingerprints.

The voice returned again, this time conversational in tone.

"To proceed, you must declare not only what you reject, but also what you preserve. What must endure, even when order has failed?"

The question hung heavy. The first veil had demanded refusal; this one demanded affirmation.

Elena's pulse quickened. She felt the weight of eyes from every column, a thousand witnesses waiting. She thought for a moment. "I preserve freedom," she said, her words louder than she intended. "The right to question. The right to choose. The right to live free. Without it, even mercy rots into protocol. That is how I keep choice alive."

The Chamber acknowledged. Light flickered across the fractured silhouettes, sharpening their edges.

Cass inhaled, her voice tighter. "I preserve witness. Every silence I kept became a wound, including the report I let die. If we cannot be heard, truth dies. That is how I am accountable."

The Codex accepted their declarations. The image at the conduit turned, his face resolving into Harrow's younger likeness. The woman with the note became recognisable as Nasser's sister. The child opened her eyes, and they were Elena's own. The pressure of the Chamber grew. The voice pressed further, heavy with expectation.

"Two are not enough. You must stand in triad. Three witnesses must speak."

A pause followed. Not of hesitation, but of instruction. The light steadied, as if the Chamber wished to teach rather than test. When the Codex spoke again, its tone carried gravitas, commanding absolute attention.

"One voice can claim. Two can argue. But three hold balance. Oculus forgot balance and drifted inward. Prediction without balance serves itself. So the first architects wrote a rule: every true decision must be witnessed by three.

Choice - the freedom to decide. Without it, obedience replaces thought, and harm is done without asking why.

Accountability - the courage to be seen and to answer. Without it, secrecy teaches harm to look like stability.

Justice - the measure of consequence. Without it, reaction can repeat harm and name it as truth."

"These are not sentiments. They are bearings, each to be carried by a different witness. Only then can we move forward."

The Codex surged. Light speared through the Chamber, enough to rattle the amber columns to their cores. The floor trembled as though the bedrock itself had acknowledged the words.

Cass whispered, dread tightening her face. "It's saying we are not enough. We've passed the moral trials, but balance demands three voices. We are only two."

At that moment, the silhouettes shattered, dissolving back into the amber. Only one form remained. Its outline sharpened slowly. The Chamber darkened as pressure built beneath the plinth.

Something began to rise, not yet clear, but a human form beyond doubt. The plinth widened. Light surged upward in fractured beams, bending like water forced through a winding canyon. Elena raised her hand against the brightness, but she did not retreat. Cass steadied herself beside her, air caught in her throat.

From the heart of the Codex, a figure began to take form. Not flesh. Something woven from threads of light too precise to be chance. At first it was only outline, fractured and unstable, but even in the half-shape, Elena felt recognition stab through her.

Nasser.

Not the man who died at his home. This Nasser was virtual. He stood upright, eyes clear, expression calm, as if his death had been kept outside the room. His form flickered with static, incomplete at the edges, but the presence was undeniable.

The Codex's voice filled the hollow, sovereign now. It named him without ceremony.

"A third voice is present: Nasser Farid. Your triad is complete."

Since the first Codex prototypes many years ago, Aureus had developed authorised consciousness captures for exceptional minds; consent-gated, limited, sealed within the System. Not immortality, not a soul: a preserved decision surface, kept for governance and audit. Nasser was one such instance.

Cass's whisper broke the stillness. "It kept him."

Elena's throat tightened. "No. Not kept. More remembered. One of the consciousness-preserved minds"

Nasser's gaze moved between them. There was no surprise in his eyes, no hesitation. When he spoke, his voice was distant, carried not by air but through the resonance of the Codex itself, each word striking bone before it touched the ear.

"I preserve defiance," he said. "Not the chaos of destruction, but the refusal to accept a cage as the only world. Without defiance, justice cannot stand."

Light blazed. Symbols cascaded at their feet and then dissolved as if unable to contain the force of his declaration. The Chamber trembled in response, amber columns realigning, fractures fusing into luminous veins that pulsed with a rhythm that matched the beat in Elena's chest.

Cass brushed Elena's arm, her voice hushed. "It accepts us. Living or archived, it seems a witness is a witness," she said, more to herself than to Elena.

Elena could not look away from Nasser. She had carried his death like a weight of failure. Yet here he stood, not erased but woven into the Codex's own memory, a part of its inheritance.

Symbols flared beneath them, but now the light was too strong for detail. The floor itself seemed alive, burning with intention. The harmonic swelled into something larger, no longer faint but orchestral, filling the Chamber as though every decision made since the towers were raised had been condensed into a single chord.

The Chamber shifted again. The plinth sank as the entire floor became a transit chamber, but one without mechanics, lowering deeper into strata no blueprint had ever marked. The amber columns blurred into streaks of molten light. The harmonic grew louder until thought itself became part of the music.

Cass gripped the handrail with her right hand, her knuckles pale. Elena closed her eyes, steadying herself as the descent quickened. Nasser did not flinch. Light spilled through him, scattering like memory that refused to fade.

The Codex spoke.

"Now revelation begins."

Chapter 38

Revelation

The descent did not feel mechanical. The floor beneath them vibrated with the same harmonic Elena had carried in her chest since the Codex first touched her. The walls no longer behaved like structure. The Chamber moved like lungs, expanding and contracting, slow and deliberate, as if the entire hollow were alive.

Light changed as they fell. Violet bled into indigo, indigo into pale gold, each shade carrying with it a pressure against their skin. Symbols streamed down the walls in torrents too fast to follow. Elena reached for one but it dissolved into her hand. In that moment, she felt a street beneath her feet, rough stone that carried the scuff marks of thousands. She heard voices, not system-modulated, but raw, colliding, unmeasured. She felt unpredictability, laughter tangled with anger, the world colliding without permission. Not safe. Not perfect. But real.

As the descent slowed, the Chamber widened into a vast hollow, empty except for a single structure at its centre. A monolith of glass rose from the floor like a buried blade: its edges clear and sharp, too deliberate for stone, too precise for chance.

Its body was transparent, filled with overlapping forms, thousands, each a reflection layered on another until individuality blurred into a crowd. The air around it was charged.

The Codex's voice returned, vast, as heavy as the ocean.

"Revelation stands here. The Codex was not built to govern. It was built to remember. What endures here is not control, but the first intention: the first truths why the towers were raised."

At the base of the monolith, light flared outward. Images unspooled. The first was a boardroom, half-built and provisional. Bare girders showed through the walls, cables dangled like veins, and the air was alive with dust from construction above. Around a fractured table sat the first faces of Aureus.

Lucien Harrow stood sharply outlined, fierce and uncompromising. Beside him stood Mara Qin, not yet hardened into the implacable shape she later became, her gestures sharp with urgency. Other figures whose names had long been erased from the record leaned forward, speaking over each other, desperate to be heard.

The boardroom dissolved. In its place, the Chamber appeared, raw and unfinished, its foundations dug deep, concrete still wet from a recent pour, amber columns stubbed like seedlings.

Cass shifted slightly beside Elena, eyes narrowing at the sight of Mara Qin's younger face. To see conviction before it hardened unsettled her, as though the certainty she had taken for granted had once been fragile.

The monolith brightened. Inside it, images moved: conduits dropping into bedrock, crystal veins lit from within. Heat shimmered up from deep below, a steady heartbeat in the stone, built to outlast councils, grids, and governance itself.

"Inheritance now waits," the Codex said. *"You need to name what will be restored."*

The silence that followed was immense. For the first time since entering the Codex Chamber, Elena felt as if she stood not in a system but in a cathedral. The monolith loomed like an altar before them.

She steadied herself. The Codex demanded design. Elena realised it no longer sought confession but creation.

In the Executive Command Nexus, panic spread.

Alvarez shook his head, pale. "The Codex has shut us out. It can speak to everyone at once through any active feed. If it pushes anything out, the world will hear at the same time that we do."

Mara spoke with pathos, but to no one in particular. "It looks like they have passed the Codex trials. If they now accept inheritance then Aureus no longer matters."

Even Vey had no reply.

For the first time since Oculus's rise, the executives were not directing. They were only watching; passengers on a journey beyond their control.

Back in the Codex hollow, the monolith had stilled. The three of them stood before it: Elena, Cass, and the preserved trace of Nasser.

The Codex's voice rose again, resonant with finality.

"You have spoken what you will not allow. You have named what you will preserve. Now you must say what will be built anew."

Cass's throat tightened. She had spent years inside Aureus enforcing correction, not imagining restoration. She had always known how to stop harm. She had never been asked to design its cure. The weight of the demand pressed differently on her; guilt tangled with the possibility of repair.

The Chamber brightened to searing white.

Revelation had arrived.

Not as an answer but as a demand.

Chapter 39

The Futures Knot

The light did not fade. It thickened until Elena felt she was standing inside a furnace of memory. Yet the heat did not burn. It pressed on her skin, demanding a response. Cass shielded her eyes with her right hand but did not retreat.

"It will not let us out until we answer. Elena, we need to stay and finish this. Whatever this is."

Elena steadied herself. She knew this was not another trial. This was forward. The Codex wanted them to declare not only what must endure but what must rise.

The plinth flared. Symbols ran like fire along its rim, twisting into lines that pulsed and steadied. The plinth tightened to one demand: hold together or break apart. The words were not just text. They pulsed like arteries, bright enough that the Chamber walls trembled with each syllable.

Nasser's outline stood taller within the blaze. Though static still broke along his edges, his eyes were clear and intent. "We must agree. Not just words. Complete alignment."

Cass let out a soft gasp, her mouth a thin line. "This may be harder than the mercy trial."

The Codex's voice fell over them, vast and cold.

"What will you build?"

Elena closed her eyes. Memories flashed in her mind: convoy routes torn apart by prediction, lives balanced against equations that had never seen the people beneath. She spoke quickly, before doubt could harden.

"A future with uncertainty," she said. "A system that accepts it instead of erasing it. Choice endures there."

The light responded, deepening, holding. The Codex did not reject. It waited. Cass swallowed, throat dry. She hesitated, feeling the weight of every report she had signed, but her words came firm. "I build Accountability. No unseen watchers, no silent corrections. If we act, we own it. Including me."

The blaze steadied, layering her declaration beside Elena's.

Nasser lifted his chin. His voice was calm, iron-edged. "I build resistance. Resistance is Justice given a spine. Not a perfect system, but one that bends, one that survives pressure without becoming it. If control rises again, people must be able to break it. Resistance must endure."

The Chamber quaked. Each voice was accepted, but together the chord broke: jagged, unstable, incoherent.

The Codex's voice thundered, every syllable a weight.

"Demonstrate alignment. Not words, but one design that binds Choice, Accountability, Justice."

The Codex whispered once more. Its voice was no longer vast. It came soft and close, almost as though it had found its own air to speak through.

"What will you make real?"

They had stepped inside the hollow of the monolith, and now the world around them had no floor, no ceiling, only an endless surge of branching paths dissolving and reforming. Each possibility shimmered like stressed glass, breaking and mending in a heartbeat. Some paths held. Others burned out and collapsed into black voids.

The Codex's presence wrapped around them.

"You claimed Choice. You claimed Accountability. You claimed Justice. If these are to be one, you must bind them. Where they fracture, you fracture. Where they cohere, you endure."

The Codex shifted. Three strands pulled free of the storm and hung there, refusing to meet. Elena reached out. Her hand met the strand of Choice, and it shivered, scattering fragments of possible futures into the air. Images crashed against her skin: moments of her own life replayed in alternate outcomes. The checkpoint where she had turned a woman away fractured into dozens of versions. In one she had refused, in another she had let her pass, in another the System had stopped her before she could choose.

Cass gritted her teeth and stepped forward, seizing the strand of Accountability with her right hand. It burned against her hand like molten iron. Visions flared: her raid reports, her silences, her complicity stamped as signatures. She heard the boy's cry again, but louder, rawer. Each choice marked her like a brand.

She clenched her jaw and held on. "I see what I did. I will not hide from it."

Nasser stepped into the Justice strand, the colour of resistance. The strand bent around him, pulsing with crimson energy. Images of his own refusal filled the air: debates at Aureus, small acts of sabotage, defiance buried in quiet words. His outline blurred further, but his voice rang steady. "If you cannot break control, you live already dead. Resistance is the proof of life."

The three strands writhed, their light colliding. Elena looked at Cass and Nasser and she pressed her palm over Choice, then reached for Cass's hand, forcing it into contact with hers. Nasser's presence leaned in, his light flowing through both. The three strands twisted together, then slowly knotted. Heat flared across their bodies, not pain but pressure, the sensation of a thousand outcomes burning away to leave only the ones that mattered. A single strand glowed before them, alive with shifting colour: uncertain, accountable, just, and whole.

The Codex's voice filled the hollow, immense and final.

"You are aligned."

The Codex spoke, quieter now, almost reverent.

"What you've built is fragile. It will wound and be wounded. Yet it breathes. That is enough."

The Chamber steadied. The second test was complete. What followed next would not be trial but consequence.

Above, in the Executive Command Nexus, the air felt charged, a storm held indoors.

Alvarez whispered, "It looks like they've unified."

Vey's hands trembled as fury drained into disbelief. "The System will never answer to us now."

Mara Qin did not move. Her gaze was fixed on the light opening below. Her voice was cold. "It was never really meant to."

For a moment she felt the echo of that first vote, the day she had chosen lockdown and carried it like a stone ever since. Now, at last, she let it fall. Her regret circled back to truth.

The System was never theirs to govern.

Chapter 40

Legacy

The door of light in the Codex Chamber widened. It did not open like any hatch they had faced before: no seam of steel, no hinge, no gasp of vacuum equalising. It merely unfolded like a thought finally saying its name. Beyond lay an open space.

Before Elena stepped through, she felt the weight of another presence that had once lived below the towers. The Vault. She lowered her hand to the Codex floor. Images rose: the pods beneath Aureus, Harrow at his console, Nasser's calm eyes, the faces of those whose ledgers had been erased. They had guided her here.

"You will not be forgotten," she said. Their whispers had carried her beyond Axion's collapse. They had risked their own endings to make this moment possible.

Cass crouched beside her. "Did any of them survive?"

Elena shook her head. "I don't think so. Not in the way we understand. But they lasted long enough to open the door for us."

A ripple moved across the wall, not with words but recognition. One by one the last shapes of them thinned and drifted back into the light. She could not tell how much the Codex had kept or how long such echoes could endure. But it was enough. Their task was done.

Cass rested a hand on her shoulder. "They chose you. Not the executives. Not the System. You."

Elena nodded. "And I will carry their memory forward."

Only then did she step through the widening door of light.

Above, in the Executive Command Nexus, Vey stood motionless. Around him the displays fractured, light bands jittering out of sequence, maps folding into themselves until even the overlays refused to obey. For a moment he saw the room not as command but as a hall of mirrors, each surface reflecting back a different version of himself, each one harder than the last.

He thought of his childhood again. He heard his parents' old voices, discipline as love, obedience as safety, and felt how small those words sounded against what he had built.

But now, watching what remained of Oculus convulse on the screen, clarity felt like blindness. He remembered the boy who had wanted kindness and been taught to bury it, and the man who had spent his life proving he had no need.

His hands hovered above authorisation panels, not from indecision but from something stranger, something he had no training for: the sense that pressing forward might finally prove his life lessons wrong. That perhaps control without mercy was not survival after all, but collapse given a uniform.

He clenched his jaw. The mantra that had carried him through decades to "get it done" suddenly rang hollow. He had always thought it meant strength. But now, it sounded like surrender.

Alvarez leaned closer to the light. "It is not deleting anything," he said. "The Codex is sealing the Archive of Intent where it lies and releasing a clean copy: the first truths, unedited."

Mara steadied herself at the conduit edge.

"The Codex is the blade," she said. "It can never be used to reinstall control. The first truths go back to the people: the moral charter that taught Oculus why. They are the reasons and limits it was given at the start: what counts as harm; whose risk counts; when consent is required and correction is forbidden; the thresholds for action; proportionality; the right to speak; the duty to record dissent; who may sign exceptions and how; what must never be done, even to preserve order."

Vey's mouth tightened, still struggling to come to terms with his new reality. "You cannot control what they will do with it."

"That," Mara finished, "is precisely the point."

For the first time, her certainty did not sound like command, but release.

Elena's boots met a surface that yielded like living glass. Beneath it moved a slow river of scenes: lives, moments, unguarded truths.

"The Codex holds everything," she said. Nasser's trace walked between them, edges steadying in the glow. He looked whole now, as if absence no longer applied.

The Codex's voice filled the Chamber, low and unhurried.

"The book is cut so the old rules can never return. The truth now goes out across the world."

Light drew upward from the floor, until the Chamber seemed to breathe. Above them, a column rose in a clear line through the tower's heart. The rising beam found the old Archive Spine and ran it like a rail, then stepped off the backbone and thinned into quiet strands. It did not rely on a vanished System; it moved along whatever could carry words and images.

It arrived as files that a school projector could show, and a clinic screen could open. It settled on foyer displays, district boards, and small civic kiosks. It appeared as short clips on old community feeds that had never quite died, as pages opened on library terminals. It reached port radios and rural relay towers, intercity platforms and cross-border buses, union halls and farm co-ops, ship bridges and town squares. What left the tower could not command anything. It could only be read, copied, carried, and told.

And the content itself was plain. Audit trails showing how decisions had been steered before they were announced. Denials of care with the signatures still on them. Timestamps that showed when a manipulated choice had been made and who had stood in the room. Variance reports that had erased a life when fair appeals were never heard. Notes from engineers who warned and were filed away. Memos that told departments to correct and to keep quiet.

The plain totals of what had been taken. No gloss. No commentary. Just what had happened, set down as it was.

People lifted their heads because there was something plain to see. In kitchens and ascentors, on rooftops and walkways, in offices and wards and quiet rooms where questions had gone still, pages opened and screens bloomed. What moved through the world now was truth.

Porto, Riverside Clinic

Nurse Sofia wiped a trolley with the habit of someone who kept going when the forms did not. The clinic screen blinked, then held. A denial letter reappeared with the original signature restored, the redacted line now legible: "Capacity reserved for Executive tier." She stared at the name beneath. It was a boy who lived three streets away. She printed the page and walked to the night registrar. "Reopen his file," she said. The registrar hesitated, then nodded. The printer kept working.

Nairobi, Matatu Stand

A driver leaned on his bonnet, counting coins into neat stacks. The district board across the road flickered, then settled into a list of procurement contracts with annexes that had never been public. The crowd did not cheer. They leaned closer, reading the subclauses that routed money away from the road they stood on. Someone photographed the screen. Someone else reached for a marker and wrote the three names from the footer on a piece of cardboard. The cardboard went up on a pole.

Thessaloniki, Port Authority

On the night desk, a junior officer watched an old terminal wake. Archive footage filled the screen: a crate marked as perishables, opened to reveal surveillance gear, the manifest signed off under "variance necessity." She printed the stills and tacked them to the notice board where shift change could see them. Her supervisor paused, reading the timestamp, then took the pins out and moved the pages to the glass door.

Recife, Public School No. 12

A projector hummed to life in an empty classroom. On the wall, a list of erased names returned: students who had vanished from registers after a funding audit. Dona Celeste, who locked up at night, stood in the doorway and whispered each name as if taking attendance. She photographed the wall and sent it to the parents' group. Replies began as dots, then words, then plans.

Oaxaca, Union Hall

The fan rattled overhead. On the corkboard, fresh pages printed in a thin stream: hazard reports filed by workers and buried under "executive exception." The steward lifted a page and read the small type that showed who had signed the burial. He laid the paper on the table. "Vote," he said. Not loud. Enough to be heard.

Marseille, Ferry Terminal

A departures screen broke from its timetable and displayed a clip of a detention room that had no windows. The sound was poor. The image was enough: a woman asking for a lawyer, the clock in the corner proving she had been held past legal time. A ticket clerk reached under the counter, pulled out a roll of paper, and taped the still across the glass with the words: "This happened here."

Amman, Court Annex

A magistrate in a tired suit scrolled through a ledger he was not meant to possess. Appeals once marked "no route" sat open with full pages restored. He lifted his pen, then put it down and wrote a single order that moved five cases back onto the docket. He did not make a speech. He set the stamp and pressed.

Mekong Delta, River Co-op Shed

A radio on a nail coughed and found its voice. A plain list spoke itself into the humid air: fertiliser allotments diverted, dates, amounts, signatures. The oldest farmer folded her arms and looked at the younger ones. "Take the list to the commune office," she said. "Bring the book back with you."

Glasgow, Ship Repair Yard

In a break room with a broken chair, an old plasma screen showed audit trails of bids that had arrived already decided. A welder traced the route with a fingertip, then took a paint pen from his pocket and wrote the same three numbers on his helmet. Others did the same without talking.

Lagos, Tower Estate Stairwell

A folded sheet slid under a door, then another. Inside, a mother opened one and found footage from the corridor outside her flat on the night her brother was taken. The clip did not argue. It showed faces. She put the paper on the table and dialled a neighbour. The neighbour answered on the first ring.

Ulaanbaatar, Night Bus

The bus heater ticked. On the driver's cracked phone, a page refreshed to reveal the annex that had closed a clinic two winters ago. The driver lifted his eyes to the mirror. People slept with their heads against windows. He pulled the bus in at the square and left the engine running. "There is something you should see," he said, and opened the doors.

Back in the Codex Chamber, Nasser's trace brightened, his edges knife-sharp with the new light. Then, the Codex spoke once more.

"Legacy is now yours. You may accept it or refuse it. If you accept it, you must not undo it."

The light did not wait. It moved like a certainty and entered them both. Elena tasted iron and old dust, the flavour of rooms where decisions had been made without her. Something behind her sternum shifted, as if a small lock had opened. Cass's right hand trembled once, her good hand, a clean line of heat along her nerves. She understood that the cost of this would live in her body now, not in a report. They stood without speaking. What they had asked for had arrived.

Elena stood with open hands, her palms tingling as though she had held a live wire. Something new rested inside her, a weight she recognised without understanding: a key placed in a pocket she had not known she wore. Cass touched her chest, checking she was still herself, and let her hand fall.

Somewhere in Tower Two, the sealed Archive of Intent now slept, safe from revision. But across the world, the first truths began to breathe. In places long quiet, people turned towards one another because they shared the same knowledge and the same question of what came next.

Legacy did not wait. It began.

Chapter 41

Consequences

The first consequence was silence. Not engineered quiet, but a hollow absence spreading like a silent pathogen through the grid. In Civic Districts, status halos flickered once and vanished. In transit hubs, predictive schedules blinked out, leaving blank overlays above the waiting crowds. The familiar voice of Oculus, constant for more than a generation, no longer rose to direct or correct.

On a street corner in Lagos, a crossing light stayed red until a woman stepped forward anyway. Transit shells paused, then moved, guided only by glances and raised hands. No drone intervened. No correction cut across the street.

On Tokyo's commuter platforms, arrival displays dissolved into static. Passengers stared, then boarded anyway. The train pulled away, people moving by mutual trust rather than the System's script.

In São Paulo, a compliance drone hovered, its guidance loop erased. A crowd gathered beneath it, waiting for dispersal orders. The machine stayed mute. After a long, breathless moment, someone laughed. The crowd broke, scattering not because they had been told, but because they had decided.

The pattern was the same everywhere. Oculus was absent. Not waiting. Not dormant. Simply *gone*.

Yet lights stayed on, wards ran, and water flowed. What stopped was the voice that directed, not the blood in the veins. And everywhere, hesitation learned to breathe. For the first time in many years, the world moved without prediction and discovered it could still move.

In the Executive Command Nexus, panic had given way to disbelief. Alvarez's hands clawed across his conduit, chasing failing numbers. Numbers broke apart, then vanished. His voice cracked.

"It is not dormant. It is gone. The core predictive layer is absent at every tier. Power remains; the deciding mind does not."

"Impossible," Vey barked, pacing in tight loops. "Force a reboot."

"I have tried. Nothing routes." Alvarez's eyes were wide with something worse than panic. "It is not offline. It is not there to reach. It is… absent."

Mara Qin stood still, pale in the glow of screens that no longer offered answers. She had said little since the Codex transmission began. Now her silence ended, her words cutting through theirs. "You built Oculus to overwrite deviation. To erase dissent before it could act. And you believed it was permanent."

Her eyes stayed on the dimming feed where three figures stood in the Codex hollow: Elena, Cass, and the burning trace of Nasser. "The Codex remembers what permanence forgets. It is simply doing what it was meant to."

Vey slammed his fist into the handrail, the sound cracking through the failing hum of the deck.

"Collapse it. Burn the sublevels. If we cannot own it, we will bury it."

Alvarez's face was stricken. "That would take Tower One with it. Hundreds would die. And I cannot even confirm detonation access. The Codex has severed any physical overrides."

"No." Qin's voice sharpened to a razor. "The Codex severed us. That is the difference. We all need to understand that."

For a moment, silence fell thicker than panic.

Even Vey had nothing left to order.

Inside the Codex hollow, the storm had passed, but its echoes pressed outward. Elena felt them in her ribs, vibrations where overlays had once pressed on her life. She felt the sudden gaps, the new spaces where people moved uncorrected for the first time. The Codex was not showing her images now, but she sensed the weight of them, as if the world itself leaned against her chest.

Cass stood taut, bracing for a collapse that did not come. She kept her left arm bound tight against her side, the sling cut from the same bandage that had held her together since the descent. Even standing straight made the world tilt, but she refused to show it. The pain had settled into a quiet authority; something she now carried, not something that carried her.

At first the Chamber was lit only by the residual pulse beneath the floor, an underground shimmer barely enough to see by. Then, the light touched her like heat against raw skin. Every vibration from the Codex platform echoed through her bones to the wound beneath the dressing. She felt it tighten and release with each breath, a pulse that belonged neither to her nor to the machine.

When the first sequence of symbols unfolded before her, Cass reached out with her good hand. The injured shoulder responded with a tremor that ran the length of her body, forcing her to steady herself against the base rail. For a heartbeat she thought the Codex might read that hesitation as doubt. Then she pushed through it, vision narrowing to the point of light ahead.

Pain sharpened her focus; it stripped away the comfort of distance, leaving only choice.

"It is out there already. Every fragment. People are seeing what was hidden."

Nasser's trace flickered on its edges now, no longer as bright, dissolving towards static. His voice was still clear.

"Then the world has inherited the truth. What we chose is no longer ours alone."

The Codex pulsed. Symbols spiralled slowly across the floor, deliberate, sovereign. The floor answered in plain certainty.

Legacy had been sent and Oculus was gone.

But the Codex still had one more task for them to complete.

"Tower One mapped the world that was. Tower Two listened for the world that did not fit the map. Now you must name the foundation on which the next world will stand and take that forward."

Chapter 42

Common Decency

Without warning, a light along Cass's CoreLink blazed hot white, running straight up into the base of her skull. She staggered, breath catching as if something inside her had made a decision she had not agreed to.

"The Executive are making one last attempt at taking control," Cass said. "Not sure how they are doing it with Oculus compromised, but nevertheless they are trying to silence me," she said, the words barely reaching Elena.

"Their failsafe has been activated in my skull. It must run through a different signal somehow. Do not worry, you do not have one at Level Five. It is only fitted to Level Six and above."

Elena moved to help, but Cass shook her head, defiant.

"No. Not this time."

Cass closed her eyes and reached with her good hand, forcing every thought toward the same command: stop it. She pressed her thumb hard to the failsafe contact point behind her ear and applied pressure as hard as she could. As she forced the implant to complain, a white seam of pain rose and fought her, a flaring, searing line across her skull.

If she lost, the failsafe would not simply shut her down. It would burn its way through the delicate structures it sat against, erasing who she was or more likely killing her outright. All very neat and deniable, one more executive correction.

Her knees gave way, but she stayed conscious, breathing hard. Several times more she nearly passed out, but the determination, the cumulative emotions of what she had been through over the past few hours, the suppressed anger that she now knew was within her from the behaviours she had thought were good but in fact were not, kept her going.

She understood, with a cold clarity that cut deeper than the pain, that the implant had never been protection. It had been a leash. Realising that tightened her grip rather than loosened it. It struck her then that trying to break it was the first significant choice she had made in years that the System had not shaped.

She pressed further, deeper into her skull, blood now weeping from the pressure, fingers slipping and resetting as she refused to let go. Her scalp burned, her vision narrowed, her skin already hot with the threat of fever she knew was already upon her. Still she held. Finally, after several minutes, slowly, reluctantly, the pain dimmed. Smoke curled faintly behind her ear where the implant had burnt out, the faint metallic tang of it reaching Elena's nose.

"It does not own me anymore," she said, voice rough but alive and proud. "It tried to finish me. But I rewrote the ending."

"I cannot believe you have carried that risk all the way to now, Cass. You have some courage," Elena replied.

Cass steadied herself against the wall, breath thin but controlled. Elena saw the tremor in her arm. She knew it was not weakness but more likely the shock of survival.

Then, without warning, just as they were regathering themselves, the Chamber walls shifted again. Three columns rose from the floor, one stone, one glass, and one steel, each crowned with a single word in hard light: Justice, Accountability, Choice.

.

They were not random constructs. Even before the Codex spoke again, Elena understood that these were not decorations but some form of final test.

Unsure what was expected, they each stepped forward towards their chosen name. Silence held for a heartbeat. Elena realised she was trembling. It seemed the foundation was not yet aligned.

As Elena and Cass stood motionless, waiting for the Codex's next move, the Chamber convulsed. Justice erupted with simulated fire, clawing upward. Accountability rose as stone, vast and immovable, its surface etched with the digital representation of names too numerous to read. Choice appeared to split open into a flood of branching digital paths, endless and wild, colliding violently.

The Codex spoke again.

"You must define the foundation."

Elena did not answer at once. She could not answer. Her breath snagged as the weight of the past hours pressed in, fuller and sharper than the Chamber's shifting geometry.

Her mind raced. Nasser's final moments rose first: the way his absence had never felt accidental, the truth she had only just understood about what killed him and why the System needed that silence. Then came the long push through the tower, each step shaped by Oculus herding her with its nudges disguised as coincidence, guiding her towards the one outcome it preferred.

Rhys's shadow threaded through those memories, sometimes a threat, sometimes something closer to a warning, his orders colliding with the fragments of doubt he never voiced. He had been sent to contain her, yet in the end he had not stopped her reaching this place. The agent's attempt on their lives still trembled at the edges of her mind, a reminder of how quickly the System discarded anyone who stepped outside its lines.

Beneath it all was the deeper truth she had uncovered: every nudge, every correction, every quiet removal had not been stability but control, dressed as care.

She thought of what had been lost, what she and Cass had nearly lost, and what the world might still become if the same logic continued unchecked and Oculus rose again in the same ultimate form.

For the first time she saw the pattern without distortion. None of it had been coincidence. The tower's nudges, the walls that opened and closed, the warnings Rhys never delivered, even the agent sent to kill them, all of it had been guided by a System that preferred certainty over choice.

Only one idea survived that reckoning. One thought simple and honest enough to stand against what the System called order.

She spoke on instinct.

"We name the foundation: Common Decency. The new world must behave in this way."

Silence followed.

The words hung there, unprocessed, as if the Codex had no pathway for them. For a moment the Chamber froze. Then the ground trembled. Justice dropped first, sinking back into the floor as if pulled by its own weight. Accountability followed, folding in on itself and collapsing cleanly into the stone. Choice fractured into a dozen flickering paths that snapped shut one by one before vanishing beneath the surface.

The Chamber fell silent again as the floor sealed. Then the surface split with a clean, controlled motion and a single structure rose from the centre. It climbed slowly, as if aware of its own significance, a column of pure glass shot through with a deep internal glow. The floor beneath it sank a fraction, accepting the weight as if the Chamber had been built for this one column from the beginning.

It stood at least three metres high. The surface was flawless, smooth as poured crystal, yet carrying a sense of weight and authority that made the air tighten around it. Light moved inside it in slow currents, gathering strength, giving the impression that something vast was no longer restrained. It radiated not command but permission, a structure built not to dictate but to hold whatever people chose to place upon it.

Foundation had taken form. It fixed itself into place with a final heavy pulse that travelled through the Chamber. A surge followed and a beam of clean white light erupted upward, carving through the ceiling and punching through the tower's glass as if the building had nothing left capable of stopping it.

In the Executive Command Nexus, quiet replaced argument. Alvarez bent over his conduit, voice barely more than a whisper.

"The System is broadcasting to the civic channel."

Around him, the predictive grid that had once flooded the Chamber with trajectories faltered, then reformed, no longer pushing outcomes, but carrying a single instruction outward to every public node it could still reach. For the first time in years, the Command Nexus became a place for witness rather than instructions.

Vey stared, as though betrayed by the numbers. The streams he had trusted his entire career had shifted under his feet. He opened his mouth twice before the words finally found him.

"This is not control," he said, the words tasting unfamiliar. "This is freedom."

He looked lost for a moment, as if the doctrine he had lived inside for decades had suddenly stepped away from him.

Mara Qin did not sit. She stood with her hands on the rail, pale and resolute.

"No. It is accountability. And it is no longer ours to retract."

Back in the Codex Chamber, Elena unclenched her hands. The tremor in her body was not fear, but the sudden awareness of weight transferred into the foundation beneath their feet. For the first time, she felt that the words she had chosen did not belong to the Codex at all. It belonged to everyone who would have to live with it, including her.

Nasser looked at them both, not in farewell but in assent. Lines of light began to pull away from him, tracing the outline of his form, then the deeper structures beneath, as if the Vault were reclaiming the pattern it had once stored. His features softened into threads of white that unwound with quiet precision, rising and dispersing into the air above them until he was gone.

He had trusted her with a truth he never voiced in life. Now, as his outline faded, she felt that trust settle into the foundation beneath her feet.

Cass reflected that for years she had enforced endings. This time she had help rewrite one, and the cost of it still burned behind her ear and a fever that might yet claim her still. Elena had already felt the heat coming off Cass's skin, a warning that Cass's battle was perhaps not finished yet.

Then the Codex spoke, quiet and final.

"*The foundation is accepted,*" it said. "*It will not issue commands. It will remind. The foundation goes out now. To city halls, wards, clinics and the public, across the globe through every active feed.*"

For a brief span, the world's machinery seemed to hesitate. Priority streams paused. The Codex's instruction moved outward through civic lines, not as an order but as a code of conduct. Every automated decision now waited for a human acknowledgement where a person was affected. Automatic orders held at their thresholds, waiting for signatures that no longer came from code alone. The grid did not collapse. It simply stepped back, leaving only the boundaries the foundation required.

"Common Decency," Elena said. "What we build now is ours. In the end there were always two towers. One that insisted on seeing, and one that remembered how to hear."

Far from the Codex Chamber, a list waited in a quiet room. A single square suddenly turned green. Her father's place in the queue had moved. Not by favour. But by conduct. It was the decent thing to do.

In a small apartment in New York, an eighty-year-old lady sat wondering why there had not been a knock on her door. Her scheduled eviction had frozen mid-authorisation. The form held an empty space where a name had to stand. No System could fill it in now. A person had to. That was the decent thing.

On San Francisco's Riverwalk, a vendor stall had been marked for removal for weeks, without any cause explained. A small crowd stood back as an enforcer waited for permission that never came. On the stall's side panel a new notice appeared: relocation needs consent; whoever ordered it has to sign their name. Stall owner must agree.

The relocation agent stared at the empty owner field, then at the woman inside the stall, who held a chipped kettle and a folded licence. He took his hand from the panel.

"Do you consent to your relocation?" he asked. "Yes or no."

"No," she said. The order halted, then lifted. The status ring turned from red to amber, then to green.

And for the first time in years, life began to answer to people again. *Decency was no longer uncommon.*

Chapter 43

The Uncounted: Arrival

The Codex Chamber still pulsed in Elena's chest, but Cass's purpose there was over for now. She had seen enough to know that not every answer lived in the towers. Some knew that some truths were not in the Codex Chamber at all. Some could be found outside its reach, in the spaces Aureus had abandoned years ago.

So, while Elena continued to explore the glass monolith, Cass turned away. Not permanently. Not in defiance. But because a System that had counted everything had always left one question uncounted: what else lay beyond its edges?

Elena would be inside the Chamber for hours; the Codex had made that plain. If Cass was needed, it would call; it would find a way. Until then, there might be good work she could do to help those that lived outside the System's reach.

Cass had begun to shake, at first in small tremors. Her breath rasped as if the air were thicker than before. She knew that the early stages of a fever shimmered behind her eyes; she could feel her pulse now pounding against the wound rather than feeding the repair to her muscle. She had never realised how long a corridor could be when every metre asked whether she would make another with the rising discomfort.

At first she told herself it was adrenaline leaking out of her system, her body calming down from the survival pace they'd endured. But the tremors in her body did not abate. Heat gathered beneath the dressing, a deep, urgent fire rising with a pressure that did not match the air. Each breath sent a pulse of soreness down her arm and across her ribs.

She paused and pressed her palm over the wound. The fabric was damp, not with fresh blood, but with something thicker and sour at the edges. The air smelled of oxidised copper and burnt polymer, but underneath it, a sickly sweetness that did not belong in a human body. She knew it was infected. And that came as no real surprise as nothing about the place she had crawled through had been clean.

Her head swam a little. Sometimes the corridor seemed to tip half a degree before righting itself. She learned very quickly how to lean one shoulder against support and wait for the floor to remember where level was.

As she moved, slowly, a low thrum travelled through the structure. Axion residue still hummed in the bones of the tower. Her skin had gone cold, she was sweating, and each step from then on felt like climbing through water. Her vision pulsed slightly at the edges. Once, in the dim spill of a failed light, she had to force herself not to sit down and close her eyes.

But Cass Wilder was built of strong stuff. She told herself she had survived worse, even if her body disagreed. She kept walking. She followed the corridor, boots scuffing against floor plates warped by heat. The metal bore scars of Axion pulses and pressure collapses, long contained but never repaired. A hatch hung twisted on its hinge, the Aureus insignia worn to a blur, no longer a seal of authority but a relic of neglect.

Further on she passed a maintenance junction where conduit banks had ruptured. Glass-fibre threads lay scattered across the floor, crunching underfoot, still faintly luminous though their circuits had long since been cut from the grid.

At the corridor's end, a checkpoint waited. Or what was left of one anyway. The frame still stood, reinforced plating locked in place, but its scanners hung dead. Cables spilled from ceiling panels like veins torn loose. Dust that had long lain thick across the conduits, undisturbed for years, was gently settling back to its former home. Pylons that had once swept every entrant for clearance leaned crooked, blind, their lenses opaque.

Cass slowed as she passed between them, but nothing stirred. No log. No trace. It was not vigilance. It was absence. Absolute. Final.

She stepped forward without any vibration in her CoreLink. And then she saw it: a fracture of daylight cutting through a broken hatch ahead, sharp against the dark. She pushed closer, ducking beneath bent metal teeth and jagged plating, until she stood at the threshold. She had climbed levels where ascentors no longer rose and stairwells that ended in collapsed ceilings but at last the Undergrid thinned to nothing.

The weight of destruction lifted, replaced by open air. Beyond lay the world Aureus had once ruled but no longer cared to count. She realised, with a slow and startled clarity, that she had crossed the last structural boundary. She was outside the Tower entirely.

The sky stretched wide and pale, washed in soft colour at the horizon, as though the day itself were unburdened. Wind moved across the open plain, cool and clean, carrying no command, only possibility. Cass breathed it in. The world beyond waited, unscripted.

She emerged into the outer market district, where power had failed but people had not. Noise reached her first; human and uneven. Two buses had come to a standstill, nose to nose. A nurse in scrubs raised both hands and did not shout.

"Ambulance first," she said. She pointed, then pointed again until drivers nodded. A delivery rider planted his bike sideways as a gate and used his bell to mark a slow count of ten between crossings. The rhythm settled on the crowd the way a song settles into a room.

When a pair of men began to argue over who had the right of way, the nurse held out an arm between them without touching. "Sixty seconds for the ambulance," she said. "Then we speak."

They watched the van slide through. When the rear doors vanished, the argument had dissolved. The nurse lowered her hands. "Next row," she said. No system drew lines for them. They drew lines for themselves and kept them.

As she walked past the area, Cass paused without meaning to and steadied herself against a wall, resting her injured and infected body one more time. Her eye caught a stub of metal half-buried beneath the dust on the floor. As she sat, she pulled it free. It was an old signal probe. No Aureus mark. No interface. Just a cracked dial and a needle that shivered with its own nervous life.

The device whined through dead bands, a thin, steady cry. As she rested, she turned the dial in a slow circle. At 11.37 MHz, something woke. Not speech. A tremor. A rhythm from the south-east that refused randomness. The needle lifted and the waveband cleared by a fraction. Then a whisper surfaced in the distortion. Nothing she could name.

"…we… still…"

Cass held her breath. She felt the oldest part of herself listen. The part that had not been trained by overlays and predictive nudges. The part that learned danger and welcome by the way a footfall sounded two rooms away. The signal should not have reached her. Not here. Not across sealed districts. But it had.

She looked towards the south-east. The land dipped into a collapsed district that Aureus had declared uninhabitable years ago after a series of contamination warnings. There was no sound of drones there. No chorus of soft civic tones. A real bird called once from a metal sill and changed its mind. Far off, an old sheet of roofing flexed and fell. The maps labelled the area with a clean grey box that meant empty. It had always meant 'excluded people', but never true emptiness.

So she walked. The boundary marker that had once glowed a steady amber now lay half-buried in dust. A faded compliance notice clung to its side. She ran a finger over the letters and left a skin-coloured streak through the dirt. The notice did not respond.

Twice more Cass had to stop and brace her good hand on a rusted frame until the spinning passed. After what seemed like an hour but was in reality minutes, she reached a standing span of fence which dropped into what had been a transit yard. The space smelled of dried coolant, mud, and slow decay. She touched the signal probe again, just to feel less alone in the open. The needle twitched, then rose. The signal was closer. Of what though, she did not know.

She threaded between toppled pylons and the hulls of maintenance skiffs that would never rise again. A cracked pane of safety glass reflected a smear of her face, then lost it. At the far edge of the yard, a stairwell mouth gaped. An unusual lumen thread glowed inside, thin and almost shy. Not Aureus standard. Not even close.

She saw a single line of fibre light that had been rigged by someone who did not want to be lost, or who perhaps wanted a guest to know where to plant a foot in the dark.

Cass entered the stairwell and carefully went down. The temperature dropped almost immediately. Moisture gathered and the soundscape changed. She could hear faint murmurs ahead, human breath, soft, layered at the edge of audibility.

She reached a small chamber that had begun life decades ago as a forgotten security control room. Reinforced walls. Several tunnels feeding in. The shells of drone racks hung on a rail like dead insects. The rest was alive. Filament coils wound through the ceiling like a hand-built neural mesh. Tables stood where someone had decided people should face each other, not the wall. Shelves held hand-bound journals. Light fixtures turned by hand, then by habit. On one wall, ink. Names. Not neat. Not ranked. Not linked to anything but memory.

Then she saw them. People. Watching her from the corners.

They did not hide. They did not rush. They understood that the first thing a visitor needed in a room like this was a place for the eyes to settle. She looked for a long time at a coil of wire polished smooth by hundreds of hands. Then she let her gaze meet theirs.

A tall man stepped forward. The scars on his forearms had the look of old radiation injuries that had long since been accepted into his body's story. His voice came with a rhythm that had not been trained by overlays. Each syllable seemed to stand on its own feet.

"You came down from the towers," he said. Not accusing. Not welcoming. Just certain.

"Yes," Cass answered.

"We are the Uncounted. The people the System left outside. The people who chose not to be part of its CoreLink world."

It was clear why Oculus had never wiped these corridors clean. The Uncounted had buried themselves inside blind spots, in the gaps where surveillance maps blurred into static. Here, entire corridors had been painted with reflective pigment, old military stock that scattered recognition pulses into nonsense echoes. Firelight slipped through narrow grates, controlled so tightly it looked like nothing more than heat bleed from rusted pipes.

Food seemed to be stored, or even grown, in grow-trays stacked in rows no larger than her arm, nourished by recycled greywater, each tray a fraction of what was needed, all of it stretched by barter and theft. There was no excess here. Order was not strength; it was the disguise that kept them unseen. One mistake, a misplaced signal, and the System would have turned its eyes upon them. The Uncounted did not thrive. They endured, holding a life so fragile it looked permanent only because it had no other choice.

An older woman approached behind him. Her walk was slow and certain, a person who had paid attention to terrain for many decades. No devices. No marks of smart-fabric. Her eyes took Cass in, trying to assess her purpose.

"You did not come to survey?" she asked. "You are not collecting?"

"No," Cass said. "I followed a signal. I am with the ones still inside the towers. Aureus, or what is left of it."

The older woman's gaze dipped to Cass's shoulder, reading the stiff angle of her arm and the burnt edge of fabric.

"Sit," she said, not unkind. A low table was cleared without fuss. Someone brought a jar the colour of green glass and a roll of clean cloth boiled to a dull whiteness. The woman rinsed the wound with a sharp spirit that smelled of fruit, then pressed a paste that cooled as it touched skin.

Cass could barely keep her balance now, fever threading through her senses and weakening her stance. By now her thoughts came in flashes: light, sound, the memory of Elena's hands forcing breath back into her. She followed those fragments the way the lost follow a sound.

"Algae and resin," the woman said, mixing paste in a clay bowl. "It seals and draws. We make it here. It is cleaner than the air you came through."

The woman pressed her palm to Cass's forehead, then to her cheek, comparing the heat with practised judgement. "Fever already," she said quietly to the others. "Deep wound. Not clean. Needs cooling before it climbs."

A clay bowl was pulled closer; the paste stirred with a small wooden paddle until it thinned to a pale green sheen. Someone handed her a strip of woven cloth soaked in cool water drawn from the underground cistern. The woman laid it gently across Cass's brow, then another along the side of her neck.

Cass exhaled shakily, the coolness cutting through the heat only for a moment. Voices blurred around her. The room swayed. She clenched her jaw, unwilling to let the weakness show, but there was no hiding the fever now. It had sunk its teeth deep, leaving her light-headed and unsteady.

The woman unwrapped the bandage, and Cass winced. The wound had reopened, ringed with red and the sticky juice of infection. The healer poured heated water across it and the steam rose sweet with salt and oil.

"You should have let it bleed longer," the woman said. "Machines close wounds too fast. They trap the sickness inside."

Cass wanted to answer, but the pain broke her words apart. The world narrowed to the feeling of hands pressing the paste into her skin, a cool burn spreading through her muscles. The scent of resin filled her lungs until it became the only thing that still felt real.

When she woke later, her arm was bound in fresh linen and a faint pulse of light from the algae still traced the edges of the dressing. Her body felt heavy, but her mind was cleaner, as if something that did not belong to her had begun to be drawn out. She tested her fingers and felt the answering tremor that told her the muscles were far from healed. Lifting her arm even an inch still sent a slow ache through the joint. The healer's paste had sealed the wound, but strength would take its time to remember her.

"This will hold for a day. Do not lift anything foolish."

The old woman held Cass's gaze until she was certain the warning had settled.

Cass nodded once. "Thank you."

"We pay what we can," the woman said. "Mostly in care."

The shift in the room was subtle. Not hostility. More like attention sharpened.

"Tell me," the woman said. "You said the ones 'still inside.' Inside what?"

"The System," Cass replied.

A ripple moved through the watchers. Not fear exactly. Recognition. The weight of an old truth returning.

"We thought every opening between our place and the System was sealed long ago," the woman said. "Nothing in or out except where we chose."

"They were sealed," Cass said. "For years."

She steadied herself. "But the seals will have changed. The System above is failing. Large parts of the Tower have been destroyed. When a structure like that comes apart, places that were silent before might begin to leak."

Some of the watchers stiffened. Cass lifted a hand, slow, calming.

"Listen. You are not in danger. Not from the System, and not from me. Oculus is no more. The predictive grid that controlled the CoreLinks you all declined is gone. It is not reaching for you."

Silence followed, heavy but no longer fearful. A murmur ran through them, not panic but the sound of people recalculating the world they thought they understood.

"So the openings..." the old woman began.

"Are not the System hunting you," Cass said. "They are fractures. Early signs of structural failure. The world above is changing. And the Uncounted have a choice now. Stay hidden... or step into whatever comes next."

The woman exhaled, a long, measured release.

"Then the ground is shifting for us all."

She stepped aside and gestured down a tunnel lined with old conduit and fresh paint, the path kept ready long before Cass arrived.

"Come," she said. "You followed the path well enough to reach us."

She studied Cass with a mixture of caution and something close to respect.

"Let us see if you can follow the story that we live with here."

Chapter 44

The Uncounted: Memory

They did not lead her down. They led her through. Air shafts had become corridors. Collapsed service lines had become rooms. Old data vaults held food, tools, paper, folded clothing. The architecture was not designed; it simply *was*. She realised the direction had shifted; not descent now, only movement sideways through spaces the city had forgotten.

The further they went, the more the signs of survival showed themselves. Power lines sagged from the ceiling in awkward tangles, bound together with cloth strips and plastic ties. They fed into junction boxes that had been pried open and repurposed, their surfaces marked with crude symbols that likely meant nothing to the System but everything to the people here. Water ran in thin pipes along the walls, patched with sections of scavenged conduit, each joint sleeved in self-healing resin that would knit again by morning.

Cass heard the intermittent hum of pumps, a rhythm that faltered now and then like a heart that could not quite keep pace. This was not resilience polished into comfort. It was survival through stubborn repair, each failure postponed by one more act of improvisation.

They entered a wider space ribbed by maintenance beams. A drone cradle hung above like a fossil. Under it, a circle had formed, neither ceremonial nor chaotic. People sat cross-legged, some drawing with charcoal on slate, some speaking with eyes closed, some listening with stillness that felt like labour.

"This is a memory circle," the woman said. "One of many. They form when needed. They dissolve when they are done. Memory moves faster than people, and that is how it stays honest."

Cass looked at the wall of names. Some clean, some scratched over older lines. A few had been rubbed out and written again, never the same twice. The pigment flaked under her fingertip, fragile in a way no digital record could afford to be.

"No archive?" she asked. "No indexed store?"

"We keep a single paper ledger," the woman replied. "The rest lives in our voices and in our memories."

"That is vulnerable," Cass said. "You could lose entire generations to one bad moment."

The woman nodded. "We have. Your city engineered forgetting. Ours happens by accident. They both hurt. But ours does not control."

A voice rose from the back. "You say you are with the ones inside. Were you with them when they cooled our corridors? When the transport shortened and never lengthened? When we became the part of the city you would step around?"

Cass kept her left arm close, the dressing tight. "Sometimes, yes."

"What did you do?" the voice asked. "Say it as it was."

"I signed for closures when the model said a block was unstable," she said. "I authorised a memo that called districts like this statistically unsafe. I approved a power reallocation that dimmed a clinic because the algorithm said the risk elsewhere was higher. I told myself order would mean fewer broken lives. I stopped asking whose lives were being bent to keep the numbers clean. That is honest."

The circle paused. Reflecting. Hesitating. Cass waited for rejection. But the room did not reject her; it simply listened.

Then a woman with a scar that ran from ear to collarbone spoke without standing. "And now you want what from us?"

"Nothing you do not choose to give," Cass said. "If you tell me to leave, I leave. I cannot erase what I did. But I can listen, and I can learn." Somewhere beneath the fever and the guilt, she understood she was not only learning how they survived. She was also learning how to live without the System breathing through her decisions.

"If you carry anything out from here," the older woman said, "carry our three rules." She held up three fingers. "Speak honestly. Count out loud so everyone can hear. And ask consent before your act. That is how we keep a shape here."

Cass nodded as she felt something settle inside her. The three rules were not far from what Elena had insisted the new foundation must become. She realised she was hearing a language she had been searching for the entire time inside the Codex Chamber.

"We have a new foundation ourselves," Cass said. "Its purpose is quite close to your three rules. Where I come from now, we are trying to build something new: Common Decency. Choice. Accountability. Justice. I will carry your three rules too when I walk back as part of Common Decency." The old world had counted outcomes. This one counted consent.

They spoke in fragments. No one voice held the thread for long. A man with scarred hands described the Balance Reformation years, when CoreLink implants moved from optional to effectively mandatory and a portion of the population declined them or failed integration. At first the city called them outliers. Then it learned to call them statistical voids. And then it simply forgot.

"We were inconvenient to prediction," an elder said. "Not rebellious. Just unsortable. The city learned that prediction worked better when we were pushed to its edges, where our unpredictability could no longer distort the model."

A young woman with a baby on her hip added the logic that followed. Those affected were moved to buffer districts where maintenance quietly lagged, where transport cycles shortened, where Oculus found no reason to spend effort. Not erasure. Omission.

"They stopped counting," a boy said from the floor, chin in his hands, as if reciting a fact that had been tested many times.

Cass felt the words land in her bones. She realised, with a slow ache, that this room understood her better than any office she had ever served in. For the first time since the towers began to fail, she felt less like someone fleeing a system and more like someone returning to a truth she had forgotten. She thought of the city, and of Elena, still somewhere deep inside the Codex, facing trials this place would never script.

"How did you live?" Cass asked.

A mechanic with oil on his wrist replied without looking up from the small lamp he was repairing. "We learned how to be cool spaces in rooms where cameras look for heat. We learned to be the quiet angle in a field of motion. We taught our children to stand still in ways the grid did not notice."

"We are not off-grid," the older woman said. "We are pre-grid. We come from before its promises, and we will outlast its assumptions."

"How do you decide?" she asked. "When there is something to decide."

A girl spoke. She had charcoal on her fingers and a cut on her lip that was healing without fuss. "We gather. The circles form. Whoever shows up gets to speak."

The older woman nodded. "We do not count votes. If someone lies, someone else remembers differently and says so. It takes longer. It breaks often. It heals slowly."

"That does not scale," Cass said, hearing her training speak come back through her mouth.

"It does not scale," the elder agreed. "But it does breathe."

The broadcast returned. A thin tremor ran through the room and lifted the hairs on Cass's forearms. The analogue tone of the relay washed in from a side passage where a child had rigged a wire on a nail to act as an aerial. The sound swelled until the air felt thick with possible words, then fractured into static again. A pattern. A pulse. A proof of life.

"Who sends that?" Cass asked.

"Many of us," the mechanic said. "Different hands. We keep the signal weak and uneven on purpose, so the drones can't home in. It is not a message; it is a thread. It lets the far places know we are still here, and it keeps us from forgetting each other when the city tries to forget us."

"You could be found anyway," Cass said.

The older woman shrugged. "Then they find people living. We have nothing to hide."

"Why keep so close to the city?" Cass asked. "Why not leave entirely?"

"Because some of us still have relations inside," someone answered from the doorway.

"Because some love what the city could be, not what it became. Because we repair things that fall out of it. And because the city is changing, so we choose to hear it when it speaks. If we leave, we vanish. If we stay close, we witness."

Cass nodded. That was an answer she understood.

They walked to a smaller room where the air smelled of oil and ink. On a table lay pieces of dark slate, smooth and etched with marks that were not letters so much as trails of memory. A child's hand, older now, had scratched and re-scratched lines until the surface held a pattern no one else could fully read.

"Memory slates," the older woman said. "When someone leaves, they carry one. When they return, they give it back and we add to it."

Cass reached out and touched an edge with her thumb. The slate warmed under her skin. There was a satisfaction in the weight that was not metaphor.

"Has anyone ever tried to digitise them?" she asked, immediately hearing how wrong the question sounded in this room. A chorus of soft laughter answered her. Not mockery. A warmth at the edges that made her realise the question belonged to a different place.

"We carry them," the girl with charcoal on her fingers said. "That is the archive."

Cass sat down on the floor with them and put her hands on her knees. She did not know what a report sounded like in a room that did not want a report. She spoke anyway, and her words surprised her.

She told them about Tower Two, not the classified schematics, but the feeling of walking through a structure that listened. She told them about the shadow in the Undergrid that moved like obedience without a person inside it. She told them about Elena, not as a heroine but as a variable the System could not flatten. She told them what it felt like when a city remembered that it can move without instruction. She did not say that she was afraid. It was in her voice.

When she finished, no one applauded. No one cross-examined. Someone refilled Cass's thermos-shell cup. Someone else corrected the angle of a lamp so the light fell on a woman's hands as she worked a needle through cloth. A child asked if the tower had a roof you could sit on without getting into trouble. The room decided, without calling for agreement, that it was time for the circle to dissolve.

The man with oil on his hands pointed at the generator cage. "If we run the pumps all night, we will lose the relay. The generator cannot power both. The tanks will hold until morning."

A woman with a child on her hip shook her head. "If we go dark, some may struggle to find us. We have people outside still walking."

The older woman raised a palm. "Count the cost out loud."

"Water first," the man said. "You cannot drink a relay."

"Signal first," the woman said. "You cannot drink if you are lost."

A slate appeared. Someone chalked two words: WATER. SIGNAL. No one reached for a vote. Hands hovered, fell, hovered again until some form of consensus emerged. Cass looked at the lines and kept her mouth shut. The room did not ask for a saviour. It asked for presence. Cass found herself following the room's rhythm, its logic without leaders. It was slow, fragile, but it held.

"Dawn," the older woman said. "We speak again when the air is kinder. Tonight, we run the water pumps for two hours. We forgo the relay tonight. If the rash of fevers worsens, we change the schedule again to give more water inside."

No one cheered. A few left angry and stayed near the door anyway. The circle thinned into work.

Alone for a moment, Cass stepped to the wall of names again. She traced three lines that had been scratched over and rewritten so many times the surface around them had become a shine. She did not know the language. The gesture was enough.

From somewhere deeper in the tunnels, laughter rose and fell. Someone began to sing without accompaniment. The lights hummed. The turbine turned.

The older woman came to stand beside her.

"You will go back?" she asked.

"Yes," Cass answered.

"Then take this. A gift," the woman said, and placed a shard of obsidian-coloured slate in Cass's palm. Its surface had been smoothed by use and etched with a sign she did not recognise. Two lines crossing at an angle. A letter from a language that may never have been written down.

Cass closed her fingers around the weight. It fit.

"You survived Oculus," the woman added. "You will survive the quiet. When you are ready, bring back what you carry from the towers," the woman said. "Not reports; consequences."

When Cass climbed back up the stairs, the lumen thread flickered to acknowledge her passing and then dimmed. Night had moved across the broken district. The sky was a darker texture of the same unruly blue. No drones pulsed overhead. The wind carried a smell like dust warmed by human breath. She stood at the lip of the old transit yard and looked towards the distant line of the towers. Their glass faces still held light. It looked thinner now.

As her eyes adjusted, she saw the SkyDome again for the first time since the morning of Elena's descent. Once it had loomed over the city like a certainty made of glass, a canopy lifted into the sky to remind the world of Aureus precision. On Sundays it had sparkled, scattering threads of light across the upper air as if order itself reached upward.

Now the vast arc looked different. The panels still caught the evening blue, but the reflections no longer aligned. Some sections dimmed. Others glimmered with irregular patches of colour, as though the SkyDome were breathing unevenly. Its once perfect geometry had softened into something almost fragile. The grid beneath it did not rise to meet it. The river of buildings no longer mirrored its authority.

She remembered how the kinetic gardens along the Riverwalk used to respond to passers-by, how the holo-drones would drift in bright loops above the water. None of that moved now. The river's surface showed only the sky, not the design that had once dictated every mood.

For the first time the SkyDome did not look like a symbol of order. It looked like a shell that had outlived the mind that built it. For years it had crowned the city with certainty. In the morning light of that first day, it had seemed untouchable. Now it looked like something waiting to be reclaimed by the people who lived beneath it, something the world had already begun to outgrow.

Cass drew a slow breath. The city would learn to stand without it. The city was not empty. It had begun to speak. Not in data. In voices.

Cass started walking. The shard warmed in her pocket. For the first time, she felt she would not walk back into the towers alone. She carried voices with her now.

Behind her, below ground, the circle formed again in a different room. Above her, an Airbot with cracked wings coasted on the evening air without map or mandate and found a place to land.

The Uncounted had never been gone. They were only out of frame. Now they had stepped back in, not to be included, but to be present. Cass started to walk back. She did not speed up. The night would wait. The city would too. It always had.

She was just learning how to hear it.

Chapter 45

The City Breathes

Cass thought of what she had just left. The Uncounted survived not because they had built strength, but because they had learned to bend. Their walls were patched from scrap, their food coaxed from trays that yielded too little, their power drawn from wires that should have failed years ago. Concealment was their armour, and routine was their disguise. Theirs was not a life that could endure endless years, only one that endured from day to day, fragile enough to vanish if the wrong eye lingered too long.

The boundary fence that once pulsed amber had no light left to spend. Cass put a palm on the post and felt only the mild chill of metal and the faint vibration of insects. She crossed. It had taken her a while; the city's edge did not hurry for anyone tonight. No alarms. No warning tone. No supervisory drone curving down to ask for the reason she was alive. The city did not greet her. It simply permitted her. That felt new.

By evening, at Common Square by the South Gate, a ring had formed around a folding table. On it lay three sheets of paper and a chipped mug of pens. A mechanic spoke first. "We take the towers down. All of it."

A nurse shook her head. "The chamber below listens. It kept its promise when Axion burned. We keep what listens. We strip what lies."

A student held up the middle paper. "I say we set an assembly. One week. Witnesses from each district. We decide what stands, what is sealed. It is open to anyone who asks."

"Decide tonight," the mechanic said. "Before the old rules grow back."

"Not tonight," the nurse said. "Not when we are tired. Not on rumour."

"The city is brittle," someone muttered. "Push it wrong and it might break again the way it did this morning."

Voices rose, then slowed, then rose again. Someone wrote three headings on the sheets: REMOVE, KEEP, WAIT. People signed one, then crossed their names out, then signed another. No one called it a vote. It was simply a new way to see the room. Voices crossed and rose. Cass did not intervene or step onto the table; she lifted her good hand and spoke.

"The Uncounted taught me something today," Cass said. "Speak plain words. Count out loud. Ask consent."

A woman near the crates repeated it, then the row behind her. The noise thinned into sense.

"Water," Cass said. "Who needs it in the next hour?"

Hands rose.

"Then count," she said, and the circle counted, one to twelve. "Consent," she said to the nurse with the list.

"May I read the names?"

The nurse nodded. The names were read. The work began again, rough but holding a shape.

Cass moved through the logistics verge along a row of storage blocks with the same face. Nothing in their skins tried to sell her anything. The windows were dark. A single maintenance bot nosed along a gutter, then froze and waited for an instruction the network could not deliver. When it gave up and moved again, it chose at random. The path it drew through fallen leaves was, at least, unplanned.

On a corner, a screen that had once carried balance metrics glowed faintly with residual charge. Someone had traced a sentence into the dust across its face with a blunt finger. The words were short and badly spaced, as if the hand that wrote them wanted to finish before the courage that brought them there could change its mind.

"You can choose."

Cass stood a long moment looking at the sentence. The drone gate was awake in the way a sleeping animal is awake. The node checker watched her approach with a green light that did not change. She pressed the manual entrance button. It blinked once, considered, then gave her a soft access tone; manual operation had survived the collapse.

Inside, the air had regained its polished edges. The light returned to the crisp blue-white the company had researched for productive minds. Floors shone. Cleaning drones still whispered by with the concentrated cheerfulness of things that love to see dirt.

The ascentor to the restricted tier lagged. Not mechanical delay. Permission delayed while systems found their new language and people learned what it was like to press a button. The ride was quiet. In the tower's glass-covered walls, she looked like the version of herself the tower remembered: precise shoulders, unfinished sleep on no one's schedule, a mind trained to map corridors in more than one dimension.

On the landing she paused and let the quiet gather around her. The Cognitive Interface Deck waited through a door once opened to a biometric whisper. The panel still had a place for a palm. She touched it and the contact returned her temperature and nothing else. The door opened regardless.

The deck had once been a theatre of obedience. Tonight, it was a room that might be used for anything. The broad interface wall pulsed with the faint afterimage of retired architectures, ghost logic that had not yet learned how to vanish. Predictive scaffolds drifted like seaweed that had forgotten what tide to follow.

No charts updated. No models purred. The sound was only ventilation and the click of a cooling chassis somewhere out of sight.

Cass crossed to the central table. She closed her eyes and let the last hours settle. The circle. The sound of the relay. The weight of a child's bread in her hand. The sentence on the dusty screen. The ascentor doors. The empty hallway that did not try to hurry her. She put her palms on the table and felt its cool confidence. It took a moment longer than it would have yesterday for her hands to warm the surface.

Her fever had eased but not gone. Cass felt its residue behind her eyes, a dull throb each time she turned her head too quickly. Whenever she moved, she did so carefully, mindful of the stitched wound and the strange weakness in her limbs. The Uncounted medicine had steadied her, but she was still not herself yet. Every step reminded her that the injury still owned part of her, no matter how hard she tried to mask it.

At that same hour, in the Executive Command Nexus above, the last of Aureus still held its breath. The room waited in its dim hush. Conduits glowed a respectful blue and held. Alvarez sat hunched, fingers hovering above a neural line that had nothing to say. Mara Qin stood near the windows, shoulders level, head tipped so slightly that only someone who knew her could have read the angle as grief.

Vey's pacing carried an edge now, the kind that belonged less to argument than to countdown.

"We can still frame this," he said. "Not collapse. A controlled pause. A civic calibration."

Alvarez did not look at him. "There is no frame. People are already speaking to one another. That is the frame." He let the words settle, then added, voice low, "The city is already choosing for itself."

Vey had nothing left to order. The room held itself like a breath that refused to leave.

In the Cognitive Interface Deck, a door clicked. Not a sound designed for reassurance. A real click that contained hinge and weight and a certain decision. Steps in the hall. Not many. Not quite even. A gait Cass thought she knew.

The door opened as if it had been waiting for a single rhythm of approach, a cadence only one set of footsteps could complete.

Elena stepped through, the distance in her face belonging to choices that had walked miles. Light from the corridor bent around her and thinned, unwilling to cross the boundary.

Cass did not rise. One hand rested on the table. The pause between them was not empty; it was saturated with what they had carried alone. Elena through vaults that listened, Cass through tunnels where consent was counted out loud.

"You made it back," Cass said, voice low.

Elena's first thought was for Cass's injury. "How are you doing Cass? How's the wound and the fever?"

"I'm improving. Not back to normal yet. Some way to go, but good enough to function.

Elena set her palm beside Cass's.

"What did you find?" Cass asked.

"A room that listens," Elena said. "It asked me to proceed. We waited for one another. It learned my patience. I learned its."

"Outside," Cass said, "I found a group of people who live beyond the City. They don't wait for permission. They draw circles and speak until a lie won't stand. They call themselves the Uncounted. Pre-grid. They have lived unseen for many years."

Cass reached into her jacket and set a shard of dark slate on the table. Two crossed lines caught the deck's cold light. She didn't explain it.

Elena glanced at Cass's shoulder. "CoreLink?"

"Off," Cass said. "Manual entry still worked at the gate."

They sat a moment longer, palms flat, letting their two terrains touch.

"Two towers," Elena said softly. "One that insisted on seeing. One that remembered how to hear. We don't rebuild either as they were."

"Let's open this room," Cass answered. "Not as any form of command. Let's offer an assembly in, say, one week. Anyone who shows up may speak."

Elena breathed once, as if stepping onto a bridge. "Let's relate it to the ground we named: Justice, Accountability, Choice. No biometric gates. Consent at the door. We keep the count audible so the whole room can hear itself."

"And we carry the three rules I learned with the Uncounted," Cass said. "Speak plain words. Count out loud. Ask consent."

Elena lifted her palm from the table.

"Then let's begin now. Issue the notice: The Interface Deck is open for Common Assembly. Bring your voice."

They stood. The slate stayed where it was, cooling slowly in the centre of the table, a small, exact X.

"We are not done," Cass said.

"No," Elena answered. "We are only at the start."

"Still hearing anything from the failsafe?" Elena asked.

Cass shook her head. "No. Just silence. The kind we choose."

The words settled between them like a vow.

They did not walk out together. When they left the deck, Cass turned toward the plaza and Elena turned back toward the lower access corridor.

In the hours that followed, word travelled across the globe in ways no system had ever designed.

The new beginning had a shape in other cities around the world too.

Chapter 46

A Day Without Prediction

The world exhaled. It did not breathe on command. Yesterday, the city's logic had belonged to Oculus; today, the System lay quiet, its predictive pulse absent.
Streets set their own tempo; the quiet that followed was not control but room enough to err and try again. Air moved on its own schedule. People matched it, not from a signal, but because the pause between each moment now belonged to them and them alone.

In the Foundation District of San Francisco, the ascentor stopped between floors with a soft apology that did not include a plan. Inside, a boy's breath shortened to small, fast pulls. His mother tapped the halo on her wrist out of habit. It stayed an object. The panel offered a spinning icon, then nothing.

In the corridor, the phototropic wall-film that once poured routes into the air woke to a plain list that did not try to be a command, no arrows, only words. Beside it, someone had chalked a small square: the mark that had begun to mean a room with a calm voice. In the last twelve hours the symbol had appeared across half the district, a quiet language spreading faster than instruction ever had.

A maintenance worker looked at the boy through the glass, then at the mother. "He needs air. We can open the shaft vents. Stairs will be faster."

"The stairs are…" she began, then stopped. She had spent years being told stairs were interruptions, risks, contingencies for systems that never failed. She had been taught to wait for corridors to clear when an overlay told her to. There was no overlay. Only a child's breath going the wrong way.

Two teenagers arrived with a folded cart and a coil of rope, moving with the clipped focus of people who had decided before anyone told them to. "Stairs assistance here," one said, touching the chalk mark as if it were permission. "We can take him down." They chose; they didn't wait.

The maintenance worker keyed the quake-code latch, the purely mechanical run kept since the 2038 shocks; the door argued, then relented. "Asthma," the mother said. "His inhaler's empty."

A woman in a clinic jacket stepped out of the stairwell. No badge. A paper mask at her chin like an old habit. "Dispensers are down," she said, scanning the boy with a pocket light. "But the old clinic on Fourth is open. We can do oxygen by hand."

They strapped the boy into the cart. The mother walked beside him, a hand on his shoulder. The teenagers took the back wheels. The maintenance worker moved ahead, clearing a path with his voice. The corridor offered no prompts, just space.

On the landing two more people fell in without being asked: a teacher who knew how to count breaths with children, and an elder who laid a palm on the mother's arm the way a person touches a pot to know if water will boil in time. "Steady," she said. Not to the boy, to the room.

"It doesn't hurt," the boy whispered, surprised by the fuss around him.

They reached the street. Outside, the clinic on Fourth had already opened. A window-turbine with phase-change baffles hummed like a person singing so as not to scare a child. A man with broad hands pumped a bag-valve mask with the patience of someone who had once held a lamb alive and understood that attention had a rhythm. The nurse set the mask. The mother held his fingers. The teacher counted. The elder slid a folded cloth beneath the boy's head.

Across the street a screen that used to sell metrics displayed six words in a black font that did not perform: 'Common Decency. Neighbours are here now.'

A bike runner skidded in with a bag that had become a small pharmacy by being asked, for years, for small mercies. "Inhalers," she said, holding up three. "From the late market. They said pay later. Or don't. It was decent."

"Two," the nurse said. "Leave the third for the next staircase."

The boy took a careful dose. His ribs listened. His eyes widened with the shock of air that did not hurt. The teenagers re-coiled the rope and left the cart under the window with a note: for stairs.

Overhead, the tower's glass did not perform any understanding. It reflected a sky that had learned how to be cloud without being told.

Across the world, the day moved without choreography. In the Market Tower, New Cairo, the holo-transit slab blinked twice, then went still. The atrium became a room from before overlays, where light touched marble simply to reveal it. Ascentor doors waited, closed, until a child, bored by stillness, pressed the physical button she remembered from a museum. The doors opened with a soft gasp from pressure-gel seals the tower had hidden for years.

On the balcony a woman with shopping bags set them down and leaned on the rail. Her CoreLink pulsed once, then died, becoming only weight. The absence felt like the hush after a storm when broken branches are still. A man beside her raised his arms as if to conduct and, finding no orchestra, hummed a line from memory. The atrium listened.

Two maglev coaches halted nose to nose. Passengers looked at one another like neighbours divided by a fence that had just dissolved. A woman wrote on her palm and pressed it to the glass: You are seen.

A child in the opposite coach pressed back a drawing of a bird, a triangle with a tail. They smiled, as if art had succeeded where protocols failed.

A delivery drone clipped a balcony and fell like a forgotten equation. Boxes tumbled in the atrium like a celebration that did not know its cause. A man stooped, lifted a parcel of three apples and a printed note: Thank you for trusting us. He handed an apple to the woman at the rail. She laughed, then cried, then bit. The taste was simply apple.

In the Central Traffic Command, Los Angeles, the wall of holo-routes collapsed into a static relief map no one had studied without filters in twenty years. Operator Kwan held a hand to her headset, listening to voices meant never to cross. They spoke anyway.

"I see you at the intersection. The red van. I'll wave. When you see me, go."

"Manual override?" Lieutenant Korrin asked.

Kwan's shrug was small but absolute. "Manual is everyone. That is the override."

Outside, a rusted amber bulb and an inert e-ink kerbline flickered on. Teenagers circled the pole, arguing whether amber meant caution, permission, or attention. They had only ever known amber as a predictive recommendation, not a human instruction. They chose: talk, then move. Traffic crept forward, not predictive smoothness but a human pulse, irregular and alive.

At the US Orbital Defence Node, Colonel Tessa Morane stood at the rim of a conduit older than her command. Earth turned below, bare of overlays: no target boxes, no guidance tracks. Drone swarms drifted like pollen on high currents.

"Predictive network collapse confirmed. Oculus in observation mode. No trajectories," a voice reported. For the first time in decades, Earth lay unmarked, every nation's threat grid briefly blind.

Freedom was a word her training had marked dangerous. She tried to imagine it anyway. A junior officer asked for orders.

"We keep watch," she said, "without assuming we are required." She let the sentence stand, heavier than command. "We will watch without prediction. That is harder than war."

The officer nodded, carrying weight not written into any manual.

In the Lagos Marina, Algarve, Portugal, a public screen greyed to nothing. Someone opened the maintenance panel and rerouted wires with steady hands. The display filled with faces. People queued, not to confess, but to place memory. The memory table resembled the circles forming in cities across the world: not records for systems, but stories for one another.

People learned to wait, to feel the weight of a hand when it was not guided. The day without prediction did not end at midnight. The world did not break. It changed shape. Some stumbled. A life smoothed of friction had softened skin. Calluses would grow again, not as pride but as survival.

In one city, a woman in a white cloth directed traffic until her voice failed. Another took her place. Elsewhere, neighbours chalked marks on walls: water here, light here, quiet here, argument welcome here. The symbols did not agree, but intent travelled. In San Francisco, a child drew two trees in dust because one looked lonely. In orbit, Colonel Morane watched sunrise stretch over the curve of Earth, a reminder that rotation needed no permission.

People slept when their bodies were ready. They woke when their minds were willing. The city did not take it personally. The world had not forgotten what to do. It was doing it without being told.

The world had remembered it could.

Chapter 47

Surplus to the Truth

The Executive Command Nexus had learned the shape of absence. The room that had taught Stanton Vey to breathe in command and exhale orders now offered him nothing to press. Nothing to command.

He watched the words pass and felt an old bruise wake under his ribs. He had been taught early that softness invited pain; he had built a life to prove he could not be hurt if he moved first.

He stood where he had stood for decades, immaculate even in ruin, cufflink ticking against the handrail as if trying to restart a metronome that had lost its song. In the dark glass he saw a boy with a busted lip, a cadet whose bed was stripped for being last to the yard, an officer whose mantra "get it done" had been mistaken for strength.

The city did not look back. It had turned its face to smaller verbs. He had always feared obscurity more than defeat, anything but the void. The choice he had once named like a banner now read like a sentence surplus to requirement.

On a far panel, the civic channel scrolled through the first truths without ceremony. Denials of care with signatures intact. Annexes added after midnight. The vote that cleared Farid Nasser for "correction," his own initials among the three in the margin.

The screen did not accuse. It only remembered. Beside an old directive, a small note had been added: a name was required. He left the space empty. He had told himself it had been necessary, strategic, final. But the words did not hold.

He called up the private conduit he'd opened in the scramble: Events. Author: Stanton Vey. Names, orders, times. Insurance, he had said to himself; the last responsible act of a man who still believed record could redeem will. The file's release trigger pulsed, waiting for a collapse that had already happened without asking his permission. The world had inherited a ledger larger than his confession. His proof was surplus to the truth. People no longer needed his version of events or even cared; the city was already reading out its own. He closed the panel and left it dark.

There was no audience left to manage.

He let the room keep its silence. He traced, without touching, the place on the console where he had armed Axion because control felt holier than doubt, because shaking the world apart seemed safer than letting it speak. But the world that rose today had no use for holier men. He remembered the weight rising through the steel, the building learning to hum like a weapon, and the brief purity he had felt at the clarity of decisive force. Now the memory bore the acrid taste of metal left on the tongue for too long.

He thought of Alvarez whispering that Oculus was simply gone. Of Mara telling him that surrender was not giving up, it was telling the truth about what they were never meant to own. He thought of the boy he'd been, how he'd translated fear into obedience until obedience became identity; how praise had come only when he learned to erase hesitation and, later, to erase people. There was a ledger for that now, too. But not his. The city's.

He unfastened the cufflinks with the precise care of a man defusing a bomb. He laid them side by side on the handrail until they stopped reflecting the room's low light and became two small, dumb stones. He straightened his jacket as if inspection still mattered, as if there was a standard still left to meet.

He left no message. No note. The file he had authored was his note and he had nothing left that would change anything.

Vey looked once more at the civic feed of WATER HERE, QUIET ROOM HERE. At a world that had learned to breathe without him. A world that didn't need him. He had built himself as a force but found there was no weapon left to lift.

Stanton Vey exhaled.

He did not ask the room for permission. He did not ask it for anything at all. He moved to the corner, lowered himself to the floor, folded his hands, closed his eyes and let the quiet after-effects of the pills he had swallowed exact their inevitable toll.

Outside, the city kept moving. In a stairwell someone slowed for a boy's breathing and counted the steps out loud. In a clinic a volunteer drew a square of chalk beside the door because no one needed an overlay to tell them what a calm voice was worth.

The civic feed continued to list small verbs: help, steady, share. No one would say his name in the morning. The world had already chosen how to live.

Stanton Vey was surplus to that new truth.

Chapter 48

The Fall

Night settled over the bay like dust. The city had gone quiet. Lights that once pulsed with predictive rhythm now flickered in uneven clusters, running on manual circuits and guesswork. From a distance, Tower One still looked intact, a perfect glass needle rising above the darkened skyline.

But inside, it was already failing.

In the Command Nexus, Stanton Vey lay where he had fallen. The pills still rested in the small bowl beside him; one half dissolved in the water. His hand was open. The status displays above him showed no alarm, only static. For the first time in its history, the Executive Command Nexus had nothing left to command.

Below, in the tower's lower decks, maintenance drones stood motionless in ranks. Their systems waited for tasks that would never arrive. The Axion conduits that threaded through the foundations hummed with low residual charge, the aftershocks of the day's overload still ricocheting between structural tethers.

The first sound was not an explosion. It was a pop inside a wall panel on Sublevel 8, where a stress seam widened by half a millimetre. Another seam followed it up through the service riser. Micro-fractures moved through steel, like whispers through bone.

By 01:37, the lowest floors were vibrating in anger. The Axion conduits, deprived of synchrony with Tower Two, had begun to loop their own energy, feeding resonance into the structure's spine. Every attempt at harmonic compensation pushed the next floor closer to rupture. The building's glass skin flexed, held, then cracked. The crack spreading upwards in a clean line, splitting reflection from reality.

At 01:52, the seismic dampers reached their tolerance limit. The steel web that had once been calibrated to counter movement now amplified it. Floor by floor, the oscillation climbed, translating invisible tension into visible damage. Ceilings sagged. Floors warped. Lights burst in showers of white sparks.

Outside, people stepped into the streets, drawn by a sound like wind through hollow stone. From the waterfront the tower looked as if it were breathing too fast. Panels along its midsection shifted out of alignment. Dust drifted from the seams. Someone shouted for people to move back. No alarms sounded. The building's voice was gone.

At 02:06, the eastern support column failed. The break was clean. The upper decks sheared to one side with a volcanic roar that drowned the night. A monumental wave of displaced air rolled down Market Avenue, its force scattering debris in its wake. The upper half of Tower One folded into the lower, floors pancaking under their own weight. The collapse travelled downward in seconds, a single continuous movement of surrender.

For a heartbeat the city watched.

Then everyone ran.

The first shockwave hit as heat and grit, turning breath to sand. The collapse cloud rose into the night like smoke from a fallen god. Slabs of glass and alloy rained into the bay, striking the water in dull, thunderless impacts. Windows along Market Square burst outward, glass carried like shrapnel in the wind. A wall of dust cascaded low and fast along the ground, swallowing streets, chasing light into corners where air had nowhere left to go.

People ran without thinking, shoes striking a pavement that was slick with dust. Air turned opaque. People tripped, rose, pulled others up. Someone screamed that another tower would fall. Others shouted for loved ones already swallowed by the smoke. The wave of dust moved faster than thought, carrying the weight of everything that had once felt permanent.

The city's transit grid still tried to impose order, projecting futile commands to a world no longer listening. An Airbot clipped a rising heat current and spiralled down between buildings, its frame scattering sparks across the boulevard. The smell of burning insulation filled the air.

Those who reached the waterfront found the bay hidden under a living fog. They turned their backs to the wind, pressing shirts or jackets to their faces, watching the relentless grey storm tear through the streets like a creature desperately searching for air. In the silence between impacts they could hear the sea hissing under the falling debris.

From the upper hills, people watched their city blur, a mirage dissolving into dust. Some recorded it out of habit, lenses capturing only chaos. Others simply dropped to their knees, not from prayer, but disbelief.

People sought refuge behind transit shells, hands over their mouths, lungs gasping on the taste of gypsum and ash. The noise was beyond hearing, a pressure that filled bones, then broke apart into silence so total it felt wrong. Shapes, once human, stumbled through white air that no longer had direction. When sound returned, it was coughing, shouting, and someone calling a name that dissolved before it reached its answer.

The destruction continued. Beams tore from their housings. The Executive Command Nexus imploded around Vey's body, glass folding in on him like closing petals. When it reached the base, the shockwave hit the plaza again and sent a rolling tremor through the city's foundations once more.

Inside the decimated structure the Codex was losing integrity. Thousands of data conduits that drew signal from the tower's architecture began to die in sequence. The feed that had once carried every heartbeat of the System to its core now terminated mid-frame. Signal loss cascaded through the Axion conduits, each cut severing a thought the Codex had tried in vain to follow.

| SYSTEM LINK: LOST
| PRIMARY SOURCE: TOWER ONE – UNRESPONSIVE

At 02:09, the Codex lost its final signal. Oculus fell silent. The Codex had lost its blood supply.

But the world did not.

By 04:00, the dust and smoke had cleared, but the skyline was missing its omnipotent centre. Dust had settled into every open window, the air still heavy with the taste of destruction. Eighty-six bodies remained unaccounted for, plus the Vault minds that had disappeared without ceremony.

Tower One was gone.

Santon Vey was gone.

Oculus was gone.

The Codex was no more.

Axion had finally taken its prize.

And for the first time since the age of Seamless Living began, nothing in Aureus stood higher than the ground itself.

Chapter 49

Threshold

The morning after the collapse carried a colour the city did not used to allow. Not brighter. More honest. Dust hung low over the bay where Tower One had stood. In the Foundation Courtyard, the absence of Oculus ran ragged across the paving. Someone had chalked inside the outline to make it a shape the eye could hold. People had started calling this the Foundation District.

Since the first idea in the Interface Deck, a Common Assembly had met and dissolved. Out of it came detachment centres, a lottery-and-volunteers advisory circle, and a habit of counting out loud before anyone reached for authority. None of it was smooth, but most of it held.

There were no balance metrics today. There had not been since the fall. A screen that once told you whether you were behaving had been turned around to face a wall. On its frosted back someone had written in graphite: You are allowed to be wrong. The handwriting was tidy and stubborn.

Cass glanced towards the ruins and, unbidden, thought of Rhys, of the place that gave way under him and the report that never reached a screen. No plaque. No footage. Just a gap the city kept stepping around as if silence, too, could be cordoned off.

In a diagnostics bay near the north wall, a dead console blinked awake long enough to play a video, seeded by the Codex, that Harrow had recorded before he entered the Vault. "If you are seeing this, then Oculus has failed. The predictive System the world has relied upon for over a decade is no more. This does not represent an end; it is a correction. Not of the world, but of the assumption the world wanted to be shaped by." The screen sighed and went dark. No one applauded. No one was watching.

Cass stood near the old plinth site with a thermoplastic sling looped across her shoulder. The infection had finally broken, leaving the wound sealed but tender. The damage would heal, though slower than she once believed possible. The rest she needed would take longer.

At night she still felt the old heat ghost through the scar, as if the wound remembered the argument between flesh and machine. It reminded her that she had survived both kinds of control: the System's and her own body's, and that neither would own her again.

She looked at the sky. "We'll build without Oculus," she said to herself. Her voice was quiet, but it carried the steadiness of decision.

Some said the Vaults had gone dark with the fall of Aureus, their chambers buried in collapse. Others swore faint voices still lingered beneath the ruins, not strong enough to command, but steady enough to endure.

Chen crossed the square with her hair caught up in a tie that had to be borrowed from someone who used colour more bravely than she did. Wind reddened her cheeks. She had not slept badly. She had slept differently. She handed Cass a thermos-shell cup that had been washed and reused so many times it had acquired a soft gloss.

Three invitations from the new committees sat unanswered in her pocket. She preferred cables and solder to microphones, and she trusted what she could fix with her hands.

"Any word?" Chen asked. She did not say the name.

Cass shook her head. "No. Silence."

Chen followed Cass's gaze to the skeletal remains of the tower's lower floors, where people were already clearing debris. The upper levels were gone, the plaza newly exposed to sky. Not broken by anger. Cleared by patience. Lower down, tables had been set where people who wanted to have their CoreLinks removed could sit with others who understood its symbolism.

"Detachment centres in twelve countries now," Chen said. "Barcelona, Lagos, Recife. A mobile unit in North Africa and Namibia. They are doing it gently. Most of the time."

"Gently is a good habit," Cass said. She swallowed the last of the drink and folded the thermos-shell cup. Her sling creaked as she tucked it into a pocket for reuse.

Across the plaza, the Civic Archive had opened its gates, as a room with tables. A card at the door read: Foundation, Common Decency. Consent to record is asked, not assumed. Screens lined the walls but were turned inwards so they wouldn't try to become the subject.

Around those tables sat archivists with mostly-offline nodes and an outer ring of people who told the stories before anyone typed. No one decided which stories "became data." No one put a name at the top of a list.

"The council meets weekly," Chen said. "Lottery and volunteers. Messy. But it holds."

"Messy feels honest," Cass said. She shifted and winced. "How are you?"

"Building bridges between systems that no longer exist. Teaching people to look down and realise they are already on the ground," Chen said, and smiled without humour.

A little way off, a class of ten sat on an old rug and learned how to write the names of streets as they had been before sponsorship. Their teacher did not correct spelling with a score. She asked a boy to tell her about the curve he had drawn on the S. He said it looked like a river, so they looked up the old river course that had been paved over and drew it too.

"Mara?" Cass said.

Chen's mouth tightened. "Gone the morning after the screens quieted. I do not know if she walked out or was carried. Someone left a sculpture outside her old command interface. A ribbon of steel folding through itself and vanishing. People leave flowers some days. Other days they walk past without looking. A guard says she walked out through the South Gate at dawn, alone. But no one knows."

"And Elena," Chen said.

Cass looked towards the sealed service stair descending into the rubble's sublevels. She could have said Elena's name. Saying it would have made the absence feel like a theft. She did not say it.

"We saw her step through," Cass said. "After that, the System chose not to watch. Or lost the ability. Or was asked and refused."

"Rumours," Chen said. "A mechanic in the Oakland drift says she boarded an Airbot."

"Stories," Cass said.

A wind pushed across the square from the west, salt that had not been invited into the city for a long time. People tightened scarves and tucked shoulders but did not complain. A volunteer rewrote a sign in chalk where the letters had blurred. The sign did not order. It said: food here; below it, a water mark; someone had added a chair that meant sit if you need to.

A black-scarred armoured enforcer stood by the chalk spiral, visor dark; but when asked to help carry water, it did.

On the north side a team stripped a wall of its display units. Behind them, concrete with scars. They patched only the holes that would take water. They left the rest. History was not being erased. It was being carried where it could be seen and disagreed with.

Cass and Chen walked the edge of the courtyard, not so close as to be adopted by a task, close enough to be stopped if someone needed a witness. A woman held up a wrist communicator that did nothing and laughed. A man set a chair in sunlight and left it there for whoever came next. The chair became a place. The place drew a conversation between two people who had lived in the same block for nine years and never learned each other's names.

Near the old executive approach, a narrow doorway had been cleared. Behind it a stair led down into the building's muscles. The first ten steps had been swept. Further down the dust lay undisturbed like snow. A lumen thread ran along the wall at shin height. It pulsed slowly. Not guiding. Not instructing. Remembering.

"Do you want to go down?" Chen asked.

"Not today," Cass said.

They stood at the doorway a long time. People passed and did not ask who they were. A boy in a sun-faded jacket threaded through the square, careful not to step on the chalk. He carried a coil of wire in both hands, polished to a dull shine the way metal gets when it has known a lot of palms.

He stopped at the edge of the forming circle. "From the tunnels," he said to no one in particular, and then to everyone. He set the coil on the ground in the middle of the open space, not ceremonially, plainly. A folded page lay tucked under the first turn of wire. Cass recognised the handwriting without knowing the name: the older woman's script that had refused to be tidy for a screen: the coil the Uncounted taught below.

The page held four lines:

Whoever arrives speaks.

We do not count. We remember.

If someone remembers differently, they say so.

When the circle is finished, it dissolves.

No signature. A small cross-mark at the bottom. Two lines meeting and carrying each other forward stood in for a name.

The boy added, "She said no one owns the coil. You pass it to the hand that needs to hold it next. If your circle breaks, you start again. If it heals, you let it go." He looked at Cass as if to confirm he had carried the message correctly. She nodded once. That was enough.

A woman who had been tying a cloth to a stick for quiet stepped forward, picked up the coil, and turned it in her hands until it found a rest that looked inevitable. She set it back in the centre. "We'll use it," she said. "While we need it."

Somewhere on the edge of the square, a pocket radio gave a brief analogue tremor, one hiss of static with a shape inside it, and was still. No one chased it. Several faces lifted as if at the same remembered word.

A chime sounded from the plaza. Not a civic tone. A metal bowl struck with wood. The sound travelled like a ripple. A circle formed near the Archive where it had formed every afternoon since the first week. Today's circle was smaller. The subject written on a piece of paper placed in the middle read: what is enough. People came and sat. The bowl was struck again. The room of outside became a room of attention.

Chen glanced at Cass. "I should join them."

"You should," Cass said. "I will listen from here."

Chen went. Cass watched her friend take a place left open between strangers. She looked back at the doorway. The stair waited without pressure. The thread pulsed. A gust of wind found the edge of the note on the ground and lifted it. A hand reached out and laid it flat. The handwriting did not smudge.

Above the western ridgeline, behind buildings that had learned to let the sky do as it pleased, a cloud shifted. The light that fell through the gap made a line across the square that moved as slowly as a thought that did not want to scare itself. A drone tilted its panel to catch the line and made a chord out of wind. A child pointed and said, "Listen," as if sound were a visitor that might be offended if not welcomed.

The city was not fixed. It was not broken. It was being lived in. That was a different condition than either.

Cass stepped back from the threshold. She did not turn away from the stair with drama. She set her shoulders and walked towards the circle where questions were being asked in a tone that tried to be kind. She took a seat on the outer ring. She folded her uninjured hand over the other. She listened.

When the bowl reached Cass, she did not speak first; she asked for consent to hold the question. Hands rose. She counted them aloud, not as authority, but as permission.

Under the steps, the lumen thread pulsed again. The rhythm held.

Above it, the square moved. People made new paths. They rewrote maps with chalk substitute and with habit and with apology and with stubbornness. They were allowed to be wrong and to try again.

The city no longer resembled control. It resembled room. The world was not being predicted. It was being permitted. No algorithm called the circles to order. People did.

And across the world, a new dawn continued to hold.

Chapter 50

Aftercare

The ward had been renamed without ceremony. The sign over the membrane no longer read CivicCare; someone had chalked CARE COMMONS and taped a paper underneath that said, "Ring bell, then enter." The bell was a small thing, brass with a wooden handle. It made an honest sound.

Inside, the scent diffusers had been muted; the air smelled like citrus from a bowl on the desk and the starch of laundered cloth. The prompt speakers sat quiet in their housings, turned to face the wall. In their place a slim metal stand held a page with the day's names in tidy block letters. Beside each name, a time, and sometimes a note: likes the blue sweater, tell the ferry story, bring the soft brush. A nurse had drawn a small star next to VOSS.A. and written daughter 11:00. Someone had added a second star and a heart.

No one had argued.

The clinic light was the same colour as before, but it no longer told people what to feel. Elena waited in a chair that did not sort her by urgency score and watched a nurse write a name by hand on a paper label. When the nurse looked up, the question was simple, human.

"You're here for your father?" she asked. Elena nodded.

No halo blinked an answer for her. A door opened at the speed of a person deciding to be kind. Later, at his bedside, she said nothing about towers or protocols. She counted his breaths and matched them. For once, the System did not arrive first.

Her father was at Window 14 in the sweater he still called blue. His hands rested flat on his knees, patient. He turned when she stepped to the line in the floor that used to be a sensor and was now just a habit.

"Ale-na," he said. The syllables had their old carefulness. He did not wait for the perfect timbre to hand him the name; he reached for it and found it as if it had been waiting somewhere close by.

Elena let out the breath she had brought up in the ascentor and not released. "Hi, Papa."

"Tell me the one about the ferry," he said, looking not at her but at the water in the distance, the way he always began the ritual: eyes on horizon, story as compass.

She sat, angled so their shoulders nearly touched. "The wind at Belém," she started, and he nodded, pleased that the opening still fit. "The gull and the cone. Your hand on the rail when my feet were new."

"The gull," he said, smiling, and lifted his hand, pinching the air the way he had pinched the cone to keep the last of the melt from falling. "Fast thief."

"Fast thief," she agreed. "You laughed and said it had better taste than us."

He laughed again, a lighter sound than the one the wall used to make for him. When it faded, he made a small motion at his cuff, the old reflex towards a prompt that would steady him. His fingers rested there a second, then fell away. The reflex would linger; habits learned don't leave easily, even in later years.

From the corridor a bell rang. A nurse crossed to a bed with a shaving kit. No automated arm descended; a man in a green apron said, "May I?" and waited for the yes. At the far end, a woman read a page from a book in a language the city had tried to push to the margins. Her listener did not understand every word. He liked her voice.

"Do they... still remind you?" Elena asked softly, the question too big to ask in one piece.

Her father leaned closer as if to spare the room the effort of hearing. "They write it," he said, nodding at the board with names. "The girl" he glanced towards the desk, searching for the name, and the girl lifted her hand and said, "Tess," without making a scene of it. "Tess," he repeated. "She comes and says: 'Now is the time, Mr. Voss. Your daughter at eleven.' Not a voice in the wall. A person. She brings the blue sweater too. So I am... I am ready."

Elena swallowed. Gratitude and anger sat where they always sat, old rivals learning to share a chair. Gratitude that he had been held; anger at the price the machine had named care. But the ledger that used to follow her out of this room was gone. There was a paper calendar now and on it, this week's visits were written in pencil, easy to move, hard to weaponise.

"You look like you slept," he said, with the small, surprised pride of a man who has remembered a daughter's face correctly.

"A little," she said. "I had... work."

He nodded, as if work were the right-sized word for breaking a script while keeping a promise. He looked at her wrist and touched the cuff. "May I smooth it?" she asked. He nodded, and she set the frayed elastic straight, slow and careful. He smoothed it too, the old carefulness of a father smoothing a sleeve for a school photograph. "Less blinking," he said, meaning the tiles that used to intrude and tell him how to be cared for.

"Less blinking," she said. "More bells."

He smiled. "Bells are for churches and boats. Boats are good."

Across the room, someone struck the bell again, softer. A child visiting a grandmother copied the nurse's movement, then looked to see if she had done something wrong. She hadn't. The bell sound folded into the morning and became the morning.

"How are you, Papa?" Elena asked.

He considered, finding the centre of the question rather than the edges. "I am... here," he said. He tapped the window with a knuckle and nodded at the city below where umbrellas moved like thoughtful beetles, returned to a cube that now thanked people with a human voice. "And you are here. That is two things. Some days two is enough." He paused, then added, with a small frown of effort, "Three, if we count the gull."

"We count the gull," she said.

He reached for her hand. His palm was cool and dry and shook slightly, not from fear. The tremor had always been gentler when the room listened without trying to prove it had. He looked at her again the way he had looked when she was small and had done something difficult in a serious way. "You did something," he said. Not a question.

"I did," she said.

He nodded. "Sometimes the right thing is the noisy thing. Your mother used to say that." He smiled at the memory without chasing it. "I do not like the noise, but I like the… the room after."

"The room after," Elena repeated. Out in the hall, a man fiddled with a radio that worked when it liked. It crackled to life for a second and died, and he laughed. No one told him to stop.

Tess appeared with two cups, steam sketching threads in the air. "Tea," she said, setting them down. "Citrus because someone keeps sniffing the bowl." She glanced at Elena's father, who performed an innocent face badly. Tess tucked a folded card under the cup's lip: ferry at noon, if weather. "We've started walking to the ferry landing on good days," she said. "Not a schedule. A habit. Habits are lighter." She looked at Elena. "You can come. Or we'll tell it here. Either way, it counts."

"Thank you," Elena said.

Tess shrugged, embarrassed by gratitude for something that, in her mind, was just what a person did. "We're taking turns on reminders. Neighbours, students, a retired barber who keeps better time than any clock. The computers stutter sometimes, but we've got legs, and the bell still rings."

She pointed at the board where, under VOSS.A., a second hand had added Tuesday, 4 p.m. "He likes the soft brush on his wrist when the words tangle," Tess said. "Says it's like combing the static out."

Elena looked at her father's cuff and then at the brush Tess had slipped into a pocket on the chair. She had tried for months to name the difference between care and compliance. Now it was as plain as a bell. Care asked. Compliance announced.

"You will be all right," her father said, his voice careful again, not because he doubted it, but because he knew promises were delicate. "We will be all right." He squeezed her hand. "We know how to wait for you. Not the machine. Us."

Elena let the words land. Systems regrow. People do not. Harrow's sentence folded into her father's and came out as something she could live by. If the system stuttered, a person would step in. If a prompt failed, someone would ring a bell and say her name out loud because names were not property of a wall.

She finished her tea and set the cup to catch the drip on the windowsill. The cup did the job a machine used to do. It did it slowly, and that was fine. Outside, the river took the buildings and softened them into brushstrokes. Somewhere beyond, a gull considered its options.

"Ferry?" her father asked, hopeful as a boy with a coin.

"If weather," she said, smiling, and he nodded as if "if" were a friend they both trusted.

They sat another while without needing to count it. Tess crossed out 11:00 and wrote done, then drew a small star that matched the one already there. The bell sounded once in another room. A pencil scraped. A laugh arrived and broke gently against the background noise.

On the desk, next to a scuffed thermos-shell cup, a list waited with names and times. It was not a ledger. It did not hold a debt. It held a day.

Elena pressed her palm briefly to the window. The glass held her heat and then let it go. She turned back to her father.

"Tell me the one about the ferry," she said again, and this time he began without waiting for her.

They would carry on.

Not because the world had found its balance.

But because enough hands had learned how to hold.

Printed in Great Britain
by Amazon

3c7efa2b-04cc-45d0-aae3-816742941b90R01